I JUST CAN'T SAY I LOVE YOU

DEBBY MELTZER QUICK

ISBN- 979-8-9871874-1-8
Cover and interior design by: Jai Design
Author photograph: Milana Gilligan Photography
Printed in the United States of America

To Al, because I'm a lot and you still love me.

PART ONE:
THE THINGS WE LEAVE BEHIND

LET'S MAKE A PACT

SOPHOMORE YEAR, APRIL 1984

"I think the prom is stupid," Kim Drake lamented out of nowhere.

Carl Bishop was picking a tiny fleck of shriveled Frosted Flakes off the hem of his Black Sabbath T-shirt. "What?" he responded, looking up to find the source of the comment. Kim was sitting next to him in English class, like always. She was frowning. "What did you say?"

"I said the prom is stupid," Kim repeated, turning in her seat to face him. She'd been hoping Carl would respond. She didn't want to be observed talking to herself before class. It was just weird. "I mean, I think it's stupid. It's so fake. Kids dressing up like they're going to a royal ball or something. I don't even want to go to the prom."

"Maybe you won't," Carl said, instantly regretting his choice of words.

Kim glared at him. "Why would you even say something like that, moron?" she demanded. "You don't think anyone will ask me to the prom? Why? Do you think something's wrong with me?"

Carl almost reached up to shield his face with his hands in defense. He was no stranger to being shoved hard by Kim after saying something dumb. When they were seven, she had shoved him down in the sandbox when he made a comment about her hair looking like a rat's nest, and he spent the next two days finding sand in his body's crevices. She was much stronger than her petite frame let on. This time, she let him off the hook.

"I didn't say no one would ask you," he said. "I just mean maybe you'll decide not to go. Maybe you'll turn down like eight guys or something."

"Yeah, right," Kim said, pouting. "That's another thing I hate. So if no one asks you to prom, you don't get to go? That's just not fair."

Carl agreed. He had been on the receiving end of rejection a time or two, and it was no fun. And now his best friend and cousin, Chris Mahoney, had a serious girlfriend, Rhonda Jenkins. They were so happy and touchy, and it made Carl feel creeped out. Or envious. He hadn't decided yet. If he had a girlfriend, too, he wouldn't even have to think about prom next year. He would just go with her.

"Maybe we can start a petition or something," he suggested to Kim. "So that anyone can go to the prom, even without a date."

"I don't think there's actually a rule against going without a date, moron," Kim said. "But I mean, who would want to even be the person to try to find that out by doing it? That would be pretty lame."

Carl thought about it. Yeah, it would be lame to go alone. He could see himself standing against the wall of the gym, his hands in his tuxedo pants pockets, one formally clad foot perched up against the wall, watching all of his friends slow dancing with girls. No, he wouldn't go if he didn't have a date.

"Yeah, maybe I won't go to the prom either."

Kim looked at him with a touch of sympathy. That was unusual. Usually she looked at him with contempt. Carl didn't like it when Kim acted unusually.

"Carl, why don't we make a pact?" she asked him.

"A pact? What kind of pact?"

"Well," she started, grasping her hands together and grinning at him maniacally. "Why don't we say that, next year, if it's getting close to prom, and we both don't have dates, we go to prom together, you know, as friends?" She seemed very pleased with coming up with this idea on her own. "That way, we both get to go, and we don't have to stress out all year about finding dates."

Carl considered this. "But what if one of us gets a date, and the other doesn't? Won't that be weird?"

Kim nodded. "Yeah, but I'll try to find a friend to go with you if that happens." She laughed.

Carl glared at her. "So you're saying I'm probably gonna be the dateless one. Thanks." He scratched the back of his head, then glanced at his fingernails. "I don't know. Maybe. Yeah, okay, let's do that. Let's make a pact. I could do that. But we also have to promise that if one of us does get a date, they'll do everything they can to help find a date for the other one."

"Okay, moron," Kim agreed. "We can do that." She spit a little into her palm and held it out to Carl.

Carl didn't hesitate. He spit in his palm, and they shook hands firmly.

"Don't even think of falling in love with me or anything," Kim warned. "If we go to the prom together, it'll only be as friends."

Carl grunted. "Don't *you* go falling in love with *me*."

Kim guffawed. "I don't think we have anything to worry about, Carl," she told him. "I've known you all my life. You're okay, but you're still a moron. I could never see us as anything more than friends. Gross."

"Yeah, gross," Carl agreed. Well. Maybe not gross. But at least weird. He was pretty sure he didn't want a girlfriend whose nickname for him was "moron."

IMPACT OF THE PACT

JUNIOR YEAR, MARCH 1985

"So I need to invoke the pact," Kim said as she slipped into the desk next to Carl's in biology class.

"Say what?" Carl responded.

"The pact, moron, the prom pact," Kim said in an irritated tone. "I need you to go to prom with me. I don't have a date. And it's next month. It's getting too late to find anyone else."

"Why do you still want to go to the prom with me if I annoy you so much?" Carl asked.

Kim sighed. "Sorry, okay? I didn't mean to offend you. But we made a pact. Do you have a prom date? If you do, you need to find me a date, remember?"

Carl shook his head. "No, I don't have a date yet," he admitted. "I don't know if I'll find one at this point. And yes, I remember the pact. I'll respect the pact. We can go to the prom together since we don't have dates."

"How romantic," Kim mumbled sarcastically. "I can hardly wait."

"Wait," Carl objected. "Now I'm confused. You specifically told me that if we went, it would be as friends. Do friends have to be romantic with each other? Or do you want to go to the prom as actual dates?"

Kim rolled her eyes dramatically. "Friends, of course," she responded. "Okay. So we'll go to prom together. It's settled."

"Just one rule," Carl told her. "You can't call me a moron at the prom."

"Fair enough," Kim agreed. "You get a moron reprieve for one night."

"So what do we do now?" Carl asked. "Do we have to buy tickets?"

"Yeah," Kim told him. "We get tickets. We each pay for our own. And then I get a dress. And then you get a tux that matches my dress. And then right before prom, you have to get me a wrist corsage, and I have to get you a boutonniere. And we have to make plans to go out to dinner with our friends. It's all traditional. Oh, and Traci's getting a limo, so we can all go in the limo. And Dougo, her date, is renting a hotel room for after, so we can go there after and sort of have a party and sleep over so no one has to drive home after drinking."

"Uh," Carl said, "I think you might need to write some of this down for me. That's a lot to remember. How much is all this gonna cost?"

"I don't know!" Kim told him. "You can ask Chris or James. They're going, too, so they might know. I just need to go find a dress and stuff. But you know, I think it will be fun. Going as friends."

"Yeah," Carl responded cautiously. "Fun. But it also sounds like a lot of work for one night. But all our friends will be there, so yeah, it'll be fun. But yeah, maybe still write it all down for me."

"Moron," Kim whispered under her breath. "I honestly don't know how you make it through each day."

PROM GREETINGS

Carl straightened his maroon bow tie and smoothed out his cummerbund. He brushed a speck of dust off the lapel of his black tux jacket. He reminded himself how grateful he was that Kim had not decided to wear some bizarre or obscure color, like prune or aqua marine. His brown eyes and tan complexion looked good with maroon. At least that's what his mother told him when he put it on earlier. Now, she was dropping him and an overnight bag off at Kim's house before prom so they could fulfill the pact they had made sophomore year.

Carl had asked one girl, Debbi Fields, to the prom, but she had politely declined. At least she hadn't laughed at him. Maybe there was some pity in her eyes. He was kind of glad he was going with Kim. He didn't have to act a certain way to impress her, or worry all night about her regretting her choice of dates. Carl and Kim knew each other, and well. They had been in school together since kindergarten and pretty much friends since the first time they had met at age five. He just had to ignore the fact that she found him dumb as dirt. He knew pretty clearly he was not dumb as dirt.

His cousin Chris had arrived already with his girlfriend, Rhonda. Carl joined them on the lawn, carrying Kim's wrist corsage. Darlene and Charlie, Michelle and Joey, and Traci and Dougo all wandered over to them. They had all already exchanged corsages and boutonnieres before he had arrived. Kim was nowhere in sight. They were still waiting for one last couple, James and Sally, to arrive in James's ancient Vista Cruiser station wagon. Everyone else, except Darlene and Charlie, would be traveling by limo to dinner and the prom.

The front door of the house opened, and Kim stepped out. Carl barely recognized her. She was a sight in her maroon dress with off-the-shoulder puffy sleeves. Her dark brown bangs were feathered back high off of her head, and she had curled spirals into her long hair. Her makeup and accessories made her look older, more mature. Her high-heeled maroon shoes gave her some height, but at a petite five-foot-two, they didn't work miracles. Carl sometimes forgot that Kim was pretty. To him, she was always just Kim.

Carl stared at her along with the rest of his friends as she walked toward them, making her entrance, but suddenly he remembered that he was her date and he was supposed to be doing something now, too. He stepped forward and greeted her. She had his boutonniere, which she fastened on his lapel. Then he slipped her corsage onto her wrist. They smiled at each other.

"Looking good, you two," Chris said proudly, as if he were responsible for their appearance.

James and Sally pulled up, parked, and then joined them, and they broke up into groups of girls and boys to chat as they waited.

Mrs. Drake came out to take pictures. When it was time to take couples shots, Carl slipped his arm around Kim's back gingerly, worried that he might break something on her fancy outfit. The part of her back that he touched, near her waist, was bare with a fabric cut-out, and her skin was smooth and warm. He expected her to pull away at his touch, but she stood still and smiled for her mother behind the camera.

The limo arrived, and they all left for dinner. They dined at Tony's Italian Cucina, which was crowded and hot but still good and fun. Carl was prepared to pay Kim's bill, but she declined.

"We're here as friends, moron," she reminded him. "You're not obligated to pay for me."

Carl shrugged and did not object. He knew that once Kim decided something was a rule, it was written in stone. Plus, he had offered. He came close to reminding her about her promise to refrain from calling him a moron, but he decided to let it go, for now.

Finally, they left for the school to attend the main event. Kim gasped as they walked into the gym and were quickly inundated by the Prince "Purple Rain" theme. The gym had been transformed by purple, gray, and white decorations, and Carl could hear his friends making impressed noises. He milled around the gym with Kim and their friends, and when they all went out to dance, he followed. He knew dancing wasn't one of his strong points, but his friends didn't care, and there were others there who were far worse than him.

They danced, ate, and socialized for about two hours. Michelle's date, Joey, poured shots of vodka for everyone who wanted some from a flask he had carried into the building in his inside breast pocket. Later, Chris also produced a flask from his pocket and shared. Carl wondered when everyone had suddenly gotten flasks. He felt a slight buzz and decided to pace himself. There would be beer and champagne at the hotel after. He didn't want to be the guy who vomited in the limo.

Soon, they all started to discuss heading out to the hotel. But first, "Purple Rain" came on, and everyone went out to the floor to dance to the prom theme. Carl took Kim's hand and led the way, and they danced close in the crowd. Carl could smell her floral perfume. Next, the DJ played "Crazy for You," and Carl felt Kim relax in his arms. She pressed her head up against his chest. He felt the taffeta of her dress and the warmth of her skin, and he smiled. He liked the feeling of dancing close, and Kim was just the right height to nuzzle below his neck. He couldn't see her face buried in his tux, but he felt she was enjoying the dance. He let his body move freely to the music.

Before they left the dance, the class president, Rob Novak, announced class awards, leading up to the announcement of the prom king and queen. To no one's surprise except the recipients, their friends James and Sally won The Cutest Couple award. Carl had never seen anyone look so horrified to win anything, but James and Sally were both very private people. He envied their closeness and their sureness about their feelings for each other. They'd never had any doubts that they were right for each other. Carl hoped that someday he would feel so sure that something was just right.

When the awards ended, they headed for the exits. They were going to the Marriott for the night. The limo dropped them off in the loading and unloading zone, and Charlie and James parked their cars in the garage. Doug O'Leary, who everyone called Dougo, checked in. He was over eighteen and was legally allowed to rent a hotel room. Carl guessed that any of them probably would have been able to get away with renting a room, but Dougo gave them a sense of legitimacy, especially with their parents.

The room was crowded with six couples and only two full-sized beds, but they all managed to find places to sit. Carl and Kim sat next to each other on one of the beds, shoulder to shoulder. Soon, Carl went into the bathroom to get himself beer and a wine cooler for Kim from the stash on ice in the bathtub.

Everyone was in a good mood, and no one was too drunk at that point of the night to participate in conversation. They drank and joked around for about an hour. Everyone teased James and Sally for winning their award, and everyone, including the lucky couple, laughed along. When James and Sally got up to leave for James's house, the tone of the party changed. Everyone got up for more drinks. Michelle and Joey found their way into a corner and started to make out. There was more room on the bed now, but Kim still sat pressed against Carl. He was watching her, making sure she was okay. She was pacing herself with her drinks, and Carl was glad. He wanted to be able to have fun without having to worry about peeling Kim off the floor the next morning.

Kim was smiling. He could tell she was having a good time. He was, too. Kim was being nice; she had danced with him to all the slow songs and had been willing to touch him without pretending to gag. He had enjoyed touching her as well, remembering the smoothness of the skin on her back. He wondered what it would feel like to touch it again. He resisted as long as he could, and when their drinks were nearly empty, he reached out lightly and brushed his fingers against her.

"I'm gonna go get us another drink, okay?" he said. He felt slight bumps rising on her skin. She didn't pull away.

"Okay," she said.

He rubbed his fingers together on the way to the bathtub. He hadn't realized how erotic back skin could be. He shook his head back and forth. He had to shake out these thoughts. This was Kim. She felt more like a sibling to him than his own brother. He could not allow himself the luxury of thinking of her in any other way. Even if he could think of her that way, she would never allow those thoughts to become reality. He needed another drink.

When he came out of the bathroom, he could see Kim still sitting on the bed, laughing at something that Traci had just said. Her laugh caressed his ears, and he blinked his eyes slowly. Kim looked beautiful tonight. There was no denying it. She was hot. And he'd been touching her bare back just minutes ago. He thought of how he might be able to do that again.

THE BISHOPS AND THE FARMERS

It took a few moments for Carl to pick back up on the threads of conversation in the room after he sat down. Chris was talking about one of their cousins, Josh Bishop, a senior at Murphy High who was going to UConn the next year to study chemistry. He was thinking of becoming a doctor, much to the pleasure of his relatives.

Traci spoke up. "Chris and Carl, I know the two of you are cousins," she started, "but how exactly are you related to each other? I mean, you look so much alike, but Carl, you're darker skinned than Chris. There's got to be a story in there somewhere." Traci had only been part of their friend group for about two years, while the other friends had known each other since kindergarten.

Kim laughed. "Traci, you've never heard the story of the Bishops and the Farmers?" she asked.

Traci looked confused. "Uh, no, should I have?"

Darlene piped in. "I thought everyone in Eastboro knew this story. Chris and Carl's great-grandfather, Jerome Farmer, used to be the mayor of Eastboro, like early in the century. He was beloved by everyone in town. There's actually a statue of him downtown."

"Oh!" Traci exclaimed. "I've actually seen that statue. But I don't know the story."

"Carl, do you want to tell it, or should I?" Chris asked.

"Oh, can I?" Kim asked. "I want to see if I can get it right after all this time."

Both Chris and Carl waved her their permission. Kim was the group's best storyteller.

Kim cleared her throat. "Okay, here goes," she said. "So Jerome Farmer was the mayor in like 1915 or something. He had a bunch of kids. Two of them were identical twin daughters, Missy and Cissy."

"They were not called Missy and Cissy," Traci objected. "You're making that up."

"No, really," Kim insisted. "Right guys?" Chris and Carl nodded. "They're nicknames for Melissa and Cecilia. So anyway, they're beautiful girls, and when they graduated from high school, they went to business school to learn to type, and other office-type secretarial skills. So Missy, or Cissy, I don't remember which one it was—"

"It was Missy," Carl interjected, representing his grandmother.

"Okay, Missy," Kim went on. "Missy's in a classroom before class, and one of the younger teachers walks by and sees her sitting there. He's overtaken by her beauty and goes in and starts talking to her. She seems pretty into it, and they talk for a while. So then, class is about to start, and not wanting to walk away without making plans to see her again, he asks her out. She says she will go out with him, but only if he brings a date for her identical twin sister, too. So Saturday comes along, and Missy and Cissy go out on a date with this guy and, as it turns out, his younger brother. They go on a bunch of dates over the next few months, and eventually, both couples fall in love, and both brothers propose to both sisters! They said yes, of course, and then they all got married at a huge double wedding. A newspaper reporter came to the wedding and took pictures, and the story was featured the next day on the front page of *The Eastboro Journal*. 'Clyde and Cecil Bishop, brothers, marry identical twin daughters of the mayor, Cissy and Missy Farmer.' Then the paper in Boston picks up and runs the story, and the next thing you know, the story has become a nationwide human-interest story!"

"Oh my God!" Traci exclaimed. "Kim, how do you know all this?"

Kim smirked. "Those of us that went to DeMarco Elementary have all known each other for years and years. I don't remember a time when I didn't know this story. So anyway, Missy and Cissy eventually had children, and these kids are first cousins, but genetically, they're kind of like half-brothers and half-sisters because their moms have identical genes, and then their dads are brothers! So they're like double cousins, too. And they all have the same grandparents! So when Chris and Carl had to do their family trees at DeMarco in fourth grade, there were whole branches missing!"

"So Carl," Traci said, trying to work this out in her head, "your dad is a Bishop. And Chris, it must be your mom who was, too, since your last name is Mahoney. So they're first cousins, and you two are second cousins, but also you're more like first cousins because your parents are like brother and sister. And your grandmas are identical twins. Can you tell them apart?"

Chris shrugged. "I think so," he said. "I don't think they've ever tried to trick us, but if they did, the joke's on them since we had no idea!"

"They go everywhere together," Carl put in. "They don't live together, but they definitely travel as a pair. My Grandpa Cecil died ten years ago, but Chris's Grandpa Clyde is still kicking around. He's like the king of the Bishop clan."

"And Chris and Carl have hundreds of Bishop and Farmer cousins," Darlene added. "Any time you see anyone with those names in Eastboro, you can pretty much assume they're Chris and Carl's cousins. Both the Farmer twins and the Bishop brothers came from huge families."

"I've heard you guys talk about your cousins a lot," Traci admitted. "It just never occurred to me that you weren't talking about the same people over and over."

"And Carl's darker skinned because his mother's from Puerto Rico," Kim explained. She put her hand to her mouth. "Oh, Carl, I'm sorry, is it okay that I said that?"

"Why wouldn't it be?" Traci asked.

Carl shrugged. "I don't know what things were like at Fremont Junior High," he said, referring to Traci's previous school, "but at Randall, there was a lot of tension between different ethnic groups. I never knew there was anything 'wrong' with being Puerto Rican until I went to Randall Junior High in seventh grade and mentioned to someone that my mom was from San Juan. He said something back to me that I didn't understand, and when I asked my mother about it later, she cried and told me not to repeat it, because it was a really mean thing to say about people from Puerto Rico. I, well, kind of stopped talking about it at school after that. I liked having the image of being a bad boy and all, but I really didn't want to get in any kind of fist fights about where my mom came from. That just seemed way too big and dangerous. It scared me."

Everyone in the room was silent for a moment. Carl took a swig from his beer bottle. "Hey," he said lightly. "C'mon, it's okay. It's all a good story, about the Bishops and Farmers. Someone should write a book. Maybe I will someday."

Kim reached out and put her hand on his knee. Carl froze. He tried not to tighten his leg muscles. He took a deep breath. He knew that Kim was only comforting him. It meant nothing to her. They were friends. She was trying to help. It did kind of help, just not in a way she probably knew.

Ten minutes later, they were on a new subject, and drinks were getting lower again. This time, Carl let his fingers linger a bit on Kim's back when he let her know he was going to get more drinks. She turned to face him, and her face came close to his. His breath sped up, and his feet tingled. He had to push it down, push it away. Feeling attracted to Kim wasn't going to do him any good. It was only going to lead to frustration and confusion.

SEARCHING FOR CHANGE

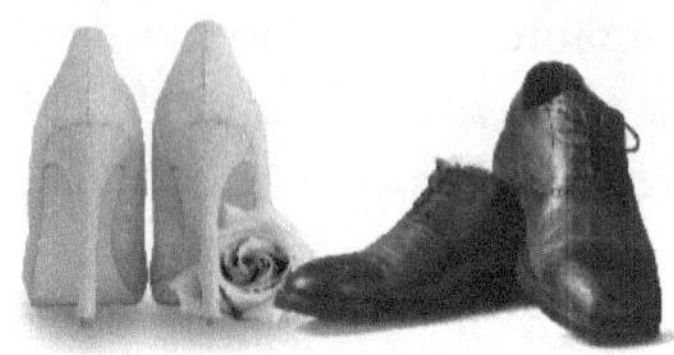

When Carl came back with the drinks, he opened the wine cooler and handed it to Kim. She smiled her thanks and took a chug. She gathered her thoughts, then excused herself to use the restroom.

Kim grabbed Darlene around her upper arm and pulled her off the bed, away from Charlie and along with her into the bathroom. She shut the door and made sure it was latched.

"Darlene," she said, breathing hard. "Here's the deal. I need you to get Charlie's car keys for me."

Darlene rubbed her arm gingerly where Kim had been grasping her. "Are you out of your mind?" she exclaimed. "I'm not gonna let you drive his car. He's not gonna let you drive his car. You've been drinking all night!" She looked at Kim like she had two heads.

"Uh, hello?" Kim responded. "I'm not gonna go anywhere in the car. I just, uh, I think I left something in the back seat earlier."

"What are you talking about?" Darlene said, shaking her head in confusion. "You weren't even in Charlie's car earlier. I don't think you've ever been in Charlie's car."

Kim rolled her eyes. "I don't know, Darlene," she said through her teeth. "I think there's something in there I need to get," she said desperately. "I was thinking, I could just walk down there with Carl, and, like, see if maybe there's something there I need to get."

"What . . ." Darlene stopped midsentence. "Oh," she said, leaving her mouth in an "o" shape even when sound stopped coming out. "You wanna go dig for change in the back seat of Charlie's car with Carl??" Now she laughed. "Oh my God, Kim, are you even drunker than I thought you were?"

Kim averted her eyes and stepped back. "No!" she insisted. "I've still got my wits. I'm fine! I've had like three wine coolers and one glass of punch at the prom, over like four hours. No, it's just . . . Carl has been so sweet tonight. I mean, did you see the way he was looking at me when I came out of my house in my prom dress? Then he danced every slow dance with me. He keeps getting up to get me drinks. And when he was talking about being scared at Randall? I never knew that about him. He was being so vulnerable. I mean, how can there be something I don't know about Carl? And he keeps touching me on this one place on my back. It's driving me crazy! I mean, it's getting me all hot and horny! I kinda want to get him out of this room and alone and see what happens!"

Darlene changed her expression from one of levity to another of concerned empathy. "I get that," she told her friend. "Listen, I'll see what I can do. No good being horny on prom night and not being able to cash in. I just hope that Carl's not too drunk to cash in!" She erupted once more in laughter.

Kim smacked her on the upper arm with an open palm. "Cut it out! Just go talk to Charlie. I'm gonna go suggest to Carl that we go for a walk."

Darlene took two deep breaths to compose herself and rubbed her arm again. "Lay off my arm, Brutus," she said. "My mom is gonna go batshit if I come home with a huge bruise. She'll never let me see Charlie again!"

Kim opened the door, and they reentered the room. Carl was still sitting on the edge of the bed, now with his legs sprawled open and his shirt untucked. He looked a bit rugged. Kim bit her bottom lip and walked over to him slowly. She sat down by his side, and he turned to her with a smile. She smiled back.

"Carl," she whispered more loudly than intended in his ear. He leaned closer to her, seemingly to be able to hear her better in the noisy room, touching her back again in the same place. She felt a whoosh through her body. "Do you wanna go for a walk outside with me?"

Carl's eyes opened wider, and she could practically see his pupils dilating. "Okay," he said and stood. Kim stood, too, in a slow and hopefully dignified manner. She glanced toward Darlene, who discreetly showed her Charlie's keys in her hand. She grabbed her purse.

"We're going for a walk," Kim announced to the group, walking toward the door. Darlene slipped the keys into her purse as she walked by.

"You're coming back, right?" Chris asked. He and Rhonda were now sharing a one-person armchair, and Rhonda was looking dangerously close to tipping her wine cooler bottle onto Chris's lap. He noticed, took it from her hand, and placed it on the desk next to them. "You know, Carl, I'm responsible for making sure you get home in one piece tomorrow. If anything happens to you, I'm gonna be a Bishop-Farmer outcast by morning."

"It's just a walk," Kim said, looking at Chris and shaking her head. "I'll make sure he's back and safely tucked into bed before you know it."

Chris gave her a sardonic grin. "I'm sure you will," he said.

Rhonda lifted her head from his shoulder. "Be nice, Chris," she said with a slight slur. "It's prom night. It's still prom night, isn't it?" She giggled.

Kim grabbed Carl around the wrist and headed for the door.

As she closed the door from the outside, Carl pulled his arm free. "Hey, easy there," he said. "Slow down. Where are we going?"

Kim grabbed his left wrist with her right hand, more gently this time. Then she grabbed his right one with her left. She pulled him toward her so his hands would rest on her hips and kissed him on the mouth.

Carl recoiled like he'd been hit. "What are you doing?" he said.

Kim smiled. "What does it look like I'm doing?" she asked. "I'm kissing you. And now I'm taking you for a walk." She pulled Charlie's keys out of her purse and jingled them in the air.

"Wait a minute," Carl said guardedly, his eyes fixed on the set of keys. "You made it very clear to me that we were at the prom as friends. Remember? How is this just being friends?"

"Carl, you really are a true moron," Kim told him. "I'm basically handing you an invitation here. I'm going to Charlie's car now. I was trying to give you a preview, but I guess you're not interested. . . ." She started to walk down the hall toward the elevator.

"Wait, hold on!" Carl called after her. She stopped. She turned around and faced him. In a moment of buzzed courageousness, he took hold of her waist, pulled her close, and kissed her back. She rested her hands on his elbows, and they stood kissing like that for a few minutes before breaking away.

Kim held up the keys again. "Wanna go see if Charlie lost any change in his back seat?" *Please, please, please,* she thought, *don't let him think I'm really talking about finding loose change.*

Carl grinned, showing large, straight, white teeth. "So there's treasure in Charlie's back seat? Okay, let's go see if we can find it."

Kim let out a sigh of relief. It seemed like they were finally speaking the same language. For once. Maybe Carl wasn't such a moron after all.

TWO TICKETS TO PARADISE

They walked out through the hotel exit into the parking garage. It was a chilly night, and the wind blew through the open walls of the structure. Kim looked around for Charlie's car, a light blue four-door Chevy Cavalier with a Harvard University decal peeling off the back windshield. She spotted it and walked purposefully toward the parking space, Carl trailing behind her.

She stopped at the passenger-side front door and unlocked it with the key. Suddenly her heart started pounding. She was nervous. She was not used to being in situations like this. She was a planner, a plotter. She didn't often go off with boys to the back seats of cars. In fact, never. Something stopped her from opening the door right away. She was feeling desperate to initiate physical contact with Carl, but she didn't want to rush it. She reached for him and kissed him. They kissed each other hungrily and messily, hands moving freely over each other's bodies through their clothes. Kim felt Carl's hands on her breasts and bashfully worried that her off-the-shoulder dress might start to inch down. She opened the car's front door and reached back to unlock the back door.

Carl opened the door and stepped aside to let Kim get in first. Then he followed her and clumsily reached to kiss her as she fell backward on the seat. He reached up to stroke her hair, but his fingers got tangled in her hairspray. She laughed and grabbed her head. He gently freed his fingers, and then Kim guided his hands back to the front of her dress. He pulled the satiny fabric down lower on her torso and massaged and kissed the sensitive skin on her chest. Kim moaned involuntarily with pleasure. Then, she reached for his belt buckle. Once she had liberated his pants, she helped herself to a good caress of what in them. She let out another sound.

"Carl," she whispered, "look what you've been hiding down here all this time!"

Carl smiled in surprise at her response. Kim reached down to hike her dress up to her waist. She wasn't wearing anything underneath. Carl's smiling face transformed into a look of wonder and awe. Now that they were free of any barriers, they resumed kissing, and very quickly, they joined together. And then very quickly, much more quickly than Kim anticipated, it was over, and Carl was panting on the seat beside her. Kim immediately knew what had just happened. She felt sick.

"Carl," she said. "Oh, Carl, this was your first time, wasn't it? Oh my God, it didn't even occur to me—"

"No, Kim, it's okay," he told her. "Yeah. It was my first time. I should have told you, but there just didn't seem to be enough time. I'm sorry."

Kim propped herself up on her elbows. "No, Carl, it's me who should be sorry. If I had known . . . this would have been different. I never thought . . ."

Carl sat up on the seat and pulled his pants up. "It's fine. I mean, it's prom night, right? I mean, guys are losing their virginity all over town right now, right?"

Kim closed her eyes briefly, then opened them again. "Your first time on prom night. And you'll remember it the rest of your life."

"I'm okay with that," Carl told her. "I mean, I've known you forever. It's not like I just picked someone up off the street. You're my prom date! I'm just sorry I couldn't, you know, hold out longer." He turned to face her. "So judging by your reaction, I am assuming this was *not* your first time."

Kim sighed. "Oh, Carl. No, it was not my first time. But it wasn't like my thousandth time either, you know." She was not expecting to have to talk about this on prom night in the back seat of her best friend's boyfriend's car.

"Who was it?" he asked her. "Who was your first? I mean, obviously you get to know who my first was. It's only fair I should get to know yours."

Kim put her hand over her mouth and paused a moment, considering her next words. "It was at a party sophomore year. It was just some guy. I was high. I didn't plan it. It just happened."

"Wait, what party?" Carl asked.

She froze. She knew she had to say it. There was no way around it now. "It was at Jake Pierce's house. It was right before Christmas." She waited for him to work it out in his head.

Carl thought about it.

"I was there. I remember that party. I was there with Chris. He hadn't started going out with Rhonda by then, but he was planning on asking her out. I remember James was off making out with Cyndi Wells under the mistletoe. A group of us were passing a joint around, and Chris said he had another one in his jacket pocket and was gonna go get it. He was gone for a long time. You were there with us. You went off to try to find him. Later, Chris told me he hooked up with some girl in one of the upstairs bedrooms, which is why he didn't come back for so long."

Carl stopped.

"Oh my God, Kim, it was you. You did it with Chris?" He looked at her face, and her look of horror showed him the truth. "You two hooked up in a bedroom while I was sitting down there waiting for him to bring back a joint. Not only did you hook up, but he was your first!"

He lowered his elbows to his knees and put his forehead on his palm. "You did it with a guy who's not only my cousin, but also my best friend, and neither of you ever told me!"

Kim's face crumpled and she felt she would start crying, but instead she swallowed. "I asked him not to tell anyone," she told him. "I didn't want anyone to know. I didn't plan it, Carl. I really was just gonna try to find him because I wanted to smoke that joint. I figured he had hooked up with someone and forgotten about us, but when I went upstairs, he was coming out of the bathroom, and we were both so high, and we literally just started kissing without saying anything, and next thing you know, we were on some bed and we were doing it! It happened so fast!"

Carl stayed still and thought about what he had just heard. He knew people could do things they regretted when they were drunk or high. He had found himself in similar situations in the past, but luckily, they had never gotten that out of control.

"You guys didn't do anything wrong," he admitted. "I mean, neither of you were dating anyone. It's not like you were cheating on anyone. It's just so . . . I don't know. I mean, I'm here with you tonight, and we just . . . it's just weird. You must have known it would be weird."

"I thought it might be," Kim said softly, tears running down her cheek. "It crossed my mind. But sometimes, I just want things, and when I want them, I can usually make them happen! I didn't want to hurt you, Carl, I never would. I just

. . . I felt close to you tonight, and I wanted to show you, to let you know somehow how much I appreciated tonight!"

"A simple thank-you probably would have sufficed," Carl said.

"Okay," Kim said, wiping her cheek and nodding. "I deserved that. But I don't regret tonight. I didn't do anything I'm ashamed of. And I'm not wasted, if you're thinking that. I had a few drinks, but not enough to make me do anything I didn't already want to do. And I know you've only had like two or three beers. I was with you the whole time. And I could feel the vibes coming from you, too. You weren't just touching my back over and over in the same place by accident. So I'm not gonna feel bad about this. I'm not gonna let it ruin the whole night. Yes, I went all the way with your cousin, but it didn't mean anything. I don't even ever think about it, or about him. And obviously, he moved on, too. We were just stupid, high kids. I mean, I've never even really been that close to Chris."

I have actually resented him for years, she thought.

Carl felt his anger start to melt away. She was right. It was nothing. But he was confused. Why was Kim getting so defensive? Wasn't she the one who kept insisting they were there as friends? And didn't she think he was the biggest moron who ever lived? She had been telling him that since grade school. So why was Kim getting so emotional? He figured she would have been the type to laugh something like this off as nothing. And why, he really wanted to know, did she bring him to Charlie's car in the first place?

Carl opened the car door. "C'mon," he said. "Let's walk around a bit and get some air. Then we can stop in the lobby so you can go wash your face before we go back."

Kim sniffed. "What are you gonna say to Chris?" she asked.

He shrugged. "I don't know. Maybe nothing. Maybe something. I'll figure it out. But don't worry. If I do say something, it'll just be between me and him, I promise."

Kim gave him a grateful smile. "Thank you, Carl." She took his hand and squeezed gently. "I'm sort of flattered that you're going to remember this night forever. But I hope you just remember the good parts."

PULLING IT TOGETHER

Kim splashed water on her face. Then she did it again, and again. An older woman walked into the lobby bathroom and looked at her with concern. She forced herself to smile. The woman turned away and stepped into a stall. Kim grabbed some paper towels and dabbed at the mascara running around her eyes. The makeup came off on the towel, leaving her eyes looking undefined with red streaks. She decided not to care. There was no way her friends wouldn't work out that something happened. She would just have to decide what she wanted them to hear. She was good at telling stories. Not to hurt people. Just to protect them. And herself.

After several minutes, she decided she had left Carl in the lobby long enough. She took one more glance at the mirror, smiled tentatively, and then stepped out of the bathroom.

Carl gave her a gentle smile. "You okay?" he asked.

She nodded. "I don't think we'll fool anyone when we go back, but that's okay. Just let me take the lead, okay?" Carl nodded. "You okay?" she asked.

Carl allowed himself a grin. "Kim," he said, "no matter what happens now, or what happened before, something huge happened for me tonight. I feel like beating on my chest like a gorilla!"

Kim laughed. "A gorilla. Sounds about right."

They caught the elevator and rode to the third floor. As they approached their room, they looked at each other and tried on their most convincing smiles. Then Carl knocked on the door.

Michelle opened the door with a smile. Then she looked at Kim, and her smile fell. "You okay?" she said softly. She glanced accusingly at Carl.

Kim spoke quickly. "Oh, yeah, Michelle, I'm fine," she said. "I just had a couple too many. I got a bit sick. I had to wash my face."

Michelle looked at her closely. "Okay," she said tentatively. "If you say so." She stood aside and let them in. Everyone looked up as they entered the main area of the room.

Darlene gave Kim a look of concern. They had a certain way of communicating without words. She let Darlene know that she was okay.

"Everything's fine, everyone," Kim said to the group. "I'm fine. I just got a bit sick. You're just not used to seeing me with my makeup off. I know! It's a scary sight!" She walked over to the bed and grabbed her overnight bag from the floor. "I'm just gonna go to the bathroom and change," she announced. She walked away, and no one spoke.

Chris looked at Carl. Carl looked back and tried to keep his expression blank. He was afraid to show any feelings at the moment. He knew Chris was not to blame, but it sure felt like he was guilty of something to Carl.

AFTER THE FALL

Eventually, Darlene prodded Michelle and Joey, who were back to making out in the corner, and everyone got up to change and get in bed. Carl watched Kim as she sank into an exhausted slumber, wearing a long T-shirt with a teddy bear on the front and sweatpants. Then he pulled back the sheets and got out of the bed, careful not to step on Traci and Dougo on the floor between the beds. He found the key to the room on the dresser and let himself out into the hall. He leaned against the wall outside the room and slid down to the floor. He pulled his knees to his chest and held them to his body. He let himself remember all the details of the night, starting with picture-taking at Kim's house before dinner, and ending with them coming back to the room after their walk and everyone giving them suspicious looks. He tried to sort the good from the uncomfortable but realized they came as a package. This would be his memory of prom.

He heard the door open beside him and Chris slipped into the hall. "I was wondering where you went," he said to Carl. "Rhonda is pretty much passed out in there. We can't talk out here. C'mon, let's go for a walk."

Carl got up, and they walked to the elevators. They traveled down to the first floor and took seats in the large empty lobby, away from prying ears.

"Something's wrong," Chris said. "Something happened with you and Kim, and it wasn't good. What was it?"

"No, Chris," Carl told him. "Something happened with me and Kim and it was great. But then I found out something that wasn't good." He looked at him with a sneer. "Something I should have known a long time ago. Something that might have made things a lot different for me."

A look of horror came over Chris's face, similar to how Kim had looked earlier when Carl figured it all out.

"Oh my God," he said. "She told you, didn't she? Oh my God, Carl, I'm so sorry."

Carl shook his head. "It's okay," he told him, even though it might not have been. "She told me everything. She told me it was her idea to not say anything. I know there's nothing between you. But God, it was horrifying, Chris. You know it was my first time. It wasn't so mind-blowing for her, I don't think. But then we talked, and she cried. It's not how I imagined it at all. I wasn't expecting fireworks or anything, but I sure as hell wasn't expecting crying."

Chris shook his head forlornly. "Dude, I know you're saying it's okay, but it's not," he said. "I don't make a habit of doing things like that. It was a total fluke. It was like the timing was there. I've never thought of her in any romantic way. We never even talked about it after. And I've never done something like that with anyone else. You know everything else there is to know about me. I really never keep things from you. God, I feel awful. Your first time."

"She felt awful, too," Carl told him. "She didn't know. How could she not know? I mean, I've been on like five dates my entire life." He shook his head. "But I still don't even understand. I mean, why? Why did she even want to? She's totally the one who initiated it. It was definitely planned out to some degree. And she's never expressed any interest in me whatsoever. And I don't think I've ever expressed any interest in her besides just being friends. We've always been friends."

"Carl, man, I hate to tell you this," Chris stated. "But we all saw the two of you slow dancing tonight. Rhonda and I were both saying we've never seen the two of you looking so relaxed and loose. It looked so easy for you. You were smiling, and she had her eyes closed. Dude, there was something going on there, maybe something chemical, I don't know. We were surprised you two didn't start making out on the dance floor!"

"Really?" Carl responded. "No, we were just comfortable with each other. It's because we've known each other for so long. And because we didn't have anything riding on it. We were there as friends."

Chris laughed. "Yeah, like Sally and James were there as friends. That's what they'll say at their wedding. No, Carl, there's something there. You just need to find out what it is. A girl just doesn't decide to go all the way with a guy if she's not feeling something. It could just be that she wants to do it with you, but is that such a bad thing? Kim is pretty hot. You could do much worse. Please, no matter what happens, please don't let what happened with her and me get in your way. And please, don't tell anyone about it, okay? It was definitely too close to the time I started going out with Rhonda. No overlap, but she might not like it if she finds out. It's definitely an ancient and insignificant history."

Carl sat and looked at his knees for a minute. "You really think there could be something there?" he asked. He trusted Chris's judgment, sometimes more than his own, but now he didn't know what to think.

"Carl," Chris said, "we all saw Kim when you came back from your 'walk.' It was so clear that the girl was feeling some emotions. Not the kind you feel for someone who's just your friend. Yeah, man, there's something there." There was a pause. "C'mon, let's go back to the room. I'm exhausted. We both need to get some sleep."

"Okay," Carl agreed, standing. He felt slightly woozy. He hoped he wouldn't wake up with a headache in the morning. He had too much thinking to do.

They went back to the room, and Carl crawled stealthily into the full-sized bed next to Kim. She was sound asleep and rolled onto his arm as he adjusted his position on the bed. He could feel her body rise and fall against him as she breathed. It was reassuring. He let himself drift off to sleep and hoped that he didn't start to snore.

MORNING AFTER

When Kim woke up, her head was resting in the crook of Carl's arm, and she did not remember how it got that way. Carl was still asleep. She was able to see his profile, and it looked relaxed. She felt relieved. Then she felt the guilt return. *My God,* she thought, *what have I done to Carl?*

After a few minutes, Kim picked up on movement around her. Her friends were getting up. Most had slept with their dates on the floor, with Darlene and Charlie taking the other full-sized bed. They were all standing up from their nests and stretching their arms and legs. Kim felt Carl's body shift, and he opened his eyes. He glanced down at her and smiled.

"Good morning," he said hoarsely.

"Good morning," she said. "You sleep okay?" That was what her father asked her each morning when she came down for breakfast. Sometimes, he'd ask her more than once.

Carl stretched his arms behind his head. "I could use three or four more hours of sleep, but yeah, I guess so. You?"

"I slept like a baby," she admitted. And she had. She felt rested. She didn't have a headache. Her body felt at ease. She had slept all night in Carl's arms. That was something new.

They both got up, and Kim went to the bathroom to wash her face. Traci was at the sink brushing her teeth when she entered. "You okay?" Traci asked her around her toothbrush.

Kim nodded. "Yeah, I'm okay. Everything's good." She splashed water on her face. It felt good.

"Do I need to have Dougo go kick Carl's ass or something?" Traci asked with concern.

Kim laughed. "No, I think I did a good enough job of that myself last night. Verbally. I think I wounded him." She strained to keep the tears in but failed.

"Oh, oh Kim," Traci said, putting her arms around her shoulders. "I'm sure it's okay. I'm sure he's fine. It'll be okay."

"He'll be okay," Kim agreed. "I just hope I can say the same. If I lose Carl as a friend, I don't know what I'd do. I don't remember a time before Carl. I feel like I punched a hole in my own heart."

Traci handed her a tissue from the box attached to the wall. "Here," she said. "Splash your face again. It will help. And we'll get the girls together later, and we'll all talk it out."

"No," Kim told her. "I can't today. I promised my mother I'd help her get ready for her open house this afternoon. But it's okay. I'll talk to Carl later. I'll work it out with him. I just hope I can make it right again."

They checked out of the hotel at eleven. Charlie and Darlene drove Chris and Joey back to Kim's house to get their cars, then they all drove back to the hotel to get Carl, Kim, Traci, Rhonda, Michelle, and Dougo. They headed to IHOP for breakfast, and then headed home. Chris and Rhonda drove Carl and Kim back to Kim's house. Kim asked Carl to hang around for a bit, and then she would drive him home. She wanted to talk.

"I thought you had to help your mom with an open house this afternoon," Carl said.

"I just made that up because I didn't want to have to talk to my friends about last night," Kim admitted. "Actually, my mom's at her open house right now until five, and my dad's at my aunt's house. He won't be home until tonight. Let's go inside."

"No one's home?" Carl asked. "Where are your brothers and sisters?"

"They're at Aunt Karen's, too. Mom set it all up because of the prom this weekend, so I didn't have to worry about anything. We have the house to ourselves."

Carl followed Kim into the house cautiously. He lived about a mile away, and had been here dozens of times, but never alone with Kim, and never the morning after having sex with Kim in a car after the prom.

Kim went into the den and sat on the couch. She motioned for Carl to come sit next to her. "We need to talk," she told him.

Carl sat down stiffly. He wasn't sure where this conversation would lead, but he guessed it was a good idea to get it over with. "Okay," he said. "You start."

Kim sighed deeply. "First of all, I'm sorry," she said. "I've been leading you in all sorts of crazy directions the last few weeks and I know it's confusing, but it's confusing for me, too! I never meant to do anything to make you uncomfortable, or to hurt you. You must know that."

"Sometimes I don't know what to think," Carl admitted. "Sometimes you're like two completely different people. I don't know who I'm with from one time to the next."

"I know," Kim sighed. "I've been that way to myself, too. But I do want to tell you something. Last night wasn't random. It wasn't an impulsive thing. I had thought about it, even before prom. I wasn't sure it would happen, but I wanted it to happen. And I'm glad it did. I just wish it had happened differently."

"How differently?" Carl wondered.

"Well, for one thing, we wouldn't have been so rushed," Kim started. "We would have taken our time. And we wouldn't have been drinking. And we would have been someplace more private."

"Yeah, those things would have been good," Carl agreed, feeling himself starting to respond physically to her words.

"Carl, I have to tell you," Kim said, sliding closer to him on the couch. "What happened between us last night might have happened, uh, a bit quick, but it was actually pretty enjoyable while it lasted. It felt really good."

Carl jerked his head back. "It did?" he asked. "I can't imagine you had time to even notice."

Kim laughed. "Carl, when something feels right, it feels right. And we felt right. Even for the briefest time, I felt it. And," she moved even closer and ran her hand across his cheek, "I want to try to feel it again. This time, the right way."

Carl closed his eyes briefly and took a breath. "Kim, I really want that, too," he admitted. "But first I need to know, what's going on with us? Why now? Why me? You've been so clear about us never being more than friends. What changed?"

Kim put a hand on his knee. "I don't know, Carl. To tell you the truth, I don't know if anything's changed. It's possible I've just been lying to myself and you about me wanting us to just be friends. Maybe that's not what I want."

"So what do you want?"

"I want to be around you, I guess. I feel safe with you. I always have. Maybe too safe. Maybe that's why I kind of want us to be, you know, something more now. Like maybe we should take a risk with each other." She squeezed his knee. "What do you want, Carl?"

Carl thought about it briefly. "I don't know, Kim. I mean, we've been friends for so long, and you've never given the slightest hint that you wanted more than that. I'd pretty much removed it as a possibility years ago. And you're always putting me down. I mean, you call me a moron all the time! That's not usually the best sign that someone thinks highly of you."

Kim smirked. "I know. I've been horrible to you. For years. But you wanna know a secret? If I really thought you were a moron, I probably wouldn't have come within twenty feet of you. You're no moron, Carl. Sometimes, I think you're actually the smartest one among our friends. You get the best grades, and you barely even have to try. It's just that you're always standing in Chris's shadow. Always letting him take the lead. It's like he's the boss of you. It's hard to get past Chris to get to you." She remembered what she had told him about her and Chris the night before and cringed. "That didn't come out the way I wanted it to."

"No, but I know what you meant," Carl told her. "Chris has always been the one to take control of our group of friends. I don't mind so much, but it is kind of like standing in a shadow. I do depend on him a lot to know what to do next."

"Carl," Kim said softly, "when I ask you what you want, what I wanna know is what *you* want, not what you think I want you to want, or what anyone else, even Chris, would think. So what do you want, Carl?"

He put his hand over hers. "I think I want to see what could happen to us if we were more than just friends," he told her. "But I think if we're gonna do this, we should do it right. We should go on dates and stuff. Hold hands. You know, stuff people do when they're together."

Kim nodded. "Are you asking me out?"

"I am," Carl affirmed.

"Okay, then, yes, I will go out with you," she told him.

"Good."

Their hands were still on Carl's knee. "Now that we've decided to go on a date and give it a try," Kim said, "do you think we can get back to talking about the fact that my family is all gone for the next four hours and we're alone in my house? And we have all the time and privacy in the world?"

Carl had no doubts that this information interested him greatly. He leaned toward her and they kissed, slowly, thoroughly, gently, and deliberately.

After several minutes, Kim whispered, "Do you want to go up to my room?"

Carl wanted to go up to Kim's room. He continued to kiss her, and then said, "Kim, we didn't talk about it last night, but are you on the pill? I mean, I obviously didn't have anything with me last night, and . . ."

Kim smiled. "Yes, I'm covered," she told him. "We are free to do whatever we want. And what I want is to do it very, very slowly."

I'VE GOT YOU COVERED

They took the time to explore over their clothes, and then slowly undressed each other and explored what was underneath. Hands continued to return to each other's faces, and through each other's hair, and then back to their bodies, finding each other's most erogenous places. They used their kisses and words to express their appreciation of each other's bodies. Finally, Kim took Carl's hand and led him to the bed. She lay down and pulled him on top of her. She whispered her thoughts in his ear and moved slowly below him. He moved slowly, at times being totally still, and moved when she told him to. He used his breath to pace himself, and finally, knowing that their second time was in no way going to be a marathon session, he let himself release, feeling waves and waves of pleasure, and seeing the same on her face as she looked at him. When it ended, he held himself over her, his elbows propping him up so he wouldn't crush her with his body.

"Can we call this my first time?" he asked her softly. "I think this is the moment I want to remember forever."

"Only if we can call it mine, too," Kim whispered back with her eyes closed. "Carl, that was amazing. I told you that you were the smartest person I know. You are a fast learner."

Carl smiled. "And you are an amazing teacher."

They kissed some more, and then lay on her twin bed beside each other, staring at the Bon Jovi poster tacked on the ceiling above Kim's bed. Eventually, they decided to get off the bed, get dressed, and go downstairs to get drinks and watch a movie on video.

They sat together on the couch, while previews played, eating microwave popcorn from a bowl. Suddenly, Kim squealed.

"What?" Carl said, almost upending the bowl in surprise.

"Carl!" she exclaimed. "We just had sex! We had, like, really good sex! And, we're, like, cuddling on the couch after sex, eating popcorn!"

Carl laughed. "I guess we are!" he agreed. "I never would have imagined this would be happening twenty-four hours ago! What are our friends gonna say when they find out?"

Now Kim laughed. "They are not gonna believe it! I mean, they think we'd be the last ones to get together. I always call you a moron, and you tell everyone I'm like your sister!" She sighed. "Maybe we'll win Cutest Couple at next year's senior prom!"

Carl turned to look at her. "I didn't think you cared about that kind of stuff! You always make fun of it! I saw the way you were teasing James and Sally when they won last night."

Kim rolled her eyes. "We all were! They were practically asking for it, being so damn cute all the time. They're a cliche. We're a novelty. Plus, I was just jealous. You have to remember from now on, when I'm mean, or sarcastic, I'm usually covering for something else. I'm very insecure. If you remember that, it will save us from a lot of future arguments."

"Good to know," Carl said.

The movie started, and they turned their attention to the TV. They snuck glances at each other from time to time, sometimes catching each other's eyes and smiling embarrassedly at being caught. At five o'clock, Kim's mother came home, dressed in a gray skirt suit and carrying a briefcase. She saw Kim and Carl with their limbs curled together on the couch and her eyes went wide.

"Well, this is something new," she said with a smile. "I take it prom was good."

Kim and Carl laughed. "Yeah, mom," Kim told her. "Prom was very good. The movie's almost over. We'll tell you all about it when it's done."

Mrs. Drake shook her head as she walked toward the kitchen. "You'll tell me some of it, I would guess," she accurately predicted. "I'll be in the kitchen making us something to eat. I'm starving. Dad and the kids won't be home for dinner. Carl, you like Hamburger Helper, right?"

"You know me so well, Mrs. Drake," he answered, smiling at Kim. They turned their attention back to the movie, both feeling warm and happy.

SCHOOL DAYZ

It was lunchtime before anyone talked about prom details. "We're splitting up tables for the day," Michelle announced when they all arrived at their regular table with their trays. "Girls, come with me."

Darlene and Traci shrugged to each other, but they all complied, picked up their trays, said goodbye to the boys, and followed Michelle to a table halfway across the room.

Once they all sat down, Sally looked at each of her friends. "Okay, what happened after we left?" she asked. She and James had left the hotel early on prom night to have a sleepover at James's house, since his parents had conveniently gone out of town for the weekend. They'd missed all the action but had quite a bit of their own.

"We should be the ones to ask you," Kim responded. "What's that really shiny thing around your neck?"

Sally reached up and touched the triple heart charm that rested on her chest. "Oh, this little thing?" she said. "Oh, it's just a little token of Jamie committing to spend the rest of his life with me, no big deal!"

The other girls gasped, and Michelle and Sally both smiled. They had talked on the phone the night before. "Make sure they see the tiny diamond," Michelle instructed.

They all admired her necklace and asked more about their night and their promises to stay together.

When Sally was done with her story, Michelle turned to Kim. "What I want to know, Kim," she said, "is what happened with you and Carl at the hotel?"

Sally put her hand to her face. "Something happened at the hotel?" Michelle had not filled her in on anything but her own prom details yet.

Kim looked from face to face. "There are some things you just can't talk about, even with your best friends," she told them. "But yeah, things happened with me and Carl at the hotel. And things happened with me and Carl again at my house the next day. And things are gonna happen over the weekend when Carl and I go out on a date." She squealed. Now all the girls put their hands to their faces.

"You're going out?" Darlene exclaimed. "On a real date? With Carl Bishop? I thought you guys were 'just friends'! I mean, I can get being friends who do it, but friends that date??"

Kim smiled. "Big announcement," she told them. "I no longer think of Carl Bishop as just a friend. We're gonna try it out, see how it goes. Kind of like an experiment."

"Wait, you and Carl did it?" Sally asked in a hushed voice. She tended to shy away from talk like this, but this news was too gigantic to ignore.

"A little," Kim responded with false modesty. She glanced over at the boys' table and made fleeting eye contact with Carl. They both smiled.

"A little," Traci responded. "Great answer. You did it a little at the hotel, and a little at your house? That sounds like it adds up to kinda a lot!"

They all laughed. "But seriously, Kim," Darlene said gently, "you looked so sad when you came back in the room, like you'd been crying."

"You were crying?" Sally asked. "Remind me to stick around next time. It seems like I missed a lot!"

"I was fine," Kim assured her friends. "Carl and I were just talking, and some stuff came up from the past, and I got all emotional. It's all good. We're good, I promise."

"What are you gonna do on your date?" Michelle asked. "I mean, first dates are usually awkward, and you try to get to know each other. You've already known Carl for over ten years! You're gonna need to do something extra special."

Kim shrugged. "I don't know. It doesn't matter," she told them. "We can do anything. Maybe we can go bowling or something."

"Bowling," Traci repeated. "I bet if last week Carl had asked you out to go bowling with him, you would have called him a total moron!"

Kim grinned. "Yeah, he's such a cute little moron. But seriously, Traci, that's a good point. I need to work on calling Carl by his real name from now on. It's only fair. Did you guys know he made the honor roll last term? That's really not moron behavior."

The boys could hear the excitement coming from the girls' table, even from so far away. "What do you think they're talking about?" Chris asked James and Carl. "There was so much going on at that hotel, it could be anything."

"It sounds like I missed some stuff by leaving early," James lamented. "Any big news I need to know?"

Carl and Chris glanced at each other, and Chris deferred to Carl with a wave of his hand. Carl cleared his throat. "Well, yeah, there might be some news you might hear about."

"Let me guess," James said with a smirk. "You and Kim hooked up on prom night?"

Carl looked at him quizzically. "How did you know that?" he asked James. "I don't think it's public knowledge yet."

James laughed. "Are you kidding?" he asked. "I think anyone who saw you two dancing to Madonna at prom would disagree! It was obvious there were vibes going on that were more than just friendship vibes. If you told me you didn't hook up, I would have been more surprised."

"Well, okay then," Carl replied, feeling slightly embarrassed. "Then I'll tell you something you both don't know yet. Kim and I didn't just hook up, twice, by the way, but we are also, like, together now, like, going out together."

Chris spit out a bit of his milk on his tray. "What?" he asked. "You're like boyfriend-girlfriend going out now?"

Carl gestured to James. "Do you have anything to say, or spit out, about this before I go on?" he offered.

"Uh," James said. "Uh, I don't know. Congratulations? I mean, I'm a bit surprised, seeing that she thinks you're a total moron. At least that's what she's been saying since second grade!"

"She's rescinded that opinion now," Carl announced. "I'm not a moron anymore, apparently. I guess maybe I never was. I suspected, but, you know, I didn't want to challenge her opinion. We just won't tell her I already knew."

Chris laughed. "Oh my God, Carl," he said. "This is wicked awesome! You and Kim! I never would have put the two of you together, but now that I'm thinking of it, I should have! You're perfect for each other!"

Carl nodded. "We might be," he agreed. "We really kinda need to find out. So I'm taking her out this weekend." He paused. "Or, I guess she's kinda taking me out, since I don't have my license yet, and she has a car. Where should we go? I need some good ideas. And it has to be some place where we can't just, like, go off and do it instead. It has to be a real first date."

James smiled at Carl. "Dude, first, I just have to say," he lowered his voice, "seriously, congratulations on the first-time thing! That's kinda a big fucking deal. And second, there's nothing wrong with just going off and doing it at any time. But if not, maybe take her to a movie, or skating. Or maybe bowling? Something you can do together that's fun."

Carl nodded. "Yeah, those are good ideas," he agreed. "I mean, it's not like we have to do the first-date routine of asking about each other's family and stuff. We already know so much about each other. Yeah, I like the idea of going bowling. I'll see what she thinks about that."

BOWLING FOR DOLLARS

The bowling idea went over well, and Kim saw the fact that they both had the same idea as being a good omen. They went to Chandler Lanes on Saturday night and bowled two frames. Then they went to the arcade area and played video games. Kim was particularly good at Ms. Pac-Man, and Carl cheered her on from the side, laying quarters on the machine so she could play again and again. After the quarters ran out, they went to the snack bar and ate steamed hot dogs and greasy fries.

As they walked back to Kim's car later, Kim was all smiles as she held Carl's hand. "That was so much fun!" she exclaimed. "I can't remember the last time I went bowling when there wasn't a big group. It can get so boring waiting for your turn. But this was fun!" She twirled herself around in Carl's arm like Ginger Rogers with Fred Astaire, dancing happily in the parking lot.

Carl grinned. "I had fun, too. And your ass looked really hot bending down to bowl in those tight little jeans of yours!"

Kim laughed. "You know," she told him, "sometimes I forget you're one of the original bad boys." She stopped in the middle of the lot and put her arms around him. "Come here, bad boy," she said seductively, and she reached up to kiss him.

He put his arms tightly around her and lifted her slightly off the ground as they kissed. He set her back down, and they continued back toward her car. "Best first date *ever*," Carl declared.

"How many first dates have you been on where you've already gotten lucky with the girl twice before the date even started?" Kim inquired, reaching into her purse for her keys.

Carl pretended to think. "Uh, just the one!"

They both got into the car, and Kim started it up. "Where to?" she asked.

"I don't know," Carl responded. "Anywhere. Someplace quiet, I guess?"

"Well, then not my house," Kim said. "I would guess there would still be little kids bouncing around trying not to go to sleep over there."

"My house?" Carl offered. "My dad has been working nights, and my mom's probably out. My brother might be there, but he won't bother us if we don't bother him."

"I haven't been to your house in ages," Kim said. "Yeah, let's go there. Maybe just hang out for a while."

They rode for ten minutes, listening to the local rock station and singing along to the songs they knew. Kim pulled up in front of the Bishops' house, turned off the engine, and switched off the headlights. They both stayed in the car.

"There are no cars here," Kim said, looking in the driveway.

"No, it kinda looks like no one's home," Carl agreed.

"Hmm," Kim contemplated. "This might be dangerous."

"I live for danger," Carl informed her.

They opened the car doors and rushed to the house. Carl unlocked the door, and they stepped inside. They were greeted by darkness and silence, and then a hungry meow. Carl switched on the light. An orange tabby approached his legs and rubbed up against his ankle.

"Hey, Tiger," Carl greeted the cat. "Looks like no one's been home for a bit. Let me just go give him some food."

Carl went into the kitchen as Kim roamed around the familiar front hall. She could see the purple, fluorescent lights of an aquarium emanating from Carl's brother Scott's room, but aside from that, all the bedroom lights were off. Carl came out of the kitchen alone and took her hand. He led her down the long hallway to his room and pulled her inside. There, wordlessly, he kissed her, and she responded. Carl shut the door and turned the lock. They didn't speak until all their clothes were off and they were on the bed.

"I was so looking forward to doing this again," Kim said softly.

"Me too," Carl admitted. "I totally owe the rest of the Bishop clan for having the good foresight to give us some privacy."

This time was even better than the last. Carl felt he was getting the idea of how things worked and what felt good to Kim. She urged him to experiment, and he gladly obliged. He felt the pleasure lasted even longer this time, and he could tell she felt the same. He thought to himself that he could not imagine a time when he would ever get tired of doing the deed with Kim. He was addicted. It was his drug. But now, inexplicably, he felt that he needed a cigarette. He asked Kim, and she agreed to get dressed and go outside for a smoke with him.

"I hardly smoke anymore since I got caught at school in the fall," Kim told him, "but now does seem like a good time."

"My dad said he quit, but my mother still smokes," Carl told her. "I maybe have a few when I'm out with the guys, but I don't make a habit of it otherwise."

He went into his mother's room and found an open pack and a lighter. They went outside and sat on adjacent lawn chairs in the yard.

"It's so nice out here," Kim observed. "It's almost summer. I can't wait."

"It's gonna be our last summer in high school," Carl said.

Kim faced him. "Will you and Chris be going to Webster Lake all the time like usual? I think you were gone most of the time last summer."

Carl shrugged and thought about it. The idea did not appeal to him as much as it usually did. When he visualized the beach at Webster Lake, Kim's naked sexy body was not there with him.

"I don't have to," he told her quickly. "Or you can come out there with me if you want. I don't know Chris's plans. He was talking about getting a job. I might be thinking about that, too." He thought that he could use some extra money now if he was going to have a steady girlfriend.

"Hmm," Kim responded. "A job. Maybe I'll look for a job, too. Maybe some babysitting or something. Or an ice cream shop would be fun." She leaned up against his arm. "And long, hot summer nights with you, that would be fun, too."

"Yeah," Carl agreed. "Long, hot, slow summer nights."

Kim smiled up at him. "Best first date *ever*," she said softly, and then took his hand and led him back inside to his bedroom and locked the door.

Mrs. Bishop came home at 12:45. She poked her head into Carl's room, where the teens were playing video games on Carl's small black-and-white TV. She greeted Kim familiarly.

"Mijo," she said to Carl, "it's late. Time for Kim to go home."

Kim got up, put on her shoes, and said good night to Mrs. Bishop. Carl followed her out the front door and to her car.

"I'm gonna go down to the Registry this week and try to get my license," he told her. "So maybe soon, I can drive you around. I just wish I had my own car."

"You can always borrow from your mom or brother," Kim suggested. "Or I'll let you drive mine. Maybe one of your dozens of cousins has a car they can give you, or sell you for cheap. I bet your grandma could find someone to do that."

"Maybe," Carl replied thoughtfully. "Would your mom ever let you sleep over here?" he asked hopefully.

"Maybe if we were still just friends," Kim replied. "But she knows we're not anymore. But I don't know. I've never asked before. I mean, I think she knows I'm not a virgin anymore, but she probably doesn't want to know the details and stuff. But I'll ask. Would your mom let me stay?"

Carl shrugged. "I don't know," he admitted. "Dad's gone all night, and most of the time Mom goes to a friend's house and just stays over. I don't think she likes it when Dad works nights. And like I said, Scott doesn't care. He probably wouldn't even realize we were there."

"I didn't realize you were so unsupervised all the time," Kim said. "Sounds kind of lonely."

"It's fine," Carl said, brushing it off. "That's why it's so great to have Chris and my big family. If I get lonely, I just go to his house. Or Gram Missy's. I don't even have to call first."

Kim smiled at him. "Yeah, I guess it's good that you have your family." She thought sadly of how lonely she felt sometimes, even when she was home with her dad and the kids. But she pushed the thought aside for now. "Well, a sleepover would be fun. I'll try. If not, we can always take off for a weekend together. That way, we'd be out of everyone's hair for a bit."

"I like that idea," Carl agreed. "Let's do that anyway." He held her tight, then kissed her hard, then more gently. "Don't get in an accident driving home," he told her. "You need to maintain all your working parts!"

Kim laughed as she climbed into her car. "I'll call and let it ring once to let you know I made it home," she promised. "That will be our code."

Carl waved as the car pulled away. He felt good about their night together. Kim seemed happy, and she didn't insult him even once. That was a good starting point.

Back inside, his mother was sitting on the couch, lighting a cigarette. She inhaled deeply. "Carlos, mijo," she said, making eye contact and blowing out smoke. "Is there something going on with you and Kim that I might need to know about?"

DARLENE AND KIM

"Now that prom's over," Darlene told Kim as they stepped carefully over the slick log crossing the stream, "I need to decide if I want to break up with Charlie."

It was the day after Kim's first date with Carl, and she had a euphoric glow that couldn't be dimmed by her friend's announcement. "Really?" she asked as she grasped onto an extended branch and used it to steady herself as she jumped onto solid ground.

The stream was rain runoff that ran through a small, wooded area in the center of their residential block. For years, the kids in the neighborhood had been pulling fallen logs into a ring in a clearing, and they would often hang out on nice nights, drinking beer, smoking cigarettes, or passing joints. Now, it was just Kim and Darlene, looking for some Sunday afternoon peace and quiet to talk.

"I didn't realize things weren't going well with you and Charlie. We haven't talked much since all the fuss started with prom."

Darlene found a dry area on a log and sat. Kim sat down across from her on a felled pine tree trunk. "It's not that things aren't going well," Darlene said. "It's more that things just aren't going anywhere. I just don't think he's that into it. You know how it is. I always end up measuring every relationship up to Sally and James. It's probably unfair to compare anyone to Mr. and Mrs. Adorable and Happy, but I can't lie to myself. I want a relationship like theirs. And I just don't see it happening with Charlie. But there was no way in Hell I was gonna bring it up until we were safely through prom."

"I understand," Kim said with empathy.

Darlene was her best friend. They had been neighbors and playmates since they were born. Their mothers were also best friends. They trusted each other with their fondest wishes and worst fears. Kim didn't think Darlene would have made it through prom season without a date, and Darlene didn't like Kim's idea of a prom pact with a friend. She would have been devastated if she'd had to stay home, her self-esteem shattered.

"I get the whole holding yourself up to the standards of a perfect couple. I hate that I like Sally so much. Sometimes I wish I could be jealous of her *and* hate her, but I like her too much. But I also think she and James give me something to strive for."

"Are you talking about Carl?" Darlene asked, still with some disbelief in her voice regarding the events that had occurred since prom. "Kim, this is so unlike you. I mean, making yourself so vulnerable to a guy, letting your feelings out. Being so happy! I just hope that Carl will live up to your big expectations."

Kim felt slightly deflated by Darlene's words. She, too, was in disbelief about her feelings and thoughts, but she was willing to let them flow and see where they went. "I don't know, Darlene," she said slowly. "I mean, I think there might really be something there. What if I don't pursue it, and end up missing out on the best thing that could ever happen to me?"

Darlene shook her head. "Kim. I will never forget how Carl hurt you, way back at DeMarco Elementary. I don't think you ever fully recovered from that. What would it be like now, if he did something to break your heart again? I know what he would do. He would run back to Chris. But what would become of you?" Darlene looked her in the eyes. "I mean, I really hope things work out for the two of you, but please, just protect yourself, okay? I will always be here to help pick up the pieces, but it would be so much better if the pieces just stayed where they're supposed to be."

Kim bit her lip, and then quickly brought out her best coping mechanism. Denial. "So, Carl and I were talking about going away somewhere together for a weekend trip," she said. "But I'm worried about what would happen if my mom needed me to stay with my dad and the kids if she had to go to work unexpectedly. She has it all set up during the week, but sometimes on the weekend, she has unexpected showings. And she never wants to leave him alone with the kids for longer than, like, a half hour."

"Has he been leaving the stove on again?" Darlene asked.

Kim sighed. "No. Thank God. Mom unplugs it now when she's not using it. But she's worried that he'll forget how to feed the kids, or forget the kids are even there, or even exist. It's better now that they're a bit older and know right from wrong, but they don't know what to do when they find him just standing there not knowing what he's supposed to be doing. She needs someone responsible enough to be able to at least get him to go sit down or something, and then distract the kids. And someone who knows what to do if he has a seizure. Those don't really happen that much, but they do every now and then. He's better than he was when he first came back from rehab, but we just don't know if there will be a point where he just stops getting better."

Kim stopped and swallowed. She felt a lump in her throat. She didn't talk about her dad very often. It made her miss her old, intact dad all that much more. She wanted him back, and she didn't know if he could ever come entirely back to her.

Darlene reached out and put her hand on Kim's arm. "Kim, I know you miss him," she said, "but remember, your dad would always want you to have a happy childhood, and he would hate it if he understood that he was the reason you weren't. Talk to your mom. You can figure something out. And Kim, just so you know, I am rooting for you and Carl. I want both of you to be happy. He's funny, and cute, and I know he would be super loyal, and you would treat him like royalty. Well, like your prince, like back in first grade. I would happily be the maid of honor at your wedding someday." She paused. "But I swear, if he breaks you again, so help me, I will do everything in my power to ruin his life."

OUR LIVES ARE HARD

"Can I come over for a while?" Carl asked Kim on the phone after dinner. "My mom has all of her friends over and the whole house is filled with fast Spanish and thick cigarette smoke. Scott bailed like an hour ago."

"Sure," Kim said, "but can you walk over? I'm still helping Mom feed the kids and clean up. I can drive you home later."

"Okay," Carl agreed, reaching for his socks and sneakers. He threw on a clean T-shirt and headed out through the den.

"Carlos!" he heard a chorus of women's voices call out as he tried to make a clean escape. Tia Tania—they all insisted that he call them Tia—waved her hand at him. "I hear you're hot and heavy with your friend Kim now," she said loudly.

Carl noticed glasses with amber liquid and ice on the coffee table in front of his mother and her friends. Someone was mixing drinks. No wonder the volume was increasing exponentially.

"Make sure and keep it covered, okay," Tania went on, "'cause your mama's too young to become an abuela so soon!"

The whole group burst out with laughter. Mrs. Bishop blushed and said something cryptic to her friends in rapid Spanish. They laughed even louder.

"Bye, tias," Carl called as he opened the door. "Have fun." He couldn't get away from these obnoxious women fast enough.

"Be home early, mijo," his mother called after him mechanically. "You have school tomorrow!"

Carl jogged to the sidewalk and headed the mile to Kim's house. It was a brisk, early May evening, with a light wind, the clouds obscuring the warmth of the sun. Carl zipped his hooded navy sweatshirt up to the top and shoved his hands in his pockets. He knew Kim's house could get noisy with her four younger brothers and sisters, but it was a kind of happy noise, not the jaded, bitter noise of women talking about their inattentive husbands or the rising cost of groceries at the neighborhood market, which is at least what Carl assumed his mother and her friends would talk about at their gatherings. Carl knew very remedial Spanish.

His mother had only spoken to him and his brother in English as small children, a time when it would have been much easier for them to learn to be bilingual. Carl had taken three years of Spanish at McKinney High, and he was no closer to understanding what his mother and tias were saying than on the first day of class. Carl picked up most things quickly, but foreign languages did not come easy for him. He also knew that Puerto Rican Spanish was a different dialect than what was taught in school. He sometimes wondered if the women were talking about the lives they had given up in their homeland and were sharing regrets about leaving their families behind in San Juan, only to not experience the promise of wealth and prosperity on the mainland that they'd hoped for. Or maybe they were talking about sex and other men. He might never know.

His thoughts had him arriving at Kim's house sooner than he had expected. When she let him in, she had to hustle back to the kitchen and told him to follow. She had lost the glow of euphoria she had worn the night before when they had been together and alone, but she still looked happy to see him. She had left the sink running to soak the dishes and rushed back to turn off the faucet before soapy water ran over and onto the floor.

Mrs. Drake smiled from her place at the kitchen table, where she was sitting next to her husband as they both sipped on hot tea. "Hello, Carl," she said to him. "You remember my husband, Gerald?"

Mr. Drake stood. "Hello, I'm Gerald. You're Carl?" he asked. "You must be a friend of Kim's."

Carl had not seen Mr. Drake for several months, but he remembered the routine. "Hi, Mr. Drake," he said. "Good to see you again."

Mr. Drake reached out his hand. "Have we met? I'm Gerald Drake."

Carl shook his hand.

"Kim, why don't you just let the dishes soak for a while, okay?" Mrs. Drake offered. "You and Carl can go visit in your room."

"Thanks, Mom," Kim said gratefully. Kim took Carl's hand and led him toward the stairs.

As they walked away, Carl could hear Mr. Drake saying, "Didn't Kim have a friend named Carl before? I don't think I've met this young man."

Carl felt a small piece of his heart break as he took this all in. "So things are pretty much the same with your dad, huh?" he asked softly.

Kim nodded. "He almost always knows who my mom and I are," she started, "because we don't change too much, but there are times when he has no idea who my siblings are. It's so sad, and they just don't get it. Then later, he might recall a story to them about something that happened when they were little, and they get so confused. They don't know what to expect from day to day. They were so young when the accident happened. They have no memory of who he was before."

"I remember your eighth birthday party," Carl said as they settled, sitting on Kim's bed. "Second grade. Your parents made you invite the whole class to your ice-skating party. Pete and I were in your class. I wanted to go because I had never been to an ice-skating party. Pete and I were gonna go together, but at the last minute, he got sick and couldn't go. So I went by myself. I'll never forget. I think that was the first day you ever called me a moron. I was a terrible skater. I tried to skate over to you and Darlene, but I tripped over my own blade and fell. The two of you laughed at me. My pants were all slushy and wet, and I was trying so hard not to cry. And I didn't want to get up off the ice, because I was embarrassed and hurt, and had no one to skate with. Then, I felt someone lifting me to my feet. It was your dad. He skated with me over to the side and made sure I was okay. That's when I started to cry. He thought I had been hurt by the fall, but I told him about you and Darlene laughing at me, and how we were supposed to be friends, and friends don't laugh when their friends fall down and then just leave them there. He sat me down at a table and got me a cup of hot chocolate. Then he explained to me that sometimes, things change with boys and girls for a few years. That even friends can seem mean to each other. He told me that he envied the friendship we'd always had and asked me to be patient. He told me someday you would come back to me. He told me not to take any abuse from you, but to let it roll off my back, like water off a duck. I've always remembered that. And the next time I saw him, he checked in with me to see how things were going. It meant so much to me. That was a couple years before his accident, I think."

He paused and looked at Kim. Her eyes were glazed with tears.

"I guess thinking about it now," Carl continued, "I really regret that I can't just go tell him that he was right. You did come back to me."

He and Kim locked eyes. Then they reached for each other and embraced. Kim started sobbing. Carl held her tight. He could feel her loss along with her guilt for mourning over someone she had lost but who was still drinking tea with her mother in the kitchen.

When her sobs subsided, Kim pulled away. "Carl, I never knew about that," she said. "He never said a word to me. He probably didn't want to confront me on my birthday. But it sounds so much like him."

She pulled a tissue from the box on her nightstand and wiped the tears from her cheeks.

"I can't believe I laughed at you when you fell," she said, looking remorseful. "I was horrible."

"Hey," Carl said, putting his hands on her shoulders. "The point of that story wasn't to make you feel bad about something you did when you were eight. The point was, he was . . . is a good man, and he loves you so much."

Kim nodded. "He loves me as if I was one of his own," she said. "Just as much as he loves my stepbrother and sister. And my half-brother and sister. He's more of a real dad to me than anyone else ever could have been."

"He is your real dad," Carl agreed.

"For the record, I'm not the one who walked away from us," Kim said under her breath.

"What?" Carl asked.

"Oh, nothing."

They sat on the bed cross-legged, in silence. Then Carl got up and put some albums on Kim's stereo. They propped themselves up against the headboard, and Carl put his arm around her shoulder. They listened to the music without talking for a long time, both lost in private thoughts.

At seven, there was a knock on the door. "Kim?" her mom said from the hallway. "Don't worry about the dishes. Stella and Chip agreed to take care of them. I'm gonna take everyone for a walk over to Scoops on Grand Street for some ice cream. Do you and Carl want to join us?"

"No thanks, Mom," Kim called out. "And tell Stell and Chipper I said thanks, and I owe them one!"

"Okay, babe, we'll be back in about an hour."

Carl laughed. "You guys still call your brother Chip?" he asked. "I thought for sure he would reject that nickname when he finally realized how you came up with it!"

Kim smiled. "It's not my fault his parents named him Simon," she said. "Or that he developed buck teeth like a chipmunk! But by now, I don't think he has a choice. Everyone calls him Chip, even his teachers! I just wish my parents had named Zach 'Alvin,' and Sophia 'Theodore.' We could have called her Teddy."

Carl realized they had an hour home alone, but he didn't make any suggestions. He left it up to Kim. And Kim didn't move from her spot. She kept her head perched on Carl's shoulder, and they stayed together in that manner, listening to the music, chatting, and sharing a copy of *People* magazine until they heard Kim's family return. Only then did they both reach for kisses.

"Kim," Carl said softly.

"Hmm?" she answered.

"Can I ask you something personal?" he said, turning to face her.

"Okay," she answered, sitting up straighter.

Carl sighed. "You told me who your first was on prom night," he said, "but I never asked who else—"

Kim quickly put a finger to his lips. "No one, Carl," she whispered. "After that first time, no one. I wanted to wait for the right person, for you. You were the one I wanted for my first. But since that couldn't happen, you were my second. If I could go back in time to make that first time never happen, and make you my first, I would, but I can't." She paused. "But don't tell anyone, okay? For some reason, people have certain ideas about me. I have a reputation to uphold, you know."

Carl smiled as she reached to kiss him. Now he wished they had their hour of privacy back again. Now he would do it differently.

BACK TO SCHOOL

The school week began like any other, but this week, Carl and Kim discovered many of the places they could go between classes to make out without being discovered. There were closets, unused classrooms, utility rooms, and, of course, Kim's car. Now they sat beside each other at the lunch table each day, and their friends became aware that they were hearing much less of the word *moron* coming from Kim's mouth when she referred to Carl. In fact, her tone was soft and often complimentary. Chris still drove Carl to school in the morning, but Kim drove him home. The three bad boys from Randall Junior High, for the first time, were all finding themselves with girlfriends and less likely to hang out at the convenience store for hours after the last school bell rang.

On Thursday, Mrs. Bishop brought Carl to the Registry of Motor Vehicles for his written and road driving tests. Carl had been practicing his parallel parking and three-point turns for months. He was nervous as the test car left the lot. He knew he made mistakes. He was sweating as they pulled back into the Registry lot, prepared to receive his failure. The examiner handed him his stamped form. He had passed. He was getting his license.

Mrs. Bishop let him drive home. It wasn't as much fun with her in the car, but he still took the opportunity. When he pulled up at the house, he saw his Gram Missy's car in the driveway. "Why is Gram here?" he asked his mom.

"God bless her, who knows why that woman does anything?" his mother responded, rolling her eyes. She had never been even remotely charmed by the Bishop-Farmer appeal.

They went into the house and found Gram Missy along with her identical twin sister, Cissy, sitting at the kitchen table, drinking mugs of hot tea. Tiger was purring on Cissy's lap.

"Make yourselves at home," Mrs. Bishop mumbled dismissively, throwing her purse on the couch and retreating to her bedroom.

"Thank you, Rosa, I think we will," Gram Missy replied with a smug smile. "Hello, Carl, I assume we are correct to congratulate you on passing your driving test?"

Carl smiled. "Thanks, Gram," he said. "Yeah, I passed!"

Aunt Cissy clapped her hands together. "Wonderful, Carl," she said. "I knew you could do it."

Gram Missy stood. "We've just been to see Steven Bishop," she told Carl. "He's your grandpa's cousin Jeffrey's boy, so he would be your, oh, I don't know, second cousin once removed? Anyway, to make a long story short, he helped us pick you out a gift."

"A gift?" Carl asked, looking around the room for any tell-tale clues. "For getting my license? That wasn't necessary."

"You're not going to find it in here, Carl," Aunt Cissy scolded. She handed him a bulky envelope.

Carl suddenly knew what he was holding. He ripped open the envelope, and inside the greeting card, along with a check for twenty-five dollars, was a large key with the word *Ford* etched on top.

"Oh, my God, you two, what have you done?"

"We put a car key in an envelope, Carl, it's not rocket science," Gram Missy said mischievously.

"But I didn't see any car outside when we pulled up," Carl told them.

The sisters looked at each other and smiled. "So this is our resident honors student, hmm," Gram Missy quipped. "Carl, go look in the garage. It works much better than wrapping paper for a car."

Carl ran to the inside garage door and threw it open. Where his father normally parked his ancient Chevy pickup, Carl found a red four-door Ford Escort.

"It's a 1982," Gram Missy announced. "Good year for Fords. Steven Bishop always gives us a very good deal on the best cars in his lot."

Carl was awestruck. "Gram! Aunt Cissy! I can't accept a car from you," he told them. "This is too much! I was not expecting this at all!"

"Why wouldn't you?" Aunt Cissy asked him. "I assumed you knew that we gifted Christopher his car when he got his license." Seeing the baffled look on Carl's face, Aunt Cissy laughed. "Oh my goodness, we did tell the boy not to let on, so it would be a surprise for you when it was your turn, and it seems he took our words to heart!"

Gram Missy laughed. "Go on, Carl, start it up. I'll open the garage door and move my car. Go take it for a spin. All the paperwork is in the glove box."

"And this is all okay with Mom and Dad?" Carl asked, unlocking the driver-side door. The inside looked pristine and detailed.

Gram smiled. "They have always known that this day was coming. They know that Cissy and I like to provide our grandkids with wheels. It's something nice we can do, that we know that you all will appreciate. Except for Scott. He had already saved for a car, and he wanted a lizard. So get in, Carl! Turn the key!"

Carl got in the car, turned the ignition, and listened to the engine fire up. It didn't purr like a Rolls-Royce, but the sound was like music to his ears. He rolled the window down. "What time is it?" he asked his aunt.

She glanced at her watch. "It's four o'clock, Carl," she told him. "Your young lady should be home from school by now."

Carl grinned. He backed slowly out of the garage and out of the driveway. He waved to his grandmother. "Thank you so much, Gram!" he yelled out through the window. "I'm gonna go show Kim."

Gram waved. "Have a good time, Carl! Come by over the weekend to say hello. And you can bring Kim along. I'll bake a chocolate cake!"

Carl drove the car around the neighborhood a few times, testing the brakes and the accelerator, and vowed to take it out on the highway to test its power later. Then, he drove the short distance to Kim's house and parked in front. He ran to the door and hit the doorbell.

Mrs. Drake answered. "Oh, hello, Carl," she said with some surprise. "I just sent Kim to the store to get some milk, but she should be back in a few minutes. Would you like to come inside and wait for her?"

"No thanks, Mrs. Drake," he replied with a grin. "I can wait out here. I have something to show her."

"Suit yourself, Carl," Mrs. Drake said. "But the two of you come in for a snack after." She looked over Carl's shoulder. "Oh!" she exclaimed. "Nice car, Carl. Yes, why don't you wait for Kim out here. And congratulations on getting your license!"

"Thanks, Mrs. Drake," he responded, and he doubled back to his car. His car! He would never take the bus again if he didn't have to.

Carl leaned up against the Escort's passenger-side door and crossed his arms in front of him. Within five minutes, he saw Kim's car approaching the house, and she pulled into the driveway. She opened the door, and without even closing it, she ran up to him. He grabbed her in his arms.

"Oh, my God!" Kim burst out, pulling away and peeking in the car windows. "Carl! A red Escort! It's beautiful! And it's bigger than my car! And it has a nice roomy back seat!"

Carl laughed.

"Carl! Your parents got you a car?"

"Oh, no," he corrected her. "This was a Bishop-Farmer family deal. You were right! There is a family car dealer! Apparently, all of the grandkids get a car for getting their license. But no one ever bothered to tell me! Not even Chris or Scott. It's like a big family surprise thing."

Kim gave him a knowing look. "Yeah," she said, "I always suspected there was some story behind Chris suddenly getting a car last year. Now it all makes sense! Man, I wish I was a Bishop-Farmer! There are a lot of perks, being part of your family!"

Carl grinned at her. "And there are lots of perks of being a Bishop-Farmer girlfriend, I promise. My Gram is gonna make a cake for us if we come over this weekend. You've had my Gram's cake. It's wicked good. But your mom also promised us a snack. Should we go inside so you can put the milk away and we can have a snack? I'm kinda hungry. Then I'll take you out for a drive."

"Let's do it!" Kim agreed. She went back to her car and removed the gallon of milk. "And let's figure out if there's someplace we can go to christen your new back seat!" She took his hand and led him into her house.

SUMMER IS COMING

There were three weeks left in school. The days ran into each other. Finals were approaching. Everyone was studying and making plans for the summer. Chris called his cousin, Chester Farmer, who managed the yard crew at the local medical university's large campus. Chester informed him that he did have openings on his crew, and Chris and Carl were welcome to apply. They both did, and they were both quickly hired on. They were informed that it was hot and grueling work, but they would be making well over minimum wage, which would buy them enough gas to get around over the summer with their girlfriends and have some fun on weekends.

Everyone passed finals, and their junior year came to an end. Sally's parents invited the whole group of friends and their dates over for a barbeque, and they all went to the Bachmans' on Saturday evening for burgers and hot dogs. Mrs. Bachman made her famous potato salad and coleslaw. They spread blankets over the back lawn, and everyone sat down picnic-style with full plates to eat. Sally's parents gave them space and ate on the screened-in porch.

Pete came to the party with his girlfriend, Carolyn. It was the first time that everyone in the group was paired with a partner. They listened to music as they ate, and after dinner, they attempted to play badminton with defective birdies. They talked about their summer plans, made arrangements to hang out together on weekends when they could, and to meet at Hampton Beach one day in July.

Everything felt like it was shifting. It was their last summer in high school. James and Sally were going on vacation with James's family in Newport and would be looking at colleges while they were in Rhode Island. Michelle and Traci were going to rental houses on the Cape with their families for a couple of weeks. Chris, Carl, James, and Sally all had jobs lined up, and the others were still looking or considering their employment options.

"I put in an application at Scoops, over by my house," Kim told her friends as they sat in a large circle in the yard as the sun started to set. "We go there all the time, so I might just take my pay in ice cream!" They all laughed.

"Maybe I'll apply there, too, so we can work together," Darlene suggested. "It might be the only time we get to see each other all summer."

"We'll see each other all the time," Kim insisted, knowing it probably wasn't true. She was hoping to spend most of her free time with Carl. "We're neighbors! We'll make it happen."

Kim knew that Darlene was planning her breakup with Charlie for the next week and would need support at some point, but for the moment, he was sitting in their midst in blissful ignorance about his relationship coming to an end.

"Things will change," Sally said wistfully. "We all have boyfriends and girlfriends. We'll do our best to see each other, but it will be hard. We just have to remember that we're all friends, and even if we go a while without seeing each other, it doesn't mean we don't still care."

Michelle stated what they were all thinking. "It's good practice for after we graduate."

They would all be heading in different directions. After graduation next year, things would never be the same. Dougo would be leaving for college after Labor Day.

"We'll all always be friends," Carl told them. "We'll be apart, and we'll have different lives, but when we see each other, it will be like we were never apart. At least I hope so."

"We'll all go to each other's weddings," Darlene sighed. "Who do you think will be first?"

They all laughed, and all eyes went to James and Sally. Sally blushed. She grabbed James's hand and he smiled. "Yes, Jamie and I are hopefully going to get married someday," she agreed, "but there's no guarantee we'll be first. We both have things we want to do with our lives. We'll do them together, but that doesn't necessarily mean we're in that much of a hurry to walk down the aisle. We have all the time in the world."

Everyone sat silently for a few moments. Carl took Sally's words to heart. *All the time in the world.* She said it like it was a gift. Carl felt it could also be a trap.

Time kept passing. The future was unclear. He didn't know what he wanted to do with his life. He hoped Kim would be in it, but as of yet, he didn't know what would happen. It had been two months since prom. They were happy together. But neither had declared their undying love to each other. He knew his feelings got stronger all the time, but he still didn't know how to define romantic love. He figured he would know it when he felt it, but what if she didn't feel it back? They had promised to give their relationship a try. Were they still trying, or were they there yet? And if it didn't work out, what would happen to their friendship . . .

"Hey, Carl," Kim whispered into his ear. He drew his attention back to the moment and realized that everyone had broken off into side conversations. Kim was smiling. She put her arm around his back and rested her head against his shoulder. "Welcome to our long, hot, slow summer nights."

Carl smiled and reached over to kiss her. He guessed that long, hot, slow summer nights were as good a place as any to kick off his unknown future plans.

THEY CALL ME THE WORKING MAN

Carl collapsed onto his bed in exhaustion after his first day of work. He smelled like grass and mulch and his arms were covered with dirt mixed with perspiration and gasoline. He knew he would have to hit the shower hard in a few minutes, but for now, he needed to be horizontal on his bed. Landscaping was hard work. Harder than any work he had done in his life. Even Chris was feeling it at the end of the day. They were barely able to grunt goodbyes to each other when Carl dropped him off at home after their shift, and he nearly fell out of the passenger seat getting out of the car. Carl didn't think they'd make it through the summer.

He could see the framed picture of himself and Kim at prom on his nightstand. He didn't even have to turn his head. He was doing all this for her. He was a working man. He was making money so he could treat his woman right! He laughed at this thought. But it still motivated him. He would do it again tomorrow. And the next day. And maybe, just maybe, it would get easier. Before it killed him.

When he got out of the shower, he heard the phone ringing. He wrapped his towel around his waist, modest even in the empty house, and loped to the living room and grabbed the receiver. He made himself sound halfway pleasant as he said, "Bueno," his mother's preferred telephone greeting in their home.

It was Kim. The sound of her voice soothed him momentarily. "I got it!" she exclaimed. "I got the job! At Scoops! I start training on Wednesday. Oh my God! I'm so excited!" She squealed a little. "But Carl! How was your first day on the crew?"

"It was . . . intense," Carl admitted. "A bit more than I thought. But nothing more than I can handle. I hope."

"I know it's a little early to plan our days off," Kim said excitedly, "but by August we should be able to put aside enough money to go somewhere and stay overnight, or maybe two nights! We should look at the calendar. Where should we go? Newport? That's probably too expensive. Maybe New Hampshire? Maine? The Cape?"

"Kim!" Carl interjected. "Hold on a sec. How much caffeine have you had today? You're all wound up!"

Kim laughed. "I had a coffee milkshake from Scoops after my interview. I guess they use real coffee. Anyway, can I come over? I'll bring my calendar."

Carl sighed. He didn't know if he could physically handle that much Kim at one time, but he was willing to give it a try. "Yeah," he told her. "I just got out of the shower. You're in luck. It wasn't pretty before the shower. But I can't promise you I'll have much energy tonight."

"That's okay," Kim replied. "I think I have enough for the two of us! I'll be over in ten minutes."

She was there in eight. Carl called for her to let herself in. She found him in his room, lying on his back on his bed, having pulled on his jeans but not having the wherewithal to fasten them or put on a shirt.

"I can't move," he moaned. "My arms are noodles."

"I imagine a half a mile away from here, Chris is noodles, too," Kim said. She sighed. "Roll onto your stomach," she ordered.

Carl did as she commanded, groaning the whole time. She crawled onto his bed and straddled his back. Ninety-five pounds of girlfriend on his spine was nothing compared to the machinery he'd been pushing around the grounds all day. She began to massage his shoulders, working her way down his arms. It hurt, but it felt so good.

"It's gonna feel worse tomorrow," Kim warned him. "It always does."

"But I have to go back there and do it all again tomorrow," Carl despaired.

"I'll come back tomorrow to give you another massage," Kim promised, "but then, after I start working, you'll have to pay me back. I'll be hauling big giant containers of ice cream in just a few days."

Carl felt himself almost say "I love you" in gratitude for the massage but stopped himself quickly. His eyes sprung open, then he quickly closed them again. Those words had never tempted his tongue before, but somehow, Kim's hands on his shoulders had unlocked something in him. He didn't know if it was real, or just lactic acid being released from his muscles, weakening his brain. He decided to keep the words to himself. But it made him think.

Kim massaged his neck, his back, and the top of his thighs. Then, she told him to roll over on his back. He did as he was told. She began to knead his bare chest with skilled hands. He moaned with relief.

"Carl," she told him softly, "I'm gonna give you another kind of massage now," she said as she worked his jeans down his hips. "And you don't have to do anything. You just need to lie there and relax."

Oh my god what's she gonna do, were the words that rushed through his brain, but soon his brain stopped functioning. He was a giant nerve ending. He was nothing but sensation. He let himself go with it, and soon, his earlier thoughts of Kim began to surface, and his feelings intensified. After a few minutes, she pulled off her shorts, and again straddled him, this time so he could see her face. He felt he would explode with gratitude and emotions. Instead, he eventually settled for physically. He felt his blood rush through his body, pumping endorphins through every vein, and again making him feel like a noodle, this time, a relaxed and fulfilled noodle. Again he thought those words, but held them in. He still didn't know. Was this real? Now she was kissing him and he could taste coffee. It was sweet. His girlfriend was physically made of ice cream. It was the best dessert he had ever experienced.

Kim collapsed on the bed next to him. Suddenly she realized the door to the bedroom was open. "Oh my God, Scott's not here, is he?" she asked.

"No," Carl reassured her. "Scott's never here anymore. I don't know where he goes. I just hope he's still feeding his lizard. But it might be a good idea to shut that door. People seem to have keys to our house."

Kim jumped up and hastily shut the door, then returned to the bed. Carl held out his arm, and she cuddled into him. Both of them were still without pants. Carl had decided he was never, ever going to move from this spot. It might not be physically possible.

"Didn't you say you were going to do this again tomorrow?" he whispered in her ear.

Kim laughed. "I do recall saying that," she admitted.

They lay on the bed in silence. Finally, Kim wanted to look at the calendar. She pulled on her shorts and helped Carl get back into his jeans. "Let's pick a weekend in August," she said. "And we'll travel together. We'll go away for the weekend. We'll escape from everything, except each other. It will be exquisite."

Carl smiled. Kim was high on endorphins, too. And caffeine.

They chose the third weekend in August, and both vowed to ask for that Friday off. Kim would look into motels at Old Orchard Beach and ask her mother if it was okay.

"She owes me some time off," she told Carl. "I deserve this."

MOVING THROUGH THE HEAT

Kim's mother did say yes to the trip, but it involved a mother-daughter talk about relationships, and being careful, and protecting herself. Kim listened to her mother and nodded obediently. She knew her mother had things she wanted to tell her, and she was willing to oblige, as long as it meant she had her weekend away with Carl.

Darlene didn't get a job at Scoops, but she did get on a shift at Friendly's. Kim did the best she could to support Darlene and be there for her after her inevitable breakup with Charlie, but they often worked different shifts, and Kim had to make time for Carl on weekends. Sometimes, they invited Darlene along, but she didn't want to be the third wheel. Kim wished Darlene would meet a new boy, so they could have a double date. She wished she was like Gram Missy and could insist she would only go out with Carl if he provided a date for her friend. But Carl didn't have any single friends. And his brother, Scott, was not an option.

June ended, and July rushed in bearing oppressive heat. As Carl dug in the dirt and pushed heavy mowers, Kim hauled gallons of ice cream from the big freezer to the counter. Even the icy freezer air didn't stop the sweat dripping down her forehead and her lower back. She had known that the job would entail physical work, but still she had pictured herself spending all her work time smiling at small children as she dished scoops of ice cream into cones and cups. She did have those moments, too, but she felt the customers must all be gawking at her messy ponytail and her cheeks, now a permanent pink from the exertion. And they must be smelling her rancid odor, too. At the end of the night, she had to sweep the floors. So much sweeping.

Carl and Kim spent many evenings sitting in front of the TV at the Drakes', or playing video games at the Bishops', having no excess energy for anything else. They put their money away but did treat themselves to movies and fast food on the weekends. They switched off whose car they used to travel around town, but now Kim just let Carl drive, no matter which car they had.

On July Fourth, the majority of Eastboro headed for the airport for the fireworks display and music show. There was no parking up on airport hill, so Carl and Kim hiked a mile from the lower road on the high incline along with their friends. They pushed out a space for themselves in the crowd. The temperature had peaked at ninety-six that day, and it was slow to decrease as the sun started to set. It was good to see James and Sally, Pete and Carolyn, Michelle and Joey, Traci and Dougo, and lastly Darlene and Chris. Rhonda was in Florida with her family, and Darlene was still on her own. She felt better that Chris was on his own, as well, since it made them an even number of boys and girls.

After the fireworks, they all descended the hill and made their way deep into the school yard in the neighborhood below. Some broke out cigarettes, others flasks, and they talked about their summers thus far. Some of them were having the time of their lives, others working harder than they had ever worked before, and a couple were looking forward to the school year starting again, just for some normalcy in their daily routine. They parted that night with promises of phone calls and future plans.

Carl and Kim spent a humid day and evening on Webster Lake with Chris and Rhonda. Carl and Chris's aunt, Marjory Farmer, had never married or had children, and relished having her many nieces and nephews come visit her at her lake house. They swam in the lake and ate a picnic dinner at the table in the backyard, facing the water on the private beach. For the first time ever, Aunt Margie allowed Chris and Carl to drive her motorboat around the lake unaccompanied as long as all involved wore their life jackets, and wore them correctly, the whole time. When they were boys, they were allowed to steer while sitting on their fathers' laps, but this was a whole new level. As the evening progressed, the sun began to sink, and Kim marveled at the fact that there was a Mobil Gas Station along a dock in the lake for boats to gas up.

In late July and early August, their friends went on trips, and some toured a few colleges. Carl and Kim began to contemplate what would come after high school.

"I think I'm just gonna go to one of the local community colleges for the first two years," Kim told Carl as they sat in his yard on a balmy night, listening to heavy metal on Carl's boom box. "I don't know what I want to do, like for a job someday, but I do know that it's not working in the ice cream industry!"

Carl laughed. "And I know I never ever want to run over a snail with a lawn mower again as long as I live!" he admitted. "But I just don't see myself doing anything in particular. Like, James wants to be a chef, and Darlene's always wanted to be a biologist. Michelle's looking into nursing school, and Chris is gonna apply for the teaching program at Eastboro State."

"Sally's probably gonna be a writer," Kim continued, "and Traci talks about getting into retail management. And she already has a job at the Gap."

"Are we the only ones who don't know what we want to be when we grow up?" Carl asked, taking a drag from the post-coital cigarette they were sharing and flicking the ashes on the ground.

Kim shook her head. "I don't think Pete's made up his mind yet. I don't think we're alone. And I don't think a lot of our friends will actually end up doing the things they say they want to do now. Maybe James and Sally. You know, they're so intense."

"They're just intense in a different way than the rest of us," Carl stated. He stubbed out the cigarette on the metal arm of the lawn chair. "You could make a good living as an underwear model," he told Kim. "I know I would buy whatever you were selling!"

Kim smirked. "Very funny, moron." She caught herself. "Oh my God, I can't believe I just said that! I don't think I've called you a moron for months!" She laughed. "Old habits die hard, I guess." She paused. "I should come up with a new nickname for you."

"How about 'genius'?" Carl joked.

Kim smiled. "Okay, genius," she said sarcastically.

Carl groaned. "Oh, I stepped right into that one, didn't I?" They laughed together.

They got up and started walking back toward the house, their arms across each other's backs. "I think we'll be okay," Kim assured him. "I think we'll be something, someday. We will be fine."

Carl knew that she was talking about finding purpose in their lives after high school, but her comments could apply to a lot of things. He hoped they would be fine, as well. He hoped it would all become clear someday. And someday soon.

THIRD WEEKEND IN AUGUST

Summer vacation was quickly winding down, senior year looming just around the corner. It was time for Carl and Kim to go on their weekend away to Old Orchard Beach. They drove the two and a half hours to the coast of Maine in Carl's Escort, which supplied ample air conditioning and powerful stereo speakers. They drove up and down local streets, poring over a map, trying to find their motel. They finally pulled over to a pay phone, and Kim called to get directions from their current location. Five minutes later, they used their newly work-formed biceps to lug their bags into the office to check in. Then they were on their way to their home away from home for the next two nights.

They threw their bags to the floor, then threw themselves down on the bed. They lay there staring at the ceiling, holding hands, reveling in their freedom and their privacy. They got plenty of time alone at home, but never this sort of sense of privacy. It felt divine.

"No brothers! No sisters!" Kim cried out.

"No mother! No brother! No tias!" Carl cried back.

Kim's stomach growled loudly. "No food!" They both laughed and sat up.

"I was imagining us getting naked and weird first thing," Carl admitted, "but now I'm thinking lunch. Then naked and weird."

"I second that," Kim agreed. "Plenty of time for nakedness and weirdness. Now, lobster rolls and steamers!"

"I don't know why, but that sounds kind of dirty!" Carl told her, reaching to move her hair off her neck so he could kiss below her ear.

She slapped his hand away. "Carl!" she protested. "Plenty of time. Here's our schedule: lunch, naked and weird, then beach. In that order."

"Yes, ma'am," Carl said. "We'll hit a steamer shack. But in my thoughts, we're getting naked and weird first."

They had budgeted for one expensive meal, so while they were out scavenging for lunch, they stopped at a seafood restaurant that looked fancy and made a reservation for the next night. Then they found a roadside clam stand and had their fill of steamers, lobster rolls, and fries. When they returned to the room, they both felt stuffed and greasy. They decided to try their hand at couples showering for the first time. They found it was to their liking. That took care of naked and weird.

Finally, they got into their swimsuits, gathered their swim covers, flip-flops, towels, and suntan lotion, and headed the one block to the motel's private beach area. The wind was constant but light and took a bite out of the oppressive August heat. They walked toward the waterline and placed their towels down on the sand along with their belongings. Then, they ran down to the water and let the tide wash over their feet. The water was chilly, but as they stood in the sun, it began to feel warmer, like bath water. Carl got a wild hair and ran into the waves, diving over a crest and coming up with seaweed on his shoulder. Kim was impressed with his nerve. She decided to go back to their spot and bake in the sun to get nice and hot before trying to inch her way into the sea. She was wearing a small string bikini and was horrified to think she might lose a piece in the tide. Carl had nothing to worry about in his long neon orange swim trunks, which were bright enough to scare away any nearby sharks.

Kim lay on her stomach and grabbed a magazine from her bag. Carl lay down next to her, face up, soaking the sun into his chest. He put his hands behind his head. "This is the life," he said as he watched a seagull float by on a wind current.

"Yeah, I could get used to this," Kim agreed. "My family doesn't go to the beach that often, what with all the little kids for so many years and not enough adult eyes to watch them. Even at the pool, we're always looking around, counting heads."

Carl looked over at her, seeing her in a new light. "You've just never been able to be a true teenager, have you?" he asked.

"Not since age ten," Kim confirmed. "I had to grow up fast." She smiled. "But I'm making up for lost time now. The kids are growing up. They don't need as much supervision. They can do more stuff to help Mom. I don't have to worry as much."

Carl shook his head. "But you still do, don't you?"

Kim nodded. "I always will," she agreed. "That's something that may never change."

Carl reached out for her hand. He held it as the sun baked their skin, and Kim read an article. Soon, she was feeling hot and sticky. She jumped to her feet. "Race you!" she challenged. Then, before Carl could even stand up, she ran to the water, kicked through the surf, and dived over a wave.

NEXT YEAR

"My job ends next Friday," Carl said later that night as they were lying in bed naked, both feeling proud of their latest encounter. "I can't believe I made it through the whole summer."

Kim played with Carl's fingers, lightly pulling each one, one at a time, like her own private toy. "I don't know what to do about my job yet," she told him. "They said I could work a couple shifts per week during the school year if I want, but I'm not sure yet if I want to make that kind of commitment. It's senior year. I might want to devote every day to being with my friends and enjoying the last days of school."

Carl nodded. "Yeah, I get that," he told her. "I'm not gonna look for a job for the school year. At least not right away. There's enough time for all that after graduation. I guess. I still don't know. "

Carl was thinking of the word Kim had said: *commitment.* It meant so much in so many ways. And yet it was so elusive. Commitment. It also meant being locked up in a mental hospital. Or promising to stay with someone for the rest of your life. Like his parents. He tried to remember the last time he'd seen them embrace. Or kiss. Or have a regular, everyday conversation without snapping at each other like alligators.

Commitment. Carl couldn't even commit to saying the three words that sat there in his heart. He was still waiting, waiting for something. Some kind of divine sign. But what?

Kim heard the word *commitment* come out of her mouth. She almost tried to swallow it back, but it was too late. Luckily it came out talking about work.

Because they never talked about it. They had made a decision to try to be more than friends. Obviously, they were way more than friends. But what were they? They were boyfriend and girlfriend, that was not up for debate. Kim felt enormous feelings for Carl, but when she let them flow through herself, her defenses kicked in. Love meant pain, and loss. Love was wonderful, until it was gone, taken from you. Carl had not gone anywhere, and maybe he wouldn't if they just stood still, stayed in the moment.

She knew that every word she said to herself was a lie. She knew she loved him. She adored him. She always had. She would be completely lost without him. But she'd be damned if she ever let him know that.

SUN, GLORIOUS SUN

The sky was as bright as any they had ever seen. The sand was warm and springy beneath their toes. The birds sang with perfect pitch. The children who built castles and moats were adorable and perfectly behaved. It was idyllic.

They had found a spot that was equidistant from the parking lot and the water. The public beach was crowded with families longing to catch the last rays of their summer vacations, to brown their skin just a touch more before returning to their everyday humdrum jobs and classes. School and work were the furthest things from Carl and Kim's minds as they baked in the sun and smelled the coconut tanning oil so popular with the tourists that year.

Kim had switched to her one-piece, low-cut red bathing suit, and Carl had reused his orange trunks. Kim could see the contrast of his sun-toasted skin against the bright neon swimwear. She loved the line of soft dark hair that went from his navel to the waistband of his suit. Carl tanned so beautifully. His skin looked radiant and exotic, while spots on her shoulders and thighs appeared blotchy and red from overexposure the day before. But still she beamed. They had spent the night together and had one more night before them of delicious and sweet solitude. And Carl was looking smoking hot.

They planned on staying at the beach until the heat got to be too much, and then they would walk through town and explore the cute little shops. Kim wanted to get ice cream at a place where she would never have to strain an arm muscle. Later, they would keep their reservation at the Lobster Pot before retiring back to their room for a late evening romantic rendezvous. Or just regular, soft-bed, private-room sex. That would work, too.

THE LOBSTER POT

Kim bought a loose, bellowing purple sundress with spaghetti straps at one of the made-in-India clothing shops in town. It had a black design throughout the pattern. It felt cool and gauzy on her skin, and the breeze lifted the light and airy fabric surrounding her legs. Carl was wearing his khaki pants and a navy short-sleeved shirt. He looked sharp in his dress shoes and black belt, his hair neatly combed, and his skin glowing from sun exposure. Kim couldn't resist touching him. She didn't even try.

They walked proudly into the Lobster Pot right on time and were escorted to their table. They were seated in the center of a dining room, which was framed on one side by a large picture window. They could see the ocean, and sailboats and ships passing on the horizon, just by turning their heads slightly. Carl picked up a warm roll from a basket on the table and smeared some soft butter on the side. He held the roll up to Kim's lips and she took a bite. She smiled at him while chewing, then watched him consume the rest. She took a roll for herself and dug in. She had never tasted anything so wonderful. Or it might just be the company she was enjoying.

They ordered shrimp cocktail to start, and then both had salads. Then the server brought them baked stuffed lobster, and they could barely speak as they partook of their elegant entrees. For dessert, they shared a giant slab of chocolate cake with a dish of ice cream, and neither of them even flinched when they saw the bill. They had been ready. And it had been totally worth it.

They left a generous tip and walked arm in arm out of the restaurant. The evening was balmy, and the sun was setting fast. They could see reflections of its last rays to the west of the road, where the excess tide water gathered and later receded back into the ocean.

Carl and Kim held hands and watched the ocean waves. They were both engaged in private thoughts, and both of their thoughts contained the same words. The same three secret, powerful, elusive, forbidden words. But only forbidden by themselves. After some time, they turned back to the road and walked back to their motel.

What they did that night could only be defined as making love, although neither of them defined it. They held each other, holding on to their last moments of summer, their last precious hours of being alone and together, their luscious alone time. They eventually fell into a deep, satisfied slumber, still in each other's arms. The next day, they would drive back home. But they still had their one last night. And they both had perfect dreams.

SCHOOL STARTS

The boys ended up under the stairwell next to the water fountain before the school day started. It was their sophomore-year morning meet-up spot.

"Well, here we are again," Chris said.

"School still looks the same," Carl said. He sniffed. "Smells the same, too."

"It was exactly a year ago that I saw Sally walk through that door and everything changed," James said, gesturing toward the front entrance with a reminiscent smile.

Carl smirked. "I do think Sally coming back started all the changes," he said. "She became friends with our old friends, got them all excited about things, and got us all actually motivated to do stuff. She even got all of us to eat lunch together."

Chris nodded. "A lot changed last year," he agreed. "But it was good change. We probably needed some change."

"Hey, Chris?" Rhonda approached the group, carrying her books and looking like she had something on her mind. "I need to talk to you for a sec." She started toward the empty hallway near the bathrooms.

"I'll be right back, guys," Chris told Carl and James as he followed behind Rhonda. They waited, chatting about their big vacation getaways with their girlfriends over the summer until the bell rang for first period to start. Chris had not come back.

Carl and James were in Spanish class with Kim and Michelle. The teacher called out Traci's name for attendance, but she was not there. Kim and Michelle made eye contact and shrugged. They hadn't heard anything about Traci being out sick. Charlie was also in Spanish class, but he avoided eye contact with the whole group.

It was lunch before they were all due to be together again. One by one, the friends placed their trays on the table and greeted each other fondly. Carl took out his brown paper bag.

"Is your mom still making you peanut butter and jelly?" James asked with a smirk.

Carl frowned. "No. She says any self-respecting person who can do manual labor forty hours a week all summer can make his own damn sandwich from now on." He pulled his sandwich from his bag. The jelly had soaked through the top layer of bread. "I guess I didn't get the proportions right." He took a bite and nodded. "Still tastes the same, though." Kim laughed.

Traci came through the cafeteria door and walked straight to the table without getting any food. Darlene greeted her. "Where have you been?" she asked. "You were supposed to be in my math class this morning!"

Kim could see a look of distress on Traci's face. "What's wrong?" she asked, dreading the answer.

Traci's eyes teared up. "Guys, I have bad news," she started. "I knew this could happen, but I didn't tell you all because I was hoping it would all go away." She stopped and tears rolled down her face.

Sally stood and put an arm around her shoulder. "Just tell us," she encouraged softly.

"My dad," she started, "well, a couple months ago, he put in a request for a job transfer. They have an Aries Corps subsidiary that works on car motors in Detroit, Michigan."

"Michigan!" Darlene exclaimed. "No!"

Traci nodded through her tears. "They contacted him Thursday. His transfer went through. He flew out on Friday afternoon. My mom and my brother and I spent the whole long weekend packing up the house. The moving trucks came yesterday. We're leaving today. Aries is supplying us with an apartment until my parents can find a house." She sniffed loudly.

Michelle handed Traci a Kleenex from her purse. She wiped her eyes and blew her nose.

"I begged my mom to let me see if I could stay with one of you for senior year, just so we could graduate together, but she said no. My brother's gonna be in college now, and she wants the rest of our family to be together. So I told her I at least wanted to be able to stop by school to come say goodbye to you guys."

Kim felt her eyes water. "Traci, oh my God, I'm gonna miss you so much!" She sniffed. "I can't believe I'm not gonna see you every day anymore. It's just not gonna be the same without you." She stood and embraced her friend. "You've been such a good, supportive friend. I can't believe you're leaving!"

One by one, all the girls approached Traci to say goodbye. The boys expressed their regret, although they hadn't become as close to Traci in their two years together as the girls had.

Traci took a book out of her purse. "My mom got me a new address book," she told them. "I want all of you to put your addresses and phone numbers in here. I can call you and give you my new number and address when I know them. I'll do my best to write. Sally, you like to write. Please write to me."

Sally wiped her eyes with her hand. "I will, Traci. I'm really good at that."

Darlene blew her nose. "Traci," she said softly, "what about Dougo?"

Traci looked down. "I just don't know," she told her. "He's still my brother's friend. We didn't break up or anything, but I just can't imagine a scenario where we're ever gonna see each other. He's going to college in New Hampshire, which wasn't gonna be too bad if I was here, but in Michigan! I don't know why anyone would want to come to Michigan."

Her tears continued to flow. "I still want to be invited to everyone's weddings," she pleaded, glancing at Sally. "Please. Even if we fall out of touch. I'll just need to see you all again. It will be like a reunion."

They all made promises to stay in touch, and they all hugged again. Finally Traci had to leave. They waved to her as she stepped out the cafeteria door. They watched her through the window as she got into her mother's car and then drove away.

There was silence at the table until Kim spoke up. "That sucks so bad," she understated.

"Poor Traci," Michelle pouted.

"I don't know anything that could be worse than having to move out of state for your senior year," Darlene stated.

Carl looked around. "Where's Chris?" He suddenly realized he hadn't seen his cousin since before school.

Two minutes later, they saw Chris enter the cafeteria. He, too, walked up to the table without stopping for food. He sat down and folded his hands on the table. He looked at his friends.

"You guys look like you got some bad news," he observed. "She already told you?"

"Yeah, she was just here," Kim said. "We all felt so bad for her. She was crying. We all were crying. It was so hard to say goodbye."

Chris looked at Kim quizzically. "What?" he exclaimed. "I for sure thought that you all would be on my side on this. And she wasn't crying to me. Why would she come cry to all of you? You're not even that close!"

"Uh," Kim said, looking from friend to friend, "Chris, I don't think we're talking about the same thing. We just said goodbye to Traci. Her father got a job transfer to Detroit. She's leaving tomorrow. We're not gonna see her again."

Chris stared at Kim. "Oh," he said. "Yeah, okay. We're talking about different things. That makes sense." He nodded. "That's really too bad about Traci. I really like her."

Carl and James exchanged worried glances. "What the hell were you talking about, Chris?" Carl asked.

"Rhonda," Carl sighed. "She broke up with me before school today. Just out of the blue."

WHERE THE BOYS GO

Everyone sat stunned for several seconds looking at Chris. Chris stared at his hands.

"Dude," Carl finally managed. "Are you okay? What the hell happened?"

Chris chuckled. "You got me. I have no idea. I thought we were doing great! We had a great summer, we hung out, we talked about the future, we did fun things together. I even played golf with her stepfather one time because he didn't want to play alone! Not something I will ever do again, I can promise you. And now, all of a sudden, summer's over, and she's wanting her space. She says it's her last year to have fun with her friends, and do new things before college, and she just doesn't want to be tied down anymore. Anymore. Like she'd been tied down all this time." He shook his head. "I mean, I just don't get it. There was no warning. We weren't fighting or anything. I thought we were good together."

The stunned silence continued. No one knew what to say. Chris was their unofficial leader. He always seemed to say and do the right thing. But he didn't know what to say now. Or do. Darlene went to the lunch line and got a cup that she filled with water. She put it down in front of Chris. He looked up at her and managed a small grin. "Thanks," he said.

Kim stared at Chris. She didn't know what to make of this information. She was still reeling from the idea that Traci was gone, just like that. Now Chris and Rhonda. It was like an alien ship was circling above their heads, sucking up all of their friends. Another thought occurred to her. Chris was always the alpha dog in his relationship with Carl. He was the one with the moves, the one with the girlfriend, the one with connections. He was even the first to be with Kim. She flinched at that memory. Now the tides were turned. Chris was alone, and broken, and Carl had Kim. He had her good. She wondered if this would shift their dynamic. She shook off the idea. This was Chris Mahoney. The captain of the bad boy posse. Not one to let a mere setback, well, set him back. He would be back on his feet in no time, probably dating several girls.

Carl pushed his uneaten apple toward Chris. "Eat something."

Chris picked up the apple mechanically and took a bite.

"So did you just blow off your morning classes, then?" Carl asked.

Chris nodded as he chewed. "I just went out to my car and sat there. I didn't know what else to do. I had no idea how long I was out there. My car smells like Chanel #5. That's gonna fade away, right?"

Kim saw Sally blink and a tear rolled down her face. She felt her own throat tighten. Suddenly, this all felt so real. Their problems weren't little-kid problems anymore. They were real-world problems. Kim knew real-world problems. They hurt. And the smell didn't fade away too quickly. It lingered.

They all checked their schedules for the afternoon. At least one friend was in each of Chris's three classes the rest of the day. They decided to take turns looking out for him and making sure he got where he needed to go. Carl had English with Chris last period. After class ended, they found their way out to the parking lot. Chris's car was two spots away from Kim's. Kim came out to meet them soon after.

"I'm gonna ride with Chris if that's okay with you," Carl told Kim after giving her a quick kiss.

"Of course," Kim agreed. "I'll give you two some time together, but I want to see you tonight. It's all just too much. I don't really want to be alone."

Carl wrapped his arms around her. He didn't want to be alone either. And he knew he didn't want her to be alone. They had been excited for the start of their senior year, and now, their whole group of friends was subdued and feeling kicked in the gut.

Chris let Carl drive his car. They sat quietly for the first few blocks. Carl didn't know what to say, so he waited. Finally, Chris lifted his head and looked at him. "What the hell, man?" he said. "What happened? I just . . . I don't know, I don't know what to do, what to think. What could I have possibly done to make this happen?"

Carl shook his head as he turned a corner at the light. "Nothing," he said. "You didn't do anything wrong. You two were always great together for what, almost two years?" Chris nodded. "I don't know, man, I don't know what happened. It's weird. And she didn't act unhappy or anything?"

"No," Chris said surely. "I saw her on Saturday night. We went to a movie. Then we went back to her house and did it in the basement, like we always did. It was good. She said all the same things she always said. When I left, she said she loved me, like she always did. I said it back. No clue. It's like I don't even know the person who broke up with me this morning."

"I know," Carl agreed. "It's totally fucked up. I don't get it."

They resumed their silence. They were close to home. "Should I bring you home, or do you want to go to my house?" Carl asked.

Chris thought for a moment. "Gram said she was coming over this afternoon to help Melanie make some cookies for Girls Scouts or something. That probably means Aunt Missy is there, too. No, I can't handle that today. Any other day, but not today. Let's go to your house."

"Yeah," Carl agreed, putting on his turn signal as he approached the left turn onto his street. "Today is no day for double Grams."

They went inside and were surprised to see Scott sitting on the couch in the den. "Yo, losers," Scott called, stubbing out his cigarette in the clear glass ashtray. "Don't worry, I was just leaving." Ash sprinkled from his lap when he stood.

"Do you even live here anymore, Scott?" Carl asked sarcastically.

"According to the post office I do," Scott replied. "And my lizard still lives here, so yeah."

"Where do you go all the time?" Chris asked curiously.

"Places where no one gives a crap if you're a Bishop or a Farmer, I'll tell you that much," Scott shared. "Guy's got to pay his bills somehow." He squeezed past Carl and Chris at the door, mumbling "Later."

"Well that answers all my questions," Chris said.

"Well, at least I know he's feeding Smokey," Carl said with relief. "I really didn't want to have to go in there someday and find his rotting reptile body, legs up. Gives me some hope."

"Maybe Scott's selling drugs," Chris guessed.

"Drugs? Nah, not Scott. He's not into that stuff. I'd guess that maybe he's doing some under the table work for one of the tia's husbands or something. That's more his style."

"Scott's always been a strange one," Chris said.

"You don't know the half of it," Carl informed him.

They went into Carl's room, and without any discussion, switched on his game system and started to play video football. Carl turned the volume low so they could talk if Chris wanted.

After about ten minutes, Chris resumed his thoughts. "It's not like I was thinking about marrying her or anything," he stated.

"Yeah, you never mentioned that," Carl agreed.

"But I don't know, I guess I just never thought about it just ending, you know? Like, if it did, I guess I thought it would be me doing the breaking up, or the leaving, or something, and then there would be someone else right there. Like I was the one with more control."

Carl could not relate to that sentiment. He never felt like the one in control. But he didn't know if Kim was in control, either. No, Kim was in control most of the time. But sometimes, he had her number. Was it possible they had the same amount of control in the relationship?

Carl looked over at Chris and shook his head. He sighed. "It sounds like she knocked you down a few pegs, dude," he told him.

Chris's head bobbed up and down. "I guess. I mean, I thought I knew myself so well, but it's like today, I have no idea who I am. I want to go back to yesterday, and be that guy again. That guy had a lot of confidence in himself. Now, I don't know if I'll ever get that back."

"You will," Carl assured him. "You'll bounce back. Maybe not right away, but I can tell you, these things don't last forever. I know from experience. Just give it some time."

Chris made eye contact with Carl. "Do you think, maybe, she might be interested in someone else? Or worse, even already seeing someone else?"

Carl shrugged. "I don't know," he said honestly. "I hope not. That would be a really shitty thing to do if she was."

"Yeah," Chris agreed. "I've done some bad stuff in my life so far, but one thing I have never, ever done is cheat on someone. I can't see how someone can do that to someone they supposedly love. I would never put up with that. First offense would be the last offense, right?"

Carl nodded. "Yeah," he agreed. He thought of his parents' marriage. By Chris's calculations, if the first offense was the last, then there was a good chance their marriage would have been over long before Carl would have even been born. Luckily, he had pretty good evidence that he was related to his father. He looked too much like a Bishop-Farmer to be from any other family. But what he didn't know was if there were any Bishop-Farmers running around town who had no idea what a famous family they were illegitimately born into.

Carl had kept his mouth shut his whole life about his knowledge of his parents' infidelities. He had never even told Chris. He realized it was probably the only secret he had ever kept from his closest cousin, except for the ones that he also kept from himself.

He needed to turn these thoughts around. "Kim wants to come over," he told Chris, "but she wanted to give us some time. Can I call her and tell her to come by now?"

"Sure," Chris said, bringing his focus back to the video game he was playing. "Maybe it would be good to do something else. I really don't want to keep talking about it anymore, at least not today. I kinda want to do something else."

TO THE RIVER

When Carl saw Kim pull up outside his house, he excused himself and went outside to meet her. They greeted each other with grateful smiles and a slow kiss. Carl embraced her. "How are you doing?" he asked her, genuinely wanting to know.

"I'm okay," she said honestly. "Sad. I talked to Darlene. She was in tears. She was the one to bring Traci into our group sophomore year, and I think they were probably the closest. And with the Chris thing on top of all that, it's just a lot. How is he doing?"

"He's kinda knocked out emotionally," Carl told her. "He's confused. He's not used to being on the losing side of anything. He's kinda humbled. It's weird. I hope he can get past this. I don't really want to have to be the strong one of the two of us."

Kim shook her head. "Carl, you have always been the strong one," she told him. "He's just the one with the charisma. I mean, yeah, you have charisma, too, but it's like Chris's superpower. Without it, he probably has no idea what to do with himself."

"Yeah, that sounds about right," Carl agreed. They went into the house holding hands and joined Chris in the bedroom. Kim grabbed his upper arm and gave him a gentle squeeze.

"Do you guys wanna go somewhere or something?" she asked.

Chris reached into his pocket and pulled out a slightly bent joint. "Sure. Where should we go?" he asked Kim.

"I know just the place. Let's grab Darlene on the way."

They made their way to the center of the woods near Kim and Darlene's houses. They crossed the stream and dodged the low-hanging limbs across the trail. They found the circle and made themselves comfortable on the logs. "I haven't been here for a long time," Chris said, looking around. "Hasn't changed much. Maybe a few more mushrooms and weeds."

"Kim and I come here sometimes to talk," Darlene told him. "No one is ever here during the day. It's different here when we're alone. Almost spiritual."

Kim nodded. "It's like some kind of holy circle," she said.

"Maybe we'll have mystical visions," Chris predicted, resting the joint on his lower lip and holding the flame from his lighter gently to the tip. He inhaled deep and passed the joint to Kim. They made their way around the circle twice, which was all they needed.

"Okay, I feel better now," Chris announced.

"Did you love her?" Darlene asked abruptly.

"Darlene!" Kim said, shoving her in the arm. "Why would you ask him that?"

Chris shrugged. "It's okay, Kim," he said. "It's a fair question. Did I love her? Yes. And no. I loved the idea of her. I mean, I really liked her. I liked her a lot. I was happy with her. But did I ever think of a future with her? I'd say, I don't know, maybe. But I don't really think so. I think she was holding some sort of place for me in my life. I liked her holding that place, though. I wasn't ready for her to stop. Maybe I would have loved her, someday. But maybe she didn't love me. She said she did. But then again, I said I loved her. I don't know. Does that make any sense?"

"Actually, yeah," Darlene told him. "Love is hard. It's confusing. I don't know if there are any real answers. I guess maybe it wasn't fair of me to ask you that. I'm sorry. I'm just . . . it's a sad day, for all of us."

"Yeah," Kim agreed. "It really is." She breathed a sigh of relief. She was worried that the next question out of Darlene's mouth was going to be if she and Carl loved each other. She had no idea how she'd answer that question.

Yes, she did. Yes, she thought about them in the future. No, she hadn't told him, and no, he hadn't told her. No, she didn't know if he loved her.

But Rhonda had told Chris she loved him, and then she broke his heart. And Chris had told Rhonda he loved her, and now he was admitting it wasn't quite true.

Maybe the words didn't really matter anyway. Maybe it was okay to keep your feelings to yourself. But they wanted to come out, so badly.

Suddenly, Kim longed to be alone with Sally, in a very private place, to talk about love.

HAPPY BIRTHDAY, CARL

September fifteenth was Carl's seventeenth birthday. Gram Missy had a party at her house for Carl and his friends and a few local first and second cousins. She made him a chocolate cake with white frosting and provided plenty of strawberry ice cream.

Carl's father, Jack Bishop, showed up unexpectedly with a six-pack of cheap beer and pulled Carl to the built-in grill in the side yard for a birthday drink. "I take it I'm not sharing your first beer ever with you, Carlos," he said with a guffaw.

Carl gave him a thin smile. His father always called him Carlos ironically. He did not approve of his legal name. "No, Dad, I think Tio Paco gave me my first beer when I was like twelve. It was gross, but I drank it. I've had a few since."

"Who the hell is Tio Paco?" Jack spit the words out at him.

"Uh, I don't know," Carl said honestly. "I always just assumed he was the husband of one of the tias. Maybe Tia Maria? I'm not sure."

"Whatever. You still a virgin, son?" Jack asked, giving him a wink. "You got a hot little number over there. I hope you've gotten a piece of that."

Carl felt disgusted. He was not very fond of his father, especially his father on alcohol. "Dad, please don't talk about Kim that way," he said. "You've known her since we were five. I don't really feel comfortable talking to you about this."

"So, not a virgin anymore then. Okay." Jack cracked open another can of beer. "Still don't know about Scotty though. I think that boy might be asexual. Or maybe he's into reptiles!" Jack laughed at his own attempted humor. "I don't think he's a homo, though. So how's your mom doing? I haven't seen her in a while."

"Uh, she's okay," Carl said. He hadn't actually seen his mother for a few days. He had found some cash left on the kitchen table and had been picking up fast food and snacks at the convenience store on his own. "What about you, Dad? I know you've been working the night shift, but where have you been during the day, every day?"

Jack looked confused. "Night shift?" he said. "Who told you that? Naw, I'm not working the night shift anymore. That ended in June. I'm working days. Did your mother tell you I'm still working the night shift?"

Carl was silent. He wanted to walk away. He didn't want to hear anymore.

"No, no night shift," Jack repeated. "I've got other places to go. Or staying at Ma's house sometimes. Rosa seems to like it when I stay away, so I thought I'd give her an early anniversary present and give her some space. But I'll be back eventually. She always asks me to come back. Eventually. You know those Catholic girls, always wanting to keep up appearances."

Chris came over to join Carl and his father in the side yard. "Hey Jack," he said cordially. "Throw me a beer?" Jack broke a can off the six-pack and tossed it at his cousin.

"Just don't let my Ma or your Gram see you with those," Jack told Chris. "They might think I'm a bad influence." He laughed again at his own wit. "I'm going in the house. Carlos, happy birthday, man. Next time I come by, I'll put some gas in your car for you. Chris, don't be a stranger." He sauntered away and went in through the front door.

Chris looked at Carl. "Is he drunk?"

Carl gave him a look. "What do you think?" Carl put his beer can down on top of the grill. "My dad's a prick. Did you know he's not working the night shift anymore? My mom lied to me. He's just sleeping around somewhere. It's like he's homeless or something. What the hell is wrong with him? What's wrong with both of them?"

Chris looked at him. "No wonder you're so jaded, man," he said sympathetically. "Your parents are a huge mess. I'm so sorry."

"Yeah, whatever, it's okay. Thanks for coming over and saving me from him. He was over here asking me really inappropriate questions about Kim. I wish we had just gone roller skating for my birthday like last year. Next year, just friends, no family."

Chris put his hand on his cousin's shoulder. "Next year," he reminded him, "everyone's probably gonna be gone to college by your birthday. But if we're still here, it'll be you and me and Kim. And my new hot girlfriend, what's-her-name. If I've met her yet." He sighed. "Don't let the old man get you down, buddy. Let's go find Kim. She'll cheer you up."

Carl let him lead him back to the group in the backyard, where Kim was waiting for him with a wide smile. "It's the birthday boy!" she exclaimed, giving him a big hug and kiss. "This is just a preview of your gift. You can unwrap it later."

Carl smiled despite himself. Chris was right. Kim cheered him right up.

DAYS GO BY

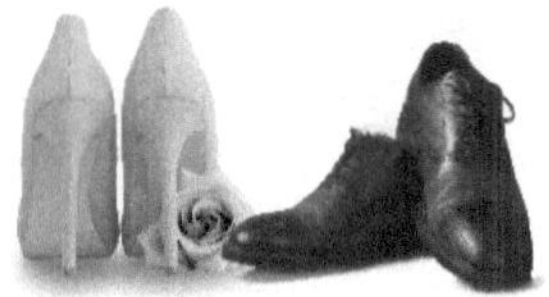

Carl, Kim, and their friends settled into the new school year, and everyone got into a routine. When homecoming approached, the girls went to the mall and bought new dresses. They all agreed to go as a group and not as dates this year, and they made a reservation for eight people at Benihana for the night of the dance. This year, the weather held out for the football game, and it was partly cloudy and sixty-seven degrees. They went to the game and cheered on the McKinney High Tigers. Their star quarterback had graduated the previous year, and this showed in their performance. The final score was 21–9, in favor of the opposition.

After the dance, they all went to James's house. The Newells didn't allow alcohol in their home due to James's brother's issues with addiction. James and Sally also didn't drink, and the group decided to dedicate their night to group sobriety in their honor. Mrs. Newell had made homemade cannoli, and they feasted on sweets and juice. It was a low-key night, and they enjoyed not having the pressure that came with being with someone new at a special event. Sally had the earliest curfew, and no car, so Kim agreed to drive her home so James could host his guests a little longer. Kim watched James and Sally kiss goodnight, whispering soft words into each other's ears before hugging and saying goodbye. Then Kim and Sally stepped out into the cooling night.

They had a lengthy drive, as Sally lived in a completely different part of Eastboro than James. After Sally instructed Kim where to go, Kim concentrated on the road until she got her bearings.

"Sally," she finally said.

"Yeah?" Sally looked over at her friend in the driver's seat.

"Sally, what do you think of me and Carl?" Kim asked cautiously. What she really wanted to ask was if Sally thought Carl loved her.

"I think you two are great," Sally answered sincerely. "I mean, I liked both of you before you hooked up, but together, you're both so much happier. And you both seemed to have grown up so much. I always thought of Carl as being the baby of the bunch back in junior high, but now, he seems, I don't know, wiser, like there's a new layer to him that was never there before. I think you're good for him. And for sure, he's good for you."

"Why do you say that?" Kim wanted to know.

"Well, Kim, you've always been a little bit, I don't know, abrupt? Remember that time we went to see *The Terminator* and you straight out asked me in the middle of the parking lot if Jamie and I had done it yet?" Sally laughed. "Kim, I could not see you doing that now."

"Oh, my God, Sally," Kim moaned, "of course I wouldn't! I can't even believe I did that then! I can't believe you didn't tell me off and never see me again. That was so inappropriate of me. I'm so sorry!"

Sally grinned. "It's okay, Kim, really," she assured her. "Yeah, I was horrified at the time, but you know what? It was more because I was dying to do it with Jamie and embarrassed to talk about it! I think I've changed enough now, and I know you so much better, that I can safely tell you that yes, Jamie and I have done it. Many, many times."

Kim laughed. "Yeah, I would hope so!" she replied. "You and James. Sally, the two of you. You know, Darlene and I were always so jealous. I think we still are. Everyone wants a love like yours. I wish we could all be as confident as the two of you. I mean, how do you know? How do you know that someone is, you know, the person that you want to grow old with?"

Sally looked surprised. "Kim, don't you know?" she asked. "It's a look in the eyes. It's a light that you see when you look at the other person. I'm not sure if it's their light, or your own light reflecting in their eyes. If that light is there, you know."

"Why did you think that I would know that?" Kim asked.

Sally nodded. "Kim, the light is there with you and Carl. Even I can see it. And I think you can see it, too. Don't you see a future with Carl?"

"I . . . I don't know," Kim admitted. "I think so, but I'm not sure. I . . . I don't think I trust the light as much as you do, Sally. Or if I see it, it doesn't look like what you see. I mean, I don't remember any of my life before Carl, so it's hard to imagine him not being there in the future. But what I don't know is, what is he in my future? Is he my friend? Is he my husband? Is he just some guy I used to date in high school? How can I know? How can I be sure?" Kim was starting to let herself feel a sense of panic she hadn't felt before.

Sally reached out and put her hand on Kim's arm. "Kim," she said softly. "You don't always know. You can't always know. Anything can happen in the future. Hell, something could happen to me and Jamie, God forbid. But in my mind, I see him in my future. I see him as my future. That's where my faith comes in."

"Like religion?" Kim asked.

Sally laughed. "Yeah, I guess it kind of is, but not like any specific one. Jamie and I know that we love each other. We make each other better, stronger people. Just like you and Carl do. And for us, that's enough. It's more than enough. It's more than I ever could have expected. You just have to find a way to believe in you and Carl."

"Sometimes," Kim said softly, "you can believe in all sorts of fairy tales and fantasies. But then later you learn that they're not real. That's my fear, Sally, that one day I wake up, and none of it is real. And I'm alone. Or even worse. There are definitely worse things than being alone."

WHAT'S NEXT?

As fall progressed closer to winter, and the holidays started to approach, the seniors prepared themselves for SATs and began their college applications. Sally fussed over her essays and helped her friends to collect their thoughts and ideas for theirs. Chris worked to get his math and science grades higher to bring up his GPA. Carl got his SAT scores back, and he scored 1480. His friends were blown away.

"Oh my God," Kim said at lunch when he revealed his scores along with everyone else. "You really are a genius! I hit the mother lode!"

Chris snickered. "I think it's a Bishop thing," he told the group. "The brains. But not everyone gets them. It's like a crap shoot. Carl's the one from this generation. I hope you use it for good, man."

Carl shrugged. "It's really not a big deal, guys," he said. "So I'm good at taking standardized tests. Everyone has something they're good at."

Darlene shook her head. "Uh uh, Carl," she protested. "You're just smart. But you don't talk about it, so no one knows. You hide it well. You could probably go to any college you want."

"If I wanted," Carl corrected. "I'm not sure I want to go to college. I mean, not yet. I mean, what's the rush?"

"Starting life with a good job, that's the rush," Chris said. "Having some goals. Making some money. Being able to do something you like to do for a living. Do you want to be on the lawn crew all your life?"

"Dude, after last summer, I don't want to even look at a lawn again," Carl admitted. "But maybe college just isn't for everyone. There's got to be a way to be happy in life without having to spend so much time in school."

"My parents would never let me get away with not going to college," Sally said. "Education has always been something that was expected of me and my brother and sister. I guess I never even considered thinking about doing something different."

Carl shrugged. "Well, my parents don't really care much about what I do, as long as they don't have to be involved. They kinda don't give a shit."

"I'm not ready for a four-year college either," Kim said quickly to distract from Carl's last statement. He had shown a part of himself he usually kept buried deep below the surface, and she didn't think he would welcome follow-up questions. "But I do want to go to school in the fall. I think I'm gonna just go for an associate's degree, and then if I want, I can transfer to a four-year school. Maybe I'll do some kind of healthcare program. I can be a phlebotomist, or a CNA. Maybe a dental assistant."

"Those are all really good things," Sally agreed. "And they're all about helping people. I can see you doing that, Kim. I'd let you scrape tartar off my teeth anytime."

James laughed, making Kim smile. James thought Sally was hysterical. Kim felt the same about Carl. She always laughed at his jokes. But now she worried about his more serious side. She wished he would consider some sort of plan for after graduation. It was like he was afraid to decide. He had no one at home encouraging him to pick a direction, so he was just standing still. She didn't care if he was a landscaper, or a bricklayer, or a hot dog salesman with a cart in front of city hall. She just wanted him to find something he could relate to, to make him feel productive and useful. He had all this intellect floating around in his brain, and she was afraid it would grow stagnant. But she knew he had a good head on his shoulders. He would figure it out. He would find his place. And she would do whatever she could to stand by his side when he found it.

TIME TO GIVE THANKS

Mrs. Drake liked to have Thanksgiving at her house and keep it low key. There were a couple of aunts and uncles and cousins, one grandmother, and Carl. He had had a long talk with Gram Missy about the holidays, and she had agreed that Kim needed him more than she did this year. Neither of his parents inquired about his plans. He was pretty much on his own now.

The day was sunny, and the air was crisp. The Drake kids were giddy and anxious for food. Sophie and Zach buzzed back and forth between all the rooms of the house, playing and roughhousing with their cousins. Stella and Chip were more dignified pre-teens, helping their mother with the food and rolling their eyes whenever she said anything they found even vaguely embarrassing. Kim watched them all from her seat on the couch with Carl and smiled. She realized they were growing up. They didn't need her so much anymore. They had each other and their friends from school. They didn't feel like they were alone, like she had at their age. But she wasn't too sure that she was done with needing them to need her, not just yet.

Her father sat in his recliner, watching an NFL game. He appeared to be following the action, and he would cheer if someone on his team scored or made a good play. He remembered football; he just didn't know who the players were anymore. The game kept him occupied while her mother and aunts cooked. Kim had wanted to help, but her mother waved her away. "You do enough the rest of the year," she told her. "Go sit down and relax."

After dinner, while the adults cleaned up and prepared dessert, Carl and Kim took the kids outside to toss around a football. Kim could not remember ever seeing Carl hold a football, and it became him. He had a strong arm and good aim. He made the kids go out for a pass, and he threw the ball in an arc, predicting where they would be when it came down. After some time, Mrs. Drake called them inside for pie and cake.

Kim grabbed hold of Carl's arm as they walked toward the house. "They love it when you come over," she told him, referring to her siblings. "You treat them like equals, and you actually play with them. Carl, you're gonna make a fantastic dad someday."

Carl felt chills in his veins to hear Kim talk about him having a family. But he also knew that this was something people said. It wasn't guaranteed that he would have kids someday with Kim. But in his mind, he imagined what they would look like anyway. They would have dark hair and brown eyes. They would be beautiful.

"If I have a son someday," he told her proudly, "I want to name him Pedro."

"Pedro?" Kim said with a laugh. "That's so specific! Where did you get Pedro?"

"It was my grandfather's name," Carl told her. "Pedro Valdez. I never met him. He died in Puerto Rico. I don't know. I mean, my name is really Carlos and I have always been called Carl. Maybe I should have gone by Carlos. Maybe I should have been proud to be named Carlos. But maybe I can have a son someday who would be proud to be called Pedro."

Kim nodded. "Carl, that's as good a reason as any I have ever heard for naming a baby anything. I hope to meet Pedro Bishop someday."

It was the closest thing she had ever said to talking about the future. She hoped that she would not just meet Pedro Bishop, but that she would love him more than life itself, because he would be her son, too.

YOU CAN RELAX NOW

December inched toward Christmas, and college applications were completed, signed, stamped, and sent in. There was a sense of relief to meet deadlines, but it was replaced by a sense of anticipation and dread, no one knowing where they would get in or what the next year would bring.

Christmas break began, and the Randall–McKinney gang and Pete trooped to the mall to go Christmas shopping. They ate buffet style at the food court and shared bags of cookies from The Cookie Place for dessert. They split up into pairs to shop for each other. Kim went off with Darlene.

"What are you gonna get for Carl?" Darlene asked as they wandered around deciding which shops to go into.

"I don't know," Kim admitted. "He likes funny T-shirts, but his Gram always gets those for him. Maybe a video game for his game system?" She wanted to get him something romantic, but she was stymied as to what that could be.

"You have to get him a stuffed animal," Darlene informed her. "Y'know, something with a big heart on it that says *I love you*."

Kim stopped short. "Darlene," she told her friend, "Carl and I . . . we've never said . . . that . . . to each other."

Darlene stopped next to her friend and stared at her in disbelief. "Are you kidding me?" she exclaimed. "You've been together since prom! You've gone away together. You practically live at his house on the weekends. The two of you just glow when you're together. How is it possible you haven't said I love you yet?"

Kim shrugged. "It's never come up?"

Darlene glared at her. "Kim, that's a lame excuse! Don't you love him?"

"I . . ." Kim paused. She should have been prepared for someone to ask her this question at some point, but she hadn't thought of what she would say. "I feel so much for Carl," she said. "I really do. He makes me happy, and we're best friends. I want to be with him all the time. I mean, he's so much. I just don't know if I'm ready to say those words yet. And he hasn't said them either, so . . ."

"Oh, my God," Darlene said, rolling her eyes. "You can't even say the words *I love you* about Carl, even just talking to me about it! The two of you are hopeless. Don't you think—"

"Look, there's the engraving store," Kim cut in, desperate to change the subject. "Carl's been talking about everyone having flasks. Maybe I can get him a personalized flask. Let's go in."

She walked toward the store with purpose, Darlene still standing in the hall, shaking her head at her.

Carl picked up a stuffed giraffe from the shelf at the Hallmark store. "Kim has stuffed animals, but I don't think she has a giraffe," he told Chris, who was leafing through greeting cards in the To Grandparents from Grandson section.

"You can't go wrong with a giraffe," Chris agreed. "But not *just* a giraffe, right?"

"Oh, yeah, of course not," Carl agreed. "But I have no idea what to get her. I've never had to buy a Christmas present for a girlfriend before. Her birthday isn't till February, so I haven't done that yet either. I think the last birthday gift I gave Kim was a Barbie in third grade."

"Yeah, no Barbies this year," Chris instructed. "What about some jewelry?"

Carl contemplated. "I don't know, won't that be a little much? Especially after James gave Sally that super expensive and meaningful promise necklace last year?"

"You can't just rule out all jewelry because James overdid it at the jewelry store," Chris said. "You don't have to get her an engagement ring, or a promise gift. Just something nice so she knows you're thinking about her."

Carl sighed. "That's like all I do," he admitted.

Chris laughed. "You sound like one of the girls. That's not an insult, I promise!"

They made their way to the cash register and paid for their items.

"Let's go to the jewelry store," Carl decided. "Not the expensive one with the rings and diamonds. The other one. And you can help me pick something out for Kim."

"Let's hit it," Chris agreed. "Are you coming to my Gram's for lunch on Christmas?"

Carl nodded. "Kim and I are planning on going there for lunch, and the Drakes' for dinner. But I'll tell you right now, if either of my parents show up and start making any kind of scene, we're out of there so fast. I'm so done with them, man. I hope they just do the right thing and stay away."

Chris gave him a look of sympathy. "Yeah, I don't think Gram will put up with any shit from your dad this year. It just keeps getting worse. My mom is so devastated by how he's turned out. They used to be so close when they were younger, like us. What happened to him?"

"He's just an asshole" Carl replied matter-of-factly. "And he's angry and resentful of the world, and especially my mother. And she won't ever divorce him. She says it's because she's Catholic, but I don't think that's it. I think there's more. Their relationship has always been so fucked up. It's like a big game to them. I think they've both finally forgotten that they even have kids."

They continued walking in silence and soon arrived in front of the jewelry store. "Let's go find something pretty for Kim that will get you lucky on Christmas night," Chris said, stepping into the store.

Carl looked around before entering the store. He saw Michelle and Sally sitting on a bench in front of Sears, peeking in the shopping bags they had already collected. Looking the other way, he saw Darlene and Kim about to enter the Hallmark store. Kim glanced up and saw him. She smiled and waved. He smiled and waved back, then followed Chris into the store. He was already feeling lucky, without even giving her any jewelry yet. But he would still take the lucky sex on Christmas night; he obviously wasn't stupid.

Christmas went off without a hitch. Carl and Kim spent the night on Christmas Eve alone at Carl's house. The house had basically been abandoned by the others except that Scott came home to change his clothes and feed his lizard. Tiger the tabby was still in residence. They watched Christmas cartoons and claymation on TV and cuddled together in bed under warm wool blankets and comforters. On Christmas day, they went to Gram Cissy's for lunch. They hung out with Chris and the other cousins and opened gifts from the family. Jack and Rosa did not come. Scott made an appearance right before dessert, and he made small talk with his extended family. He exchanged a smile with Carl, which gave Carl some hope that maybe all was not lost yet, at least with his brother.

That evening, they went to the Drakes' for a family dinner with Kim's immediate family along with Mrs. Drake's mother, Grandma Susan Lester. Carl and Kim ate lightly after having had a large lunch but gorged on desserts with the kids. After dinner, they opened their presents from each other in front of the tree.

Carl looked wide eyed at his new silver flask. "Oh my God" he said. "I wanted one of these! It's so cool!"

Kim smiled. "I had it engraved," she told him, turning it over in his hand and pointing to the etched words across the bottom. *Carlos Bishop.*

"Kim," Carl said softly. "Thank you so much. I love it. I really do." *I love you, Kim,* he thought.

He opened the other gift, which was a small brown stuffed bear holding a heart that said *Hug Me.* He squeezed the bear and then squeezed Kim. "Thanks, Kim. I'll put it on my nightstand next to our prom picture."

Kim opened her bigger gift first. She laughed when she saw the giraffe. "I love this giraffe!" she exclaimed. "When I saw it in the store, I told Darlene I hoped you'd get it for me! Thank you!"

He handed her the smaller box and smiled. She ripped off the paper and took the lid off the small white cardboard box. Inside, she found a thin silver necklace with a pearl and rhinestone charm.

"Look under the cotton," Carl instructed her. She lifted the fluff, and below was a pair of stud earrings that matched the necklace. "They're not diamonds, but I thought they would look pretty on you," he said.

Kim reached over and put her hand on his cheek. "They're beautiful," she told him. "I've never had anyone buy me jewelry before. These are just what I'd pick for myself!"

She kissed him slowly and gently, and they heard a young voice say "Ew, gross" in the background. They both laughed. Kim took out her earrings and replaced them with her new ones. She put the necklace around her neck, and Carl helped her fasten it.

Mrs. Drake was sitting with Mr. Drake on the couch, holding his hand. "You look beautiful, Kim," she said, beaming. "Doesn't she, Gerald?"

"Kimmy is a beautiful girl," Mr. Drake agreed. "She's gonna be a heartbreaker when she grows up. Just don't grow up too fast, okay, Kimmy?"

"I won't Daddy, I promise," Kim told him softly. At that moment, she was her father's ten-year-old girl again.

Carl squeezed her hand.

I love you, Carl, she thought.

KIM'S BIRTHDAY

February twenty-eighth was a date forever etched in Carl's brain. It was Kim's birthday. When he was a small child, it meant a birthday party with a white cake and pink frosting, balloons, and unicorn party favors. He remembered the first year he wasn't invited to Kim's birthday party. It was third grade. It was a girls-only party. Even so, Carl had felt rejected, not being included. Chris had told him he heard it was a princess party and would be lame anyway. "Yeah, lame," Carl had agreed. But it wouldn't have been lame, and he knew it. And just like that, they were in totally different social circles, because she was a girl, and he was a boy.

Now he was the one responsible for fulfilling Kim's birthday wishes, and it was a task he took to heart. She was turning eighteen. She would be able to vote in the next election. She would be considered an adult in the eyes of the law. She would be consorting with a minor until Carl's birthday in September. But he wasn't going to turn her in.

She didn't want a party. She wanted a nice dinner out and a movie with Carl. She wanted to go to Luigi's, and her birthday was on a night that James would be working. They made a reservation and asked for James's section. Neither had been to Luigi's before. James had told Carl it was a very nice place for a romantic date.

They arrived at six, and the hostess brought them to a small, elegant table in the dining area. Kim was impressed by the low lighting and simple decor. She remembered that this was where James and Sally had gone on their first date. She could understand why Sally had raved about the place later.

James approached their table, in full waiter gear. He used an extended lighter to light the tea candle on the table and took out his order pad. "Hello, you two," he said professionally. "I am Raul, and I will be your server tonight." Kim laughed. "By any chance, does anyone in your party have anything to celebrate tonight?"

"Why, yes, Raul," Carl replied pretentiously. "It is the young lady's eighteenth birthday today. We would like a bottle of your finest champagne, please, sir."

"Okay, sparkling apple cider and two champagne glasses, coming right up," James replied. "Please, take a look at the specials menu, and I'll be right back with your drinks from the bar."

"Thank you, Raul!" Kim called after him, giggling. "Okay," she said to Carl. "Just that exchange with you two made the whole trip worthwhile. I knew it would be fun."

Carl looked into her eyes and smiled. He saw the candlelight reflecting in her eyes and he had to blink. She looked beautiful with the gleam in her eye. He wondered why he had never looked so closely into her eyes before.

Kim turned away. Carl's stare was too intense. She could feel prickly warm sensations from the back of her neck to the soles of her feet. She shook her head lightly. She felt a bit dizzy. She picked up the menu. Carl followed suit.

"What looks good to you?" she asked.

"I like chicken carbonara," Carl told her. "I'm also a sucker for good spaghetti and meatballs."

"I'm thinking chicken parm," Kim said.

"Pick an appetizer, too," Carl told her. "Get whatever you want. This is your night."

James came back to the table with a fancy bottle of cider and two glasses, unscrewed the pop-up cork, and poured the sparkling drink for them both. He held up the bottle. "Happy eighteenth birthday, Kim Drake," he said warmly. Carl and Kim raised their glasses, clinked them to the bottle, and drank.

"Ready to order?" James asked.

"How's the chicken carbonara here?" Carl asked.

"Everything is good here," James told him and then lowered his voice. "But knowing you like I do, Carl, I think you might prefer the spaghetti and meatballs."

Kim ordered mozzarella sticks to start and a salad with her chicken parm. Carl took James's sage advice and ordered the spaghetti and meatballs and a side of steamed mixed vegetables. James took their menus and left the table.

"This is really nice, Carl," Kim told him, reaching for his hand. "I feel so grown up when we go out. Like we did at Old Orchard. That one night, well, that was almost magical."

"It was," Carl agreed, squeezing her hand. "I'll always remember that night. I can still see that sunset when I close my eyes."

"We should do grown-up things more often," she said. "I mean, we're really good at some grown-up stuff." She winked at him.

"That's the part of your gift you'll get after the movie," Carl said softly. "Which reminds me, when do you want me to give you the rest of your gift?"

Kim squealed. Carl loved it when she squealed. James was heading toward their table with a tray. "How about with dessert?" Kim suggested. Carl nodded.

James placed the tray on a stand and set the plates in front of them.

"Salad with Thousand Island for Kim, and mozzarella sticks for the table, and," he reached into his apron pocket, "a little gift from me and Sally. It's not much, but we just wanted to let you know we were thinking about you."

He put a small gift-wrapped package down on the table.

Kim picked it up. "Thank you so much, James!" she exclaimed. "I really do have the best friends."

She tore the paper off. It was a plastic baggie filled with chocolate-dipped toffee, her favorite candy. "Oh!" she said. "Did one of you make this?"

James smiled. "Both of us made it. We like to make stuff together sometimes. We remembered how much you like toffee."

"I love it," Kim said warmly. "Thank you so much. I'll call Sally tomorrow to thank her."

"You are very welcome," James responded. "Kim, I'm glad we became friends all those years ago, and again in high school. And I'm really glad you're friends with Sally. Now eat your mozzarella sticks before they solidify back into string cheese. I'll be back in a while with your entrees." He stepped away.

"I want to eat this now," Kim confided to Carl. "But I want to save room for dessert. Here, hold this for me."

Carl took the baggie and stuck it in his jacket pocket. "I'm just glad I didn't get you the same thing," he teased. They both laughed.

They ate their food and talked about their upcoming spring break. Pretty soon, their friends would be hearing back from colleges and declaring where they chose to go. Kim was still researching programs and community colleges, which had more lenient deadlines. Their entrees came, and Carl decided that he was right to have gone with James's advice. He ate every bite of his spaghetti and meatballs. Kim was quiet while she concentrated on and enjoyed her chicken parm and linguini. Both let out loud, satisfied sighs when their food was gone.

Soon, James came back to take their plates and give them dessert menus. He brought their dishes to the kitchen, then came back to take their orders. They both ordered chocolate cake, the house specialty.

"Do you guys have anything fun planned for tonight?" James asked.

"We're going to see *Pretty in Pink*," Kim told him. "It's opening tonight. It's the new Molly Ringwald movie. If it's half as good as *Sixteen Candles* and *Breakfast Club*, I know I'll love it."

James chuckled. "So at least I know now what Sally and I will be doing tomorrow night," he told them, and he left to put in their dessert order.

"Thanks for agreeing to see a chick-flick for my birthday," Kim told Carl.

"Hey, I'm man enough to admit I enjoy a good chick-flick," Carl said. "I liked the other two movies you mentioned. Hey, look behind you."

Kim turned around. James and his coworkers were heading in their direction with a piece of cake with a lit candle. "Oh, no, I forgot about this part—" Kim started.

The crew began to sing, and James put the plate in front of Kim. He had used an icing tube to write *Happy Birthday, Kim* on the frosting.

"Okay, you two, enjoy," James told them as he went back to the kitchen.

Kim made a wish and blew out her candle. Then she dipped her fork into the cake and took a bite. "Oh, this lives up to its hype!"

Carl hadn't tasted his cake yet. "Can I give you your gift now?" he asked.

Kim thought his enthusiasm to please her was adorable. "Yes!" she said, and she put her fork down.

Carl pulled an envelope from his jacket pocket and handed it to her. "Happy birthday, Kim," he told her with a grin.

She opened the envelope and pulled out a card. She could see event tickets remaining in the envelope but decided to read the card first. It was a funny card from boyfriend to girlfriend, and she laughed at the pun. Carl had written her a sweet note, and signed it *Love, Carl*.

She never knew what that meant. Was it "love you, my friend," or "I love you romantically," or something else entirely? She smiled and thanked him. She reached in and pulled out her gift: two tickets to see Aerosmith and Ted Nugent at the Centrum on March eleventh. Less than two weeks away! Kim loved Aerosmith.

She got up from the table and walked around to Carl to give him a grateful hug. "Thank you so much, Carl! These are great! I'm assuming it's you coming with me, right?"

Carl laughed. "Well," he said, "I didn't want to make any presumptions, but yeah, I'd really like to! It's a Tuesday night, the last week before break. We'll just need to check to see if we have any midterms on Wednesday and work around them. I hope that's okay."

"Hey, if I'm not prepared for a midterm by the night before," Kim told him, "I won't be ready at all. We can study over the weekend. Carl, this will be so fun! I haven't been to a big concert in so long. And Aerosmith! So cool!"

Carl knew he had scored with the tickets. He knew he had scored with the birthday festivities. Now, they just had to get through the movie, and he would score again. He liked getting good scores on something other than standardized tests.

WHAT DO WE DO NOW?

College acceptance and rejection letters started to arrive. James got into Johnson & Wales and was ecstatic. He planned to attend the culinary program, and then get his MBA. Sally got into most of the schools she applied to and opted to go to Providence College, where she could study journalism and be near James. Chris got into the teaching program at Eastboro State and expressed his relief. It was the only school he had applied to, and his backup plan was to get a job for a year and then reapply. Darlene was going to Ithaca College and planned to go ahead with her plans to become a biologist. Michelle got into UMass and Boston University, and figured UMass would be better suited for her goal of working in nursing and public health. Pete had decided on Boston College and hoped to declare a major in sports management.

Kim requested applications for three local community colleges and started to fill out forms to apply for school and financial aid. Carl watched this all happen around him and felt empty and lost. He wasn't sure who to go to for guidance anymore. Everyone had just kept telling him to apply to any school he wanted but didn't offer any other avenues for him to pursue. Now it was too late. Now he would have to consider something else to do. But what?

Midterms went by, and Kim and Carl attended the Aerosmith concert. They bought T-shirts and saved their ticket stubs. Everyone started to prepare for prom. And Michelle announced an unfortunate change of plans.

"So he did it," she said to the group as she sat down at the lunch table with a tray filled with French fries and ketchup only. "Joey turned eighteen and marched right down to the Marine recruiting office, and he signed up. He joined the Marines."

"Oh, no," Darlene said. "When does he leave? After graduation?"

"Nope," Michelle reported, stabbing her French fries with her fork and leaving the fork in there. "No, they're gonna have him take a high school equivalency test, so he can leave sooner," she said. "So yeah, he leaves in like two weeks."

"Before prom!" Sally exclaimed. "How could he do that?"

"Well, he always said he was thinking of joining the Marines," Michelle admitted. "I shouldn't really be that surprised. I guess he has his priorities."

"Did you break up?" Darlene asked.

"No, we didn't," Michelle said, "but I definitely was not consulted about his plans, so I'm not ruling it out yet. But I can't believe I can't go to prom now!"

"But you need to go to prom," Kim said sadly. "It won't be the same if you're not there!"

"I don't want to go if you're not going," Sally said.

"We could all just skip it this year," James suggested. The girls all gasped at the thought.

"Or," Carl suggested, "we could be trailblazers."

"What do you mean?" Chris asked. "Go hiking instead?"

Carl laughed. "No," he said, "but two years ago, when Kim and I made our prom pact, we also talked about the fact that it's not against the rules to go to the prom without a date. But is there any rule about going with six dates? I mean, no one in our group is dating anyone from outside of McKinney anymore, right? Why can't we all just go together as a group?"

They all sat and thought about it. "I mean, why not?" Sally asked. "It's not like they force you to only dance with the person you came with, and once we're in the door, we can do whatever we want! We can all dance together for the fast songs, and we can switch off for the slow songs. Chris, you could be unofficial dates with Michelle and Darlene, and we can just make sure there are no times when anyone is left alone."

"I guess I would be willing to go along with that," Michelle said. "It's senior year! I don't want to miss prom."

"Me neither," Darlene stated. "I'm in. Chris?"

"I don't know, guys," he said. "I'm not sure I could handle going without a date, and seeing Rhonda there with her new boyfriend. I mean, it's not like I want her back or anything, but I also don't want it rubbed in my face. I mean, I really haven't made any effort to go out with anyone else all year, so it's pretty much on me, but still."

"Chris," Darlene said reassuringly and placed her hand over his. "I promise you, if anything makes you uncomfortable with Rhonda at the prom, I will French kiss you right there on the dance floor so everyone can see, especially Rhonda. I really don't want to do this if we're not all gonna commit. C'mon, Chris, do it!"

"Yeah, Chris, do it!" Michelle insisted.

"Do it! Do it!" Carl started to chant, pounding his fist in the air. The other friends joined in.

"Do it! Do it!"

"Okay, okay," Chris said, laughing. "I'll do it! But only if you guys promise to never gang up on me like that again! Everyone's looking at us." Everyone went quiet. "But thanks, guys. I really appreciate you all looking out for me. I don't know if I could have made it through this year so far without you all. It's really been a humbling time for me. But having the best friends in the world has made it bearable. So thanks."

Everyone smiled at Chris, and Carl and James patted him on the shoulders.

Sally took charge immediately. "Okay," she said, "I'll check with the school to make sure we do everything by the rule book, or if not, how to change the rules. Girls, we need to go out shopping for dresses for those of you that don't have them yet, and accessories for the others. Chris, why don't you just get a black-and-white tux that matches all the girls. We need a plan for after prom, and we need to figure out how we're all gonna get around. James, why don't you take charge of the transportation, and Michelle and I can work on the afterparty. And then we'll regroup next week and do an update. Everyone knows what they need to do?" Everyone nodded. "Ok, good huddle guys. Go team McKinney!"

"Go team McKinney!" Michelle and Carl echoed back.

James laughed. "Sally, it may be time for you to back off a bit on all the sports pep talk movies!"

PROM TIME FUN TIME

Sally was told that a request for a group date to the prom was highly unusual and frowned upon. She continued to push the issue until she got an audience with Principal Catalano. She pleaded her case, and Mrs. Catalano could find no rule against the request. They would have to each pay for a ticket as individuals instead of by couples, and they would all behave like perfect ladies and gentlemen and not draw attention to themselves at the dance. Sally had to restrain herself from hugging Principal Catalano.

James secured an inexpensive limo, and all the boys rented their tuxes. The girls bought their dresses, shoes, and accessories. Chris got his parents to agree to have the post-prom party at their house. The Mahoneys had a fully furnished rec room in the basement. The prom-goers would be left on their own, and everyone would sleep on the floor in sleeping bags. They were encouraged not to drink but also to drink responsibly. Pete and Carolyn were invited to the party, since their prom was on a different weekend. The agenda was set. Everyone was ready.

The senior prom theme was "One More Night." It was their last big event in high school before graduation. Kim and Carl entered a gym decorated with stars, moons, and planets, and spotlights projecting stars on the floor, walls, and dancers. There were large silver stars dangling from the ceiling, and black tablecloths covered with silver star glitter on each table. Black, white, and silver balloons filled the room.

Kim looked like an angel to Carl. She wore a sleeveless teal gown that didn't reveal too much cleavage, but clung tight to her body down to her waist and flared slightly as it extended down to the floor. He couldn't see her shoes, but she knew she was standing on two-inch heels. Her hair was swept into an updo behind her head, with little strands dangling down seductively beside her cheeks. Her makeup was not overstated, and her smile lit up her face—and his. He wore a black tux with a bow tie and cummerbund to match her dress. He felt that with her by his side, they were invincible. They could take on the world and have something left over to show for it. He felt happy to be by her side, and for the world to know it.

The couples had their pictures taken by the photographer. They were allowed group shots, and there was one with Chris with Darlene and Michelle on each of his arms. The group stayed together to dance and traded off partners. They made sure no one felt alone or neglected. They sat together at a table to eat and drink punch, and the girls traveled to the bathroom in a pack. When the prom theme song played, they all went out to the floor, and Chris, Michelle, and Darlene danced as a threesome. Carl and James cut in to dance with Michelle and Darlene, and Kim and Sally danced with Chris. They all laughed at the spectacle they were making and decided not to care that their classmates were staring and pointing fingers. They were a team. They were having fun. And no one was left out.

This year's prom did not have awards like the junior prom did, but there was a royal court with a king and queen. After the presentation, the group decided to leave. They found their limo in the school parking lot, and they were driven back to the Mahoneys' house. They were greeted when they came in by Chris's parents, who then excused themselves and went to their bedroom. Chris's two younger sisters had been sent to sleep over their Gram Cissy's house for the night.

Everyone headed down to the basement. Mrs. Mahoney, who was also Carl's cousin Kate, had set out snacks and non-alcoholic drinks for the guests. Soon after, Pete and Carolyn arrived. Pete brought a case of beer. Beer and wine coolers appeared from inside rolled sleeping bags, and everyone opened a drink. Some of them had been partaking in shots from flasks at the prom, but no one had yet to become intoxicated. They all ate snacks and talked about their favorite prom moments. Pete and Carolyn talked about their plans for the Murphy High prom in May. Kim finished her second wine cooler and excused herself to go upstairs to the bathroom.

Carl chugged down his second beer, waited two minutes, and went upstairs. The Mahoneys' house was his second home. He'd spent more time there after school as a child than he did at his house. Chris's parents treated him like their own child. He knew his way around.

He waited outside the door for Kim to come out of the bathroom. She saw him there and jumped back. "You scared me," she said, her hand over her chest.

Carl came closer to her and put his hands on her waist. "I would never want to scare you," he whispered in her ear. He pulled her close. "Did I ever tell you how beautiful you are?" *And how much I love you?* he thought.

Kim nuzzled her cheek against his. "Yes," she replied softly, "but you can tell me again and again." She reached up to kiss him and things escalated quickly.

Carl eased her into the den and onto the couch. They were very quiet. They didn't want to attract any attention. They held all sounds inside, even when they wanted to call out. They held each other close and breathed heavily in each other's ears. They whispered each other's names. Finally, they fell from each other, both panting and content, and they put their clothing back in place.

"Much better than last year's prom," Carl told her.

"Much better than last year's prom," Kim agreed. "And I'm not going to cry tonight."

They sat on the couch, curled up but sitting, for some time. A light flicked on in the hallway, and Kate appeared in the door of the den. "Carl!" she exclaimed when she saw them on the couch. "Shoo! Go downstairs. No private parties, okay? I know you feel comfortable here, but I'm still in charge. Downstairs. Kim! Go!"

Carl smiled at his cousin. "Okay, okay," he said, pulling Kim to her feet with him. "You don't have to tell me twice. We're going." They started toward the basement.

"Hey, wait," Kate called after them. They both turned around. "I just wanted to tell you two, you both looked wonderful tonight. You really are a beautiful couple."

Kim and Carl looked at each other and smiled. "I know," Carl said. "Thanks, Kate."

They walked down the stairs together. Everyone looked up as they came near. "Where have you guys been?" Darlene asked with a grin. "Looking for change upstairs?" The others laughed.

"You know where we've been," Kim said to Darlene. "We all know each other too well here. I'm not going to stoop to making something up."

Carl laughed. "Yeah," he joked, "but if anyone here needs change for a twenty, I got you covered."

Everyone else laughed. Kim shoved Carl in the arm. Then they both got drinks.

At one o'clock, everyone decided to turn in for the night. They had made a huge dent in their alcohol supply, and witty conversation was becoming more of a challenge. Carl and Kim zipped their sleeping bags together and crawled inside. Kim was feeling woozy and relaxed. Carl was feeling tired and content and quite a bit buzzed. They kissed for a bit after Chris turned out the light, then cuddled up together to sleep.

"Good night, Kim," Carl said, brushing his lips up against her cheek.

"Good night, Carl," Kim said as she buried her face between his arm and chest. "I love you."

"What?" Carl said as he turned his head to face her. He had only heard a blurred mumble.

"What?" Kim replied, having realized that the words had come out of her mouth instead of staying in her head where they belonged. She held her breath.

"Oh, sorry," Carl said softly. "I thought you said something. Good night."

Kim let out her breath. "Good night."

GRADUATION TO THE REAL WORLD

Classes ended, and finals were completed. Students were given invitations to hand out for graduation. Carl gave one to Gram Missy and held on to the rest. There was no one at home to give them to. He left them on the kitchen table. They were still untouched the morning of graduation. Underneath the invitation was a form that Carl had left for his parents to fill out months ago. Carl wadded up the paper and threw it in the trash before leaving the house.

Carl went to Kim's house to get ready for the ceremony. Mrs. Drake had ironed their robes. They put them on along with their caps, and she took pictures of them before they left. Carl and Kim drove over together in Carl's Escort, and Kim's family went in their deluxe station wagon.

There were Bishop and Farmer distant relatives graduating that day, as well, and Carl could see cousins, aunts, and uncles as well as his grandmother and her twin in the crowd. When he walked across the stage to take his diploma, the principal announced he was graduating with honors. Carl braced himself. He knew that his parents weren't there to applaud him. But the Bishop-Farmer clan came through. There was a massive eruption of cheers from the crowd. He smiled to himself.

When the ceremony ended, Chris and Carl found each other quickly. Their grandmothers approached them immediately.

"Congratulations, boys! We're so proud of you," Gram Missy said as she hugged Carl and Gram Cissy hugged Chris. Then they switched off and hugged each other's grandsons.

"Just yesterday, you two were babies in the playpen together, and now you're grown men entering the world," Gram Cissy said proudly.

"Thanks," Chris and Carl said in unison as both grandmothers handed them greeting card envelopes that they knew each contained a twenty-five-dollar check.

Gram Missy cleared her throat. She had something important to say.

"So, Carl, I was talking to our brother Rolland Farmer the other day."

Carl always found it funny that Gram Missy used her family's last name when referring to her brothers. When he was a child, he thought that they all actually worked on a farm.

"You remember Rolland's son, Laine?"

Carl nodded.

Gram went on. "He and his wife, Beth, moved to California several years back to be near her family. Now Laine has a thriving electrical business out there."

"He should have opened a bowling alley instead," Carl said. "He could have called it Laine's Lanes." Chris laughed.

Carl was sure he was getting funnier as each day went by. At least Chris seemed to agree.

"Yes, yes, very funny Carl, you are a comedian," Gram Missy said. "But seriously, Carl, Rolland says that Laine is looking for a young man to apprentice into his business, and Rolland immediately thought of you. They have a new program out there where you can get a grant to apprentice to a trade and take classes toward getting your license while you're practicing in the field. It's what they call a pilot project. If it works out, they could start offering these types of programs all over the country. Laine was able to get in on the ground floor, so to speak. And Laine and Beth have a small rental unit on their property and would be willing to have you come and stay there for free until you start making some money and can pay rent."

Carl shrugged. "I don't know, Gram. I mean, an electrician? That's not something I've ever even considered doing."

Gram Missy looked at him and shook her head. "So what are you going to do with your life then? Work at Friendly's? Have you seen the people that work there full time? They all have acne all over their faces. It's greasy. And they don't pay anywhere near enough for a young man to start his life on the right foot. Carl, if you're not planning on going to college, you need to do something! Your mom and dad aren't gonna support you, and you won't be able to survive in that house very long without a job. I can assure you."

Carl paused. He had no argument. He had no plans. If he said no, he had no alternative. But an electrician? He didn't know any more about electricity than how to screw in a new lightbulb. He would have to start from scratch. But he was no dummy. He was a fast learner. He had one of the highest SAT scores in the school. He'd made the honor roll consistently. It wouldn't take him long to learn a new skill, and do it well. But California?

"I'll think about it," he told his Gram.

"Think about it soon, Carl," Gram said. "Laine would want you to get going by your eighteenth birthday, so you would need to relocate by mid-August."

"I will," Carl promised.

Grams Missy and Cissy went off to find Chris's parents and their other graduating nieces, nephews, and cousins so they could pass out their stack of greeting cards.

"She's right, Carl," Chris told him after the Grams walked away. "You're gonna need to find something to do to make money. Your parents aren't gonna let you freeload. And I don't think you'll survive in that house if you stay there much longer. That place will kill you eventually. I don't know why you just don't suck it up and go to college. You'd just cruise through your classes. You could even just go to community college."

Carl rolled his eyes. "I don't know," he replied. "I just don't see myself sitting in a classroom all day every day for the next two to four years. I need a break, or something."

"Well, maybe an apprenticeship would feel like a break for you," Chris said. "I remember Laine Farmer. He's pretty cool. And he's pretty laid back for a Farmer. He'd probably buy you beer and stuff. Although I think he has a couple of kids now, so I don't know. I mean, I totally don't want you to leave, and I'd miss you more than anything, but this might be a really good opportunity for you. And I'm gonna be busy with school, and I'll be living in the dorms. I won't be around as much."

Carl bit his lower lip. "But what about Kim? I'm just supposed to pick up and go across the country, and leave her behind? It kinda sounds like it would be a major commitment to be an apprentice. I probably wouldn't be coming back for a long time. Would it be fair to ask her to wait for me? I don't think she'd want that."

"Yeah, I know," Chris said. "It is a big decision. But it's not like you have to make up your mind right this minute. Maybe you can call Laine and find out more. It would be pretty cool to have your own place. And to make money. And who knows? Maybe things will work out for you and Kim somehow."

Carl sighed. "She really doesn't strike me as the long-distance relationship type," he lamented. "And I don't think I'm ready to give up on her yet. I mean, it's been like three months since she's even slipped up and called me a moron by mistake. That's progress. I wish they could just do this pilot project thing here in Massachusetts."

"Just talk to Laine and find out about it," Chris told him. "Then you can decide what you want to do. I'll get his number for you from my mom."

CALL TO LAINE

Carl waited three days to call Laine. He knew if he waited too long, Kim would start to pick up on his tension and start to ask questions. He wanted to have answers. If he decided not to do the apprenticeship, it would be no big deal, but he would need to make another plan for his future. If he did decide to take the offer, he'd have to figure out what to do about Kim.

Laine answered the phone after two rings. "Farmer Electric, Laine speaking."

"Uh, hi Laine," Carl said awkwardly. "This is Carl Bishop, Missy's grandson?"

"Oh, hey, Carl," Laine said pleasantly. "I was expecting your call. Hey, congratulations on your graduation!"

"Hey, thanks, man," Carl said, and then thought he shouldn't have called him *man*. But Laine was still his cousin. Cousins were informal. "So my Gram was telling me about the apprenticeship program, and I thought I'd call to get more information from you to, you know, see if it might be something I might want to do."

"Yeah, Carl," Laine said. "I heard that you did pretty well in school. Pretty impressive with the grades and SATs. Aunt Missy said you're not planning on going to college right now. I'm looking for someone to apprentice who would be able to come in and pick up on the skills pretty quickly, and be able to work with me on jobs, not just observe. The town I live in, Seska, has started this program, where they subsidize a portion of your pay while you learn, and cover the cost of classes. They're trying to lure people from out of town to get involved in the trades. If you do this, I expect you to make a commitment to stay with the program for at least a year. If that doesn't sound like something you could do, I'd prefer to find someone who would be willing to stay. It has to be of benefit to me, too, to sponsor an apprentice. I don't just give my time away. Do you want me to tell you more? Does it sound like something you might be interested in?"

"Yeah, I'd like to hear more," Carl said. He was not making a commitment on this call. He was just learning about the gig. He could hear more.

"So Seska's east of San Francisco. It's a really small town with a small-town feel and attitude, but this is a very liberal part of California. Lots of granola-eaters settled here in the sixties. So pretty easy going. But you can't get in trouble in town without your neighbor finding out about it before you even get home. We have a house near the edge of town. By we, I mean me and my wife, Beth, and our two kids, Benjamin and Claire. They're five and two. Good little kids. I built an apartment unit in our old converted two-car garage and shop. Kind of an extended studio with partitions between the two main rooms. It's not huge, but it's pretty nice. I did all the wiring and plumbing, so you know it's done well. It's fully furnished. The rent is five hundred a month, utilities included, but you wouldn't be expected to pay until you started getting paid, and don't worry, you would make enough to afford the rent. And you'd have a guarantee that Beth would invite you for dinner at least twice a week. The work is mostly residential, but I do have some contracts with commercial business and government offices. I've also got a storefront in town in front of my shop where I sell basic electrical stuff like lightbulbs, lamps, and fuses. I'm thinking of expanding a bit when the time is right, maybe into light fixtures and whatnot. I'm not the only electrician in the county, but I'm pretty much all we've got in town. Sound okay so far?"

"Yeah, it does," Carl responded. It did. It sounded good.

"What I can do is send you some information in the mail this afternoon, and you can read about the grant and the type of work you would be doing. Once you get that and look it over, you can call me back and let me know what you think, and then we can talk more about you, and what you'd want to get out of all this. But Carl, you already have high recommendations from your local Bishop-Farmer clan, and that goes a long way with me."

Carl gave Laine his home phone number and address. He agreed to read the material, think it over, and call him back by the end of the next week. They ended the call with familial pleasantries.

Carl hung up the phone and went into the bathroom. He splashed water on his face and looked at himself in the mirror. He knew that he had to seriously consider this opportunity. He had nothing else to consider. It sounded ideal. But the thought of leaving Kim was like being stabbed in the gut. And talking to her about leaving would be the hardest conversation he would ever have to have. He wished she could just come with him, but he would never want to ask her to leave her family. He didn't think she would ever want to leave her dad. He knew he had to face this decision. He was a high school graduate now. He couldn't depend on anyone else to make up his mind for him.

But he could get advice from his Gram.

TALK TO MISSY

They were going to get together that night, but Kim needed to babysit for her younger brother and sister so her mother could take Stella and Chip to visit their biological mother's parents. The regular babysitter had gotten sick. Carl hated to be away from Kim, but it did buy him some time. They spoke on the phone after she put the kids to bed, and they promised to see each other the next day to make up for lost time.

The next morning, Carl was up early. He couldn't stay in bed. He showered and dressed, then got in his car and headed to Gram Missy's house, unannounced and unfed, like always.

Gram answered the door with a huge smile. "Carl!" she said. "Is Chris with you? Or Kim?"

"No, just me," Carl told her. He came inside. "I was hoping we could talk, you know, about this apprenticeship thing,"

"Of course, Carl, come sit down," Gram insisted. She sat him at her dining room table. "I made muffins. I'll go get one for you."

Carl took the muffin gratefully, and once he had ingested it with a glass of milk, he turned his chair to face his Gram. "Gram," he said. He sighed. "How could I leave Kim?"

His grandmother's smile was kind. "I thought that might be what was getting in your way. But Carl, how can you stay?"

"I don't know, Gram," he told her. "I don't know what to do. It's like whatever choice I make, I lose something. How do people usually make choices like this?"

Gram took his hand. "So you talked to Laine," she said, "and you liked what he had to say."

"Yeah."

"I'm sorry to have put you in this position, Carl," Gram said sincerely. "But I can't stand to see you wasting away in that house. You've had no guidance, no one to help you. No one to teach you to make hard decisions. I can't imagine that you've ever seen your mother and father work through a problem to its conclusion in a healthy way. So I understand why this is so hard for you."

"Until now," Carl told her, "there was nothing important to decide. I just had to get up every day and go to school. And it came so easy for me. I never had to ask for help. Now I need help."

"Carl, you know I adore Kim," Gram said. "And I want a happy ending for the two of you. But if you stay, I worry that you won't get that happy ending. I see you not being challenged, and becoming restless and resentful, like your father, although I don't know what happened to make him that way. I see Kim moving on with her goals, and you watching her move away from you. That breaks my heart, Carl. The thought of you losing Kim and having nothing to show for yourself. But if you do this apprenticeship, there's still a chance for you. You might still be able to make it work out. Maybe not, but maybe so. Maybe you'll do what you have to do, and she will still be there. But if not, at least you have a leg to stand on. While you rebuild."

"Why can't just being with her be enough?" Carl wanted to know.

"Was that enough for your mother?" Gram asked, not unkindly.

Carl sat silently. "No," he told her. She was right. Nothing was ever enough for his mother. Especially his father.

"Carl, think it over some more," she told him. "You don't have to decide today or tomorrow. But talk to Kim, and tell her what's going on. Don't keep her in the dark. She needs to make some choices about her life, too. Let her have all the information so she can make the right choices for her."

Carl never wanted to do anything to make life hard for Kim. It might be hard if he left, but it might be even harder if he stayed. The choice was becoming clearer. He had to talk to Kim.

KIM'S RESPONSE TO CALI

Carl didn't tell Kim immediately, but he did talk to her once Laine's information arrived in the mail and he'd looked it over.

"California?!" Kim exclaimed. "Like, the California on the West Coast?"

He had asked her to come by, so she had stopped at his house on the way back from Michelle's house. Now they stood in his driveway, leaning against her car in the summer heat.

"Yeah," Carl told her. "That California. My cousin Laine lives in a town called Seska that's like fifty miles from San Francisco, and they have a single apartment unit in their backyard that I would rent. It's a converted garage. I'd be going to work with Laine thirty-two to forty hours a week, and taking eight hours of classes a week at the technical school. He would hire me on as an assistant as he trained me, and to work in his store part of the time. I could eventually come back to Massachusetts and transfer my hours, and probably get a job pretty easily."

"So " Kim started, "you'd be gone for how long?"

"I'd need to commit to at least a year working with Laine," he told her. "He doesn't want to put in all of the effort of getting me trained and then get nothing in return. But it takes up to four years of experience and classes to get an electrician license, kind of like a degree in college, but much less classroom time."

"So at least a year." Kim stated this like she would a historical fact. "But probably more. So I'd stay here, and wait for you for at least a year. And then you'd come back, and I'd just be here, waiting for you."

"Kim, it's not exactly like that," Carl told her. "I mean, yeah, I would love it more than anything if you were here when I got back. It would be ideal. But I can't control what happens over a year."

Kim looked at him with no expression of emotion. "Is this a done deal then? You've made up your mind?"

Carl scratched his hip absentmindedly. "Well, I mean, it's not written in stone or anything. I talked to Laine, and the whole thing sounds pretty good. And it's not like I have any other prospects. I can't keep living at my parents' house. You know that. It's just not healthy there. And you're planning on taking classes or going into some training program. . . . I have to do something. I need a way out. I don't want to waste away my whole existence. And I don't want to turn out like my father. I wouldn't be able to live with that."

"So it sounds like a done deal, then," Kim said softly.

Carl pressed his lips together. "I think it is," he told her. He put his hands on her shoulders. "I mean, I would love for you to come with me, Kim, but I know that's not really fair of me to ask, with your dad and everything. And I hope more than anything that you're here when I come back. But I also don't want to hold you back, you know? Ugh, it's just a lot to think about. I just don't know. Can we keep talking about it? I wouldn't go until August, so there's still some time for us to, you know, decide things and figure stuff out."

Kim felt her "everything's okay" facade taking its place in front of her face: muscles slack, neutral expression.

"Okay," she agreed. "We'll talk more about it. What this would look like. I mean yeah, this sounds like a once-in-a-lifetime opportunity. I get it. Let's talk more later. I gotta go now, though. My mom wants me home to help with dinner," she lied.

"Oh, okay," Carl said. "So I'll call you later tonight?" He reached over to give her a kiss. Her lips felt cold, even in the hot afternoon.

"Yeah, call me later. Bye, Carl." She quickly opened the door to her Chevette, got inside, started the car, and drove away. Carl was left standing alone in front of his house. It was a feeling he might have to start getting used to.

THE PEOPLE WHO LOVE YOU KNOW

The four girls sat at a round outdoor table with a giant umbrella sticking up in the middle, scooping Blizzards out of blue paper cups with long red spoons. Michelle was the first to speak up.

"I can't believe he's going to California," she said. "I didn't think that Carl would ever leave Chris! They're almost as much twins as their grandmas! But what does that mean for the two of you, Kim?"

Kim shrugged. "I think a breakup with Chris would be harder on him than a breakup with me," she said bitterly. "I don't know what's gonna happen to us. I mean, neither of us has experienced something like this before. We've been together for over a year now, but can we make it if he's gone for a year? I just don't know." She shook her head. She was getting used to tears since being with Carl. It was disconcerting.

Sally put a hand on her forearm. "I'm so sorry, Kim," she told her. "And Michelle, Darlene, Jamie, Pete, and I will be leaving in September to go school. It's gonna be a hard time with everyone going."

"Chris will still be here," Michelle said. "I'm surprised that he decided to stay in town and go to Eastboro State after he and Rhonda broke up, but I guess he likes being around his family. Maybe the two of you could hang out. You'll both be missing Carl. You can commiserate."

A look came across Kim's face that her friends did not recognize.

"Yeah, I don't think so," she told them. "I don't see us being that close with all of you gone. We just don't have much in common besides Carl." She poked at her dessert with her spoon. "Maybe it's just not meant to be. I mean, c'mon. Carl and I have been friends all our lives. Maybe we were only meant to be friends. Maybe we were there for each other at a time when we both needed to be with someone. Maybe our futures aren't meant to be together."

Darlene looked up abruptly from her ice cream. "That's a load of crap and you know it," she said. Noting the shocked look on Kim's face, she smiled. "I have a long memory, Kim. He was your prince. You remember. He still is. You're not gonna get out of this one so easily."

"Prince?" Sally asked, intrigued.

"I'll tell you later," Darlene promised.

"I feel like when he leaves, I'll be left with nothing," Kim said, her shoulders hunching. "I didn't realize I felt that way until he told me he was leaving. I mean, I don't know what we would have become, but I feel like at least I deserve to find out!"

"Have you thought of . . . well, maybe going with him?" Sally asked gently. "They have community colleges in California, you know."

"Go with him?" Kim responded. "Yeah, I don't know. That seems pretty extreme. I mean, if I went with him, wouldn't he think that I was expecting something from him that he might not be ready for? I don't know, I mean, we might get more serious if he stayed, but what if I went out there and it just didn't happen for us?"

"Yeah," Sally said quietly. "But, Kim, just imagine if it did."

Kim was in the kitchen with her mother, helping her prepare dinner. Her dad was taking a nap, and the kids were playing video games in the den.

"Kim," Mrs. Drake said after minutes of silence, "is there something on your mind? You've seemed very preoccupied the last few days, even more so than when Carl told you he was planning on leaving."

Kim sighed. "You know me too well, Mom," she admitted. She was chopping broccoli, but now she put down the knife and looked at her mother. "Mom," she said, "I'm thinking about going to California to be with Carl."

Mrs. Drake looked up from the sauce she was stirring. "Oh!" she said. "I didn't realize that the two of you had discussed that possibility."

"Well," Kim admitted, "we haven't, really. He just assumed I wouldn't want to go, but I think maybe he might want me to offer. I don't know. But the more I think about it, the more I realize that something is pulling me toward going with him. I . . . think I want to be with him. I don't want to be away from him for a year. Not even a month, really. And it's not like I would be just going there to sit around and give him moral support. I could go to school there. I could get a job if I needed to. Mom, Carl has been my life every day for over a year now. I can't see how I can just let him go."

Mrs. Drake took the saucepan off the burner and came to sit next to Kim at the table. She took her hand. "It makes a lot of sense," she agreed. "You and Carl have gotten very close. If you feel it's the right thing to do, Kim, I support you. But I can tell, something's holding you back. It's Dad, isn't it?"

"Of course it's Dad," Kim admitted, looking down at the table. "And you, Mom. As much as I can't see not going with Carl, I also can't see leaving the two of you and the kids. What if something happened and I wasn't there?"

"Kim," her mom started, "we can't control everything that happens just by being there. We can't watch everyone every minute. You and I were both nearby when Dad had his accident, yet there was nothing we could have done. Sometimes, we can fix things, and protect people, but other times, we just have to deal with the consequences as they come up. Life will go on here at home, whether you are here or not, Kim. It's wonderful that you've been here all this time, but if it's your time to leave, you need to follow your heart. And it's such a good time to make a change. You've graduated, you're at a place where you can choose a future for yourself and not be locked in. California is known for having many great colleges and schools. You can find the right one for you if you decide to go."

"The timing *is* good," Kim agreed. "And I guess we could always come back if we need to. Or I guess if things don't work out for some reason, I could always come back. . . ."

Mrs. Drake smiled. "Kim, you'll always have a home here," she assured her. "In one year, in two years, whenever you need it. This is your home, even when you're not here."

"Thanks, Mom," Kim said as a single tear rolled down her cheek. "I have to talk to Carl. What if he says no?"

Mrs. Drake laughed. "I've seen the way Carl looks at you, Kim. Carl is not going to say no. Listen, we're all supposed to go to Aunt Karen's tomorrow night for dinner, but why don't you hang back here and make dinner for Carl? And you can talk all about it. And you can both decide together what's right for you."

"I'll make him dinner," Kim agreed, "but it's gonna be something that comes from a freezer box."

FOLLOW YOUR LUCKY STAR

"I've made a decision," Kim told Carl the next night over dinner. She had made them Weaver Fried Chicken and French fries but had used her mother's fancy dishes and silverware.

"What kind of decision?" Carl said, taking a swig of milk from his glass.

"Well," Kim told him, "I talked to my mom about my plans for the fall, and I went to the library and did some research. I talked to my friends, and I did a lot of soul searching. . . ."

"You decided what program you're gonna apply for next year?" Carl asked.

Kim bit her top lip, then looked Carl in the eye. "Carl, I made a big decision. And I want you to hear me out. I want to go to California with you. It's not some hasty decision I'm making. I've really thought it out. My mom agrees. It's a good time for me to make a change. I don't have a job. I'm not going to a four-year college. And they have everything I need in California. I can take classes, pick a program, and figure out what I want to focus on. And I don't have to live with you. I can get my own place, and we can just see each other when we want to, no pressure. But we can still see each other. To see what would happen. But I've made up my mind, Carl. I'm going to California." She made herself stop talking, even though she wanted to say more.

Carl sat silently looking at his fried chicken. Then he looked up at her.

"You want to go to California? Kim, I didn't even think going to California was an option for you. I mean, you've never even talked about moving from Eastboro. Your family is all here. Your dad. It's what you know. You'd leave that all behind to go to California because I'm going there?"

"Well . . ." Kim started. Her confidence from only moments ago was wavering. "Yeah. I mean, maybe I wouldn't if the circumstances were different. I mean, all of our friends are leaving for school. You're leaving. There's really nothing left here for me. It's like perfect timing. Then we both can have someone we know, so we'll never feel alone, and we can see where this relationship takes us."

"Okay," Carl responded.

They weren't the exact words he had wanted to hear from Kim in this situation. He had wanted her to say she didn't want to be without him. But he did want her to go. He looked at Kim's face. Her mouth was slightly agape, and she was staring at him with wide eyes. He realized that she was disappointed. "Okay" was not the response she had been looking for from him.

"Kim, this is great," he said honestly. "I would love for you to come to California. I didn't want to leave you behind. I would miss you way too much. And you're right, it's perfect timing. It's a great opportunity. And of course you'll live with me! As long as it's okay with Laine and Beth. But I can't see why it wouldn't be."

Carl found it didn't take much for him to switch gears from leaving Kim behind to taking her with him. It was easy. It was like he had already planned it all out in his head, even though he hadn't thought it possible. But he didn't really understand her motivation. Was it that she wanted to go with him, or was it just that she wanted to go because there was nothing left for her here?

"This will be great," he continued. "As long as this is what you want. I just want you to be happy. And I'll be really happy if you're there."

Kim smiled with relief. She felt her stomach muscles relax. She realized there had been a part of her who thought that Carl would say no. It was her vulnerable part, the one she hardly ever let him see. But she might have let just a bit slip by this time.

"And I promise, Carl," she told him, "I'll work hard on getting myself set up there. I've already got the names of nearby community colleges, and I'm gonna start sending out the paperwork. And I don't have to bring much, just my clothes and makeup and stuff. Anything else I need, I can just get when we get there."

Carl was aware that his life had just changed in a very drastic way, but the reality hadn't fully hit him yet. He felt fear and relief. He smiled at Kim and reached out for her hand. They still had some time. They could plan out all the details later.

GETTING READY

They decided to aim for arriving in Seska by August fifteenth, exactly one month before Carl's birthday. That way, they could learn the area, complete any paperwork they needed for the apprenticeship for Carl and school for Kim, and also spend some time in San Francisco before becoming too busy with their new work and school responsibilities.

It would take six days of driving about eight hours per day to cross the country, depending on traffic and construction delays. They gave themselves a ten-day window to allow for car problems or bad directions. They figured there might be places where they would like to stay an extra night or two. Carl called Laine and they reviewed the plan. Beth was getting the furnished unit ready for their arrival, and they would plan to have dinner at the Farmers' house on August fifteenth when they arrived. Laine was doing the paperwork to get the apprenticeship ball rolling, and Carl would need to bring his birth certificate and social security card for identification.

Carl called Gram Missy and asked her to help him find his birth certificate and social security card, as he couldn't locate any important papers in the house. He didn't know where his parents stored those sorts of things, and he didn't care to find them to ask.

"You're in luck, Carl," Gram told him. "Jack keeps his Strongbox here at my house for safekeeping. I guess his paranoia about getting his things stolen has paid off for you. I'll dig out your papers and drop them by later."

"Thanks, Gram," Carl told her.

Gram came by an hour later with an envelope. She did a double take when she saw the state of the inside of the house. Carl had been doing his best to keep the place clean and free of vermin, but still items were strewn around, clothes were draped over the couch, chairs, and floor, and leftover takeout was left in boxes on the coffee table.

"Carl," Gram said softly. "I knew things were not ideal over here, but I had no idea it had gone this far. Where is your mother?"

Carl shrugged. "I don't know," he admitted. "Sometimes, I can tell she's been by here to get something, and she leaves me some cash on the table for food, but I don't think I've seen her face for, I don't know, at least a month, maybe more."

"And your father?"

Carl shrugged again. "I thought you'd know more about where he was than I do."

Gram shook her head. "Those assholes," she hissed. "They've pretty much abandoned you, haven't they?"

"I guess," Carl admitted. "But I'm kinda used to it. I mean, they were hardly ever here anyway, and when they were, they pretty much left me alone, or made a lot of noise. It was especially bad when the tias came over. I kinda like it better with them gone."

Gram looked like she might cry, but instead, she tugged at the bottom of her shirt and stood up straight.

"Carl, you made the right choice," she told him. "I'll miss you like crazy when you go, but I'm happy that you're going. And that Kim is coming with you. I'm gonna throw the two of you a goodbye party at my house. Tell me who you want there, and I'll make it happen. And Carl," she continued, "throw some clothes in a bag, and grab your toothbrush and your video game console. You're coming to stay with me until you leave for California. We'll come back with some cousins and get you all packed up for your move later. And bring that orange cat of yours with you. We should have done this months ago."

Gram's house was in the opposite direction of Kim's house from Carl's, about two miles away. She and Cecil had raised their six children in the four-bedroom 1928white colonial. They had been the second owners. Now Gram lived alone in the house, but often welcomed grandchildren, nieces, nephews, and cousins for extended stays. It was Carl's turn. It was July tenth, and he and Kim were leaving on August fifth. Carl settled into his temporary home.

Mrs. Drake ordered them maps from AAA specific to their chosen route, and they unfolded them on her kitchen table to plan out their trip. The many maps were highlighted and marked for construction sites, but they decided to take certain detours to see sights, or to make brief stops to see relatives. They made lists of what they needed to bring and measured space in the car to make sure they didn't overpack. The decision was made that Tiger, who was technically Carl's cat, would be making the trip with them to California, so animal-friendly accommodations would be needed, along with food, water, and room for a litter box. He would roam free in the car but would need a carrier to be transported back and forth to lodgings.

Gram Missy planned the going away party for August second, a Saturday. Carl and Kim's friends would still be in town, and it would give them a couple days after to finish their travel preparations before hitting the road. Gram bought invitations, then mailed some and delivered others by car. She enlisted the help of her identical twin to help plan the menu and decorations.

Kim and Carl got together with their friends as often as time allowed. There were gatherings in the clearing, and trips to the mall. Movies and meals. Pictures taken and quickly developed. Everyone except Chris would be leaving town in the next few weeks, but no one wanted to say their final goodbyes until it was absolutely the last moment.

Kim got used to time at Gram Missy's house, with cookies and muffins provided at every visit, and stories of her childhood as a Farmer daughter with her twin and their marriages into the Bishop family. Kim loved the follow-up stories to her favorite childhood true-life fairy tale, and she got to hear all about the happy ending. She and Carl were shown the wedding album from the event where the Bishop-Farmer clan was formed when the pair of twins and their dashing brother-grooms married. Kim noticed the strong resemblance between Carl and his Grandpa Cecil as a young man. Everyone always said Carl looked just like a Bishop, and now Kim could enthusiastically concur. Gram Missy beamed when Kim said this.

Finally, the day of the party arrived. There were concerns of possible thunderstorms in the afternoon, but the front passed to the southeast, and the day was sunny and warm. Tables were set up in the shade of the backyard, and multitudes of entrees and sides lined up on top. Gram had made a ginger ale and Hi-C punch and presented it in a crystal punch bowl with scoops of neon sherbet on top. Signs declared Good Luck and Bon Voyage, and streamers were hung from the eaves and rafters. A volleyball net and a croquet set were assembled for those who wanted a challenge. There were bubble wands and soap for the smaller children, along with bean bags toss games and Hippity Hops. Basketballs lay gently on the ground below the hoop in the driveway.

Guests began to arrive around three, and a row of cars appeared parked along the street. Chris, his parents, and his two sisters came first. Then the Drakes. Then Darlene and Michelle, Sally and James, Pete and Carolyn, Cissy and Clive, and multitudes of aunts, uncles, and cousins. Gram cranked up the stereo, and guests enjoyed their food. The volume level got high. Carl and Kim mingled in the crowd, holding hands and keeping grateful smiles on their faces as they were handed greeting cards stuffed with cash.

As the afternoon turned into early evening, the food supply got low and was replaced by cakes, cookies, pies, ice cream, and urns of coffee. Small children began to whine and complain, and the cousin population thinned out. Soon, the Drakes said their goodbyes and headed home. Now only the group of McKinney friends and Pete and Carolyn, honorary McKinney friends, remained outdoors, while the Grams and the remaining family went inside to watch *Wheel of Fortune* and gossip.

"This is nice," Michelle said as they all arranged lawn chairs in a circle and settled in. "But this is also the last time we're all gonna be together as a group, until who knows when."

"Don't make me cry, Michelle," Sally warned. "I vowed to myself that I wouldn't cry tonight."

Kim was already tearing up. "I kind of feel better, knowing we're not the only ones who are leaving," she admitted. "I know that everyone had to make a choice to go. I don't feel like I'm abandoning you guys."

"Kim, no one's abandoning anyone," Michelle assured her. "We're out of high school. It's normal for us to go. It's what people do." Now she started to tear up. "I just wasn't expecting anyone to go more than three thousand miles away!"

"Hey," Carl said, "it's the same distance by phone between you in Amherst, Darlene in New York, and us in California. We will stay in touch."

"Some of us will be coming home for the holidays," Pete said. "We can get together and call the rest of you."

"Please do that," Kim pleaded. "It will be the first time ever I'm away from my mom on the holidays, and it's gonna be tough."

Chris had gone inside to use the restroom, and now he came back out and joined them. "Hey guys," he said. "Aunt Missy just stopped me in there and asked me if I wanted to help out and make some quick bucks by driving Kim's Chevette out to Cali later this month. She said I could take a friend, and she and Gram would pay for the gas and motels and our plane tickets home. I'm totally up for a road trip. Anyone wanna come with me? We'd be back before school starts."

Pete looked at Carolyn and she shrugged. Then he shrugged. "I don't have anything going on and I could use a quick buck or two," he said. "Carolyn's going to Fort Lauderdale with her friends later this month, and I don't have to be at school until Labor Day weekend. Let me just run it by my folks, but I'm sure it will be fine."

Kim and Carl looked at each other, and then at their friends. "Oh, my God, you two," Kim exclaimed. "That would be amazing! I thought we would just have to leave my car behind! Man, your Grams are the best! And you can visit us for a couple of days and see our new place. And we could all spend a day in San Francisco together!"

"And maybe you guys could haul some more of our crap out with you," Carl suggested. "We could pack up the car before we leave."

They all went quiet for a few moments.

"Man," James said, "for some reason, this all just started to feel really real for the first time."

Everyone else nodded in agreement.

The sun started to move lower in the sky, and someone produced a tightly rolled joint. They passed it around the circle, conscientiously skipping over James and Sally, who always abstained from drugs. Sally insisted she would be emotional enough without the enhancement.

They circled around and around, until all involved felt the stars were streaming across the sky like comets. "Our last joint together," Michelle lamented.

"Are you gonna do this all night?" Darlene asked her. "Our last joint together, our last shrimp cocktail, our last pee in Gram Missy's toilet . . ."

Michelle started to laugh and almost fell out of her chair. "Be careful, Darlene," she warned. "If you make me laugh too hard, it will be my last pee in my pants together!"

They all laughed and had to struggle to contain themselves. The weed they had smoked was pretty potent.

A car pulled up in front of the house. Carl recognized it immediately as Scott's and tensed up. His brother got out of the car and made his way over to the circle of friends.

"Hey guys," he said. "I see and smell that you've all been partaking in some innocent fun, once again."

Carl stood. "Hey Scott," he said, finding himself feeling more sober all the sudden. "I didn't expect to see you here tonight."

"Yeah, well, I saw Gram the other day," Scott explained, "and she told me you were heading out to California soon and she was having this party. I thought I should come check it out for myself, you know?"

"Cool," Carl said, his head bobbing up and down. "So. How ya been lately?"

Scott looked around the circle, all eyes on him. "C'mon, Carlos," he said. "Let's walk over to the grill pit, okay? We need to talk."

He took Carl's arm and led him to the opposite side yard. They both leaned against the stone wall and were silent for a minute.

"Carl," Scott finally said, "I just wanted to let you know, man, none of what happened was ever about you."

"What are you talking about?"

"None of the stuff that went on at home. With Mom and Dad. It was never about you. You never did anything to make them go. It was all them. They're both fucked in the head. They never should have been allowed to have kids. They should both be locked up, or at least someone should have reported them to the child welfare department."

"What for?" Carl asked. He thought his voice sounded slightly off, and he realized he might not have sobered up as much as he had hoped. "No one ever hit us or anything."

Scott frowned. "They didn't need to hit us with their hands, Carl," Scott said. "They fucking abandoned you. They took off. You were just sixteen. You had no one taking care of you."

"I took care of myself," Carl asserted defensively.

Scott's smile appeared warm. "Carlos, you did the best you could. I think someday it's all gonna hit you hard and you're gonna realize what happened. And I just want you to know that none of it was your fault. You were the kid, and they were the adults. And I'm to blame, too. I'm your older brother. I saw what they were doing. And I did nothing. No, I did do something. I stayed away. I pretended that if I didn't see it, it wasn't happening. Man, I am so sorry I didn't do anything. I showed more compassion to my lizard than I did to my own younger brother."

"It's okay," Carl said dismissively. "It's all good. It's over now, and I'm leaving. Starting a new life with Kim. I'm fine."

Scott looked at him sadly. "No, Carl, it's not all good. But I can see that this might not be the best time for us to have this conversation. That's fine. Someday we will." He stood. "I'm not gonna stay. I just wanted to come by and say goodbye and wish you luck, man. And also, I hate to tell you this, but I think your cat might have run away. I haven't seen him for a couple of weeks. I left some food out for him, but it hasn't been touched. Sorry."

Carl laughed. "No, Scott, the cat didn't run away," he said. "Tiger's here with me at Gram's house. Tiger decided to escape the long, cold New England winters and move to California with me and Kim. He's gonna be our travel companion."

Scott smiled and patted Carl on the shoulder. "I'm glad Tiger's alright. I'm grabbing Smokey and moving out of that deathtrap house myself next month. Maybe it'll get condemned and torn down. I hope so. Well, be safe, my brother. Take care of Kim, and look me up if you ever come back."

Carl wondered if he should initiate a hug with his brother, but his body didn't seem to know how, so he stood there with his arms by his side. "See ya, Scott," he said.

Scott went across the front yard, got in his car, and drove off.

Carl turned to walk back to his friends. He could see Kim looking at him from the circle and wondered if she had been watching him the whole time. He suddenly had a profound marijuana-induced revelation. *Look at me,* he said to himself, *walking away from my old life and toward the new.*

When he reached Kim, he knelt in front of her, wrapped his arm around her, and then kissed her, long and hard. All conversations in the circle stopped. Once the kiss ended, they all knew. The night was over. It was time to say goodbye. Their last goodbye together.

ON SUNDAY

On Sunday, Carl woke up in his bed at Gram's with Kim in his arms. They were fully dressed in last night's clothes. He didn't remember going to bed with Kim, but then he did recall asking her to call her mother and tell her she was staying over, because he didn't want to be alone. Now it was morning, and once again, he was waking up with Kim. He gently pulled his arm out from beneath her shoulders and crawled out of the tiny twin-sized bed. Had he had his wits about him last night, he would have pushed the two twin beds together, but both of them appeared to have made it through the night no worse for wear.

He let himself out of the bedroom and into the hall, then made use of the bathroom. He loped down the stairs into the kitchen and found Gram Missy at the table, drinking coffee and reading the Sunday paper.

She looked up when she heard him. "Good morning, Carl. Did you sleep well?" Carl nodded. He had no idea if she knew that Kim was in his bedroom. She met his gaze. "And did Kim sleep well?" He nodded again.

Carl was about to think that Gram knew everything there was to know, but then she betrayed that notion. "I don't know what kind of bug juice you and your friends were drinking last night," she said, "but I had to have James and Sally drive Pete and his girlfriend home, and Cissy took Michelle, Darlene, and Chris. Some of them came by earlier to pick up their cars. You kids really outdid yourself on the hooch. I should have supervised you better."

Carl smiled and could feel the bloodshot in his dry eyes. "Sorry, Gram," he said. "It was a hard goodbye. We all wanted to drown our sorrows. In hooch."

He promised himself to look up *hooch* in the dictionary later, but he suspected it was something you drank and not something you smoked.

Gram rose from the table. She was wearing a bathrobe over her pajamas, and her slippers looked like they were from 1946. She approached him and held him in an embrace.

"Sorry it's so hard, Carl. I really am." She carried her coffee cup to the counter and refilled it. "I'll make some eggs. We'll save some for Kim."

She took the frying pan out of the cupboard and then a carton of eggs and milk from the refrigerator.

"I saw you talking to Scott in the yard last night," she told him as she cracked the eggs into a bowl. The familiar morning sound made Carl's stomach rumble. He was getting the post-munchies.

"Yeah, Scott was here," he said, recalling the foggy and bizarre conversation with his brother. "We talked, but I was kinda far into the hooch by that time."

Gram looked at him and shook her head in dismay. "I hope you at least have a headache for all your trouble," she told him. She sighed. "No I don't. But just learn from your mistakes, okay? I thought it was the right thing to do, to tell Scotty you were leaving. I hope you don't mind."

"No, I don't have a gripe with Scott," Carl told her. "It's okay."

He heard footsteps behind him on the stairs and turned around to see Kim walking into the room, brushing her long bangs out of her tired, bloodshot eyes.

"Good morning, Sunshine," he said. Kim growled at him. "Gram knows we went a bit heavy on the hooch last night," he told her, "but she has no sympathy."

"I do, too," Gram protested as she flipped the scrambled eggs in the pan. "Kim, pull up a chair, you're about to get some fresh eggs and toast. And then we'll talk about the game plan for the day."

Kim groaned. "Does there have to be a game plan?" she asked. "Does the game plan include me standing under the shower for two hours, then taking a nap?"

Gram laughed. "Oh, Kim, you're as funny as a Farmer! But you're gonna need to pep up a bit if you're gonna start driving cross country in two days. We need to get you both packed up!"

"Ugh, packing," Kim said, dropping her head onto her hands. "I need to pack all my clothes. My mom agreed to help me. I haven't even started yet."

Gram dished eggs on to the plates in front of Carl and Kim and slid the toast on beside them.

"Well, the game plan includes you going home to pack with your mom, Kim," she told her. "And Carl's gonna have a Bishop-Farmer-type pack-a-thon at his old place, and we're gonna decide what goes and what stays. And then what will go in the Chevette with Chris and Pete, God bless 'em. And anything you want to keep but can't take with you, we'll stow away in my attic or basement, just in case something happens to the house while you're gone. Warren Bishop's gonna bring his pickup truck."

"Thanks, Gram," Carl said around his bite of eggs. "You've done so much for me. Sometimes I think I don't deserve you."

Gram sighed. "I know, Carl," she said sadly. "I know what you think. But you do. You deserve every good thing that happens to you. Every last bit."

Kim went home and took her long shower. Then she threw her laundry in the washer and set her suitcases open on her bedroom floor. As per their arrangement, her mother came up after lunch to help her to pack.

They folded her clothes neatly and laid them in the suitcases. Kim rolled a pair of socks and threw them on the pile.

"Mom?" she said tentatively, looking at Mrs. Drake.

"Yes, Kim?" Her mother finished folding a shirt and then looked up at her with a smile.

"Mom, are you gonna be okay? Like after I leave?" Kim sat down on her bed. Mrs. Drake sat down next to her.

"Kim," she said, "I'm gonna be fine. I promise. I'm a grown woman. But now you're a grown woman, too, and it's time for you to be out there in the world, finding what's right for you. Making a life for yourself. This is my life here. It's a life I choose every day when I wake up in the morning. But it's not the life I want for you."

"But Mom," Kim protested, putting her hand over her mother's hands. "It's so hard. So much work. And there's only so much the kids can do to help. I worry about you getting exhausted. I worry that you'll need more help."

"Kimmy," her mother reassured her. "I get so much help already. I have a flexible job schedule. I have the best sisters-in-law who will take Dad and the kids whenever they can, and I have you. You'll always be at the other end of the phone line, even if you're not here." She paused. "And I can also get help from the state if we ever need it. They have caregivers who can come to the home if needed, if we need more help. And there's facilities . . . It's all already approved. But we just haven't needed it yet." She put her hand on Kim's cheek. "Kim, I love your dad. He's my soulmate. He's my partner. I never could have imagined someone coming into our lives and seeing us for what we were at the time and not running away screaming." Kim laughed. "He is your true dad, Kim. And I owe it to him to be there for him now. And I'm not unhappy. There are moments, short, lovely moments, when he comes back to me. And those moments make it all worth it."

"Mom . . ." Kim started as tears rolled down her cheeks.

Mrs. Drake put her arms around her daughter. "I know, babe, I know. Me too." She released her embrace. "We need to get you ready now. You have a long trip ahead of you, and a new life to start."

She picked up the next shirt and started to fold. Kim picked up another pair of socks and started to roll.

GOODBYE DOESN'T MEAN FOREVER

They wanted to get an early start on Tuesday, and they didn't want their emotions to slow them down. So on Monday, they made the goodbye rounds. They stopped at Gram Cissy's, and then went to the Mahoneys'. Knowing they would see Chris and Pete soon made those goodbyes a bit easier. They visited Pete and then James and Sally at the neighboring Newells' house. They had lunch with Darlene and stopped at Michelle's house for last hugs. They shoved last-minute belongings they couldn't live without into crevices in the Escort and went to the store to stock up on drinks and snacks for the road. They went to the Drakes' for dinner, and Kim spent alone time with each of her brothers and sisters. They hugged and took pictures and promised to call and write. Stella cried and ran off to her room to be alone.

Kim was already tearstained as she went to say goodbye to her dad. He smiled as she approached him in his recliner. "Hey, Dad," she said as she knelt beside him.

"Kimmy!" he said. He reached for her hand. "All those children over there look so sad," he said softly. "Is your mom okay?"

"Mom's fine," Kim assured him. "She is a bit sad, though, because I'm going away tomorrow. I'm here to say goodbye. For now. I'm gonna miss you so much."

Mr. Drake smiled. "Are you going to sleepover camp?" he asked. "I know you worry about getting homesick, but you'll have fun. You just have to give it some time, Kimmy. You'll make new friends, and you'll have new adventures. It will be good for you! But I'll miss you. I always miss you when you go away."

"I know, Daddy," Kim's internal ten-year-old replied. "It's the right thing for me to do, to go. I know you love me. I always know that in my heart." She squeezed his hand. "Goodbye, Daddy," she whispered.

"Oh, are you going to bed now?" Mr. Drake said. "Okay, Kimmy, I'll see you in the morning."

"See you in the morning," Kim repeated. She got to her feet, waved to her dad, and headed out the door. Her mother followed her to the car with Carl.

"What he said," Mrs. Drake told her. "It's all true. It will be good for you. You're gonna grow in leaps and bounds. Kim, I'm so proud of you and the woman you've become." She embraced her daughter and squeezed her tight. Then she turned to face Carl. "Carl, take good care of her. You've always been her friend. Never stop being her friend."

They hugged, and then Kim and Carl got in the car and drove away.

The final goodbye was saved for Gram Missy. They would say goodbye before bed; they were leaving at dawn. Gram fed them cake and cocoa and gave them last-minute instructions.

"Don't forget to give Laine the package from Rolland," she reminded them. "And to call me collect every night to let me know where you are. Don't take your eyes off of Tiger when you stop. I've heard stories of pets running away at rest stops, and not all of them miraculously find their way home like in the movies."

"We'll keep an eye on Tiger," Carl promised.

Gram took an envelope out of her housecoat and handed it to Kim. "You cannot refuse this. This is gas, motel, and food money from me and Cissy. And I put an emergency credit card in there, for if you break down or lose your cash. Put it in a safe place."

"Thank you, Mrs. Bishop," Kim said warmly.

"No, no, Kim, you're moving across the country with my grandson," Gram insisted. "You've earned the right to call me Gram."

Kim felt her resolve melting away right before her. "I'm gonna lose it now," she told Carl and Gram. "I need to go to bed. Goodnight, Gram." She gave her a tight embrace. "And thank you. For everything." She let go of Gram and ran up the stairs.

Carl watched her as she left, then turned to Gram. "Thank you, Gram," he said. "For this, for the past month, for my whole life, for everything. I love you and I'm gonna miss you so much." He put his arms around her and held her tight.

Gram's eyes teared up. "You're my sweet, good boy, Carlos Bishop," she whispered. "You're going to accomplish wonderful things. I'm so proud of you. Now go out and conquer the world, okay? Now go!" She gave him a pat on the back to shoo him away. "Go on, go to bed now. Good night."

"Good night, Gram."

Carl went slowly up the stairs. He could hear crying from above and below him. He knew where he needed to go.

He went into the bedroom and found Kim face down on the pillow, sobbing. He lay down next to her and wrapped his arms around her. She continued to sob, and he felt the tears well up in his own eyes.

Eventually, the tears receded, and Carl took Kim's hand and led her to the bathroom so they could brush their teeth. They went back to the bedroom and changed into their pajamas, set the alarm for 5:00 a.m., and turned out the light. Then they cried quietly in each other's arms until they fell asleep.

PART TWO:
THE THINGS WE TAKE WITH US

TIGER IN YOUR TANK

Tiger hid under the front passenger-side seat and didn't come out. Every now and then, they would hear a low, guttural growl from below, and Kim worried she might soon feel the sharp sting of fangs around her ankle. She folded her feet beneath her as Carl drove. They exited Massachusetts, sped through Connecticut, and entered New York state. They were slowed down briefly by rush hour but experienced no stoppages through the morning. They ate Gram's muffins and drank tepid coffee from an oversized thermos. They pulled off for exits that promised McDonald's with restrooms, taking turns so someone would be with Tiger at all times. They refilled the thermos with coffee and tried to cover a good distance before stopping for lunch. Their goal was to make it to the Ohio border by nightfall. They were making good time.

The cat had not surfaced to eat or use the litter box, and Carl worried that they had made a mistake by bringing him along. It was too late to turn back now, so he vowed he would spend the rest of Tiger's life trying to make up to him for the inconvenience.

Pennsylvania seemed endless as the sky turned dark and threatening, and rain started to fall. When they saw signs for Lake Erie, they both relaxed. Soon they could stop for their first night on the road. It felt like it had been days. They felt exhausted and jittery. And they both wanted to shower.

They quickly found a motel near Erie, Pennsylvania, that allowed pets. They tried to lure Tiger out with food and soft calls and whistles, but finally, Carl had to reach under the seat and yank him out. He came out screeching and scratching but was eventually secured in his carrying case. Kim made sure all the car doors were locked, and they lugged cat, cat supplies, and overnight bags to their second-story room.

Kim pulled the drapes open and saw they had a clear view of the car. Carl placed the litter box in the corner and released Tiger. He shot out of the carrier and dashed for the underside of the bed. The bed was attached to the floor all around, so the cat jumped straight up in the air, looked around madly, and made a beeline for the bathroom. Kim laughed. She felt bad for Tiger, but she was tired, and that was hysterical.

Carl collapsed on the bed. "I'm so tired," he announced. "But I'm also wicked wired. I don't know if I can sleep. And this is just the first day." He covered his eyes with his hands.

Kim peeled off her tank top and shorts and curled up beside him on the bed in just her bra and underwear. "It's gonna get easier," she assured him. "Now we know what to expect. And I can drive tomorrow."

"I actually like driving," Carl said. "I think I should keep driving until I want to stop, and then you can take over. I don't want to lose my momentum. But I don't think it's good for us to drink all that coffee. It makes me wired, but my eyes still want to close. And we need to stop too often. And I don't want to get hooked on coffee before I even turn eighteen."

"We just need to take a shower, get some food, and chill out in front of the TV," Kim said. "Don't forget, we just said goodbye to our family and friends yesterday. We still have emotional hangovers. We're still leaving Massachusetts, but soon, we will be heading for California."

Carl opened his eyes and turned to look at her. "Did you just come up with that, or have you been saving it for the exact right moment?"

Kim grinned. "Right moment," she admitted.

"Still brilliant," Carl told her. He sat up. "Let's find a place where we can order a pizza. I could really use some pizza."

He found a list of restaurants and menus in the nightstand drawer on top of the Bible. He leafed through and found a pizza place called Maurice's. They had seen its neon sign as they pulled into the motel parking lot earlier. They pored over the menu and made their choices. Then Kim got her toiletry bag and went to take a shower, and Carl called to order their food. He put on his shoes, took the motel key, and walked carefully out the door, making sure Tiger, who had been spooked out of the bathroom by Kim, didn't dash outside in a panic.

He walked toward the neon sign, savoring the sensation of stretching his leg muscles. He waited outside the restaurant for the allotted fifteen minutes given over the phone, then went inside to retrieve the food. Ten minutes later, he was back at the door of the motel letting himself in with the key.

Kim was at the sink, brushing her wet hair. She was wearing a clean tank top, pajama shorts, and Gram Missy's 1946 slippers.

"How'd you end up with the slippers?" Carl asked her, pointing to her feet.

Kim smiled. "I told her that I liked them," she said. "She must have slipped them in my bag while we were sleeping. I just found them!"

Carl felt a wave of affection, both for Kim and his Gram.

"Let's eat," he said, putting the pizza box down on the small table. "Then I'll take a shower."

He wanted to touch her, to undress her, to ravish her body, but she was so clean, and he felt so dirty . . . he would have to wait. Focus on the food.

Kim sat at the table. "We'll call Gram after dinner to let her know where we are. And thank her for the slippers. And then, after you shower, let's see what it feels like to do it in Pennsylvania. As a matter of fact, I think we should do it in every state we stop in. We can keep a running list."

Carl looked up at her gratefully, then took a bite of piping-hot pizza. He liked that they were thinking along the same lines for their evening plans. And he liked the efficiency of keeping a running list.

When they woke up the next morning, Tiger was sleeping at the bottom of the bed. The level of food had gone down in his dish, and there was evidence he had used the litter box. Carl felt relieved, but he tried not to become too overconfident. The road was hard. They would all keep having to adjust.

They took a quick shower together to prepare for the road, packed up their things, and hit the highway. Breakfast was a car meal, as there were still muffins to be had. They started with coffee, but as they progressed through Ohio and into Indiana, they switched to water and juice.

"So we're stopping in Joliet," Kim said after they stopped for lunch. "Romeo and Joliet." She laughed. "We have two hours until the Illinois border, then we have to go through Chicago. That's gonna be interesting."

"How far is it from Chicago to Joliet?" Carl asked.

"A hop, a skip, and a jump," Kim told him. She used her index finger and thumb to measure the scale. "Less than fifty miles. Then we can add Illinois to our running list."

Looking at the speedometer, Carl realized he had subconsciously sped up ten miles per hour after Kim's comment.

From Joliet, Illinois, they cruised through Iowa and into Nebraska. They were going to stay two nights in Lincoln to visit museums and the Sunken Gardens. Somewhere beyond Des Moines, Kim felt a puff of air on her calf, and when she glanced down, Tiger was half emerged from the seat and sniffing her leg. She remained very still. By the time they reached the Nebraska border, he had leapt onto her lap and settled down. Kim and Carl both felt a sense of relief pass through them. They had passed through the center of the country. They had stopped leaving Massachusetts and were on their way to California. They would add another state to their running list. And they were more than halfway home.

ROCKY MOUNTAIN HIGH

They had arranged their trip so they would pass through Denver, off the proposed AAA route. They were going to visit Kim's cousin, Theresa Morgan, in Breckenridge, Colorado. Theresa was five years older than Kim and had moved to Breckenridge after finishing college. She was Aunt Karen's oldest child. Kim and Carl would stay with Theresa for three nights. It would be a mini vacation and a break from their road fatigue. And it would give Tiger some time to stretch his legs.

They spent the first night at Theresa's apartment eating their first home-cooked meal in days. They slept in the second bedroom with Tiger locked in, as Theresa's cat did not enjoy feline guests on his turf. The cats sat on either side of the closed bedroom door hissing at each other for the first several hours. Carl and Kim allowed themselves to sleep in the first morning, and then spent the afternoon exploring Breckenridge and shopping. Theresa was very excited about a particular Mexican restaurant in town and took them there for dinner. Neither Kim nor Carl had ever been to a Mexican restaurant before, and they found the food to be exotic and delicious. They ate deep-fried ice cream for dessert and agreed with Theresa that it was fantastic.

Kim and Carl had grown up around snowy winters, but they were both intrigued by the idea of seeing snow deep into the hottest summer months. Theresa drove them twenty-four miles to Loveland Pass along the Continental Divide, and they were absolutely blown away by the view and scenery. They took several pictures. They also enjoyed being able to stand on either side of the divide, where the flow of water diverged either east to the Atlantic Ocean or west to the

Pacific. Then they explored the top of the Pass and saw the snow. They got out of the truck and jumped into the drifts. They played in the snow until they got too cold. After a two-mile hike, they headed back to the truck and into town.

Kim and Carl bought postcards at a general store to send home. Theresa agreed to drop them at the post office the next day, so they could hit the road early. Then she brought them to Mile High Stadium to see a Denver Zephyrs Minor League baseball game. They ate hot dogs, Kim bought a jersey, and Carl got himself a baseball cap.

That night, Kim sent Carl off to read in bed while she and Theresa sat up to chat. "So how's Uncle Gerald really doing?" Theresa asked. "My mom always just tells me he's fine, and nothing has changed. But there must be something different you can tell me."

Kim shrugged. "Not really, Terri," she told her. "We waited for years for things to get better, but nothing really seems to change. I mean, he's not unhappy or anything. Sometimes he's more confused than anything, but it doesn't last long. The seizures can be scary, but they don't happen too much. I think it's hardest on everyone else. Especially the kids."

Theresa sighed. "It's always hardest on the kids, isn't it? I remember when Stella was born. Everyone was so excited for Simon to have a little sister. And then when Penny just took off on them, it was so unbelievable. It's like a miracle that they got a new mom. But then to basically lose their dad . . . Your mom is amazing, Kim. Those kids are so well adjusted for what they have been through."

Kim felt a rush of affection toward her mother. "She is pretty amazing," she said. "I'm really gonna miss her. And Dad."

Theresa nodded. "It's hard to leave home. But Carl seems so great. You really hit the jackpot with that guy."

Kim smiled. "Yeah, I really did," she agreed. They talked for a bit longer, and then Kim got up to get ready for bed. She and Carl would be heading out first thing in the morning, and they both needed to get a good night's sleep.

The last stop on the road to Seska was Reno, Nevada. It was August thirteenth, and they were due at Laine's by the fifteenth. They had almost made it. Reno was only a three-and-a-half-hour drive to Seska, and they wanted to arrive at their new lives refreshed and alert. Carl was not old enough to enter the casinos, and Kim had no desire to go without him. They would spend the last two days of their trip exploring museums, sightseeing, and adding the second to last state onto their running list. They vowed to return to Nevada again sometime after Carl's eighteenth birthday to gamble.

On Friday, August fifteenth, Kim and Carl woke up early. Today they were approaching the last, small leg of their trip. They were both excited and nervous about ending their journey. After finding an IHOP in the yellow pages and packing up the car one last time, they brought Tiger into the restaurant in his case due to the heat in the car from the desert sun, and they ate a slow breakfast of pancakes, bacon, coffee, and orange juice. Both of them were both quiet, lost in their thoughts as they ate. They used the restroom before leaving and vowed to drive straight through to Seska. They got in the car, released the cat, and put on their seat belts.

Carl turned to Kim. "Are you ready for this?" he asked.

She grabbed his hand. "As ready as I'll ever be." She smiled. "Starting tonight, we actually live together. That's kind of a big deal."

Carl grinned. "Yeah, it's really a big deal." He leaned over to the passenger seat and kissed her. Then he let go of her hand and turned the key. "Next stop," he announced, "the Farmer house."

He pulled the car out of the parking lot, entered the highway, and they were on their way to their future.

Reno was on the Nevada border, so they were quickly in California. They stayed on Highway 80 through Sacramento, then started following signs toward San Jose. Kim pulled out the directions that Laine had given Carl over the phone and called out which routes and exits to take. The last numbered exit was exit 12 to Main Street, Seska. They stayed straight on Main, passing what must have been the town center, filled with shops, restaurants, and business. After about a half mile, the commercial buildings thinned out and houses started to appear.

Kim instructed Carl to take a right at the stop sign, go four blocks, and then take a sharp left. At the end of Topeka Avenue, he took a right onto Fullerton Street. The Farmer house was the third house on the left: 45 Fullerton Street, Seska, California. It was a two-story maroon house with yellow-gold trim and a wraparound porch. And there it was, right where it was supposed to be.

ARRIVAL AT LAINE'S

Carl turned the Escort into the driveway. He and Kim could see the apartment set back in the corner of the backyard, at the end of the long driveway, as he pulled in. As Laine had said, it was a converted garage, but it had been refitted to look like it was intended to be a small house. It was the same color as the main house but with vinyl siding instead of wood. The two windows in front sported window boxes overflowing with vibrant purple flowers that neither Carl nor Kim could identify. A narrow concrete path led from the front stoop of the dwelling to the back door of the main house.

In the freshly mowed and very green backyard stood a woman who appeared to be in her thirties with short, layered, blond-frosted brown hair. She wore a loose sporty black tank top and jean shorts above pristine white Keds. She turned to face the car as Carl pulled in and came to a stop. The woman smiled.

Carl and Kim then noticed the little girl wearing a pink and green one-piece bathing suit over a diaper hopping up and down inside a small blue wading pool on the grass. The girl had tiny pigtails on either side of her head and was squealing with delight as she splashed water below her bare feet and onto her mother's previously dry clothes.

Carl put the car in park and cut the engine. The little girl looked up, noticing that something had changed. Kim grabbed Tiger tightly as Carl got out of the car and brought the cat carrier around to her side. Once the cat was securely locked in, Kim got out of the car, and they turned their attention to their host.

"Hello! Welcome," she called out, grabbing the child from the pool, wrapping her against her will in an oversized beach towel, and walking toward the driveway.

The child squirmed and kicked violently in her arms. "I'm Beth," she said, dodging a foot that came close to her face, "and I am guessing you are Carl and Kim! Carl, I haven't seen you in years. You're so grown up now! I'm so glad you're here!" She put the little girl down softly on the grass, then approached the couple, hugging each one in turn.

"Hi," Carl said with a smile. "Is there someplace we can put our cat? He's been in the car a long time. I think he's ready to be done."

"Oh, of course," Beth said. She climbed the two steps to the apartment unit's concrete stoop and opened the screen door. The storm door was open. "I was keeping the place aired out for you," she told them. "Come on in, it's your new home!"

She walked through the doorway and directly into a kitchen area. Carl and Kim slowly followed her inside, Carl toting the cat case. The little girl ran in the door and stopped in front of Carl. "Kitty!" she exclaimed.

"That's right," Beth told her. "There's a kitty in there. Carl, this is your cousin Claire. She's two and a half. She loves kitties, but I'm trying to teach her to give kitties room and to be gentle."

Carl smiled at Claire. "Hi, Claire," he said to her. "This is Tiger." He turned back to Beth. "He'll be off like a shot as soon as I open the crate, and we probably won't see him again for hours. The trip's been a bit stressful for Tiger."

"For all of us," Kim corrected. "Hi, Claire, I'm Kim," she told the tiny cousin, whose bathing suit was now dripping pool water on the linoleum floor.

"Kimmmmm," Claire hummed.

Carl opened the case, and Tiger took off. Claire laughed.

"Let me show you the bathroom," Beth said after wiping the water off the floor with a dish towel she had taken from a drawer. She stepped out of the kitchen and into a living area cramped with a couch, chair, coffee table, and TV stand. The floor was covered by a large, colorful, circular rag rug, and there were paintings and artful photos hung on the walls. A pony wall topped with a shelf separated the area from the rest of the unit, which proved to be the bedroom and bathroom. Kim excused herself to get better acquainted with the facilities, and Carl went in after she was done.

"So I'm guessing the two of you might be hungry?" Beth asked as they moved back into the kitchen.

Kim and Carl looked at each other and back at Beth. They were starving. "We could eat," Carl understated.

Beth lifted Claire in her arms. "I need to put this one down for an n-a-p," she told them cryptically, "but even though she doesn't look like it, she's exhausted, and she'll go right down. You can come with me and wait in our kitchen."

They followed Beth into the main house, and she seated them at the table. She put Claire down on the floor, and the toddler quickly ran off into another room, her tiny feet pattering on the wood floors. Beth got two glasses out of the cabinet and filled them both with water from the tap.

"I'll just be a few minutes" she told them, placing the glasses in front of them. "Then we can make some plans for getting the two of you settled in."

She went to find Claire, and Carl and Kim sat quietly at the table, sipping on their water.

"We're here," Kim finally announced.

"I can see that," Carl replied.

"Now what?" Kim asked.

"Lunch," Carl said as his stomach growled.

"And then?" Kim asked.

Carl shrugged. "I guess we're the adults now. We get to decide."

Kim laughed. "That's a scary thought," she said. "Plus, you have another month to go until you're a real adult." She sighed. "I'm really looking forward to finding my good shampoo and conditioner, and my soap. Motel soap is okay, but there's nothing quite like Zest."

Beth padded into the room stealthily in her socks. "You two are looking forward to putting your stuff away," she said. "I don't blame you. I remember when Laine and I made the trip six years ago. It was so distressing to not have my stuff available. It's also kind of strange when you see all your old stuff in your new place, but you'll get used to it. I don't have many choices for lunch for you. Do you guys like peanut butter and jelly?"

Kim and Carl laughed. "Peanut butter and jelly saved me from twelve years of school lunches," Carl told her. "Do you have strawberry jam?"

Carl ate two sandwiches to Kim's one, and they both downed large glasses of milk. Then Beth gave them Oreos.

"Sorry," she said as she put out the plate of cookies. "We cater to small children around here. I promise dinner will be more adult." She sat down at the table with them and grabbed a cookie. "So I was thinking," she said after chewing and swallowing a bite, "I can help you bring some of your boxes and suitcases into the unit, and then the two of you can take the afternoon to put things away and get to know your new space. Benjamin gets off the bus from camp in front of the house around 3:40. Laine gets home around 5:15, and I know he'll want to see you right away. Then we can have dinner around 6:30. Does that sound okay to you?"

"Yeah, that sounds great," Carl agreed. "But first, I'm gonna need to call my gram to let her know we made it here, and I think Kim probably wants to call her mom. Can we use your phone? We'll keep it short."

"Of course," Beth told him. "There's a phone on the table next to the couch in the den. Take as long as you need."

They both phoned their families to put them at ease, and Carl asked Gram to update Chris so he could let their friends know they arrived. Chris and Pete would be leaving for California in a couple of days. Carl would call Chris later to give him the names of the motels they stayed in and the best places to stop and eat. Then they all went out to the car to start to unload.

The three of them made quick work of the job, and soon, Beth left them alone to get organized. They lugged their suitcases full of clothes to the bedroom. They both looked at the fully made full-sized bed.

"Which side do you want?" Carl asked. "Whatever you pick is probably gonna be your side for the rest of your life, so choose wisely."

Kim laughed. She lay down on the right side. Then she rolled over to the left side. "When I've fallen asleep in your arms, it's always been on your left arm," she said. "I'll take the left side."

Carl nodded. "And it's also closer to the bathroom," he said. "You chose well."

Kim got up off the bed, approached Carl, and wrapped her arms around him. He embraced her back, and she closed her eyes.

"I'm tempted to add California to our running list," she said softly, "but not just yet. Tonight. When we go to bed. When we know we'll be alone. We'll break in the bed."

Carl closed his own eyes and smiled. "Too bad we can't take an n-a-p," he teased. "But we have time. Now we need to unpack." They reluctantly pulled apart, and both opened their suitcases.

"So what's the story behind the pb and j with strawberry jam sandwiches?" Kim asked as she removed a pile of folded shirts from the suitcase and placed them in the dresser drawer. "You've been eating them for lunch as long as I've known you, and that's a long time. How come you never just got school lunch?"

Carl continued to organize his sock and underwear drawer as he answered. "I tried school lunch on the first day of first grade," he told her, eyes still focused on his task. "It was gross. So I skipped it the next few days and would come home starving. My mom figured it out when she found my lunch money wadded up in my book bag at the end of the first week. So she started making the sandwiches, and I started to eat them. It just kind of became a thing."

He sat on the edge of the bed and refolded a pile of jeans.

"And as time went by, my mom stopped doing a lot of things for me, or she just wasn't there so I could ask her to. But the sandwiches were always there in the morning when I got up, in a brown paper bag, with a dollar for milk and a cookie. The guys would make fun of me as we got older, but it was okay. I know they didn't mean anything by it. It was kind of weird, you know? A teenage guy with his mom making him peanut butter and jelly to bring to school. But when I ate that sandwich every day, it was like a sign, you know? That my mom loved me. That she cared about me enough to make sure I had a lunch that I would eat. I loved every bite of those sandwiches, and every year, they got better and better, as everything else with my parents got worse."

He opened the bottom dresser drawer and placed the jeans inside.

"Then, on the first day of senior year, there was no paper bag with a sandwich left for me on the table. That was kind of when I knew things had changed. It was kinda when I knew she was really gone. I kept making the sandwiches, though. I had to. It was like a connection, to remind me it wasn't always so bad. You know?"

Kim got up from her side of the bed and walked around to Carl's side. She sat down beside him, put her hand on his knee, and leaned heavily against his side. "Yeah, Carl," she said softly. "I totally know."

Kim remembered the first day of senior year. It was the day that Traci told them she was moving to Detroit. It was the day that Rhonda broke up with Chris. But she realized sadly that it was also the day that Carl had been truly and finally abandoned by his mother.

DINNER IS ON US

After Carl's story, they were both too mentally and physically exhausted to keep unpacking. They took off their shorts and crawled under the covers of their new bed. They curled up, with Kim on Carl's left arm, and drifted to sleep.

Carl was awakened by a knock on the kitchen door. He glanced at the clock on his bedside table and saw that it was 5:20. Laine was home from work. He shook Kim's shoulder to wake her, and they both got up. "One minute," Carl called to the door. They both put their shorts on and quickly tried to neaten their hair. Then they walked into the kitchen and Carl opened the door.

Laine stood on the other side of the door, looking very much like a Farmer relative. He had closely cropped dark brown hair, with a slight receding hairline around a steep widow's peak. He had deep brown eyes like Gram Missy, the type of eyes that conveyed wisdom and warmth. He was smiling and had very slight laugh lines around his eyes. He was dressed in a white polo shirt with a company logo and tan khaki pants. His middle betrayed that he most likely enjoyed a good beer and possibly dessert now and then, but he also appeared muscular and strong.

"Carl and Kim!" he said as he stepped into the kitchen. "Good to see you! Are you two huggers? We do a lot of hugging around here."

Kim smiled and Carl shrugged. "Sure," Carl replied. Laine gave Kim a hug, and then Carl. Then he held Carl at arm's length.

"Wow," he said, his eyes widening as he looked at Carl's face. "You really do look like Uncle Cecil as a young man. I've been told there was a resemblance, but you were only about eleven when we left, so it wasn't quite there yet. I guess I had to experience it for myself."

"Doesn't he?" Kim exclaimed with a smile. "I've seen the wedding pictures. Carl is a true Bishop."

Laine looked at his face again. "Yeah, I can see the Bishop," he admitted. "But those are Farmer eyes." He pointed to the living area wall. "I don't know if you noticed the big black-and-white photo over the sofa. It's a picture of my father and his eight brothers and sisters, including the twins and their husbands, at their wedding. My dad was the youngest of the nine, and Missy and Cissy were numbers two and three. I think all the Farmer kids have a copy of that picture somewhere in their house. It's a classic. It's gonna be a different experience for you, Carl, living out here. No one knows anything about Bishops or Farmers, unless they're in a chess game or work in the vegetable fields!"

Kim and Carl laughed. Laine smiled. "I see you have some unpacking to do," he said, looking around. "You'll have some time to get settled. Beth wanted me to tell you to come over to the house at six for dinner. We're pretty casual over here. Sometimes Claire shows up wearing nothing at all, but I do expect the two of you in some sort of clothes. Well, I'm gonna run to the package store real quick before dinner to get some wine for Beth. They don't call them packies here, by the way, they call them liquor stores. There are other things I'll need to tell you about that are different here than in Massachusetts. But there's time to learn. Can I pick up anything for you while I'm out?"

Carl grinned. "A six-pack of beer and some wine coolers?" he ventured.

"Hah!" Laine replied. "Nice try. Maybe when you turn twenty-one. You're on your own when it comes to buying alcohol, but we'll share our wine with you at dinner. And I'll pick up some soda at the store. So come by at six. Just knock on the back door to warn us and let yourselves in. See you then."

They closed the door when Laine walked out. Carl sighed. "So much for laid back Cousin Laine buying us beer," he stated. "I'll need to get a fake ID."

Kim laughed. "No one would ever believe it with your baby face, Carl," she informed him. "We'll just have to make friends who can buy for us. Or we'll just have to drink milk for fun. But Laine and Beth seem okay."

"Yeah," Carl agreed, "they do. And this apartment seems okay so far."

"Yeah," Kim said as she spotted the back side of Tiger poking out from behind the couch. "I think it has potential."

Kim and Carl had wanted to shower prior to dinner, but they realized their nap had bitten into their hygiene time. Carl pulled out one of his folded pairs of jeans and a light cotton black T-shirt that looked new. Kim dug out a short summer skirt and a white silky tank top. They combed their hair, and Kim applied some eyeliner and mascara. They left food in Tiger's dish, then made the short walk to the Farmers' house. They knocked and let themselves in.

"Hi, guys," Beth said pleasantly from the stove where she was stirring food in a wok. The air smelled of frying vegetables and soy sauce. "Laine's in the living room over there," she gestured to the doorway to the right, "with the kids. Go on in. Dinner will be ready as soon as the rice is done cooking."

Kim and Carl went slowly through the doorless entryway. Kim was more nervous about meeting the five-year-old son than she had been for Laine and Beth. She knew little kids could make quick judgments based on first impressions, and she knew it would be important to be friends with the Farmer children.

Laine was sitting on the couch with Claire on his lap and Benjamin to his left. Laine was reading a book to Claire, and Benjamin was holding a book of his own, leafing through to look at the pictures. Laine looked up.

"Hey, Kim and Carl," he said, smiling. "You made it! I see you didn't get lost on the way over. My directions must have been spot on!"

Kim smiled. "I have heard a lot about the Farmer sense of humor," she told Laine. "It's good to see it in action."

"Ignore everything the Bishops tell you about the Farmers," Laine said defensively. "Farmers are funny. We're just misunderstood." Kim laughed. "You're just in time for story time. You've both met Claire already, and this guy here is Benjamin." Laine nuzzled his son lightly on the head with his knuckles, messing his hair. "Say hi to Kim and your cousin Carl, Benjamin."

Benjamin looked up from his book. "Hi to Kim and my cousin Carl," he said and looked back at his book.

Laine shook his head. "Farmer humor," he said. "The only problem is it runs in the family. Benjamin just finished kindergarten, and he learned all about reading. He's very interested in books. And he can point out the words he recognizes. We're working on sounding things out, and we're making some progress. Hey, take a seat, you two! You're making me nervous just standing there like that!" He gestured to a loveseat and two single chairs.

Kim and Carl both went straight for the loveseat and sat close, holding hands. "I like to read, too, Benjamin," Kim said. "I like books about people who lived a long time ago, and fairy tales. What types of books do you like?"

Benjamin looked up again. "I like books about dinosaurs," he said, holding his book to face her and pointing to a picture. "That's a velociraptor."

Kim was impressed, although she couldn't see the caption from where she sat to confirm if it was indeed a velociraptor. "Wow!" she exclaimed.

Laine smiled. "Benjamin knows his dinosaurs," he said. "He has them all memorized."

"Does anyone ever call you Benji or Ben?" Carl asked.

Benjamin shook his head several times, and his shaggy brown hair fanned around his head. "No," he said, "that's not my name. Does anyone ever call you Car?"

They all laughed. "Good point," Carl responded. "That's not my name. But to tell you the truth," he leaned in closer and lowered his voice. "Carl isn't really my name either."

Benjamin's eyes opened wide. "It's not?" Carl shook his head. "What is your real name?"

Carl smiled. "It's Carlos," he said proudly. "The whole thing is Carlos Jerome Bishop."

Benjamin gasped. "My middle name is Jerome, too!" he exclaimed.

Laine laughed. "All the Farmer men have the middle name Jerome. After my grandfather. It's my middle name, too."

"I didn't realize it was all the Farmer men," Carl said. "I know it's me, my brother Scott, my dad, and Chris Mahoney, but I thought it was just something the Grams did. That's pretty cool."

Pedro Jerome Bishop, Kim thought. I wonder if I'll be in there anywhere.

"Daddy!" Claire blared. "Read! Read!" She shook the book he was holding in his hands.

"Okay, okay, Clarabelle!" Laine said, grasping to keep the book from flying across the room and hitting his guests.

Benjamin looked at Carl and Kim and then slid off the couch and approached them on the loveseat. "Her name's not really Clarabelle," he whispered to them confidentially. "It's Claire. Mommy said that Clarabelle was a clown on TV." He jumped up on the loveseat, and Carl and Kim quickly made space for him between them. He handed his book to Kim. "Can you read this to me? I can tell you the name of every dinosaur."

Kim took the book and made eye contact with Carl. They both smiled.

Ten minutes later, Beth came in to get them for dinner. She found Claire in her pajamas curled up asleep on Laine's lap, and Benjamin half on Kim's lap, half on Carl's. She approached Laine, scooped Claire into her arms, and carried her upstairs. When she came back, she told everyone, "She ate her dinner earlier. It's almost her bedtime anyway. Come, dinner is ready."

They all adjourned to the dining room. Carl and Kim waited for the other three to sit down in their regular chairs and then took their seats. Dinner was family-style, and they passed around bowls with stir-fry vegetables and chicken and rice.

As they ate, they talked about themselves. Beth told them that she was an accountant but taking time off to raise her kids. "Things are easier for us here than they were in Massachusetts," she told them. "Here we have my mom, who is retired and can help with the kids, and Laine has been really successful with his business, so we can manage with only one income. But when Claire starts first grade, I think I'm gonna try to go back to work, at least part time, maybe at one of the tax preparation places where I can be around other adults besides my husband. No offense, Laine."

Laine waved her off with his hand and a smile. "Oh, no offense taken, Beth," he said. "Why do you think I got involved in the apprenticeship program so early? It will be nice to have someone to talk to who doesn't just want me to get them some of the good kitchen water in the Big Bird cup before bed, or spit their gum in my hand. I'm talking about Beth, of course." They all laughed, including Benjamin.

They had finished their main course. Beth and Laine quickly cleared the dishes, and Beth brought out a plate of warm brownies and a tub of vanilla ice cream.

"Ice cream!" Benjamin yelled out. "Can I have two scoops and a brownie?" he asked, holding his spoon in the air.

Beth smiled at him. "Okay, Benjamin, you can have two scoops, but I don't want to hear you even try to ask for seconds," she told him.

Carl wondered if he would be allowed to have seconds. He loved brownies with vanilla ice cream, and he knew Kim did, too.

After they finished dessert, they returned to the living room, and Beth put out hot water for tea and a pot of coffee. Benjamin sat on the floor playing with large plastic dinosaurs, engaging them in a turf war, while the adults continued talking.

SO WHAT DOES YOUR FATHER DO?

"I can't wait to get started with the apprenticeship," Carl said. "It seems like a much better way to learn than sitting in a classroom all day, every day. I know I'll have to go to one day of classes per week, but that's not too bad."

Kim snickered. "I don't know how they grade things in technical school," she told Laine, "but I'm pretty sure Carl will be on some sort of honor roll or dean's list by the end of the first term."

"I'm really looking forward to starting your training," Laine said. "It's like you're a blank slate, and I get to give you all this knowledge I've been saving up."

"Laine, how did you end up in the electrician business?" Kim asked. "Is it something you always wanted to do?"

"Not really," Laine replied. "I went to college right after high school and studied electrical engineering. After school, I got a job working for a company that had government contracts. There's good money in the field, but I really didn't like the work. I felt too removed from the end product. It ends up, I like the more hands-on approach. I was lucky enough to find a great mentor, and I already had most of the classroom hours from college. Once I got my license, I worked doing wiring for a contractor building houses in new subdivisions right outside Eastboro for a few years, but the work was tedious and repetitive. All the houses were exactly the same. So when we moved out here to be near Beth's mom, I decided to hang out a shingle and work for myself, and it turned out to be the right move for me. And for Seska. They had to bring in electricians from out of county, and they charged exorbitant fees for the travel, especially in emergencies. So they were glad to see me. A lot of my high school classmates and our cousins ended up on the production line at Aries Corps after high school and worked their way up to management. I didn't think that kind of life was for me, so I kind of worked my way down in my field, and I've never been happier."

"Isn't Uncle Rolland on the management team at Aries?" Carl asked. "I think he worked with my friend James's dad for a while."

"Yeah, but my dad retired from Aries last year," Laine replied, "and now he and mom spend most of their time playing tennis or planning trips they'll probably never actually get around to taking. Jack was working at Aries on the receiving dock before we left six years ago. Does he still work there?"

Carl shrugged. "As far as I know," he said. "I haven't seen much of my father for the last year or so, but I would assume so. I think he's pretty much been doing the same thing since he got out of high school. Most of the guys in his department have either been promoted or moved on. But not my dad."

"What about you, Kim?" Beth asked, turning to look at her. "What do your parents do?"

Carl looked up and glanced at Kim. "Beth," he started.

Kim shook her head. "No, Carl, it's okay," she promised him. "I can talk about my parents." She faced Beth. "My mom's a real estate agent. She's been doing that since I was a little kid and she was a single mom. Sometimes, she would take me with her to show houses before she met my dad and they got married. She had no one to watch me. It was so much fun, running around the empty houses, and rolling around on the lawns. Sometimes, the people looking at the houses would have their kids there, too, and I would play with them." She paused. "And my dad . . . well, he's my stepdad, but he adopted me when I was seven, so he's my dad. He used to work at Aries, where everyone's dad seems to work. He was a human resource manager. But that was only until his accident."

"Oh, Kim," Beth said, putting her hand to her mouth. "I'm so sorry . . ."

"I was ten," Kim continued as if Beth hadn't spoken. She had slipped into storyteller mode. "It was summer. My mother was pregnant with my youngest sister, Sophia, and was due any day. She had a list of things that needed to be done before the baby came. Sophia was the fifth kid, and the fourth kid, Zach, was only eighteen months old. Things were gonna get really hectic. Dad was working in the yard, and cleaning things up, because he wouldn't be able to get to it again for some time. He was raking, and I was helping him bag up the old, rotted leaves to haul away. I always loved to help him with yard work. He decided while he was out there to clean out the gutters, because they were stuffed with leaves from the previous fall and there was heavy rain in the forecast, and he could haul all the debris to the leaf dump at the same time. I was pulling a big old full yard bag toward the car in front when I heard the sound. Kind of like a crash, then kind of like a thud. I dropped the bag and ran to the backyard just as my mom came out the back door to see what happened. We found him on the ground. He must have lost his balance on the ladder as he was reaching for the gutter, and he fell backward. His right leg and left arms were twisted in a weird way, and his head was resting on the concrete patio. There was blood in his hair. There were rotting leaves scattered all over, and the ladder was lying on the ground. And he was unconscious. I just stood there, my arms held out, frozen, staring at him. But then Mom ran to his side, and yelled for me to call an ambulance. I ran inside and grabbed the phone. It took me three tries to dial the right number. They asked me what my emergency was, and I said 'my dad fell off a ladder. I think he's really broken!' I don't remember much more from right after that, but all of the sudden, my grandmother was there at our house and the ambulance guys were wheeling my dad through the house because the side fence was locked, and everyone was talking in hushed voices, and there was a lot of beeping and radio static. And then as they were walking toward the ambulance, my mother made a loud noise. She was having a contraction. She had gone into labor. And my dad was still unconscious."

"Oh, my God, Kim," Laine said softly.

"Dad wasn't regaining consciousness, my mom told me later," Kim continued, "and there was too much pressure from swelling on his brain, so they had to bring him into surgery. And at the same time, they were prepping my mom for an emergency c-section, because the baby was breech. And I was at home, trying not to panic, with my younger brothers and sister playing with my grandma, and eventually other relatives who came by, and me staring at the phone, not knowing that the two people I loved most in the world were in surgery, one of them fighting for his life. Mom and Sophia were fine, and out of surgery before Dad, and Mom had to wait, by herself in her room, to hear any news. It took hours before anyone was able to get to her at the hospital to give her support. It was my best friend Darlene's mom, Mrs. Feinman. She dropped Darlene off to be with me, then stayed with my mom and the baby as long as she could. And I got to have Darlene with me."

"They sound like really good friends," Beth said.

Kim's eyes got misty. "Darlene is still my best friend. I already miss her." She sighed. "Well, my dad survived surgery, and then the first night, and the second night, and then every night, but he still didn't wake up. Over the next two weeks, they had to do surgery on his arm, and his leg, and other things, like putting in a feeding tube, and removing hardware and stuff. Then after two weeks, he started to respond a little to stimuli. It wasn't like you see on TV, someone waking up from a coma and asking what day it was. It was slow. Very slow. A little at a time. And all the time, they were watching to see what he was able to do, and what he might have lost from brain damage. They started doing physical and occupational therapy in the hospital, and speech therapy for, well, speaking, and eating, and swallowing. After a while, they were able to move him to a rehab center. That's where they discovered his memory loss."

"Did you get to see him at all in the hospital?" Beth asked.

"When he was out of intensive care, I was allowed to see him for short visits a couple of times per week, but the other kids were too young. They weren't allowed. It would have been tough on them anyway. The older kids, they're Dad's kids from his first wife, and they were adopted by my mom like I was adopted by my dad. They were four and three. They would ask where Daddy was, but they could still be easily distracted. And of course the babies had no idea what was going on. Mom had to take Sophia with her everywhere so she could breastfeed her, so she pretty much spent the first three and a half months of her life at the hospital or the rehab center."

"And Kim had to take care of the other three kids," Carl added.

"Well, me and various aunts and friends," Kim said. "But I was the only consistent one. Stella and Chip, his real name is Simon but we call him Chip, would always call for me if they needed anything. Like help reaching something on a shelf, or if they got boo-boos, or when they got scared at night. It was always Kimmy Kimmy Kimmy."

"But your dad came home eventually," Laine predicted.

Kim nodded. "Three months in rehab. He worked so hard. Pretty much everything came back. You would never know from looking at him that he'd broken several bones. And he relearned how to swallow and chew, and talk. And he could still read, and write. It all looked really good to the untrained eye. But there was still the thing with his memory."

"I'll never forget hearing about what happened to Mr. Drake," Carl remembered. "Gram was friends with Darlene's grandma, and got all the news about your dad from her. She told me that Gerald Drake had recovered everything but what happened five minutes ago. I didn't get it at first, until I saw him at your house. I went over with Gram to visit, but I really just wanted to see you, Kim." He reached out and grabbed her hand. "I never saw you after the accident except in class, and you were always so preoccupied with everything going on. Gram told me what to expect, but I had no idea."

"He remembered you," Kim recalled. "At least back then. But after five minutes or so, he forgot you were there, and when he turned and saw you, it was like you had just arrived."

"Yeah," Carl confirmed. "Like three or four times. I was so thrown."

"Your mouth was gaping open," Kim said with the hint of a nostalgic smile. "I felt so sorry for you. I remember thinking how sad it must have been for you to see him like that." Now she laughed. "How sad for you. Imagine that I was even thinking about how you felt when you saw my dad. How sad for *me*, though, Carl."

Carl squeezed her hand. "That's what I was thinking that day," he assured her. "I was thinking *how sad for Kim*. I knew that you adored your dad. I remembered how proud you were to call him your dad when he adopted you. You looked at him in a certain way, a way that seemed kind of familiar to me. I wanted to do something right then, to make it better for you, but I knew right away there was nothing I could do."

"There was nothing anyone could do," Kim told him. "We just kept hoping that, with time, it would get better. Even if it wasn't perfect, it could get better. The doctors didn't know. They couldn't tell us. So we waited. And waited. And sometimes, it would get better. Even for a tiny little bit of time. Something would catch in his brain, and just stay there for a while. It gave us so much hope."

She exhaled hard.

"And that was eight years ago. And here we are. Nothing has changed. The kids have grown, and sometimes dad has no idea who they are. He might know that Sophia exists, but it's just a vague idea. He remembers that Stella, Chip, and Zach exist, but he can't connect those memories with the older kids he sees in front of him until it's explained to him, but then he forgets again. He talks to them, and is polite and cordial, but there's no real connection. But he remembers who I am. And of course, my mom. We haven't changed that much over the years, and we've been the ones to mostly take care of him."

"Those poor babies," Beth whispered, shaking her head. "Your whole family, Kim. You've been through so much. I can't imagine."

"It must have been so hard to leave," Laine said. "It sounds like you and your mother were a real team, taking care of your dad and the kids. Kim, I hope we can make you feel comfortable and at home here. Even though we won't be in the same house, I want you to feel like family. Don't be afraid to ask us for anything. Or just come in for a cup of coffee if you want to talk."

Kim sniffed. Her eyes had stayed dry. She wasn't sure if this was progress. "Thanks, you guys. I'm so sorry I just went on and on like that! I just haven't talked about the accident in so long. Back home, everyone knows each other's business. I'm sure you remember. You're the first people I've spoken to in ages about what happened to my dad. I never even had to tell my friends back then, because by the time school started back in the fall, everyone already knew."

Carl smiled. "Back home, if you tell anything to a Bishop-Farmer," he mused, "it's just as effective as putting out a full-page newspaper ad!"

Laine laughed. "Being a Farmer myself, I understand," he said "Carl, I think it's up to me, as a Farmer, and you, as a Bishop, to break the cycle. This is now a no-gossip zone. All the way from that fence there," he pointed out the window, "pretty much to the western border of Massachusetts!" Everyone laughed.

"We should probably go back to the apartment and start getting things put away," Carl said, standing up and reaching for Kim's hand to help her to her feet.

"Sounds like a good idea," Beth agreed, getting out of her chair. "You probably saw there're towels and washcloths in the bathroom, and I left some dish towels, sponges, and soap in the kitchen. And sheets on the bed. You can keep all of those. And let us know if you need the names of any stores, or directions anywhere. And here's the number for the phone company. Oh, you'll probably need to call them from our phone tomorrow to set up your service!" She handed a piece of paper to Carl. She grasped Kim's hands. "And please, please let us know if you need anything."

"We will," Kim promised. "Thank you so much for dinner. It was great. And it's so good to be off the road!"

"We'll see you both tomorrow," Laine said, escorting them to the back door. "We'll take you for a little driving and walking tour of Seska. And show you the shop. I know you can't start working until your birthday, Carl, but it'll be good to get you familiar with the territory."

"We're looking forward to it," Carl said, taking Kim's hand and leading her outside. "Good night."

They walked the thirty feet back to the apartment. They could hear Tiger calling out to them through the door. As soon as they walked in, he circled around both of their ankles. His food dish was not empty. He was marking them as his in his new abode.

"I'm gonna get in the shower and get into my pajamas," Kim said, rubbing her neck. "You're welcome to join me, but I warn you, this is just a 'getting clean' shower."

Carl smiled. "I'm good," he told her. "I'm gonna put some more of my clothes away. I haven't even found my pajamas yet. I'll shower later."

Kim shuffled into the bathroom and secured the door. Tiger immediately started scratching to get in. Carl picked him up and sat on the bed. He rubbed the cat's neck and he started to purr. Carl thought about Kim and the story of her father. He had never heard the entire story, just small tidbits here and there as a child. It overwhelmed him to hear the full narrative come out of her mouth. The daily losses she endured, the way she had needed to take a different role in her family after the accident, the forgotten children she had to comfort. Kim was starting a new life now, one far away from that pain, but he was sure she had taken much of it with her to California. He still longed to take her pain away but still didn't know how. He was hoping they would find the answers together in their new home.

BIG CITY TOUR

Their first morning in Seska was a Saturday. Kim and Carl slept until ten thirty and woke up facing each other in the small bed. They decided immediately it was time to lazily complete their running list of states. After, they fell back onto their pillows and dozed off for another half hour. They were still adjusting to the time-zone shift. Tiger woke them again with his paws padding across their chests. Carl got up and attended to the cat dish, while Kim eased slowly out of bed and into Gram's slippers. She shuffled to the kitchen and got out bowls, spoons, cereal, and milk that Beth had left for them in the refrigerator. She placed a banana she found in a fruit bowl in front of Carl's bowl for his cereal. He could cut it into rounds with his spoon.

She poured the Sugar Smacks they had brought from Gram's house into their bowls. Carl came over and peeled his banana and sat down. They ate their breakfast, chatting about their upcoming day.

"I'll finally get to see the shop," Carl said, spooning up another bite of cereal, banana, and milk. "Then, when I think about going to work, I'll know what to picture in my head."

"That will be cool," Kim agreed. "I'm gonna ask if we can swing by the community college for the same reason. When I got enrolled before we left, they let me know that I could go there on Monday to register for fall classes. I can't wait! I have no idea what classes I'll take. I can take math and writing placement tests to get out of entry-level classes, and I think I could do well on those. I did well in math and English in high school."

Carl smiled at her. "You're gonna ace those tests," he told her. "After you register for your prerequisites, you should take some fun classes, like basket weaving, or aerobics."

Kim laughed. "Well, maybe not those, but definitely something I would find interesting. I was thinking about Speech and Public Speaking. I don't know if I'd feel all that comfortable talking in front of strangers, but it might be good for me to try. To get a bit out of my comfort zone."

"That's a great idea," Carl agreed. "Kim, you're a natural storyteller. You'd do great in a class like that. You always keep everyone entranced with your stories."

Kim laughed. "Whether they want to hear them or not!" she said. "I'm so embarrassed about how I went on and on about my dad's accident with Laine and Beth last night. I just met them! I hope they don't think I go around talking like that all the time. It's just that they're so easy to talk to, and I guess I just needed to make sure someone else in California knew his story, you know? Like I kind of brought him with me."

Carl looked at her and smiled. "Kim, I can tell they liked you right away," he said. "They hung on your every word. And you were really a hit with Benjamin. Notice he handed the dinosaur book to you? He could tell that you tell a good story."

Kim smiled. "Yeah," she agreed. "That was pretty sweet." She looked at the kitchen clock. "We better get ready," she told Carl. "We're supposed to meet them outside at noon."

At noon, they set off in Beth's white Ford Taurus and headed for town. The Farmers pointed out sights along the way.

"That's my mom's house," Beth said, pointing to a small tidy ranch on the right. "She wanted us to buy a house close to her so she could watch the kids when we needed, like today."

"That's the Campbells' house," Laine said, pointing to the left. "They're an older couple whose kids and grandkids live out of state. They always seem to have some little problem with their electrical appliances. I think they're just lonely."

"That's Seska Center Grocery," Kim said, pointing at the grocery store ahead. "They have good produce, and their prices are reasonable. I usually shop there. They'll also carry your bags out for you, and they won't accept tips. They probably pay their staff well."

In this manner, they also saw the plant nursery, the hardware store, the elementary school, three Christian churches, and a Jewish temple. As they got closer to town, Laine pulled up to a street-side parking space and cut the engine. "We'll see the strip on foot," he said. "What there is of it. Welcome to Downtown Seska, California!"

They walked past a florist shop, and Kim saw the woman behind the counter wave to Laine and Beth.

"That's Callie," Laine said. "Carl, you'd do well to go in and meet her before Kim's birthday and Valentine's Day come around."

Carl laughed. "You'd better show me the bank, too," he said. "Kim's birthday is two weeks after Valentine's Day. I might need to take out a loan."

"Okay," Laine agreed with a grin, stopping at the next building. "Here's the bank. Seska National. You asked for it, you got it."

"Let's go in and get an account started for you," Beth said, pulling the door open. "They're open until one on Saturday."

Kim still had the envelope that Gram Missy had given her at the start of their trip in her purse. There was eighty dollars left inside, plus change. She and Carl decided to deposit twenty dollars to open an account, and they would transfer their savings from their banks back home during the workweek. They ordered checks with both of their names on them and agreed to use them for household expenses only. They would open personal accounts later.

The next stop was Farmer Electric. It was next door to a bakery. The bakery was currently closed, but Laine assured Carl that donuts and hot coffee were readily available each weekday between 7 a.m. and 2 p.m. Laine unlocked the door of his shop, and they stepped inside. He switched on the overhead light.

"Thank God that went on," Laine said, pretending to wipe sweat off his brow. "It would have been pretty embarrassing if the lights didn't work in the electric shop!" They all laughed. Beth's grimace indicated this was not the first time she had heard this joke.

Carl looked around the store. There were short aisles of shelves running from the back to the front of the room, and a counter against the far-left wall with a cash register on the far end. There were framed prints of old electricity-themed advertisements on the walls around the room, and a copy of the picture of the Farmer siblings at the Bishop-Farmer wedding hanging behind the register. Carl could see sections of lightbulbs of every wattage, including rods and circles of fluorescent bulbs, and party bulbs in every color. There was a shelf covered with decorative table lamps, and at the end of the aisle, floor lamps stood on display. The last row was filled with fuses, switches, various colored wires on spools, gloves, electrical tape, and other small items. The shop had a distinctive smell. Carl wondered if it was a smell specific to electrical supplies.

"You don't sell any impulse items on the counter or in front of the register," Carl said to Laine.

"No, I never have," Laine said, looking at the register. "What are you thinking about?"

Carl walked over to the counter. He shrugged. "I don't know, maybe like some batteries, some small flashlights. Keychains, maybe. At the Cape once, I saw some artsy switch plates and outlet covers at a gift shop. I never would have thought of making switch plates decorative, but I know there are lots of people who would want one if they saw them. And they would make good housewarming or baby shower gifts." He knelt down in front of the counter. "Do people ever come here with their kids?" Laine nodded. "You could put some shelves up here at kid height," Carl suggested. "Maybe some stuff to keep the kids interested. Maybe if the kid sees something they want, they might be able to get their mom or dad to buy it for them, and then they'd be more willing to buy the electrical tape they were looking at, y'know, since they have to make a purchase anyway."

Laine looked at Beth. Beth smiled at him and nodded. "Go on," he urged Carl. "So what kinds of stuff would the kids want?"

Carl shrugged as he ran his hand across the front of the counter. "Candy?" he suggested. "Like lollipops or Tootsie Rolls. Peppermint Patties. Maybe some little toys. Like toy soldiers? Kim, what else would your brothers and sisters want?"

Kim approached the counter and looked at the space. "Super Balls in a little bucket," she said. "Yoyos. Marbles. Baseball cards with gum inside. Card games. Matchbox or Hot Wheel cars. There are tons of things."

"Hmm," Laine said, crossing his arms across his chest. "So you're saying if they're buying electrical supplies, they might buy other things on impulse, like keychains or decorative items. But also if their kid begs for some bubblegum, and they have their twenty-dollar bill out anyway, they might figure that maybe they should just pick up a couple of new fuses, just in case, since they're here."

"Yeah," Carl said. "And maybe you could move the smaller items like the fuses and adapters closer to the counter, too, so they can just grab some at the last second when they're buying lightbulbs."

"You know what also would be cool," Carl went on, still sizing up the space. "If we took a wooden board, maybe a half inch by a square foot, and attached some switches, bolt locks, chain locks, and dials, and mounted it down here on the wall for the little kids, like Claire's age, so they can like, twist things and switch things on and off while their parents are asking questions and paying for stuff. Like to distract them, and keep them quiet."

"Carl," Beth said, approaching him by the register. "You've been here less than a day now, and you've already come up with some ideas that could seriously help us raise our profit margin. I really like the idea about the decorative switch plates."

"I usually only have the ability to keep the store open four hours per day so I can go out on repairs," Laine said. "I've hired high school kids in the past to mind the register a few hours per day, but they weren't really salespeople, and not worth their hourly pay. Maybe, though, maybe . . ."

He walked behind the counter and absentmindedly opened the till.

"Carl, I was planning on having you work in the store with me during open hours, but now I'm thinking . . . you have some really good ideas. Let's talk about this more. I might want to think about expanding our hours, and maybe our inventory. I think I told you I was thinking of expanding into some other items, such as different types of light fixtures, and doorbells, ceiling fans, and other things that might attract contractors. This might be something we can do. And that play board for little kids. That's just genius."

He closed the register and walked back out onto the sales floor.

"I'm getting way ahead of myself," he said. "You just got here yesterday, and you're not starting until next month. We're here to tour the town. We can talk about this later. Let's go back to the shop and I'll show you where all the electrical repair magic happens."

He put his hand on Carl's shoulder and led him through a curtain and into the back room.

Beth turned to Kim. "Wow," she said.

"What's wow?" Kim asked, lowering her eyebrows.

"That was amazing," Beth said. "I have never seen Laine so impressed by anyone, let alone a seventeen-year-old Bishop cousin! Is Carl always like that?"

"Like what?" Kim wondered.

Beth grinned. "He just came up with an entire business plan for Laine's store within a minute of walking in the door," she said. "Has he done a lot of retail work in the past?"

Kim shook her head. "Uh, no," she said. "He's only ever had one job, and it was with a lawn crew. Carl doesn't even like to go shopping!"

"So Aunt Missy was right about him," Beth said. "He's super smart. Like scary smart. We need to be able to keep him interested, keep him learning. We don't want to let him get bored. . . ."

"Beth," Kim said with a laugh, "you don't need to worry about Carl getting bored. Carl never gets bored. He always finds things to interest him. You know, none of us even knew he was super smart until like junior year in high school when I found out he was on the honor roll. He never even told us. He never raised his hand in class, or he would shrug when the teacher called on him in junior high. He was actually part of a gang of bad boys!"

"You're kidding. Carl? Really?" Beth laughed.

"Yeah, and his cousin, Laine's cousin, Chris, who will be here with my car next week, was their leader," Kim told her. "They never did anything too bad. They didn't get into fist fights or turf wars or anything. And they never bullied anyone. It was mostly skipping classes, mouthing off to teachers, and smoking in the bathrooms. They cleaned up their act in high school, though. You'll see when Chris and Pete are here. Carl is super smart, but there's a lot more to him than just that. Good stuff."

Beth smiled. "Good to know," she said. "I'd hate to have to study before he comes over each time so I can keep up conversations with him!"

They both laughed. Then Carl and Laine came back through the curtain, the shop tour complete.

"What's so funny?" Laine asked.

Beth shrugged. "Neither of us is a Farmer, so you probably wouldn't get our humor," she quipped. Kim laughed.

"Good one, Beth," Laine conceded. "Carl said you want to take a peek at the community college, Kim," he went on. "Should we take a ride over there now? Then we can stop over at Mavis's Café and get some lunch if you want."

"Sounds like a good plan," Kim agreed.

They drove about one mile, and Laine pulled into a driveway that led to a small quad. A large wooden sign read Stanislaus County Community College–Seska Campus. The driveway led to a large parking lot in front of an administrative building, and several side roads led to classroom buildings. Laine drove down the roads, and they circled a quad made up of crisscrossing sidewalks and green grass. The entire tour took about five minutes.

"What do you think, Kim?" Beth asked.

"It's a pretty campus," Kim said enthusiastically, "and it's bigger than our high school. That's a relief. I'm excited to register for classes on Monday. And it's not a long drive. I hope parking isn't a problem on busy days."

Carl knew Kim. He knew her very, very well. She was using her "eh, it's just okay but I'll make the best of it" voice. She was slightly disappointed. He didn't know what she had been expecting, but apparently, it was not this.

"I've never heard of any problems with parking," Laine said. "If you ever have any issues, you can park in front of the store and one of us will drop you off if we're not at a job."

Kim smiled. "Thanks, Laine," she said. "That's very sweet."

They had pulled back onto the road and back toward town. "Anyone hungry?" Laine asked. Everyone indicated that they were. "Okay, then," he announced. "Off to Mavis's Café!"

When they got home that afternoon after lunch, Carl and Kim got into Carl's Escort and went to buy groceries. When they got back, they organized their pantry.

"What did you think of SCCC?" Carl asked Kim as he put cans of food into the cabinets.

Kim shrugged. "It's okay," she responded as she made room in the refrigerator for a carton of orange juice.

"You seemed kind of disappointed," Carl told her.

Kim smiled. "I can't get anything by you, can I?" She sat down at the table. "I don't know," she went on. "I guess after going on campus visits back home with Darlene and Michelle last year, I was just expecting something, I don't know. Bigger. Maybe grander. But that's not why I'm going there. I chose not to go to a bigger, grander college or university. I didn't apply to any. And I guess as community colleges go, this one is kind of nice."

Carl sat down across from her. "But it's not like the places our friends are going to," he said. "You're not moving into a dorm. You're not gonna have the same experience as them."

Kim smiled lightly and reached for his hand. "You really are as smart as your Gram keeps bragging you are, Carl," she said kindly. "I knew it would be a different experience than Sally, Darlene, and Michelle would have, but this is the first time it's been right in my face." She squeezed his hand. "But it'll be okay. The most important thing is going to classes, getting credit, and if I want to someday,

I can transfer to a four-year college. It'll be good. I really am excited about registering for classes on Monday. I'm gonna try to do really well at this school."

Carl smiled at her. "I know you're gonna do great," he told her. "I'll go with you on Monday. We can go get lunch, get you registered, and maybe check out the mall in Carsonville after. It'll be fun." He squeezed her hand. "We're both gonna do great here."

CHRIS AND PETE IN CALI

Chris and Pete pulled up to the Farmer house on Monday. They had already packed for school and would need to get back home by Thursday to prepare to move into their dorms on Labor Day weekend.

Carl and Kim found Kim's Chevette parked in the driveway when they got home from getting Kim registered at SCCC and going to the mall.

"Pete! Chris! You made it!" Kim exclaimed, throwing her arms around them each in turn. Then Carl gave them both a hug.

"They got here about an hour ago," Beth told them. "They made really good time from Reno."

Chris smirked. "We actually left a bit of our summer work money there," he revealed, "so we thought we should head out before we blew it all."

Kim laughed. "We couldn't go to the casinos since Carl is still seventeen," she told them.

"I'm like ten minutes from turning eighteen," Carl said, giving her a side eye. "Sorry we weren't here when you got here."

"That's okay," Pete said. "We were going to stop to get some food before we got off of I-5, but we decided to just push through. But we're pretty hungry."

Beth had put out some chips for the guys, and the bowl was almost empty. "I'm sorry that I don't have dinner for you," she said. "I still have to go pick up my kids from my mom's house, and I didn't want to start anything until I got them home."

"That's okay, Beth," Carl told her. "We'll just take them over to our place and we'll get some takeout. I'm hungry too. Thanks for keeping an eye on them until we got back. They really aren't housebroken enough yet to be allowed to run freely." They all laughed.

"Thanks, Beth," Chris said. "We'll be back to see Laine later. I can't wait to see him. It's been a long time."

"Yeah, thanks Beth," Pete said.

"Come over for dessert later!" Beth yelled to them as they walked out to the door.

They approached the apartment unit. Carl unlocked the door, and they all stepped inside.

"Sweet little place," Pete said, looking around. "Bigger than a dorm room for sure. And you have like, real furniture and a kitchen."

Kim smiled. "All this stuff was here we got here," she told them. "All we had to do was unpack our clothes and stuff. We got pretty lucky."

"I'm gonna order from the Italian place up the road. What's it called Kim?" Carl asked, reaching for the *Yellow Pages*.

"Bella something?" Kim guessed.

Carl flipped the pages. "Bella Italia. Perfect! What do you all want? It's basic Italian."

Everyone told Carl what they wanted, and he called in the order. "Someone come with me to help me carry it out," Carl said. Pete got up and followed him to the door. "We'll be back in about half an hour or less," Carl said, and then left Kim with Chris.

Kim couldn't remember the last time she had been alone with Chris and wondered if it might have been sophomore year, at the Christmas party. The fated Christmas party. She got him a glass of water and then sat on the couch.

"So how was the trip?" she asked him.

"It was pretty good," Chris said, sitting down on the other end of the couch from Kim. "It was great that Carl told us all the places to stop. It made it much easier for us to plan when to start and stop for the day. You two kind of blazed the trail for us."

Kim nodded. "It was a really long drive," she agreed. "By the time we got here, we were pretty road weary. It was nice to know we were home, you know?

"Yeah," Chris said. "I can really understand that. I'm moving into the dorm at Eastboro State this weekend, but I'll only be like two miles from my parents' house. But you know, I didn't want to be a commuting student. They call them townies. I only stayed near home because it was the school I wanted to go to. I really like their program. They do a lot of hands-on training. I'll actually be placed in a school during my first semester. I guess it's a good way to weed out who's really serious about wanting to become a teacher."

"What kind of a teacher do you want to be?" Kim wondered. "Like what grade and subject?" She was grateful that Chris had given her a subject to talk to him about.

"I'm not positive about what subject," Chris said, "but probably science or math. Those were both classes I liked in school. And I'd really like to work in a middle school."

"Really?" Kim asked, surprised. "Middle school is so hard. All those moody kids with acne and social problems. I speak from my own experience, of course."

Chris laughed. "That's exactly why I want to work with those kids," he explained. "I don't know, I just wonder sometimes, what would have happened if we had teachers at Randall who had been more interested in what was going on with us as individuals instead of what we were doing wrong at school. I mean, what would it have been like for some kids if a teacher had just asked them some questions about what was going on at home? Instead of sending him to the principal's office all the time?"

Kim looked at Chris carefully. "You're talking about Carl, aren't you?" she asked. "I mean, I know you're not talking about you, James, or Pete. You all have awesome parents. You feel like everyone missed what was going on at Carl's house, and maybe if they knew, they could have been able to make a difference back then."

Chris nodded. "I knew about it, Kim. I mean, I didn't really know the details, but I knew something was wrong. But it never occurred to me to talk about it with an adult. I didn't want to betray Carl's trust. What did I know? I was like twelve the first time I slept over his house and realized that neither of his parents were home when we went to bed. I didn't see Jack at all, and Rosa had disappeared after heating us up some TV dinners. That had never happened before. We literally put ourselves to bed around midnight. We got tired. Scott was still up watching TV. I think he stayed up all night. Why wouldn't he? There was no one there to tell him to turn it off and turn in."

"That's awful," Kim said softly. "I can't stand to think of Carl going through all of this as a little kid."

"It wasn't always like that," Chris said quickly. "Rosa and Jack were nice to me when they were there. They fed us and talked to us. But as Scott and Carl got older, it got worse and worse. As soon as Carl got his car, it was like Rosa decided he was on his own. Her duty to him was done. And Jack was already gone. I have no idea how Carl made it through those years, and graduating with honors, no less! But I mean, if I can help some kid, just one even, and maybe get them pointed in the right direction, I think it will all be worth it. Maybe I can make up for what happened to Carl. I know Carl is okay now. I know you'll make sure he's okay. And you know, it's better that I'm not gonna have a girlfriend when I go to school. It would actually be really distracting. I probably would end up not taking it seriously enough, you know? I'd be all wrapped up in doing things with my girlfriend. Maybe Rhonda did me a big favor last year by breaking up with me."

"But it ended up okay for you, though, right?" Kim asked. "Because like you told us that day at the clearing, you didn't really love her."

Chris held eye contact with her for several seconds before speaking. "I did love her, Kim," he confessed. "I lied to you guys at the clearing. I guess I was kind of confused back then. Maybe I was in denial. But I did love her. And when she dumped me, I was lost. I didn't know what to do. Sometimes I still don't really."

"Chris," Kim said, looking at him in surprise, "why didn't you tell anyone? I mean, not even Carl!"

"I don't know, Kim," Chris told her. "Pride, I guess. I mean, I loved her, and she didn't love me back. Or if she did, she stopped at some point. I always thought of myself as some sort of prize, you know? Like some girl would be super lucky to have me. I guess I felt that way at first with Rhonda, but over time, I changed my tune, and realized I was lucky to have her. I didn't just want to be with a girl. I wanted to be with Rhonda. The relationship started to define me. Everybody saw the change. I wasn't such a bad boy anymore. It changed the whole group. We stopped doing things to get in trouble all the time. I just didn't have it in me anymore. I didn't want to disappoint Rhonda."

"I think we all mellowed out in high school, Chris," Kim said.

"Yeah, but it was kind of a dramatic change for us, to go from being the bad boys of Randall, one of us getting sent to the principal every day, to us just, like, blending in like regular kids in high school. We didn't stand out in the crowd anymore. And I didn't really care all that much. I think Carl got a little bit lost for a while, because he had found an identity and a role he was good at, and it really helped him get through the bad times. But then even he eventually settled into the new routine. And James, well, I don't know if James was ever really bad-boy material. But he was still pretty good at getting in trouble. But then when Sally came back into the picture, he basically became your local boy next door. The guys always looked to me for guidance, especially the first couple years of high school, since I was kind of the leader of the gang since second grade. But after prom junior year, I think things started to really change for us."

"Because of me and Carl getting together at the prom?" Kim asked.

Chris laughed. "Maybe partly. It was the first time that every one of us had a girl in our lives and didn't really need the whole group to feel special anymore. But it was mainly because that was the night that Carl found out the truth about me. That I'm not perfect. I always knew I wasn't perfect, but I'm not so sure he did. When he found out about our little 'encounter' . . ."

"Because I told him that night," Kim said softly. "But Chris, I had to."

"I know, Kim, it's okay. I don't blame you for anything. But to be honest, after that night, things were never really the same with me and Carl. We stayed close, and I know we'll always be close, but some level of trust was lost between us. He had looked up to me until then, and suddenly, I was just another person in the world who was able to hurt him in some way. You should have seen the way he looked at me that night. It was like he was shooting daggers at me with his eyes. And I think maybe that's where it all started going downhill for me, and for me and Rhonda. I lost my confidence. I had lost my bad boy posse. I wasn't the leader of anything anymore."

"And maybe that's the part of you that Rhonda was attracted to?" Kim suggested. "Kind of like being the first lady of the posse."

Chris shrugged. "Maybe. So I lost my posse to growing up, and then I lost my girlfriend for whatever reason she had. Part of me thought that I would just move on right away, get back on my feet, meet someone new . . . but then it just never happened for me. I wasn't any good at it anymore. I had lost my drive. I had lost that spark that drew people to me."

"Your charisma?" Kim suggested.

"Yeah, exactly. My charisma. It wasn't that girls were turning me down. It was that I just didn't see anything I liked, so I wasn't even asking. I was lonely, but I didn't think that anyone around me could make that go away. It was like my life up until then was a John Hughes movie and I was the bad boy who won in the end against all odds. Everything went right. But then senior year, it all just changed. Maybe someone switched my script. I mean, thank God I had my friends. You guys kept me going. No one ever let me feel sorry for myself or fade away. And the senior prom. You guys made me go, and I'm so glad you did. I'll always remember that night. It was the night I realized how much you all meant to me." He looked at Kim. "All of you." He paused. "Someday, I want to have a relationship like you and Carl have."

Kim laughed. "Don't you mean James and Sally?" she asked. "Everyone always wants to be just like them."

Chris shook his head. "No," he said. "You and Carl. I mean, I love James and Sally and I envy their relationship, but you and Carl . . . you've both been through so much. You're survivors. I mean, we all have stuff we've gone through, and no one's life is simple, but what the two of you have been through, and what you've overcome . . . it's amazing. And then coming out here to start your life together. Taking that risk. That's no small risk. Pete and I would have broken up after that drive alone if we were a couple."

Kim laughed.

"But the two of you made it through, and you made it an adventure. I want to have something like that in my life. I want someone who wants to go with me on adventures."

Carl and Pete came through the door carrying bags of Italian food and put them down on the table. "Hey, there's more stuff out there in the car that needs to come inside," Carl said. Chris got up and went outside to help, and Kim was left alone on the couch with her thoughts.

Kim remembered when Rhonda had broken up with Chris. Right then she had wondered if that would change the dynamic between Chris and Carl, if Chris would lose his alpha dog status. And now she realized that that was exactly what had happened to Chris, but his fall from grace didn't start with Rhonda's rejection. It started when Carl started questioning Chris's power over him. Because Kim had told Carl the truth about their night together. The truth had somehow brought her closer to Carl, but it had driven him farther away from Chris. Kim felt a wave of compassion toward Chris, an affection she hadn't felt in all the years she had known him. She had never realized how fragile Chris was. She never realized how easily he could fall. And she wondered what would have happened back at DeMarco Elementary all those years ago if she had actually ever tried to push him down.

The guys came back inside. "Look what we found wrapped up in a comforter in the back of the Chevette," Carl said, lugging in a case of beer. Chris and Pete followed behind, each carrying two four-packs of berry wine coolers.

Kim gasped. "Oh my God, you guys smuggled us beer and coolers all the way across the country?" She grinned at them. "Thank you so much! We thought we were gonna have to actually wait until we turned twenty-one to ever have alcohol again!"

"We couldn't let that happen," Chris told her, smiling. "If Laine's not gonna be the cool cousin for you, then I'm gonna have to take over that role."

"And look what else I found jammed in the back seat?" Carl held up the stuffed giraffe that he had given her for Christmas.

"Raffy!" Kim said, clutching her toy and giving it an exaggerated hug. "You made it to California!" The guys laughed, and Kim placed the giraffe on her tiny night table.

Carl put the beer and coolers in the refrigerator to get cold, and they all sat down in the kitchen to eat.

The next day, they stayed in the area and checked out Seska and the surrounding towns. They visited Laine's store, and Laine took them all out to lunch. Then they chilled at the apartment, trying out the now-cold smuggled beer and coolers. Later, they had dinner with the Farmers. Claire appeared to be infatuated with Pete. Kim could understand why. He had turned into a very handsome man, and he had a smile that could melt butter.

On Wednesday, Chris and Pete said goodbye to the Farmers, and the four friends headed west to San Francisco. They checked into a motel by the airport and then hit the town. They rode the cable car to the Wharf, ate clam chowder from sourdough bread bowls, and dipped their feet into the Bay. Then they checked out the Golden Gate Bridge and park, and they all posed for each other's cameras in front of the scenic landmark. Kim wanted to see Haight-Ashbury, so they walked around the streets and explored. They marveled at the rows of large, connected houses. Finally, they found an eat-in pizza place and had dinner and then retired to their room. Chris and Pete had an early flight back to Boston the next morning and wanted to be at the airport by six. Kim and Carl told their friends to wake them up to say goodbye.

At five thirty, Kim felt a tap on her shoulder.

"Kim," Chris whispered. She turned to face him and he smiled. "I just wanted to say goodbye. And thanks."

Kim smiled sleepily. She could see Pete saying goodbye to Carl on the other side of the bed. "What for?" she asked. "You're the one who drove my car all the way out here. Thank *you*!"

"You're welcome," Chris said warmly. "But I mean thank you for everything. For having us stay at your place. For taking such good care of Carl. And for our talk the other day. It was nice to be able to talk to you like that." He paused and lowered his voice. "What I told you," he said, "about Rhonda and everything. It's not a secret, and it's okay to talk to Carl about it because I don't want to ask you to keep things from him. I'm done with that. But maybe you can just not say anything to the girls, if that's okay. I mean, maybe I'll bring it up sometime, but later, not now."

Kim nodded. "I understand," she told him. "Laine designated this area as a no-gossip zone, and I intend to honor that."

Chris looked relieved. "Thanks, Kim." He reached out to hug her. "I'm really gonna miss you guys. Please make sure he calls me, okay?"

"I will," Kim promised, giving him a tight squeeze and then letting go. "Travel safely, Chris."

Chris and Pete traded places, and everyone hugged goodbye, with promises to stay in touch. After they left, Carl and Kim went back to sleep. They woke up around ten and looked around. They were alone in the room. They grabbed each other and held on tight. Their friends were gone, and no one else was coming. They were now officially on their own. They had planned to spend the morning exploring more of San Francisco, but instead, they decided to just go home to Seska.

KIM GOES TO SCHOOL

School started for both Kim and Benjamin on Tuesday, September second, the day after Labor Day. They were both feeling different emotions. Benjamin couldn't wait to see his friends and meet his new teacher, Miss Taylor. Kim was nervous about meeting new people and getting to the right classrooms at the right times. They met up in the driveway before school and talked about their expectations.

"I heard Miss Taylor lets kids chew gum in class," Benjamin boasted.

"She does not," Kim protested, giving him a skeptical look.

"That's what Timothy Strom told me at camp, and he was in her class last year," Benjamin said.

"Oh, okay," Kim said. "Well, I won't go against what Timothy Strom told you. What did your mother put in your lunch?" she asked.

"Peanut butter and jelly, apple slices, and Oreos," Benjamin announced. "What's in your lunch?"

Kim peeked in her bag. "It looks like Carl made me a PB and J, too! And a whole apple and three Mint Milano cookies!"

Benjamin frowned. "I only got two Oreos."

Kim laughed, then fished one of her Milano cookies out of the plastic baggie and handed it to him. Benjamin smiled and ate the cookie right away.

"Now, who's your favorite cousin?" she asked him playfully.

"Kimmmm!" Benjamin announced, and they both laughed.

Benjamin's bus pulled up in front of the driveway, and Kim gave him a hug. Beth yelled goodbye through the kitchen window. As soon as the bus pulled away, Kim started for her Chevette.

"Bye!" Carl called through the window. "You'll do great!"

Kim smiled and waved at the house. Then she got in her car and started toward SCCC.

Kim had enrolled in four classes, the most she could take in one term with her financial aid. On Monday, Wednesday, and Friday, she had Speech and Public Speaking and Biology, and on Tuesday and Thursday, English Literature and Introduction to Probability. She was most worried about the math class, but she felt confident that Carl could help her if she got stuck. But her first class was English.

After purchasing her textbooks in the school bookstore, she parked her car in the small lot in front of Building 4, as indicated on her schedule. There was ample parking. Cars were pulling in as she walked to the entrance. She looked at the other students as she walked into her classroom. Most were dressed casually in jeans or slacks and T-shirts, a few of the older women in skirts or casual dresses. She noticed a wide range of ages, most students being around her age, but some looked like they were her mom's or grandma's age. There were more female than male students, and she wondered if that had to do with the subject of the class, or the enrollment of the school. The room was filled with long, semicircular lecture tables. Kim saw an open seat in the third row, next to a girl who looked to be about her age, with her blond hair in a ponytail and a denim jacket hanging over the back of her chair. Kim put her backpack on the floor under the table and sat.

The girl looked up and smiled at her. "Hi."

Kim smiled back timidly. "Hi."

"I'm Tami."

"Kim."

Tami swiveled in her chair to face her. "I haven't seen you around before. Did you go to Carsonville?"

Kim gave her a confused look. "What?" she asked. "Oh, no, I'm not from here. I just moved to Seska from Massachusetts. Just got here like two weeks ago."

"Oh," Tami replied. "I've lived in Seska my whole life. I knew I would have recognized you if you had been here before. Everyone knows everyone in Seska!"

"Oh, then you probably know my boyfriend's cousin, Laine Farmer?" Kim asked.

Tami laughed. "Of course I know Laine! Laine and Beth, and their kids, Benjamin-don't-call-me-Ben and baby Claire! I babysat for them in high school a few times. They're really nice. So your boyfriend must be Laine's new apprentice!"

Kim marveled at how fast news got around in Seska. "Yeah. His name is Carl," she said. "We moved here together and we're living in the unit behind the Farmers' house."

Tami smiled. "I know," she said. "My dad works at the bank. My brother works at the grocery store. Everyone knows everything about what goes on here, too. I hear your boyfriend is really smart."

"Yeah, he is," Kim confirmed. "He's great at a lot of things." There seemed to be a lot of talk about Carl's intelligence in Seska. She wondered if they'd never met an intelligent person here before.

"My boyfriend, David, works at the bakery next to Laine's store," Tami went on. "Do you like donuts?"

Kim gave her a warm smile. "I don't know anyone who doesn't," she said. "I particularly like the strawberry jelly–filled ones."

Tami nodded. Kim wondered if she had already known that.

"I'll bring you one on Thursday," she promised. "I bet Laine and Beth have given you the tour of Seska and surrounding areas," she continued, "but I bet you haven't had the tour yet from someone who actually grew up around here."

"No, I haven't," Kim confirmed.

"I'll give you my number," Tami said, tearing a thin strip of paper from her clean college-ruled notebook. She wrote her number on the paper and handed it to Kim. "There are actually some fun places in Seska and Carsonville to hang out. Carsonville has an under-twenty-one club that has good music, no country, and dancing, and there are a couple of clubs you can go to if you're eighteen or over and they just stamp your hand so you can't buy drinks if you're underage. There's also other things, like a drive-in movie theater and some restaurants that have, like, normal food that young people like."

"Is there a Friendly's nearby?" Kim asked. "I didn't see one in town. I really miss Fribbles already."

Tami gave her a baffled look. "I'm sorry," she said, "but it sounded like you were talking to me in a different language for a second. You have a really thick accent. Did you say Fribble?"

Kim pulled her eyebrows together. "Uh, yeah?"

"What's a Fribble? You're not talking about that fuzzy creature from *Star Trek* that purrs, are you?"

Kim realized that this had to be one of the things that they didn't have in California or that was unique to the East Coast. Laine had already instructed her and Carl to call bubblers "water fountains" and not to look for Hoodsie Cups in the ice cream aisle. She was not sure what else she had to be aware of.

"Um, no, not a purring alien creature," she said. "Sorry. I mean like a milkshake. You know, like a big frothy milkshake from Friendly's?"

"Is Friendly's a restaurant?" Tami asked. "I don't think I've ever heard of it."

Kim's heart sank. No Friendly's? People who had never heard of Friendly's? Another thought occurred to her. "How about d'Angelo's?"

Tami shook her head. "None that I know of. What do they make there?"

Kim hesitated. "Grinders?"

Tami smiled. "Oh, yeah, grinders. I love grinders. We don't have the place you mentioned, but there are some really good local places to get grinders. Mostly pizza places. I'll show you my favorite one. Mama's Italian Pies."

"Sounds great," Kim said, relieved that she didn't need to pull the definition of grinder out of the *Webster's Unabridged Dictionary* she carried in the back of her brain. As it was, Tami might still think she was talking about an organ grinder with a monkey and not a delicious Italian sandwich.

It was ten o'clock, and the teacher started the class by handing out the syllabus. Kim took out her notebook and pen to take notes. She reviewed the assignments listed on the syllabus and saw the first book they would read would be *The Picture of Dorian Gray* by Oscar Wilde. Kim was excited to have bought it earlier in the day at the bookstore. As she had told Benjamin, she enjoyed books that took place in the past. Also listed was *Lord of the Rings* by J.R.R. Tolkien, something that Kim had had on her list of books to read in the future. Tolkien wrote the ultimate fairy tales for adults. While she looked forward to the books, she hoped the class and the teacher would maintain her interest. She turned her attention up front and started to take notes.

Kim ate lunch alone in the cafeteria. She looked for Tami but could not find her. Maybe she went home for lunch, or maybe she didn't have any afternoon classes. Kim took her food out of her bag and laid it out on the table. She half expected Carl and Darlene to come sit on either side of her with their trays, and then Chris and Michelle and Sally and James to come sit on the other side of the table. She took her sandwich out of the baggie and took a bite. Carl had gotten better at his PB and J–making skills, and the sandwich was perfect. Kim could see why Carl equated his mother's PB and Js with love. She ate her apple, and then her two cookies. She still had lots of time before her afternoon class, so she threw her trash in the garbage can and headed outside.

She decided to take a walk around the quad. It was a warm and breezy day. It was different starting the school year without the threat of an autumn chill in the air. California air was different. It felt different, it smelled different. It wasn't bad, just . . . different. She walked across one of the walkways on the quad, and along the driveways past building 1, then 2, all the way up to 7 and back to 1. Her next class was in building 3. She started toward building 3, passing by students walking in pairs and laughing. There were students lying out on the grass, catching a few midday rays. There were students sitting on cement stairways leading to the buildings, reading novels or syllabi. It looked like school. It felt like school. But California school.

Probability was in a different type of lecture hall, one with stadium seating like a movie theater and seats that popped up when you stood. The overhead light was dim, as compared to the lighting in her English class, which had bright fluorescent overhead lights and natural light through the windows. There were a few other students spread throughout the room, like viewers at a second-run theater. More students trickled in as the top of the hour approached, until about twenty students were present in the one-hundred-seat auditorium.

As the class started, the instructor asked all of the students to move up to the first few rows. Several rose reluctantly from the back, rolling their eyes, and made their way forward. Kim was in the third row, so she stayed where she was. She was pleased that she didn't get lost before the first two hours of the course had ended. She understood the concepts, and she immediately liked the teacher. He explained things in a way she understood. She knew she would feel comfortable asking questions if they came up or attending his office hours. She imagined that this man was the kind of teacher that Chris would like to become, one that spoke to the target audience in a way they would understand and would be approachable in the hallway. She felt good when the class ended, and she returned to her car.

Kim decided to explore the county library in Carsonville before heading back home to Carl. It was a five-minute drive from SCCC, and there was parking out front on the street. The library was a one-story building with wings extending from either side in an L-shape and a large patch of landscaped lawn in front.

When she went inside, she found the check-out desk to the left of the entrance. She approached the librarian, who smiled at her warmly.

"Can I help you?" she asked.

"Hi, I just moved to Seska," she told her. "I need to get a library card, and take a look around and find the best places to study."

"Are you going to SCCC, dear?" the librarian asked. Her name tag identified her as Mrs. Haas.

"Yes, I just started today," Kim told her.

Mrs. Haas handed her a form. "Why don't you go ahead and fill this out for me," she instructed. "Do you have any identification?"

Kim pulled her wallet out from her purse and removed her driver's license. She handed it to Mrs. Haas, who took a look. "Oh, you're from Massachusetts," she said, gazing up at Kim over her reading glasses. "You must be the young lady who's staying up by the Farmers."

Kim stopped herself from rolling her eyes. She reminded herself that this was a very small town. She had been warned. She smiled. "Yes, I'm Kim," she said.

"Nice to meet you, Kim, I'm Judith," the librarian said, procuring her hand. Kim shook it. "Laine does all our electric work at the library. We heard he was getting a new apprentice from Massachusetts. It will be good for Laine and Beth to have you in their backyard unit. It's always good to have family nearby. Normally, I would ask you for proof of address, but since you're Laine's family, I'll just go ahead and process your card application."

"Thanks, I appreciate that," Kim said. She didn't have a proof of address yet, so the familiarity with Laine had worked out well for her. She completed the form and handed it back to Judith. Judith then took a blank card from a stack in her drawer, wrote Kim's name on the line, and added her new library card number to the bottom. Then she handed it to Kim.

"Let me check on this young man real quick, Kim," she said, "and then I'll show you our study carrels."

Judith took a pile of books from a ten-year-old boy who had stepped up behind her with his mother, removed their cards from the back pockets, ran them through her photo machine along with the boy's library card, and wrote the due date on each of the cards before placing them back in the pockets. The whole action took less than one minute. Then Judith came out from behind the check-out desk and led Kim across the length of the carpet. Along the back wall of the library was a row of wooden study carrels lined up like diner booths. Judith pointed to the second one from the left. "That one is my favorite," she whispered to Kim. "Try it out."

Kim slid onto the chair and looked around. She looked in all directions. Very few distractions. Very little sound. Comfortable chair. She got up and tried the one to the left, and then the two to the right. The first one was better. She said so.

Judith smiled. "Told you!" she said happily. "I've worked here for twenty-six years. I know every corner of this library. Please, feel free to come in every day to look around or study. We have plenty of reference material here, as well. I know that your apartment is pretty small over there, and it might be nice to get out every now and then for some quiet, especially around exams."

"Thanks so much," Kim said. "I think I will. I've got to head out now though, so I'm sure I'll see you soon." They walked back toward the door. There was a teenage girl waiting to check out some books at the desk.

"Bye, Kim," Judith called out to her as she walked out. "Welcome to the Seska/Carsonville area!"

Kim pulled into the driveway and got out of her car. She lugged her newly purchased textbooks up to the door and let herself in. Carl was sitting on the couch, watching TV.

"Carl," she said, "don't even ask me how my day was. I'll tell you," she said. "It was the most overwhelming, and underwhelming, day I have ever had."

She told him about her classes, about meeting Tami, about eating lunch alone, the huge and empty lecture hall, her trip to the library, and her tour with Judith.

"I've never felt so alone and so crowded at the same time," she explained. "Everyone knows who we are. Laine was right. This is a very, very small town."

Kim had remained standing and holding her backpack while she spoke. Carl stood, took her bag from her, and placed it on the chair. Then he brought her back to the couch with him and sat her down. He held her in his arms quietly. She sighed deeply.

Finally Carl pulled away and looked at her. "Wow," he said. "That's a lot. I haven't done hardly anything in Seska without you yet. It's gonna be weird when I go to work with Laine. I guess it's something we're gonna have to get used to. We're gonna have to figure out a way to keep our privacy. We know we can trust Laine and Beth. We just have to be careful about what we say to who from now on."

"Yeah," Kim agreed. "No more bad boys or tough girls. We have to be good here, no matter what. For Laine and Beth's sake."

"Or if we want to be bad," Carl suggested, "we'll have to leave town."

"Pretty far out of town from what I can see," Kim said.

"And no Friendly's?" Carl lamented.

"No more Fribbles," Kim said sadly. "And no d'Angelo's deluxe veggie melts!"

"We'll figure it all out," Carl promised, putting his arms around her again. "I promise."

CARL'S A MAN NOW

Carl's eighteenth birthday finally arrived, along with two twenty-five dollar checks in greeting cards from the Grams.

It was a Monday. Kim's classes didn't start until ten. Carl's job didn't start until the next day. Kim woke him up early to help him unwrap and partake of his first present. Then she got out of bed to make him breakfast. She made eggs, bacon, and toast. Carl lay under the sheets naked, watching Kim cook in the kitchen. He couldn't help smiling.

"I can tell I'm a man today," he said in his most manly voice. "It's the first birthday I've started the day naked in bed with my woman making me food in the kitchen."

Kim made a face at him and threw an oven mitt toward the bed. Carl caught it and laughed.

Kim needed the mitt. She walked back to the bed and grabbed it out of his hand. She bent over to kiss him. "Happy birthday, birthday brat," she told him. "I would cook for you naked, but I don't want to get bacon grease burns where the sun don't shine!" She smiled and went back to tend the food.

"I'm the luckiest man in the world," Carl called after her.

The phone rang. Kim answered it and handed the receiver to Carl. It was Gram Missy.

"You're up, birthday boy!" she said.

Carl laughed. "It's birthday man now, Gram," he corrected her. In the kitchen, Kim rolled her eyes and stirred the eggs.

Gram laughed. "Sorry, birthday man," she said. "I forgot about the time difference between us. I usually try to wait until one o'clock my time to call you, but you're gonna be a working man tomorrow, so I guess you have to get used to an early start now."

"Yeah," Carl said. "And Kim's making me breakfast, so it's a good start, too."

"You're a lucky man, Carl," Gram told him.

Carl laughed. "I said the same thing to Kim not five minutes ago. Yeah, she has to go to school for two classes and a lab today, so I'm gonna have lunch with Laine, Beth, and Claire, and Kim and I are going out for dinner later. I don't think it will be a late night though, since I want to start my first day tomorrow on the right foot."

"I'm so proud of you, Carl," Gram told him. "I hope you enjoy the job. And the classes. I know you'll do well, but I hope it's something you like, too. That's the most important thing."

Carl watched Kim working over the pan of sizzling bacon in her ribbed tank top and gym shorts. "Gram, I'm working hard on only doing things that make me happy these days. Oh, on that note, thanks for the birthday gift. It came in the mail Saturday, but I opened it this morning. I'm gonna use it to buy some books I want at the town bookstore. And also tell Aunt Cissy thanks for me."

"Send her a thank-you note, Carl," Gram told him. "It's only polite. I'm gonna let you go now, Carl, so you can have your birthday breakfast. Happy birthday, my darling. I can't believe my youngest grandchild is eighteen!"

"Thanks, Gram. I miss you."

"Miss you, Carl. Love you. Bye."

Carl climbed out of bed and pulled on his boxer shorts. He walked into the kitchen and up behind Kim. He put his arms around her waist and buried his face in her neck. She tilted her head back for maximum results and then spun around in his arms to kiss him.

"No more consorting with minors for me," she whispered in his ear. "But I would like to consort with you again, after breakfast."

"I'm in favor of that plan," he whispered back. Then she shooed him away from the stove.

"Five minutes," she told him.

Carl smiled. "I'm thinking more like at least fifteen, or twenty minutes," he told her.

Kim laughed. "I think I'm really gonna like eighteen-year-old Carl," she admitted.

After they ate, they revisited their bed, and then lay together until it was time for Kim to get ready for school. "I like this morning routine," Carl said. "Laine and I need to leave for a work site at seven thirty tomorrow, so should we set the alarm for six so we can do this again?"

Kim nuzzled her head against his chest. "I would," she said, "but I don't want to." She laughed. "Maybe next birthday. So I'll give you your present tonight at dinner," she told him.

Carl looked her in the eyes. "Kim, you already gave me my present," he said, "twice. Best birthday ever."

"Yeah, but you gave me the present back," she told him. "Twice. So more presents for you. Tonight. At dinner. And then more when we get home." She kissed him again and then reluctantly got out of bed and headed for the shower.

At noon, Carl went with the Farmers to Mandarin Wok, Seska's only Chinese restaurant. Carl was pleased that the style was very similar to that he was used to in Massachusetts. He feasted on spareribs, egg rolls, beef with peapods, and chicken lo mein. He opened his fortune cookie and laughed. It read, "You will receive much luck in the coming year." He silently added, *in bed.*

Laine handed him a wrapped box. "I hope you're not offended by this gift, but if you are, you'll get over it."

Carl ripped the paper off and wadded it into a ball. He opened the box and found a red ball cap with a black and gold logo that read SF in white embroidered letters. "Forty-Niners?" he asked, and he laughed.

"No offense to the Patriots if you're a fan," Laine told him "I just thought maybe it would help you fit in. I received lots of abuse when I first moved here in my Red Sox gear."

Carl smiled at his cousin. "Thanks, man," he told him. "This is really thoughtful." He put the cap on his head. "Just make sure I'm not wearing this if any of my friends from home come to visit," he said. "Especially my friend Sally. I'd never live it down."

Beth handed an envelope to Claire. "Sweetie, give this to Carl," she told the little girl.

Claire held the envelope out toward Carl and said, "Here, Carl," and Beth laughed.

"We've been practicing that all day!" she told Carl. "I can't believe she actually said it!"

Carl took the envelope from Claire's tiny hand. "Why, thank you, Claire," he said with a smile.

"Fank you, Carl," Claire said sweetly.

Carl opened the envelope and found a crayon drawing by Claire folded in quarters. Inside was a twenty-dollar gift certificate for Main Street Books.

"Thank you so much, you guys," he told them all. "I've already been to that place twice. I have a list of books I want to get. And thanks for the picture of the . . ."

"Kitty," Beth whispered. "It's Tiger."

"Of course it's Tiger," Carl said. "Beth, I just wanted to make sure you knew!" Beth and Laine laughed.

Laine dropped Beth, Carl, and Claire off at the house and went back to the store. Carl said goodbye to the ladies and headed back to the apartment.

It was one o'clock. Kim's class went until three, and then she had a biology lab until four thirty. She was coming straight home after. So by five. That gave him about four hours to wait. He sat on the couch and thought about what to do. It was his birthday, so he played video games.

At three thirty, there was a tiny knock on the door that he almost missed. He opened the door to find Benjamin standing there holding a cookie tray with a lump in the middle and a dish towel over the top.

"Hi, Carlos Jerome," he said. "Happy birthday. I made you something."

"Benjamin Jerome," Carl said, standing aside to let him in. "Come in. Thank you."

Benjamin walked in and went straight for the coffee table and put the gift down. "You can take the towel off like wrapping paper," Benjamin instructed.

Carl stepped up to the table and pulled off the towel. It was a pile of connected LEGOs. He took a guess. "Wow," he said, "you made me a LEGO dinosaur!"

Benjamin beamed. "It's a tyrannosaurus rex," he said. "But I'm gonna need those LEGOs back, so you can keep it for your birthday and give it back to me tomorrow."

"Thanks, Benjamin," Carl said, smiling at him. "I love it! And the T-Rex is my favorite dinosaur."

"Did you know the tyrannosaurus rex could get up to forty feet long?" Benjamin asked.

There was only one right answer to that question. "No, I didn't know that," Carl said. "That's really cool."

"My mom is making you a birthday cake as a surprise, but Kim knows about it," Benjamin revealed. "But I don't think we're supposed to keep secrets. Maybe you can pretend to be surprised later?"

"Okay, Benjamin, deal," Carl agreed.

"I gotta go home," Benjamin said, "but can I come over sometime and try your video games?"

"If it's okay with your parents," Carl said. "Thanks again for the T-Rex, Benjamin."

"You're welcome, Carlos." Benjamin turned and walked out the door.

At 4:49, Kim came home. She smiled when she saw him sitting on the couch, and then she glanced at the table. "Hey, birthday man, what have you got there?" she asked as she approached him for a kiss.

"Any reasonable adult can see it's a T-Rex," Carl responded. "My man Benj gave it to me for my birthday. Or I should say it's on loan. And he didn't tell me anything about my surprise birthday cake so don't worry about it."

Kim shook her head. "Dang it," she said. She sighed. "Well, at least now I don't have to make up some excuse for us not getting dessert at the restaurant tonight."

"Yeah, I would've loved to see how you would have managed that!" He put down his video game controller, stood up, and wrapped his arms around her. "I've been enjoying your gifts from this morning all day, in my head, and I've got a very good memory." He kissed her. She laid her head against his chest. "How was your day?" he asked.

"Not bad," she said. "I really like Speech class. I think it's gonna be my favorite. We have to present a speech in class on Friday, but one that's already written, so I'm gonna go to the library tomorrow after my classes to find one. I think Biology is gonna be my most challenging class. I like it, but there are so many big words that are so similar to each other. I might need your help studying for those tests. But we need to get ready for dinner now! I totally need to change my clothes."

Carl was still holding Kim by the waist. He buried his face in her hair. "I think you need a shower," he told her. "I think I could use a shower. Let's go take a shower."

Kim looked up at him and smiled. "I really am enjoying eighteen-year-old Carl," she said. She took his hand. "C'mon, birthday brat. Let's go take a shower." She led him to the bathroom.

One hour later, they were sitting at their table at Roma Restaurant in Carsonville. They were holding hands across the dimly lit table and smiling at each other the way eighteen-year-old couples do when they're enjoying a dirty little secret they're sharing. The waiter came by with their menus, and the spell was only partly broken. This was a new restaurant for them, so they studied the offerings carefully. Carl, being a creature of habit and the birthday man, opted for spaghetti and meatballs. Kim, having had enough change in her life in the past month or so, opted for her usual chicken parmigiano.

Over garlic bread, they talked about what the coming week would bring. "Are you nervous about tomorrow?" Kim asked.

"A bit," Carl admitted. "It can't be worse than the lawn crew, right? But I just have no idea what to expect. I don't really know anything about electrical work. I hope I like it."

Kim smiled warmly. "Carl, I think you're gonna like it," she predicted. "I just have a feeling. I get such good vibes from Laine. I think you're really gonna like working with him. I think he'll be a good teacher, and we know you're a good student. You'll make a great team."

Carl took a deep breath and then let it out. "Just hearing you say that helps," he told her. "It's nice to be reassured. And to know I'll be coming home to you after work. I really am a lucky man."

The waiter came back with their food before Kim could respond. They started to eat. It was fantastic. They ate silently, looking up from time to time to smile and make satisfied noises. The waiter came back and refilled their drinks. Finally, their plates were empty.

"We're coming back here for my birthday in February," Kim announced.

"I'll make the reservation tonight," Carl promised.

Kim smiled mischievously. "Time for presents!" she said, grabbing a paper grocery bag that she had brought in from the car. She reached in and brought out a squarish package wrapped in bright paper. She handed it to Carl. "Happy birthday, my brat," she said.

Carl took the gift with a grateful grin. He slowly tore the paper aside to reveal a metal box. It was a lunchbox from the 1970s. He looked at the images, which were from the TV show *The Electric Company*, which Carl used to watch in grade school on PBS. "This is so awesome!" he exclaimed. "So perfect! Where on Earth did you find this?"

Kim beamed. "I found it over the summer, at a vintage store in Shrewsbury. I knew it was perfect for your birthday, so I hid it away in the Chevette before we left. Pete smuggled it out for me before you could see it. Open it, there's something inside."

Carl shook the box. "Ah, yes, it does feel a bit heavy. Is it a Mr. Rogers thermos?"

He opened the latch and flipped the lid. Inside was a light blue T-shirt. He took it out and shook it. On the front was the image of Lester Lightbulb, the mascot for the Mass Electric Company. It was a cartoon lightbulb with arms, legs, and a face. The caption read, "Lester Lightbulb says, 'Give Me the Day Off!'"

Carl laughed. "Also vintage store?" he asked.

"No, this one came from the Main Street Mall in Eastboro," Kim said. "The iron-on store. I just got so lucky with your gifts this year! I was kind of worried that Gram Missy would get you this, too. She always gets you the perfect T-shirts, and when I saw it before we left for Seska, I knew it was perfect."

Carl folded the shirt and put it back in the box. "You did get lucky," he agreed, "but really, I'm the lucky one. Thanks so much, Kim. They're perfect gifts. And this has been the best birthday ever. I can't wait to see how you're gonna top it next year!"

Kim laughed. "I'll come up with something that will blow your mind," she promised.

Before the night ended, they made their last stop at the Farmers' house for pseudo-surprise cake and ice cream. Beth handed Carl a card that had come in the mail earlier. It was from James and Sally, wishing him a happy day. They also sent best wishes from Michelle, who had spoken to Sally on the day they sent the card.

They were home and tired by nine thirty, but the birthday was not over yet. Carl pushed the play button on the answering machine. There were two messages. The first was from Darlene, wishing Carl a happy birthday and asking Kim to call back sometime that week to chat. The second was from Chris.

"Hey, man, I just wanted to wish you a happy birthday and congrats on finally becoming a man, haha. And I wanted to wish you good luck tomorrow. I really miss you. It's so quiet in town with everyone gone. Call me tomorrow. Talk to you soon, bye."

By the time that message ended, Carl and Kim were no longer listening. They were in front of the bed, immersed in each other's lips and at various stages of undressing each other. Finally naked and on the bed, Kim asked Carl, "Is there anything you've always wanted to try but we haven't yet?"

Carl pulled his head away from her face and smiled. "Yeah, but only if you're up for it," he said. "I don't want to do anything that you wouldn't enjoy."

Kim laughed. "You want me on my hands and knees doggy style, don't you?" she guessed. Carl nodded expectantly. "I'm willing," Kim ventured, "as long as you don't try any funny business."

She kissed him face to face and knelt down to reposition herself.

Carl looked at her backside and his respiration sped up. "No funny business," he promised.

Five minutes into this venture, Kim swore she would never have sex in any other position again, except this one. Before Carl was done, he flipped her over on her back and finished while looking in her eyes. Now Kim felt they should just do it all the time, in all positions, every time. Carl continued to attend to Kim's needs until she was grasping at the comforter and finally had to ask him to stop.

They lay on the bed, Carl's arms one below and one above her in an embrace, partaking in pillow talk.

"So that was good?" Kim asked playfully, running her fingers through Carl's sparse chest hair. She loved to caress his mostly smooth skin.

Carl nodded exaggeratedly. "Yeah, Kim, that was very, very good," he affirmed. "I am one happy birthday brat."

Kim smiled. "Yeah, for me, too," she told him. "Very, very good. I really wanted your first birthday in California to be your best ever."

Carl glanced down at her. "You succeeded," he assured her. "Best birthday ever. You made it amazing for me."

You made me feel so loved, he thought. *Thank you for that. The only thing that would be better is if I knew for sure that you loved me. You have to say it, Kim, because for some reason, I just can't say I love you. But believe me, I do.*

Kim snuggled closer to Carl's body. "Carl, I always want to make things amazing for you," she told him.

Because I love you so much, she thought, *and I want you to be happy. And I want you to never leave me.*

"We need to get to sleep," Carl said, pulling the comforter up higher over their shoulders. "I have an early start tomorrow. Thanks for all of my presents, Kim. And for being with me on my birthday."

"You're welcome, Carl," she answered sleepily. "I can't wait for my birthday now. Good night, birthday brat. See you in the morning."

Carl kissed the side of her head. "Good night, Kim."

FARMER WORK

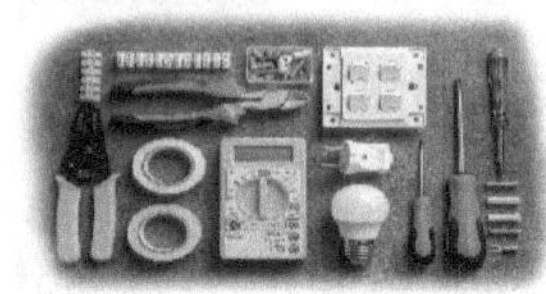

In the morning, Kim filled Carl's new lunchbox with a peanut butter and strawberry jelly sandwich, an apple, a bag of chips, and two chocolate chip cookies. She handed the box to him as he walked to the door to meet Laine at his truck in the driveway. She gave him an extended kiss goodbye, wished him luck, and promised she would be there when he got home.

Laine was walking out of his house as Carl came out. He glanced at Carl's lunchbox and chuckled. He unlocked his truck, and they both climbed into the front seat.

"This is your big day, Carl," Laine said as he pulled out of the driveway. "And it's gonna be a good one. We're heading out to Carsonville for routine maintenance of the HVAC system at the Catholic school, and then over to Severton to take a look at Mrs. Duncan's floodlights. If that doesn't take us until lunch, we'll head back to the shop and go over some stuff and then grab lunch. I didn't pack a lunch today, but I can get a ham sandwich from the bakery. After lunch, we'll head over to the Campbells'. They say they're having issues with their big old console TV, but I think they really just want to meet you. Our last call will be to the Fergusons'. I think we're looking at replacing their breaker box, which is a big job. I'll get them an estimate and get them on our schedule for next week. They'll probably have to stay somewhere else for a night if we can't get it all done in one day." He pulled onto the highway toward Carsonville. "It's the bigger contracts like the school and the town offices that bring in most of the capital," he explained, "which gives me the freedom to do the smaller jobs, like the

Campbells', and not have to schedule eight jobs a day to make ends meet. So after the Fergusons, we'll head back to the shop and finish off there."

"So, today, I'm just observing what you're doing?" Carl asked.

"Today, and for the next several weeks," Laine replied. "And meeting our frequent customers. There's a lot of customer service involved. It's good to develop a rapport. You'll need to complete your safety class before you can do anything that could hurt you, but even then, I'm still responsible for you not getting hurt, so no getting hurt, get it? And no burning down houses."

Sometimes Carl couldn't tell if Laine was joking or not, so he just smiled and promised to stay safe. "I know I have Safety and Electrical Theory this term," he said, "but what other classes will I be taking?"

"I can show you the catalog from the school when we get back to the shop," Laine said, "but I know there'll be classes on grounding, electric codes, HVAC systems, fire alarm systems, electrical metering, and a bunch if others I can't think of off the top of my head. It's a lot of facts and memorization, but also you'll get to get your hands on systems and electronics, and you'll be observing some of the same stuff with me. I might even let you carry my tools sometimes if you behave."

Now Carl laughed. "Only if you find me worthy," he joked back.

Laine laughed. "We can get your hands a bit dirtier in the store," he promised. "I'd like to start looking into some of the ideas you talked about. Maybe we can start by putting in those shelves in front of the counter and making that board for the little kids to play with. Those are easy enough to do."

"I can do both of those things as long as you have the supplies," Carl said. "Those would be fun jobs. I took wood shop at McKinney, so I learned to make basic shelves. As long as you have a level."

"I have at least three," Laine said. "Okay, we're getting off here, and we're just about at the school. I'm assuming you know how to act around priests and nuns. No swearing or sinning in the Catholic school. Make me proud, okay?"

"As long as my permanent record from junior high didn't precede me, I should be okay," Carl said. Laine laughed.

They pulled into the lot and parked near the front. They got out of the truck, and Laine pulled his toolkit out of the back. They went in through the front door. They passed some girls and boys not much younger than Carl walking through the hall in uniforms. Some of the girls checked him out and smiled at him coyly. He gave them all friendly smiles. Carl thought it was funny, since he never got attention like that from girls at his own high school. Novelty must be enticing to girls in uniform.

They entered the main office and were greeted with a chorus of women saying "Hi, Laine!" Laine gave them a friendly wave and a smile. He approached a woman who appeared to be in her sixties, sitting behind a gray metal desk. She was not wearing a habit but still had the appearance of a nun.

"Hello, Laine," she greeted him with a warm smile. "You brought your new apprentice!"

"Hello, Sister Florence," Carl said. "This is my apprentice and cousin, Carl Bishop. This is not only his first day, but also his first stop."

Sister Florence stood up and walked around her desk. She was wearing a very straight, long navy-blue dress, a dark gray cardigan sweater, and what Gram Missy would call practical shoes. She reached out her hand to Carl, and he accepted it. She gave his hand a squeeze.

"Hello, Carl. Welcome to St. Mary's," she said. "Your cousin Laine is always a sight for sore eyes around here. He always comes in with a smile, and gets the job done in no time at all! We always enjoy his visits. Would you both like a cup of coffee?"

Laine accepted a cup, and Carl, who was waiting to take his lead, followed suit. They sat down in the two seats in front of Sister Florence's desk, and Laine asked her questions about her health, her nieces and nephews, and the school. Then they talked about their 'electrical needs. It sounded basically routine, but the school wanted to be prepared in case of any change in weather over the school year. After they finished their coffee, Sister Florence gave them both Visitor stickers for their shirts and handed Laine a set of keys.

"You know the way to go, Laine," she told him. "Come on back when you're done and let me know the damage. Or, I'm hoping, lack of damage!" She and Laine laughed at her joke, and Carl figured this was a running gag between the two of them. He smiled.

As they left the office and headed for the boiler room, Carl turned to Laine. "Nice customer service," he said.

Laine smiled. "The nuns love me," he admitted. "They think I'm a choir boy. Don't let on that I'm a committed atheist, okay?"

Carl zipped his lips with his fingers. "Your secret's safe with me," he said. "Besides, I was raised by a Puerto Rican mother. At least briefly. I may not speak much Spanish, but I do speak fluent Catholic."

"Why is that not on the first line of your résumé?" Laine quipped. They reached the boiler room and Laine unlocked the door.

Ninety minutes later, they were back in the truck and headed for Severton. They were both partaking of bear claw pastries that had been handed to them in napkins by a nun on the way out of the school office. "I love going there," Laine admitted.

Carl swallowed a bite of pastry and chased it down with a sip of fresh coffee from a Styrofoam cup. "I can see why," he said.

Laine reviewed the job he had just completed, and Carl asked questions about what he had observed. Then they discussed Mrs. Duncan's floodlights. "The tricky part is making sure that the motion sensors are lined up right. If they're not, I end up with an angry message on my answering machine at 11:00 p.m. when the person pulls into their driveway and the light doesn't go on right away. I hate having to go back again to fix them. I hope the technology on these things will improve by the time you're out doing these things on your own."

"Maybe I'll be the one to improve it," Carl said.

Laine shrugged. "I wouldn't doubt it. Entering Severton," he said as they passed the city limits sign. "Don't blink or you might miss it. We won't be going inside the house, and we won't get any offers of sweets here. But there is a dog. He's big and slobbery, so brace yourself. He won't bite you, but he might lick you to death. I've asked her to keep him inside when I'm there, but she selectively forgets. Some people just assume that everyone loves their dog as much as they do."

He pulled up in front of a two-story house with a large garage at the end of a long driveway. As they got out of the truck, the front door opened, and a giant dog preceded a small woman out of the house. It bounded over to Laine and jumped up, pushing its front paws against his shoulders and almost knocking him over.

"That's not a dog, that's a bear!" Carl exclaimed, stepping back toward the truck.

Mrs. Duncan rushed out to restrain her dog. "That's his name," she told him "Bear. But he's just a big teddy bear." She had grabbed Bear around the collar and was pulling him back toward the sidewalk. "He's a Leonberger," she explained. "Very large, but very friendly. But I'll bring him inside for now. I'll be right out."

Carl had to smile as he watched Mrs. Duncan, who must have been 95 pounds soaking wet, lug the easily 120-pound dog back to the door by the collar. She gave him a treat, then closed the door and headed back toward the truck. Laine had removed a handkerchief from his pocket and was using it to wipe dog saliva off his cheek.

"Hello," Mrs. Duncan said to Carl. "I'm Eliza Duncan. You must be Carl."

They shook hands, and then Mrs. Duncan used that hand to push her glasses back on her nose and hair that had come loose from her ponytail behind her ear.

"Nice to meet you," Carl said. Mrs. Duncan was of indeterminate age and was wearing a loose white V-neck T-shirt over loose high-waisted cropped jeans and worn sneakers. She had dirt under her fingernails, and Carl could see garden tools strewn about the yard.

"Laine," she said, turning to face him, "Chuck's having trouble again with the flood lights not coming on until after he gets out of the car and starts toward the door. It wasn't a problem until the days started getting shorter and he's coming home in the dark now. I can't see up that far, but I think the birds have been nesting up there again."

"We'll take a good look and get things adjusted," Laine assured her as he stepped back to the truck to get his ladder. "Carl, grab an end for me, will you?"

Laine examined the floodlight and did find a recently abandoned bird nest. He removed the debris, adjusted the light, and encouraged Mrs. Duncan to let him know if there was any more trouble.

The next stop was the store. Carl took his lunchbox and went inside while Laine went to the bakery to get his sandwich. They sat in the shop and ate, reviewing their morning.

"It was a pretty routine morning," Laine explained. "Mrs. Duncan probably could have gotten by with a handyman instead of an electrician, but she calls me because I installed the lights and she trusts me. We'll get some juicier repairs soon for you to watch. The breaker box replacement will be a good start."

"The morning just flew by," Carl said. "It was pretty interesting watching you work, and seeing how your customers relate to you. It's so different after the way things were back home. Small-town life is like being under a microscope."

"It is," Laine agreed. "That's a good way to put it. And you're in a unique position as an observer right now. But in about a month, everyone will know everything about you that you've said out loud, so enjoy the sense of anonymity while you can."

They finished their lunches, and Carl found a note at the bottom of his lunchbox from Kim, wishing him luck on his first day, and signed with a heart. He folded it up and put it discreetly in his pocket with a smile.

The last two visits of the day were at houses in Seska. The Campbells were a spry couple of about seventy each, and they supplied more coffee and fresh chocolate chip cookies. Laine fixed the vertical hold on their television in about three minutes, basically just tightening the knob with pliers. The Campbells were very pleased by the results and were ecstatic to have met Carl. The trip to the Fergusons' house was not as joyous, as they were given an estimate for their breaker box replacement. They both sighed, then agreed to the job, which would be started and hopefully completed the following Monday. They would need to make provisions for their refrigerated and frozen food.

They ended the day back at the shop. Laine presented Carl with a key to the front door. "Guard this with your life," he instructed him. Then he showed him how to work the primitive cash register and run credit cards through the imprint machine. He walked him through the process of taking checks and warned him to only accept local accounts. He pulled out the inventory list from his binder and showed Carl the wholesale and retail pricing lists. He showed him how to use the pricing gun. Carl wasn't sure if he had stepped back into 1977 when he had come through the door of the store, but he smiled and paid attention to the instructions.

"Maybe," he said tentatively, "if we can make any money off the impulse buys I suggested, we can look into bringing the store into the 1980s. Like maybe a computerized cash register. They have some now that you can insert credit cards right into, and you don't need to imprint them anymore. And it calls the numbers right into the bank."

Laine rolled his eyes. "Carl, don't be snarky," he said. "I've been to the mall. I know there's more modern stuff out there, but this is Seska. Even if I had those things, the local system can't support them. But we get by with the old caveman stuff. You'll get used to it. Let's unlock the doors for a few hours, and then we'll head home right at five. I'll give you a rundown of the products while we wait for customers."

There were five customers that afternoon, and three bought products. The others came in just to say hi as they passed by the store. At five, Laine put the Closed sign on the door, and they headed for the truck.

"Well, that was a nice, easy first day of work for you," Laine said as he navigated the roads home. "You got to meet some nuns, carry a ladder, and learn about a new breed of dog. And you got lots of snacks. There's usually not as many snacks. People just really wanted to make you feel welcome."

"Well, it worked," Carl admitted. "I feel officially welcomed. And yeah, it was a pretty good day."

Kim was there when he entered the apartment, and he gave her a smile. "How did it go?" she asked.

"It was good," he said sincerely. "I think you're right; I'm gonna like working with Laine. He laughs at my jokes. And he explained things really well. I'm looking forward to starting classes on Friday so I can start doing stuff with my hands. For now, I just need to watch and observe what Laine's doing."

Kim smiled. "It sounds like a good day. Good. This is what you came here for." She approached him and put her arms around him. "And if you're looking for things to do with your hands," she said seductively, "I think maybe I can help you with that."

BETH THE BADASS

Kim came home from school and Carl was not home yet. It had been this way for the entire first two weeks of Carl's apprenticeship, and she was realizing that she hated walking into an empty apartment. Today, it was sunny and mild outside, and Beth was sitting in the backyard on a lawn chair reading while Claire played with her toys in the sandbox.

"Hey Kim," Beth called out. "Come sit with me." She put her bookmark into her book and closed the cover.

"Let me just scoot inside real quick to feed the cat and put on some shorts," Kim replied.

Five minutes later, Kim came outside and found that Beth had pulled up a chair for her. She sat down, and they silently watched Claire playing and singing to herself in the sandbox.

"Where's Benjamin?" Kim asked.

"Bedroom. LEGOs," Beth explained.

"Ah." Benjamin was a LEGO fanatic. He had a huge bucket filled with multiple sets and liked to build all sorts of creative creatures and structures.

"How is school going?" Beth asked, turning to look at Kim.

Kim shaded her eyes from the sun and looked back. "It's good," she said. "Nothing I can't handle. There's more homework than high school, but fewer classes. Oh, I keep meaning to tell you that I have classes with Tami Graham. She says she used to babysit for you guys."

Beth smiled. "Tami's a nice girl," she said. "But I suspect she spent more time on our phone with her friends back then than she did playing with the kids. But she was just sixteen. I was probably like that too at sixteen."

"She seems like she might have grown up a little since then," Kim said. "She brings me donuts on Thursdays, which is nice. Her boyfriend works at the bakery."

Beth nodded. "Yes, David. He's a nice guy."

"So they're safe to do things with? Like go out and stuff?" Kim asked.

Beth shrugged. "I can't see why not," she said. "It would be good for you to make some local friends, and Carl works right next to the bakery. It will be good for Tami, too. She had a really hard time, with all of her friends leaving town to go to college. Kind of like it was for you before you decided to come here."

"Yeah," Kim sighed. "Even now, I miss them. It's just not the same to only talk to them on the phone. I really miss my mom, too. We really talked about everything." She laughed. "Well, almost everything. There are some things you just can't talk to your mom about, you know?"

Beth laughed. "Yeah, I get that," she said. "Laine and I met in high school. I was at McKinney, and he was at Murphy, and we met at the community pool. He was seventeen and I was sixteen. It was a whirlwind summer romance that then turned into a whirlwind committed relationship my junior year! My mom was scandalized!"

Kim smiled. "Carl and I started dating junior year at McKinney, too," she said, "although we met when we were five. Actually, he didn't turn five until two weeks after school started, so I was the older, wiser woman. How did your mom end up in California?"

"My parents got divorced the summer before senior year," Beth explained. "Talk about scandals! My mom remarried three months later, and moved me here to Seska with her and her new husband because his family lived in Carsonville. I think she was actually relieved to get me away from my overly serious relationship, as she called it. She had heard rumors about the Farmer boys."

Kim laughed. "That's hysterical!" she said. "The Farmer boys are all so, I don't know, I guess the word is mild?"

Beth smiled and nodded. "I know," she said. "But I had the last laugh later that year when all I applied for were colleges in Massachusetts! I ended up going to Framingham State while Laine was at Boston University, and we basically moved in with each other after the first three months. Then after college, we stayed in

Eastboro while Laine was working to get his license. My father died when I was twenty-three, and soon after, my stepfather died. My mom begged us to move out here. I resisted for some time, most likely out of resentment for her moving me away from Laine in high school, but then after we got married, and I got pregnant with Benjamin, I had a change of heart. I wanted to be near my mom."

"I can understand that," Kim said.

"And Laine saw it as an opportunity to start his new business in a new place. So we came out here, and rented an apartment for a few months until this house went on the market. We loved it at first sight. We had driven by here many times, but had never been inside. It turns out, Laine had been putting away a lot of money when he worked as an electrical engineer. They can make a lot of money! So, we bought the house, Laine built the backyard unit, and here we all are today!"

"Wow, Beth, you were a badass in high school!" Kim said. "I'm impressed! And you and Laine had a little Romeo and Juliet action going on. It's very romantic."

Beth grinned. "It's my little love story, and it's still going strong. And my mother finally got used to the idea, and now she loves Laine, and adores her grandkids. She doesn't even mind that they're Farmers! It's nice to be near her now. It was easier for Laine to move away from his family. I think after growing up with so many siblings and cousins, he appreciates the quiet!"

Kim nodded. "Carl likes the quiet, too," she said. "I like the quiet, but I miss my family. I'm kind of used to the chaos, you know? And my mom and I were always right in the middle of everything."

Beth reached out and touched her arm. "You really miss your mom," she said softly. "Kim, I know we just met, and I'd never even consider that it would be the same thing, but I want you to know, I would love to be there for you when you need someone. I'm a really good listener."

"That's really sweet, Beth," Kim responded. "I appreciate that. I'll probably take you up on that. And you're actually pretty close to my mom's age. She had me when she was nineteen. She was a really young mom, and she raised me totally on her own until I was seven. She's pretty amazing."

"Sounds like it," Beth agreed. "How did your mom and your dad meet? I mean the guy you call Dad?"

"I know who you meant," Kim said. "It's kind of a cool story, although it doesn't start that way. My dad was married to another woman, Penny, and they had two kids. The kids were really close in age, and I guess she might have had some mental health problems or something. So when their second kid, my sister Stella, was born, she announced to my dad at the hospital that when they let her leave, she was taking off, and she wasn't gonna take the kids. She pretty much decided she didn't want to be a mom anymore."

"Oh my God!" Beth said. "I could never even imagine! She must have been in a really bad place to want to do that."

"Yeah, she was," Kim said. "And it was exactly what she did. Her family didn't even know where she went. Eventually she turned up, but she signed away her legal rights to be their mother. So my dad loaded Stella into the car from the hospital at three days old, went to get Chip, I mean Simon, from his parents' house, and took them home and became a single dad. I told you that he was an HR manager at Aries. He was commuting to Eastboro every day from Franklin, which had been no big deal because Simon had been home with Penny before Stella was born, but now they both had to go to daycare. And it turns out that Aries actually had a daycare on premises for employees, so Dad enrolled the kids and started to look for a house in Eastboro. He found one he really liked not too far from Carson Lake, and called for a showing. And you'll never guess who showed him the house."

"Your mom?" Beth said, her eyes wide.

Kim nodded. "Yup. My gorgeous, raven-haired twenty-five-year-old single mom, the local realtor, wearing a headband, a psychedelic-print long-sleeved minidress and tall boots, with her six-year-old daughter holding her hand. Both of us took one look at Dad, and we were instantly in love. Luckily, the feelings went both ways. Dad bought the house, and by the time he was ready to move in, he was ready to ask us to move in with him! So we went from a family of two to a family of five in less than three months. Then they got married when I was seven, and Dad adopted me, and Mom adopted Chip and Stella. I didn't start calling him Chip until two years later."

"Because his name is Simon and that's one of the Chipmunks?" Beth guessed.

Kim laughed and pointed at Beth. "Yes!" she said. "You are the first person who ever got that right away!"

They laughed together. Then Laine's truck turned into the driveway, carrying Laine and Carl. Kim looked at her Swatch Watch. It was 5:15. These guys were nothing if not prompt.

Beth sighed. "Well, here's my knight in shining armor now," she said, standing. "Claire, come say hi to Daddy!" she called out as the men got out of the truck.

Claire started to run across the yard. "Daddy!" she yelled, and then tripped on her own foot and fell on her face. She stood, brushed off her shirt, smiled, and started to run again.

Kim laughed. Carl came up behind her and started to rub her bare shoulders. She put her hands up over his, and together, they watched this sweet family scene unfold.

DEAR SALLY

October 14, 1986

Dear Sally,

I miss you so much! I hope things are going well with you at school, and with James. I think about you guys all the time.

School is going really well for me. I like SCCC so far. It's small, and the class sizes are small, which I think is good for me. Probability and English Lit are pretty good. I'm also taking Biology. It's harder than in high school bio, but I need to take it for any of the majors I might want to choose later. I'll get to that in a bit.

My favorite class is Speech and Public Speaking. Everyone has always told me I'm a good storyteller, so I thought it might be a good skill to learn more about. The teacher wants us to journal every day. I know you journal and you love it, but it's more challenging for me, and since we don't have to turn in our journals, I asked my teacher if I could journal in the form of letters instead. She said that was fine. I chose to write to you first, because I know you will be able to relate the best to what I'm going to tell you about.

So to start class, we all had to pick a speech, any speech from history, and perform it in front of the class. It was my first time speaking in front of strangers, so I was so nervous. I chose the Emancipation Proclamation. I think it went pretty well. People seemed to be able to understand me, even with my Massachusetts accent (which I didn't even know I had until I moved here) and they applauded when I was done (they applauded everyone, so . . .). The next assignment was to write and give a speech about something that happened to you in the past, something that affected your life or that you are passionate about. I had recently told Laine and Beth the story of my father's accident. I didn't know you when the accident happened, but I'm pretty sure I told you the story in junior high. If not, I can send you a copy of my speech. Anyway, I gave this speech in class, and I got a really good response. I was almost in tears, no surprise for me, but I got through. So after class ends, this older woman in my class, Ann (she's like forty), comes up to me to congratulate me on my speech. She then goes on to tell me that she has a brother who was in a car accident years ago and had a head injury and brain damage. He was never the same after that. His whole personality changed. She and her family started attending a support group, and they met some people who had formed a social service agency, and one of the things they do is educate people in the community about head injuries. It's called Head Forward. Ann is now on the board of directors for Head Forward, and she tells me she wants me to come to their quarterly board meeting and tell my story! Well, I was kinda worried about doing this, since number one, I'm not experienced with talking in front of people, two, I'm worried that no one will understand me with my "Massachusetts accent," and also three, these people know a whole lot more than I do about head injuries. What if I say something, and someone says it's not accurate? Ann assures me it's a laid back and friendly group, and not to worry, just be myself. So I tell Carl about this, and he agrees to go with me for moral support.

So I go to this Head Forward meeting with Carl, and I speak to all these men and women in suits and dresses, some that are old enough to be my grandparents! I finish talking, and these people actually start asking me questions! Like they think I know stuff! And the funny thing is, it turns out I do! So when the meeting ends, this one guy, Fred, who's in charge of public relations and community education, approaches me and Carl and asks us to come to his office. Of course, by this time Carl is nervous because it feels like being called to the principal's office, but of course it's nothing like that. This Fred guy invites me to come and tell my story at the Head Forward annual public convention in San Francisco in November! He thinks that my story is really relatable, and I tell my story with poise and grace. And he thinks I have a lot of knowledge and compassion for someone my age. And then he goes on to tell me that he wants to get me enrolled in a program they have that has classes with college credits, and works along with SCCC. There are eight classes that I can take over several semesters to learn about neurology, brain dysfunction, and traumatic brain injuries. Apparently, they are discovering new things about the brain all the time, and new tests to measure what's going on in the normal brain and one that has been injured, and even people with mental illness. The prerequisite *for the program is biology, which like I said I am taking now, and Fred says that the classes are at a level that any average college student who does their work and pays attention should be able to follow, so I won't be totally out of my league. So Carl and I go home and talk about it, and he's totally on board! So the next day, I call this Fred guy and tell him I'm in. Then he drops this on me: if everything goes well with the convention and my speech, they are prepared to offer me an internship starting next semester, where I would continue to learn about head injuries, and also give public talks at schools and other meetings, and meet with other families who are going through similar experiences! Apparently, they have had their eyes open for someone for this internship, and I guess the board members really liked me! It must be the exotic accent! It's not a paid internship, but there is a $500 stipend, which as Carl says is better than a $0 stipend! Haha! So I'm gonna do it, the whole thing! They just need my high school transcript, and if I'm approved, I can start in January.*

Sally, it feels so good to have something to focus on, and to have goals. And none of this would have happened if you hadn't encouraged me to come out to California to be with Carl. So thank you so much (plus I get to be with Carl, so thanks for that, too)!!!

Carl loves his apprenticeship so far. As anyone would guess, he's already acing all of his classes and amazing everyone. I've actually heard Laine tell Beth that he thinks Carl may be an electrical prodigy! But then, ugh, he made a joke and said it seems like Carl has lightning running through his veins. I'm really learning now why people always groan when they hear Farmer humor! Anyway, I'm so proud of Carl, and he seems really happy, and that's all I want for him.

How is James enjoying culinary school? I hope he is learning to make you lots of things with chocolate!

Have you had a lot of opportunities to write? Maybe sometime you can send me something you've written. I'd love that.

I heard your basketball team at Providence College is doing really well this year. It was on the news! I hope you get to go to some games. I know how you love your sports.

Sorry for the long letter. I'm just so excited about what is going on right now, and I knew you would get it!

Lots of love to you and James,
Kim

October 31, 1986

Dear Kim,

Happy Halloween!
   Thanks so much for the letter! Don't worry about how long your letters are. As you know, I love to read, so I was psyched to see mail in my otherwise empty mailbox! I have gotten a letter from Traci, and she's settling in well at Michigan State.
   I am so happy for you that your speech led to so much great stuff for you! All of our friends have always agreed that you are the best storyteller. I remember in 7th grade when you told me the story of the Bishop-Farmers. I felt like I could actually see the wedding through your words! I heard about your dad's accident mostly from Michelle back then, but I would love to read (or hear) your version, in your words. If you can, please send me a copy of your speech. If that's too hard to do, then maybe someday I'll hear you tell it live.
   You're welcome for suggesting you go to California to be with Carl, but to be honest, I think you would have figured that out yourself eventually. Like I told you when you drove me home that time after homecoming, the two of you have that certain light in your eyes!
   I am still journaling, and writing stories. I have a great idea for a novel, and I've been taking notes, but I haven't been able to actually sit down and start to write it. I am hoping by the time we get out of college, they'll have more affordable computers that people can have at home. It would make writing so much easier! I have been submitting stories to the Providence College literary journal, but I won't know if they get accepted until it's published in the spring. I am trying to get on staff on the student newspaper, but sometimes, that doesn't happen until junior or senior year. There are a lot of journalism students here, and it's really competitive.
   Jamie is doing great. He loves school, and he brings me samples of what he makes in class. We have been talking about maybe moving in together after second year

when he gets his associate's degree. It would be nice for him to have an actual kitchen to work in. But that's pretty far off. What's it like, living with Carl? It must be so nice to see him when you wake up every morning. That is like my dream with Jamie.

My roommate is okay, but I think she doesn't like that Jamie is always here, or I'm at his school. Oh well. We have gone to some basketball games. It is nice to have a winning team. I hope they make it to the NCAA playoffs this year!

By the way, that's weird about the Massachusetts accent thing. I think we sound normal. The people in Providence, however, have wicked heavy accents. It's hard to get used to!

We're about to leave to go to my mom's house to give out candy for Halloween. It's become a yearly tradition for me and Jamie. You know how much we LOVE noisy and rowdy parties . . . haha. It seemed like a really good weekend to get off campus.

Love to you and Carl, and best of luck with your speech. I know you'll do awesome!

Sally

BRAIN FORWARD CONVENTION

Kim spent as much time as she could each afternoon at the library, reading and researching head injuries. She knew her speech was good, but this was the big time now. Fred from Head Forward told her to back it up with facts and statistics but not to lose the human touch that made her story so relatable.

Judith, the librarian, helped her look up articles, and taught her how to use the microfiche machine to look at information that had been archived. Kim looked for other stories that were similar to her dad's and found the appropriate diagnoses that described the symptoms he displayed. She learned lots of new words about the brain, such as *anterograde amnesia* and *cognitive impairment*. She started to get excited about the brain classes she would be starting the next term.

Her other classes were going well, but she had to make sure she didn't neglect her studies in her excitement about her new venture. Carl tried to help keep her centered and focused and gave a lot of back and foot rubs when things got stressful. He played her audience for her as she rehearsed her speech and applauded and asked questions when she was done.

The conference was on Friday, November eighteenth, the week before Thanksgiving. Carl would drive Kim to San Francisco the night before, and they would return to Seska after the conference. Laine and Beth decided to make the trip to hear Kim speak and offer their support. They called to order tickets. They decided to share the car trip but get separate hotel rooms for the night.

"We haven't had a whole night away from the kids, well, pretty much since we've had kids," Beth confided to Kim. "It will be like a tiny second honeymoon!"

Kim laughed as she loaded her overnight bag in the car, and then laid her conference dress out across the top of all the bags in the trunk on its hanger. She smoothed out the fabric with her hand, and then slammed the door closed. Then she got into the front passenger seat of the Escort while Beth got in the back next to Laine. Carl hopped into the driver's seat, checked that everyone was belted in, and started to back out of the driveway around Laine's truck.

"I can't believe we live an hour away from San Francisco," Carl said as he pulled onto the on-ramp and merged into freeway traffic. "And this is only our second time going there."

"We lived sixty miles from Boston our whole lives," Kim reminded him, "and we probably only got there once every two years. It was always nice to know it was there if we wanted to go, though."

"Hey," Laine said, "why would you need to go to the big city when everything you'd ever need is right here in Seska?"

"Hah!" Beth burst out. Then she looked at Laine. "Oh, were you being serious?" They looked at each other for a few seconds, then both cracked up laughing. Kim and Carl both rolled their eyes.

Traffic was tolerable that afternoon, and an hour later, Carl pulled off the exit for the hotel where the Head Forward conference would take place the next day and where they would spend the night. Kim felt butterflies in her stomach. There was no backing out now.

Carl parked the Escort in the Hilton garage, and they all got their bags and headed to the lobby to check in. Kim informed the clerk that she was part of the conference, and he informed her that her room was being covered by Head Forward. Laine and Beth checked into their room, and they all headed for the elevators.

"So we'll meet you in the lobby at five thirty for dinner," Laine said as the elevator door opened on the third floor and he and Beth stepped out into the hall. "Don't bother calling us before that; the phone will be off the hook."

Beth slapped his arm. "Laine!" she objected.

Laine laughed. "What? We'll be taking a nap. Do not disturb!"

The elevator door closed, and Kim and Carl looked at each other. Then they both burst out laughing.

They had reservations at the hotel restaurant. It was a large dining area, and live piano music filtered in from the bar area. They were seated immediately and were handed tall, wide menus. "I'm assuming we're charging this to your free room, right, Kim?" Laine asked with a smile.

Kim shrugged. "I honestly don't know," she said, "but we should at least try!"

"I'm getting surf and turf," Laine announced.

"No, you're not," Beth told him. "You don't even like lobster. You're getting the roast chicken."

Laine sighed and nodded. "Yeah, she's right," he told Kim and Carl. "I'm a cheap date. But I'm getting coffee *and* dessert."

They all ordered their dinner and started on the bread basket.

"So Kim," Beth said as she buttered her roll, "tell me more about this brain studies certificate. What kind of job can you get with it?"

Kim dabbed at the corner of her mouth with her napkin. "It's an associate's degree," she explained. "You can become an educator or a group facilitator with it. I don't know much about it yet, but I'll learn about it during the internship, if it goes through. You also have to attend and lead a certain number of hours of groups and classes. It would be perfect if there's an opening at Head Forward when I finish, but I don't know where else I could work. I'd probably transfer to a four-year college and get my bachelor's degree after that. I guess I don't have to make any decisions yet, but it's nice to know I have options. Plus, it just feels like it might be a good direction for me to go in."

"I've never seen you so passionate about anything," Carl told her, giving her a proud smile. "You've been working so hard on your speeches and this presentation. I always knew you could tell a good story, but now everyone can see it. It's pretty awesome."

Laine and Beth glanced at each other and smiled discreetly. "Yeah, it's pretty awesome," Laine agreed.

Kim looked at her hands. She was not used to this much positive attention about something she was good at. It was slightly uncomfortable, but also slightly amazing. She looked up and smiled. "Thanks, you guys," she said. You could never go wrong with a thank-you.

After dinner, dessert, and coffee, the two couples said goodnight and retired to the privacy of their own rooms. Kim felt slightly tipsy from the night of good food and good company. She unzipped the back of her dress and let it slip to the floor. Carl watched this action with curiosity. Then Kim slowly peeled off the rest of her garments and tossed them by Carl's feet.

"You flattered me tonight," she told him as she approached and put her arms around him. "And flattery will get you everywhere with me." She reached up to kiss him.

"Good to know," Carl whispered back, walking her backward to the bed and helping her onto her back. "I love to learn new things about you."

Kim had no trouble waking up the next morning to get ready for the conference. She let Carl sleep while she showered, did her hair, put on makeup, and dressed in her fanciest dress. She went over her speech again and again, moving her lips with the words. She was looking forward to doing this but also to getting it done. She was also looking forward to the breakfast buffet.

She woke Carl at eight so he could get ready. She sat on the end of the bed and tapped her feet on the floor while he showered, shaved, and dressed. He tied a Windsor knot into the one tie he owned and looked in the mirror. Kim appeared next to him.

"We clean up well, don't we?" Kim said.

"No one will even notice me next to you," Carl said, putting his hands on her shoulders and kissing her cheek. Then he kissed her lips and told her, "You're gonna blow them all away today."

Kim smiled at him gratefully. "Let's go meet the Farmers and get some buffet." She grabbed the hotel key and led him to the door.

Laine and Beth were in the lobby waiting when they got there. They all walked to the conference area, registered, put on their nametags, and headed for the food tables.

Kim saw Fred from Head Forward scooping scrambled eggs onto his plate. He saw her there and smiled. "Kim!" he said. He placed his plate on the table and came to shake her hand. She introduced him to Laine and Beth, and then Fred turned to the man next to him. "This is my partner, Jason," he told her. Jason reached out to shake everyone's hand. "Jason has had to attend, what, twelve of these conferences over the years? This is lucky thirteen. Are you ready for your big presentation, Kim?"

Kim smiled nervously. "I think so," she said.

"Her speech is great," Carl told Fred. "I've been watching it develop from the start. She's gonna knock 'em all dead today."

Fred smiled. "We'll, that's quite an endorsement," he said, turning to Kim. "I can't wait to hear it. You'll be first up after lunch, and we'll give time for questions after. We can talk in the afternoon about what comes next. I hope you all enjoy the conference. We're very proud of what we've put together this year."

They all parted, and Kim and her group got their breakfast. Carl could see how nervous Kim was getting, and he did his best to keep the discussion light and distracting. Soon, it was time for the conference to start, and they went into the conference room to find seats. Kim was overwhelmed at how large the space was, and it started to fill up quickly. She took several deep breaths, then sat down. She put the bag containing her speech on the floor, and Carl took her hand.

The first several speakers were engaging, and the talks were easy to follow. When lunchtime came, they went back to the conference lobby and helped themselves to sandwiches, salads, and brownies. Kim felt her heart rate rising as the hour moved closer to 1:00. At 12:55, Fred approached her and walked her to the speaker's platform.

At 1:00, Fred coaxed the audience back to their seats, and when they quieted down, he introduced Kim.

"We discovered this young lady in an SCCC Speech class, giving an impassioned presentation about an event that changed her family forever. We were so impressed with her ability to convey her rich experience, that we immediately recruited her to tell all of you her story. I hope you enjoy her as much as our board of directors did. Ladies and gentlemen, Miss Kim Drake, of Eastboro, Massachusetts, and Seska, California."

Kim stepped up to the podium and waited for the applause to stop. Her eyes scanned the audience and rested on Carl. He gave her an encouraging smile and nodded. Kim smiled, then started her speech.

When it was over, she thanked the audience for listening and received thunderous applause. She didn't know where to look, so again, she settled on Carl's face. Soon, Fred came back to the podium, the crowd quieted down, and he asked for questions. There were several. Some were somewhat personal, and some more technical. Kim answered them all to the best of her ability. Finally, her time was up, and she received another round of applause. Fred pointed her to the door behind the podium, and she escaped to the hallway. There was no one else there. She sat on the floor against the wall, breathing hard, but smiling. Within two minutes, Carl was by her side on the floor, with his arm around her shoulder.

"You were so amazing," he told her with awe in his voice. "They loved you. I can't believe I get to be your boyfriend. I'm so lucky." He reached over and kissed the spot above her ear.

It was too much for Kim. It was more than she could keep inside. She burst into tears. Carl understood. He just held her.

There was a break in the conference after the next speaker. Kim and Carl found Laine and Beth, who heaped their praises on her about her speech. They all hugged.

Soon, Fred approached the group. "So Kim," he said to her with a bright smile, "can you start your internship the second week of January?"

CLOCKWORK ORANGE GIRAFFE

Laine had an annual physical scheduled the second Tuesday in December. He asked Carl to open the store at nine, close up at twelve, and wait for him to come back so they could get lunch together and finish some small jobs in the shop.

When Laine came into the store shortly after noon, he found Carl in the shop, concentrating on some work he had on the bench.

"Make any sales?" he asked him.

Carl looked up and smiled. "Hey, Laine," he said. "I didn't hear you come in. Yeah, I sold some lightbulbs and some electrical tape, and a few pieces of candy. A few people said they'd come back later when you're in to say hi."

"What are you working on there, Carl?" Laine asked, approaching him.

"I'm just working on a little Christmas present for Benjamin." Carl turned back to his work and inspected it. "I came in early today to get it started. I hope that's okay. Would it be okay if I kept using scrap wire and discarded stuff back here? I'd like to make one for Kim, too."

Laine stepped closer and looked at the project. "What is that, a dinosaur clock?" he asked.

Carl had taken a large plastic dinosaur toy similar to the ones Benjamin played with at home and had cut a circular hole in the front with an X-ACTO knife. He was inserting a small clock and securing the works in the hollow space.

"Where did you get the clock works?" Laine asked. "Did you find them buried back here somewhere?"

Carl shook his head as he remained focused on his work. "No," he said, "I made them myself from other stuff I found back here and some parts I got from the hardware store. The battery and the clock face and hands I bought at the hardware store, too."

Laine's mouth dropped open. "What?" he said. "You made them yourself? Where did you learn to do that? I for sure didn't teach you. I don't think I would even be able to do that on my own without guided instructions. I would have just bought a premade clock."

Carl shrugged and applied glue to hold the face in place. "I found an old alarm clock at the apartment," he explained, "and I took it apart. I studied it. Then I put it back together. Voila. How to make a clock." He stated this like it was akin to drawing a tree with crayons.

Laine grabbed his rolling chair and rolled up to where Carl was working. He sat down. "You took a clock apart and put it back together?" he repeated. "What would happen if I gave you a toaster?"

Carl shrugged. "I'd make toast?" he said, and he snickered. "I don't know. Do you have a toaster for me to try?"

Laine's head shook slowly from side to side. "And you're gonna make another clock for Kim?" he asked.

Carl smiled. "Yeah, but I'm gonna do a giraffe for her. It's kind of a thing with us." He set the completed dinosaur clock on the shelf for the glue to set.

"Would you mind if I watched while you did it?" Laine asked. "I mean, just to see how you do it?"

"Yeah, that would be fine," Carl agreed. "But would it be okay if we had lunch first? I'm pretty hungry. And can I use some of your wire?"

"Sure, sure," Laine agreed. "Let's walk to the café. On me, okay?"

"I never turn down free lunch," Carl told him with a grin.

When they were seated in the café and had ordered their lunches, Laine looked up at Carl. "Carl, we need to talk about something."

Carl looked back at Laine with a worried expression. Things never went well for him when someone told him they needed to talk. "What's up?" he asked.

"So, I need to know," Laine asked. "Have you ever done anything else like the alarm clock? I mean, like, taken things apart and put them back together again? Maybe fixed stuff? Or built stuff after looking at how they're made?"

Carl thought about it. "I fixed the doorbell at Gram's house once. That was pretty simple. I just looked at the back doorbell and saw how it was put together, and did the same thing for the front one. I don't know, maybe some other small things like that. An old vacuum cleaner once. Got it started, but the suction wasn't good. Why?"

"So, Carl," Laine said carefully, "did you know that most people can't actually do things like that?"

Carl frowned. "What do you mean?"

Laine contemplated. "Carl, I think you might have some sort of gift. Like a natural talent," he told him. "I don't know if it's related to electrical stuff only, but that's my only point of reference. It's like what I've read about Mozart. When he was very young, he could hear music one time and then play the piece perfectly, right after. Without even looking at the notes. Just by ear. Others would have to study for years to get the same piece right. And it wasn't like he did it mechanically. He did it with feelings, emotion. Now, I'm not saying you're the Mozart of the electricity world, or even that the story is totally accurate, but I think you have a similar type of gift."

Carl shrugged. "I mean, I can fix little things," he said. "I never thought it was a big deal."

Laine laughed. "Carl, you've seen people pay me good money to go to their houses to fix little things. Most people can't do it themselves. They usually hire professionals."

"Oh," Carl said. "So what does all this mean for me?"

Laine shook his head. "Carl, I'm afraid that there's going to come a point that I'm gonna run out of things to teach you. I mean, not right away. Of course you're gonna have to learn the basics, and you're gonna have to practice the skills, but you will ace everything I teach you in no time. I wonder if we should think about what happens after that."

"But I need to have four years of experience to get my license," Carl protested. "If I learn everything way before that, what *can* I do? I can't work on my own without a license."

Laine sighed. "I know that, Carl, but I also don't want your talent to go to waste. I wonder," he said, "have you ever thought about going to school for engineering?"

"I had thought about college back when my friends did," Carl said, "but you know the story. I didn't apply anywhere. I made my decision back then. It wasn't the right time. Maybe someday."

Laine looked at him carefully. "Carl," he said softly. "There's something else going on here that you're not telling me. I haven't really known you that long as an adult, but I've known you long enough to tell when you're not being completely up front with me. What's the rest of the story? Why did you decide not to go to college? Was it something to do with Kim?"

Carl bit his lip, then shook his head. "No, it wasn't about Kim," he told Laine. "It was about my parents." He stopped.

Laine looked at him sternly. "Carl," he said, "what did your parents do?"

Carl waited while the waiter approached and placed their food on the table. Once he walked away, Carl looked up at Laine. "Laine," he said, "I haven't told this to anyone, okay? No one. Not even Kim. Please don't tell anyone, especially your dad or Gram. Or Chris."

Laine nodded solemnly. "No-gossip zone," he promised.

Carl nodded. "Okay." He sighed. "It's not what they did, it's what they didn't do. My parents never filled out my financial forms so I could apply for college."

Laine maintained eye contact while Carl spoke, encouraging him to go on.

"We got the forms early in the school year from the guidance counselor. At that point, I assumed that I would get the paperwork done, then apply like my friends did, and then decide what I wanted to do. I had some idea of going to a school near home, to be near Kim, and maybe studying math, or science of some sort, you know, the stuff that comes easy to me. I didn't have any specific career in mind, you know, just some ideas about my education. So I brought the form home and gave it to my mother the next time I saw her. It was sometime in October. I remember because that's when she started staying away more. I didn't mind so much then, because I could get around on my own in the car Gram gave me, and she always left some money on the table for food."

Carl stopped briefly when he saw Laine wince. Then he went on.

"She took the paper and looked at it, then put it down on the table. I had even filled out the top part with my name, to make it easier for her. But she put it down on the table and said she would do it later. I was even going to hand her a pen so she could just do it right then, but she walked away and said she was going out. I asked her to please do it soon since I needed it to apply for college. Then she looked right at me and said, 'Why don't you just get Jack or Gram Missy to do it?' and then just walked out the door and left. I didn't see her again for weeks, and I haven't seen my dad since my last birthday. I don't know. My mom just wasn't herself. I didn't even know who she was anymore. Her eyes didn't even look the same. I thought maybe she was smoking pot or something, but I couldn't smell any in the house. And I didn't smell any alcohol on her breath. I think she may have been on something, but I don't know what."

Laine nodded. "Yeah, that sounds about right," he admitted. "From what you've told me about her behavior over the past few years, I've wondered if she might be on drugs. I know Jack likes his beer, but I never knew Rosa to drink to excess. I have heard rumors of an increase in people using heroin on the East Coast. Is it possible Rosa might have gotten involved—"

"Heroin?" Carl asked, his voice lowered. "I don't know. I don't know much about heroin. I've heard that street people do heroin. They shoot it up with needles in their arm. I don't know if my mom was doing that. I never saw her doing that."

"She was gone a lot," Laine reminded him. "Maybe she was using it somewhere else."

"With the tias, maybe," Carl said. He shook his head like he was shaking the thought out of his brain. It seemed to work. "I don't know. But what I do know is that my form never got filled out. It just sat on the table for months. It got food stains on it. I panicked. It was due on December fifteenth. People started asking me about college, and then my SAT scores came back really high. I didn't know they were going to be that high. I didn't even study for them. And then everyone started expecting me to apply to any school I wanted. But I couldn't. So I froze. I did nothing. I didn't know who to talk to, who could help me. Only my parents could complete the forms. I didn't know their income or any other information. I didn't think Gram could help. So I told people I had decided not to go to college because I didn't know what else to tell them. Then I did nothing. Until I got the offer to come out here after graduation. It was the first time I thought I could see a way out, and even then I didn't know what to do, because of Kim. But there wasn't anything left for me to do. I almost left her behind."

He lifted his sandwich to his mouth to take a bite.

Laine could sense that Carl was done talking. He picked up his sandwich and started to eat while he thought of how to reply to what Carl had just told him. He was amazed at how little negative emotion Carl showed when he spoke about the abuse he endured from his parents. He had really learned to block it out somehow. Laine felt sorry for Carl, for what he had gone through, but he knew pity was the last thing his cousin needed. He needed guidance, a mentor. A friend. A brother.

"Carl," he finally said as he put his sandwich down on the plate. "I can't believe you went through all that and had no one to talk to about it." He paused.

"Remember I told you that I was an electrical engineer? Do you know what an electrical engineer does?"

"Not really," Carl said as he chewed on a bite of potato salad.

Laine nodded. "Not many people do. It's a very specialized field. Electrical engineers plan and design, and develop their electrical products, or sometimes have other people, people like me, build them for them. They're like inventors or developers of the electrical future. Sometimes they work on their own or for agencies, and other times they work on contract for other companies or the government, developing products or devices as they're needed. Carl, electrical engineers are the people who took apart clocks and toasters as kids, and figured out how to put them back together, or make them better."

Carl swallowed his food. "So you're saying I would make a good electrical engineer?"

"I'm saying," Laine explained, "that you would probably be good at anything you decided to be. What you've always lacked is the ability to make that decision, because you weren't given any options. I want us to talk about options. Carl, you've turned eighteen since you've lived here. You're living on your own now, and you're earning an income. You're emancipated from your parents. I think, I'm not positive, but I think at this point, you could fill out the financial paperwork on your own."

Carl nodded. "I figured that might be the case," he admitted. "And I figured I would look into it at some point. But right now I have a commitment to work with you, to learn about being an electrician. And I really do want to get my license. I'm enjoying what we do."

"I understand that," Laine said. "But I'd be willing to let you out of that commitment if it means that you can pursue something that leads to a more successful future for you—"

"Laine," Carl interrupted. "I get that, and I appreciate it, but I don't really want to think about making any changes now. I like the way things are. And I kinda need to focus on the decisions I have been able to make on my own. I want to prioritize my relationship with Kim. The way things are right now is really good for us, I think. She's really getting into her classes, and she has the whole thing with Head Forward. She's doing so well. I need to make her my focus. To figure out where we're going from here, our relationship." He stopped to take a sip of Coke through his straw. "But I do think electrical engineering sounds pretty cool.

Maybe, when we get to the point where you're running out of things to teach me, we could start talking about it again?"

Laine made eye contact with Carl and smiled. Then he nodded. "Yeah, Carl," he said. "That sounds like a good idea. But in the meantime, I want you to feel free to use the shop. To come up with ideas, to write them down, draw them out. I can help you with figuring out the logistics. But I will help you, if you want to build something, to try something out. And I'll get you a bunch of toasters from the resale store, so you don't get bored!"

Carl laughed. "Laine, I'm not gonna get bored," he told him. "I'm really easily entertained. Really, I enjoy playing Pong for hours. But I do appreciate the ability to use the shop. And the offer to help me out when it's time for me to move on to something new." Carl took the last bite of his sandwich and washed it down with his last slurp of soda. "And the toasters would be nice, too."

"Let's go back to the shop and you can show me how you're gonna make that giraffe clock," Laine said, "and then we'll open the store for a few hours. We have a full day of repairs in the field tomorrow."

They got up, and Laine threw a twenty and three ones on the table. "See ya later, Mavis," he yelled to the kitchen.

"Later, Laine," Mavis called back.

THE FOLKS AT HOME

Christmas Eve and Christmas seemed surreal to Kim. The skies were blue, the air was dry, and the temperature spiked at sixty-one degrees. It was her first Christmas with no hint or even a thought of snow, and she was away from her family for the first time ever.

The Farmers, although atheists, made the season festive with wintery decorations, including an inflated snowman in the yard and spray snow on the windows, and traditional foods of the season, including eggnog, sugar cookies, and plenty of cocoa with marshmallows. Their house always smelled of peppermint. Benjamin wore a Santa hat around the house, and Claire became obsessed with the word *ho*.

"Ho, ho, ho," she sang out in her deepest Santa-like voice while ringing a little bell she found hanging from the Christmas tree.

"She sounds like one of those Salvation Army guys you see in front of every grocery store starting after Thanksgiving," Carl confided to Kim, who burst out laughing because she was thinking the exact same thing.

Both Benjamin and Kim loved their homemade clocks and were duly impressed with the man who made them. Carl had also given Kim a soft brown leather messenger bag that she could use for her new internship for a briefcase. She gave him a soft black suede fleece-lined jacket to keep him warm on work calls when the temperature dropped below fifty. It was apparent that they had shopped for each other in the same leather shop in town. They opened cards and letters from home and unwrapped gifts from the Drakes and the Grams. Kim talked to her family for over an hour, including all of her siblings and her dad. Stella informed her that, as of the New Year, she would be moving into Kim's old room, and would no longer have to share space with Sophia. This was a Christmas gift from their parents. Kim was happy for her sister but felt a pang of loss, even though, intellectually, she knew that it wasn't really her room anymore. Twelve-year-old girls needed privacy.

After dinner, Kim and Carl went back to their apartment. They sat on the couch, lamenting about eating too much food. Kim was feeling both happy and sad, having spent her first Christmas with a new family, but missing the one she left behind. She especially missed watching the excitement on her brothers' and sisters' faces when they ripped the paper off of their gifts and discovered something they had really wanted all year. Conversely, she reveled in the newness of coming home with Carl after a big family event and knowing they would not have to say goodbye for the night. Her emotions were in turmoil.

Carl tried to keep Kim distracted by teasing her with a sprig of mistletoe. He was able to make her laugh for a bit, but then she was quiet again. Carl had enjoyed their low-key, small-family Christmas. There were always dozens of family members at Gram's house on Christmas, and the noise level could get unbearable. It was always too cold to escape outside for a break. In the years they didn't go to Gram's, Christmas was not a big deal in the Bishop house. Often, the TV was on all day, the meal was marginal, and everyone pretty much took off after dinner. So Christmas at the Farmers' was ideal. But he wished it was more joyous for Kim.

Carl was about to suggest going for a drive, or going back to hang out at the Farmers' house, when the phone rang. He let Kim answer. It was Darlene.

"Kimbo!" she said. "I wasn't sure you'd be home yet! Hey, we're all over at Michelle's house and we wanted to say hi!"

"Who's we?" Kim said excitedly.

"Everyone!" Darlene replied. "James and Sally, Chris, Pete and Carolyn, and of course Michelle."

Kim covered her mouthpiece. "Go pick up the other phone," she told Carl. "Everyone called to talk to us!"

Carl went to the kitchen and picked up the wall receiver. "Hey Darlene," he said. "Merry Christmas!"

"Hey, thanks, Carl," Darlene replied. "I'm doing Chanukah at my dad's house this year, so double holidays for Miss Feinman. But I'm not complaining. Hey, everyone, say Merry Christmas to Carl and Kim!"

"Merry Christmas to Carl and Kim!" everyone shouted.

Carl laughed. "You all sound like my six-year-old cousin! It's so good to hear everyone's voice."

"I wish we had a speaker phone like they had on *Charlie's Angels*," Darlene said, "but I'm gonna pass the phone around so everyone can say hi. Kim, when you're all done, let's you and me catch up for a minute before we hang up, okay?"

"Sounds great!" Kim replied. Carl glanced over at her on the couch and saw that she was smiling.

One by one, or in the case of Sally and James, two, their friends got on the line, and they talked about their first four months apart. They talked about school, their dorms, the weather (there was snow on the ground in New York and Massachusetts, but not in Rhode Island). Carl talked about his work and his classes, and Kim about her approaching internship. Finally, Michelle protested in the background about her parents' phone bill. Chris promised to call Carl later, and Darlene got back on the phone.

Carl said goodbye to Darlene and hung up his receiver. Then he grabbed the novel by his bedside, waved to Kim, and headed over to read in the Farmers' den.

"What's up?" Kim asked, knowing Darlene had something to tell her.

"Well," Darlene started, "I have plans to go out with this guy from my math class after break. He's cute, but you know, I haven't even kissed a guy since Charlie. Oh, I did fake kiss Chris at the prom, but that was no big deal. I am really due for a hookup, Kim."

"Sounds like you're overdue," Kim agreed. "But you don't sound overly excited about this guy."

"Eh, it could be good," Darlene said. "I just have other stuff on my mind. I have to tell my dad something and I don't know how he's gonna react."

"What is it?" Kim asked, drawing her legs up beneath her on the couch to get in a more supportive and empathetic stance.

Darlene sighed. "I think I might have gotten a D in Biology this term. Who am I kidding? I know I got a D."

"What?" Kim said in disbelief. "But Darlene! You're always wanted to be some sort of biologist. What does this mean for you?"

"Well," Darlene admitted, "I don't really think I want to do that anymore. My God, Kim, college Biology is way more intense than high school was. And the thought of three and a half more years of classes like that? And when you're a senior, they make you dissect a cat! A cat, Kim!"

"Yikes," Kim replied, looking at Tiger, who was asleep beside her with a festive Christmas collar around his fuzzy little neck. "So what do you think you'll do instead?"

"That's the big problem," Darlene said. "I have no idea. I signed up for a bunch of liberal arts intro classes next semester to see if there's anything I would like, but I know my dad's gonna want to know what careers they'd lead to, and I just don't know. Kim, I've always known what I wanted to do, and now I have no idea! It's such a weird feeling."

Kim, having never trusted her thoughts about her own future, could relate. "It is kind of scary, not knowing," she said, thinking of her worries about her future with Carl. "But I guess it will be kind of fun, checking out new classes and stuff. I'm taking my first neurology class next semester, Intro to the Brain. I have no idea what to expect. I might hate it. But it is a good chance to find out."

"That's true," Darlene agreed. "You can't even declare a major at Ithaca in the first two years. Maybe there's a good reason for that. You must be starting your internship soon."

"Second week of January," Kim said. "I'm so nervous, but everyone has been so nice so far. And I know it's a subject that I can really relate to, so hopefully it will go well."

"Michelle looks like she's gonna bite my head off if I don't relinquish the phone. But I have to ask, how are things going with your new friend, what's her name, Tommy?"

Kim laughed. "You know very well it's Tami," she corrected. "And I already assured you, she's never gonna take over your status as my best friend. But it's good. We eat lunch together a few times per week, and we'll be in two classes together next semester, so at least there's that. She's introduced me to a few other girls, and we've been talking about having a night out with our boyfriends. Which reminds me, don't forget to call me and let me know how that date goes. What's his name?"

"Phil," Darlene said. "And of course I will. It's three hours earlier there, so I can probably even call you when I get home from my date. If I do come home! Okay, well, I miss you so much. I hope you have a great New Year."

"You too, D. Give everyone hugs for me."

"I will. Bye, Kim."

"Bye, Darlene."

Kim sat alone on the couch for a few minutes, thinking about her friends and how much she missed them. She was glad to have met Tami, and to be exploring new places to go and things to do, but no one could ever replace her first friends. And they didn't have to. Her first friends were still there, and always would be. She walked over to her nightstand and found the Ken Follett novel she had taken out of the library for fun reading during holiday break. She put on a sweater, then went back to the Farmers' house to read in the den with Carl.

When New Year's Eve came around, Kim and Carl went to dinner with the Farmers, and later Beth's mother came over to watch the kids so the adults could go watch a mini fireworks display at the high school football field at midnight. Laine pointed west, where he swore he could see flashes coming from as far away as San Francisco. It was a mild night. They sat out in the school parking lot and watched the stars, needing only to wear light jackets. Kim thought back to the crowds downtown in Eastboro on New Years Eve, and the long evenings in the freezing outdoors. Both types of celebrations had their merits, and she wasn't going to compare. But sitting on the hood of the Escort, stargazing, with Carl's arm around her shoulder and his warm breath on her cheek, put Kim in the mind of a whole new world of possibilities.

LEARNING THE ROPES

The new semester started, and Kim and Carl attended a new set of classes. Carl was going to be learning about appliances, electronics, and wiring. Kim would be taking her first foray into brain studies, along with Spanish, Intro to Psychology, and American Government. She knew on the first day that Government would be lost on her. She had no interest in politics, but it was a required class. She figured maybe it would give her something to talk about at boring parties.

She was able to arrange her classes so that she would have three mornings per week at her internship. Four hours per day. Twelve hours per week. On the Monday of the second week in January, she dressed in a skirt and a buttoned frilly shirt, and drove to Head Forward. She met with Fred when she got there, and he handed her a typed-up orientation schedule. She would have to go through the company orientation, just like the paid employees, but she could skip the parts about pay and benefits. She was given a large white binder filled with agency policies and procedures and told to read it during her free time. The only free time she saw on her schedule was during the orientation for pay and benefits, which totaled about an hour. She figured there was at least six hours of reading in the white binder. Maybe it was assumed she would be skimming through. She was shown a chair at a small barren desk in a corner where she would be able to sit and read. She left the white binder on top.

The only bright spot in the first few days was meeting the people she would be working with. She ran into Ann from school, who introduced her around on the first day. There were trainers and facilitators, nurses and social workers, fundraisers, administrative staff, and even a medical director, a seasoned neurologist. And she was a woman. Kim was immediately impressed by her strong presence and her hippy fashion style. She also met volunteers and volunteer coordinators. Everyone shared the one common thread that brought them all together: they all knew, and many loved, a person who had been affected by a traumatic brain injury. They called them TBIs for short. Kim instantly felt she was among her people.

The second week was more to her liking. She was scheduled with two employees per day, to shadow them and see what they did for Head Forward. Cassandra was the first. She was a young social worker, one year out of graduate school, and she had completed her first school internship in San Diego at an agency similar to Head Forward. She was drawn to work with this population after helping to take care of her grandmother, who had suffered from dementia. Now, she assisted people with TBIs and their families with finding community resources to make their lives easier. Kim vaguely remembered someone like Cassandra visiting her family's home shortly after her dad came home from rehab, and her mother was so grateful for the support.

She spent time with Robin, a registered nurse, who met with families and helped them find answers to their medically related questions and assisted them with getting medical equipment. Rose was a group facilitator, who led education groups for family and friends of TBI survivors and also sat in on their support groups. Kim's favorite time was spent out in the community with the volunteers, sitting at a booth at a health fair, handing out brochures and Head Forward embossed pens. Some of the volunteers were there to fulfill needed community service hours for school, and others were just there because they liked to help. But they all were friendly and welcomed Kim into their fold immediately.

By February, Kim had a good idea about what went on at Head Forward. She was allowed to attend groups and sit in with Cassandra on home visits. She met families dealing with every stage of grief and recovery due to one of their own having a recent TBI. It brought back memories, some of them hard, some of them easier, about her own family's experience. She was told she would be able to tell her own story further on in the month in group, when she was more familiar with the format and the group members were more familiar with her.

The greatest opportunity came on the day before Valentine's Day, when Kim was invited to attend a neurology clinic with Dr. Singh, the hippy medical director. Clinic was held at the medical center, not Head Forward, as patients were not seen at the agency for their medical care. Dr. Singh drove Kim to the medical center in her two-door light-blue Volkswagen Beetle, which looked like it had seen better days. It had a manual transmission, and Dr. Singh was rough with the gear shift. Kim had to discreetly roll her window down a crack to keep from feeling nauseated by her driving. She vowed if she was ever invited to observe again, she would just meet Dr. Singh at the clinic.

They had six patients to see in a three-hour period, and the time flew by. Each patient was placed in a room, each one with a family member or caregiver by their side, and one by one, Dr. Singh came in to see them. All six patients smiled when she came into the room. Each patient was different from the next. There were four men and two women. One had been in an industrial accident, two in car accidents, one had a fall like Kim's father, but at ground level, and two were survivors of hemorrhages or strokes. Some were verbal, some were very verbal, and others could not speak at all. Three were in wheelchairs. They were all adults, and they ranged in age from 26 to 84. Dr. Singh asked each group if they were okay with Kim observing, and each one agreed, as if this was old hat for them.

Kim watched as Dr. Singh asked each patient questions, even the nonverbal ones, and maintained eye contact as they or their caregiver responded. She answered their questions, reviewed medications, and did brief neurological exams. She also checked on a couple of skin sores, and even removed some stitches from a knee. She ordered new treatment for some and continued what already worked for others.

Some of the family members asked Kim about her internship, and she gave them brief responses. They all lit up when she told them she also had a loved one with a TBI. It made them into an instant family.

Finally, they were done with the clinic, and they drove back to Head Forward in Dr. Singh's tiny car.

"So what did you think?" Dr. Singh asked her.

Kim smiled through her car sickness. "It was so great," she said. "Those families were awesome. They're so tuned in to their family members. They all looked so well taken care of."

Dr. Singh smiled and nodded. "They really are," she said. "Our staff makes sure of it. They're pretty quick to pick up on when something's not right. Like bed sores. You start to see bed sores, you start to file reports and ask questions. You see dirty clothes, or you pick up on body odor, you respond. There's no being polite when people who can't speak for themselves can't speak up. You become their voice. We've had some situations we've dealt with, but I'm happy to say most of them were resolved well."

Kim sat quietly and looked at her shoes. Dr. Singh had said most had resolved well. What about the others? Dr. Singh didn't volunteer any more information, and Kim didn't ask.

"So, Kim, do you have any big plans for Valentine's Day?" Dr. Singh asked, smiling pleasantly as she changed the subject.

Kim smiled, too. "My boyfriend, Carl, and I are going out for dinner. Poor guy's got it tough. My birthday is two weeks after Valentine's Day. He doesn't have much turnaround time!"

Dr. Singh laughed. "Yeah, poor guy!" she said. "But lucky you! Isn't your boyfriend the apprentice over at Farmer's Electric?"

Kim shook her head. "How on Earth do you know that?" she asked. "I know it's a small town, but it just seems like everyone knows everything! I can't hide!"

Dr. Singh laughed again. "Kim, if you wanted to hide, you'd probably have to do something to disguise your New England accent. I went into Farmer's a couple of weeks ago to get an extension cord, and Laine introduced me to his new apprentice, whose name is Carl. And you sound just like him! I took an educated guess." She smiled. "Trust me, if you see a good-looking Indian man about my age walking into the bakery in town, you can assume he's my husband. We're the only Indian family here. There's no hiding in Seska."

"Do you ever get used to it?" Kim wondered.

Dr. Singh nodded. "To some degree. You just start to let it roll off your back."

Kim smiled. "Like water off a duck?"

"You know that one, huh?" Dr. Singh said with a chuckle.

Kim nodded. "Yeah. It's something my dad used to say."

"Your dad?" Dr. Singh said, turning slightly to glance at Kim. "The one with the TBI?"

"Yeah," Kim said. "He was always saying things like that. Helping people and giving advice to my friends. He still does it, but now it's like he's still saying it to a ten-year-old girl. But some of the stuff he tells me, it still means something to me now. It's still relevant."

They pulled roughly into the parking lot at Head Forward, and Dr. Singh whipped into a spot. She cut the engine and then turned to Kim. "Kim, I want you to always remember, it's all relevant. It's all still in there." She pointed to her forehead. "It's just locked away, and he can't get to it. But it's all in there. You're in there. And that's everything."

Kim had heard a lot of pep talks from a lot of people for a lot of years since her dad's accident, but what Dr. Singh said to her in that ten-second span left an impression like a bear paw in wet cement.

"Yeah," she responded with strength in her voice. "It is. It's everything. I just have to remember that."

Dr. Singh nodded. "And everyone here, the staff, the families." She gestured toward the building. "They'll all help you to remember. You're not alone in this anymore."

Kim headed to SCCC and sat through her two afternoon classes. She spent much of the time doodling in the margins of her notebook and thinking about the clinic. The work there seemed so important and was definitely more relevant to her than the three branches of the government.

When class ended, Tami walked out to the parking lot with Kim. "You seemed so distracted today," Tami said. "You usually seem so interested in everything that every instructor says! You must have some major plans for tomorrow." She gave Kim a knowing look.

Kim shook her head. "No, just dinner with Carl. He'll probably do something sweet. But I'm just thinking about my internship. I'm already learning a lot there. It's pretty amazing."

"It's pretty amazing that you got an internship in your first year," Tami marveled. "It's almost unheard of. I'm not gonna even start considering applying for one until next year, and you actually got *invited* to do one! Pretty cool."

They approached Kim's car.

"So Kim, some of my friends and I are gonna go see an Aerosmith cover band, Sweet Emotion, over at Margot's, the under-21 club in Carsonville, a week from tomorrow. I saw you wearing an Aerosmith concert T-shirt the other day, so I thought you're probably a fan. Do you think you and Carl might want to go with us? We'd have to get tickets in advance."

Kim shrugged. "Yeah, it sounds like fun, but I'll have to check with Carl. On the twenty-first?"

Tami nodded.

"It should be okay. My birthday is on the twenty-eighth, and we already have plans to go to Roma and just have tons and tons of sex that day. I'm so glad it's on a Saturday. Sometimes, I just can't get enough of that boy, you know?"

Tami laughed. "You don't mince words, do you, Kim? But yeah, I totally get it. And I love Roma. They're easily the best Italian restaurant in the county. So let me know by Monday, okay? So I can get tickets."

"Sounds good," Kim said, climbing into her car. "Have a great day with David tomorrow."

Kim came home to the aroma of fried chicken heating in the oven.

"Oh, Carl, bless you," Kim said, falling onto the couch. "It smells like dinner is almost ready. Come, sit with me."

She patted the cushion next to her. He sat down and put his arms around her. She closed her eyes.

"Let's talk about Valentine's Day," she said.

IS THAT CLEAR, OR EVERCLEAR?

Kim informed Tami that she and Carl would like to go to Margot's to see Sweet Emotion, and she invited Tami and David over to the apartment before the show. It was an alcohol-free club, so they decided to partake in a few adult beverages before they left. They drew straws, and Carl was assigned as designated driver.

David had gotten his hands on a six-pack of beer and a four-pack of Purple Passion. The girls tried the Purple Passion and proclaimed it tasted just like grape juice. It went down easily. Before they knew it, each girl had consumed two bottles, and they were beginning to feel kind of tipsy. David finished his second beer, Carl drank his Coke, and they decided to head for the club.

They met up with Tami's friends, Sarah and Katie, who were home for the weekend from the University of San Francisco. Sweet Emotion was entertaining, and did sound quite a bit like Aerosmith, but they made Kim feel homesick for the real band, who hailed from the Boston area. They all danced to the music, and Kim enjoyed being at the under-21 club. She thought it might be nice to go back some night with just Carl so they could dance like they did at the prom.

When the set ended, Sarah and Katie wanted to go to another club, Augusta's, also in Carsonville. The girls had not been drinking, so Carl set off in the Escort with Kim, Tami, and David to meet them at the club. Inside, they showed their IDs and had their hands stamped as being under twenty-one. They walked through the packed club, listening to blaring dance music through the giant speakers, and came to the dance floor in the back. The floor was full of dancers of all ages, some holding glasses with cocktails, others taking their dance moves very seriously.

David saw a friend by the bar and went to say hi. He came back about ten minutes later with some drinks and handed one to Kim. She took a tiny sip, and then a quick swig.

She grimaced. "What is this?"

"It's a double shot of Everclear," David yelled back in her ear.

Kim quickly handed the drink back to David. "Everclear?" she said. "Do you have any idea what that stuff can do to a little girl like me?" She instantly regretted not drawing the short straw.

David shrugged. "What do you think was in that Purple Passion you drank earlier?" he asked her.

Kim thought she might get sick. She was not a big drinker, but when she did drink, it was weak little berry wine coolers, with practically no alcohol, and over a long period of time. She looked over at Carl.

"Y'know, I think I'm about ready to head home now," she said.

Carl nodded. He was stone-cold sober and had been keeping himself amused by watching the antics of drunk people dancing. But he'd rather just be back home with Kim if that was what she wanted.

"I'll let Tami and David know we're heading out," he told Kim. She watched him approach the couple and exchange a few words. He came back and said, "They're not ready to leave yet. They're gonna hitch a ride with Sarah and Katie. Katie's driving and she's the DD."

"Okay, let's go then," Kim said, grabbing his hand and pulling him toward the door. When they got outside, Carl stopped.

"Are you okay?" he asked.

Kim nodded but closed her eyes for a few seconds. "I think maybe I drank more than I would have liked," she said. "And I accidentally drank a shot of Everclear in there." She motioned toward the club.

"Oh, that's not good," Carl agreed. "Let's just get you home and get you some water to drink."

Fifteen minutes later, Kim went right to their couch and hung her head down to her knees. "I'm not really drunk," she told Carl. "I just feel sick. Like I swallowed paint thinner."

"I think that stuff is made of paint thinner," he said. "Here." He handed her some water. "I'll get you some crackers, too, to sop that stuff up."

He went back to the kitchen and came back with some saltines. Kim carefully chewed tiny bites of the crackers, then took small sips of water. But she knew it wasn't enough.

"Oh God," she said, getting up off the couch. "I've got to go throw up."

She hurried to the bathroom, and Carl could hear her retching. It made his heart hurt. She came back out in five minutes with a wet washcloth on her forehead.

"I threw up Purple Passion," she moaned. "I'm never gonna drink that stuff again."

Carl led her to the bed and helped her undress and put on her pajamas. She got on the bed, curled up in the fetal position, and moaned.

Carl got ready for bed but sat up reading for over an hour until he knew Kim was asleep. Then he turned out the light. In the morning, she was still sleeping, and he let her rest. He made himself some eggs and toast and ate by himself. When Kim woke up, he offered her some breakfast, but she declined, clutching her stomach.

"I still feel sick," she groaned. "I must be hungover. I never get hangovers." She put on her slippers and shuffled to the couch. She lay down on the couch and groaned some more.

"I'm gonna go see if the Farmers have any Pepto Bismol," Carl said, heading for the door. "Chris swears by it for a hangover. If they don't have any, I can drive by the drug store to pick some up."

Kim turned her head to face him. "Don't leave me for too long," she said. "I don't feel well. I need you here."

Carl ran over to the main house, and luckily Beth found some Pepto in the medicine cabinet. He poured some out for Kim, and she swallowed it down. Soon, she stopped groaning and fell back to sleep. When she woke up, Carl gave her some toast and tea. Twenty minutes later, she was in the bathroom, throwing it back up.

"This isn't a hangover, Kim," he told her when she came out. "There's something else going on. Maybe a stomach bug, or food poisoning."

"Maybe," she responded, rolling back onto the bed. "Whatever it is, it's not good. I feel awful."

"Should I take you to the emergency room?" Carl offered.

"I don't think I need to go to the ER," Kim said. "But I'm going back to sleep."

When Kim fell back to sleep, Carl went back to the Farmers' house. "Beth, Kim's got some sort of stomach bug or something. She can't keep anything down. The Pepto only helped for like an hour. What should I do? I've never taken care of a sick person before!"

"Poor Kim!" Beth said. "She probably wants her mom. I would want my mom. I'll come over to check on her later. Does she have a doctor here?"

"No, neither of us do," Carl admitted. "We've both been so healthy, we haven't even thought of it. But she does have medical insurance through her mom."

Beth nodded. "That's good," she said, sitting Carl down on a kitchen chair. "I'll get you the name of our doctor, and if she's still not feeling better by tomorrow, call and make her an appointment."

Carl sat and waited in the kitchen while Beth went to find him the information. He looked around and couldn't figure out what to do with his hands. He was worried. He wasn't used to worrying. But he couldn't let anything happen to Kim.

Beth came back to the kitchen with a piece of paper, which she handed to Carl. "Here," she said. "Dr. Thomas. She's a family practice doctor, so we all see her. She's very good. They'll get you in pretty quickly. Now go back and keep an eye on her. I'll come over and sit with her after dinner to keep her company so you can get a break. And if she's up for it, help her call her mother."

Carl returned home and sat on the bed, watching Kim sleep. He finished his novel and picked up a new one to read. When she woke up, he gave her some water, which she immediately threw up in the bathroom. He got her a cool washcloth for her head and stroked her hair gently. She felt hot. He assumed she had a fever. He felt helpless. When she was more alert, he dialed her mother's number and explained that Kim was sick. Kim held the phone to her ear, and tears dribbled down her face as her mother reassured her that she would be alright. At six, Beth came over to relieve him and sent him back to the house to eat leftovers from their dinner. He sat with Laine and Benjamin, who tried to keep him distracted while he worried over Kim.

At bedtime, he walked her through her routine and helped her brush her teeth and take her pill. Then he put her to bed. Twenty minutes later, she was up again. After about an hour in and out of the bathroom, she finally fell asleep for the night.

The next day was more of the same. When Beth came to check in, they decided to call the doctor. Carl was reassured by the nurse that there was indeed a bad stomach virus going around at SCCC, but just to be sure, she scheduled her to come in to see Dr. Thomas the next morning. Beth told Laine that Carl was staying home with Kim for the day. He agreed this was a good idea. Beth also contacted Head Forward to let them know that Kim would not be in for at least the next couple of days due to illness.

Carl kept trying to get something into Kim, but she couldn't keep anything down. He made her sip slowly on water and cuddled with her in bed when she craved the company.

On Tuesday, Carl helped Kim into her sweatpants and shirt and helped her put her long hair into a ponytail. He slid shoes on her feet and walked her out to the car holding a brown paper bag in case she needed to get sick. They drove to the medical center and Carl maneuvered her into the clinic. Kim checked in at the desk and Carl helped her fill out her new patient forms while she leaned against him in her chair with her eyes closed. Carl presented her insurance card, and the receptionist took a photocopy. They were promised to be put in a room soon.

Fifteen minutes later, Dr. Thomas entered the exam room and introduced herself. She looked at Kim. "Oh, you don't look like you feel well at all," she said sympathetically.

"I don't," Kim confirmed. She listed her symptoms while Dr. Thomas took notes.

"When did it start?" she asked.

"Saturday night," Kim stated. "I thought maybe I drank some bad alcohol, but then it just kept getting worse."

Dr. Thomas put the chart down and approached Kim on the exam table. She reached out to feel her lymph nodes. "Who is this with you?" she asked Kim. Then she felt the front of her neck.

"Carl," Kim croaked out. "My boyfriend. He's been taking care of me."

Dr. Thomas looked toward Carl and smiled. Carl smiled but squirmed in his chair. "Is it okay to talk in front of Carl?" she asked.

Kim nodded. "Yes, I want him here with me," she said. "Please don't make him go."

"I won't," the doctor promised. "Any other medical issues, Kim?" she asked as she shined a light in Kim's left ear, then her right ear.

"None," Kim said.

"Medications? Say aah real quick."

"Aah," Kim said, and then, "just birth control pills."

"Good," Dr. Thomas said. She had Kim lie back and then pressed on her stomach. Then she sat her up and listened to her heart and lungs. "So Kim, I'm pretty sure you have the virus that we've seen going around SCCC. Your symptoms are consistent, and I'm not seeing anything else that's concerning me. You can continue to take in fluids and any food you can keep down, and take Tylenol for fever. If it's okay with you, I'd like to run some labs today just to get a baseline and to make sure I'm not missing anything from my exam. You can expect the symptoms to last a couple more days or so, just until it runs its course. If anything gets worse, I want you to contact my office or go to the emergency room. I'm also just going to get a quick pregnancy test to rule that out, just due to your age and symptoms."

"Really?" Kim asked. "Even though I'm on the pill?"

"We just want to cover all the bases, Kim. I'm sure you know your body best, but it's just routine. So I don't need to see you back for follow up unless needed, but you should check to see when your last pelvic exam was with your last doctor, and make an appointment with us for one year. It was really nice to meet you both."

Carl helped Kim back into her shoes, and they ended their visit at the lab. When they got home, Kim climbed right back to bed. Carl placed a glass of water with a straw on her nightstand and her stuffed giraffe, Raffy, up against her arm. Kim managed a slight smile.

Her symptoms continued into the next day, and Beth came and checked on her while Carl went to work. On Thursday, she managed to keep down some ginger ale and some crackers and seemed to be on the road to recovery. But then on Friday, the day before her birthday, Kim started to cough and complain of a sore throat. Soon after, Beth came over and announced that Benjamin's school had an outbreak of strep throat, and Benjamin was in bed, coughing.

At another trip to Dr. Thomas, Kim was informed that all her previous lab tests were negative, but it was pretty clear she now had strep. She was given a throat culture and was started on antibiotics, and her birthday celebration was postponed. Everyone from home who called to wish her a happy birthday was told to call back later in the week. Her fever spiked, and she slept most of each day, Carl and Beth taking turns taking care of her. Finally, on the Tuesday after her birthday, Kim woke up fever free and hungry. By the next day, she was up, able to take a shower on her own, and spent some time outside getting some much-needed fresh air. On Thursday, she was well enough to worry about how far behind she had fallen in school. By Friday, she was ready to reschedule her birthday. Her new birthday was Sunday, March eighth, and Carl made a new reservation at Roma.

KIM GETS HER DAY

Kim spent most of Saturday resting and eating. She wanted to be at her best on Sunday, her rescheduled birthday. When she woke up Sunday morning, Carl was ready to get her day started right.

"I thought you'd be naked," she teased as she rolled over to face him.

Carl grinned. "I know how much you like to undress me," he said. He lifted his arms. "Have at me."

She smiled and crawled toward him on the bed. "You are so good to me," she said. Then she grabbed the hem of his T-shirt with her teeth.

After breakfast, they headed out to Modesto in the Escort. It was about a half hour drive to the seat of Stanislaus County. They had no agenda but to explore, shop, and eat lunch, and maybe check out a museum or two. They had a reservation at Roma at seven, so they had nothing but time. It was a cool afternoon, and Carl was wearing his black suede jacket. Kim was wearing a peasant skirt, a T-shirt under her denim jacket, and her knee-high black boots. She laced her arm through Carl's as they walked through town, window shopping and going into stores that caught their interest.

At noon, they found a little bistro set apart from the crowded main drag. Kim got a chicken salad sandwich and a fruit cup, and Carl had a French dip and steak fries. They shared a brownie a la mode before moving on to their next stop, the McHenry Museum. After the tour, they returned to the shops. Kim found a quilt in a vintage store that matched their bedroom decor, and Carl decided to get it for her as an added birthday gift. When they were done shopping, it was close to three o'clock, and they were ready to be done with Modesto. They walked back to the car, which they had parked in the far end of the municipal lot under a shady tree. There were no other cars nearby.

"Carl," Kim said, turning to look at him, "we've been remarkably restrained for one of our birthdays. I think we've only done it once today?"

Carl feigned shock. "I think you're right," he confirmed. "We're running out of daylight. What should we do?"

Kim smiled. "Well," she said, shaking her bag with the quilt in her hand. "I think we're gonna get a lot of mileage out of this quilt over time. Should we take it for a test drive?"

"Are you suggesting doing it in the car, prom style?" Carl asked.

"Car, yes," Kim said. "Prom style, no. Back seat, yes. Quilt, yes. Me on top?"

"Yes," Carl said softly, grabbing her around the waist and kissing her. "Yes, yes, and yes."

He moved her toward the car, and they discretely got in the back seat.

Twenty minutes later, they were on the road back to Seska. "That's gonna be a new birthday tradition," Kim said as she neatened her hair while looking in the visor mirror. "Sex in the back seat."

"I'll make a reservation for next year," Carl promised.

They got home, and Kim wanted to take a nap. She took off her skirt, and Carl took off his pants, and they crawled under the covers. Carl pulled the new quilt up over them and spooned her. Tiger jumped up on top of them, and together they all slept.

Before they left for dinner, they took advantage of their shared shower, and Kim's knees almost buckled beneath her. She reached up and whispered in Carl's ear. "Best birthday *ever*," she told him.

"Best birthday girl ever," Carl whispered back.

Roma's was as wonderful as they remembered, and they partook of the same entrees they'd had the last time they were there. They finished off by sharing a chocolate lava cake. They drove home feeling full and satisfied, but it being Kim's rescheduled birthday, they had room for a little more satisfaction.

"Your turn," Carl told her as they stripped each other of clothes. "Anything new you want to try?"

Kim nodded. "There is," she told him, "but I'm kind of embarrassed to say it out loud."

"Can you whisper it to me?" Carl asked. "No-gossip zone. I won't tell."

Kim nodded and reached up to whisper in his ear.

Carl looked her in the eyes. "Both of us at the same time?" he asked.

Kim nodded shyly. "Yeah," she confirmed.

Now Carl smiled. "I'm game if you are," he said, and he pulled her down with him on the bed.

KIM BITES OFF MORE THAN SHE CAN CHEW

Kim had missed a lot of school and her internship, and she spent the next couple of weeks doing everything she could to catch up. She volunteered to attend an educational event for Head Forward on a Saturday, to give out brochures and pens. She met with her instructors to get extra-credit assignments to help raise her grades. Since the virus had been so prevalent on campus, everyone was willing to help students catch up, especially those as motivated as Kim.

As April approached, Kim started to feel draggy and tired. She figured she'd been pushing herself too hard.

"Kim, you've taken on a lot more than most first-year students," Carl told her. "Four classes and twelve hours per week at your internship is a lot. Maybe next semester, you can either cut your hours back at Head Forward, or only take three classes. You'll still be getting enough credits to stay on track."

Kim shook her head. "I'm just worn out because I was sick, and I had to do so much to catch up," she protested. "I want to take on more hours at Head Forward over the summer and take two classes. I just need to structure my time better."

Carl sighed. "It's like you're trying to do it all at once," he said. "You have time. You're not gonna miss anything if you slow down a little."

Kim nodded, but she didn't agree. She felt like she could easily fall behind. She felt like everything good that had happened to her this year could somehow go away next year, and she'd have to start all over. She wanted to do as much as she could right now, to take advantage of what she was being offered.

Laine had gotten four tickets to the San Francisco Giants opening day game at Candlestick Park. He asked Carl and Kim to come with him and Beth to watch the Giants play the Padres. Carl had accepted, but as the time got closer, Kim started to beg out.

"I don't really feel like going to San Francisco," she told Carl the day before the game. "I'm tired, and I really have too much homework to do. Why don't you just go with Laine and Beth and I'll stay home."

Carl protested. "But I want to go with you," he told her. "It's our weekend. I want to spend time with you. We can both just stay home." He put his arms around her and held her to him. She closed her eyes.

"Carl, I think you should go to the game," she said. "I'm tired and cranky, and I just want to study. I really want to ace my Intro to Brain class final next month, and I have a lot of reading to do. I'm not gonna be any fun to be around anyway."

Carl finally relented. "I'll ask Laine if we can bring David," he said. "He's a big Giants fan. But I get you all to myself next weekend, though, okay?"

Kim smiled at him. "Yes, of course," she said.

On Sunday, Carl got ready to go while Kim lay on the bed, reading her neurology book. "Don't forget to eat," he told her. "You lost some weight when you were sick. I'm worried that if I don't make you lunch, you'll just forget to eat." He leaned over to kiss her. "I wish you were coming with us," he whispered in her ear. "I'll miss you."

Kim kissed his cheek. "You'll see me when you get back," she told him. "I'm not going anywhere."

After Carl left, Kim put down her book. She wasn't following the words. It was like she was reading them backward. She got up to go to the bathroom, and the room started to spin. She sat down quickly. Then she ran to the bathroom and threw up.

When she came back, she felt panicked. She knew she was sick again. She knew she could not afford to be sick again with all the work she had to do. But she had to admit to herself, she'd known something was going on. She let herself do too much, and now she was having a relapse of her virus or her infection. She picked up the phone and called her mom.

"Mom," she said when her mother answered. "I'm getting sick again. I'm dizzy and throwing up. And I just feel awful."

Her mother sighed. "Kimmy," she said, "this is just your luck! To have a stomach virus, then strep, then to get sick again! I'm worried that you're not taking care of yourself well enough."

Kim started to cry. "But I am, Mom," she said. "I'm taking my vitamins, I'm eating what I'm supposed to eat, and I'm trying to get enough sleep, but it's been so hard to fall asleep! I just want to feel better already!"

"Kim, you need to go back and see that doctor," her mother said. "Just to make sure there's nothing wrong. You're probably just working too hard, or maybe that virus is just getting passed around again. Will you promise me that you'll call tomorrow to make an appointment?"

Kim sniffed. "I promise, Mom."

"Good," Mrs. Drake said. "Have Carl make you some toast and soup for lunch. They might help settle your stomach."

"Carl's not here," Kim told her mother. "He went to the baseball game in San Francisco for the day."

"So you're alone all day?" her mother asked, sounding annoyed.

"Mom, don't get upset with Carl," Kim said. "He wanted me to go with him, and when I told him no, he wanted to stay home with me. But he's been taking such good care of me, I just wanted him to go and have a good day. I didn't tell him I was feeling so bad."

"Kimmy," her mother said softly. "Carl wants to be able to take care of you when you need him. And just like usual, *you're* the one trying to take care of *him*. You've been this way since you started helping me take care of Dad. Kim, you've got to let people take care of you. You know what they say about caring for the caregiver, right?"

"What?" Kim asked.

Mrs. Drake laughed. "Well, basically that. That you have to take care of the caregivers!"

Kim laughed, and then sniffed again. "Okay, Mom, I'll tell him when he gets home tonight. I promise."

"Okay, babe, good," her mom said. "I'm gonna go check on Dad. Do you have someone there you can call if you need help right away?"

"Beth's mom is at the house with the kids," Kim told her. "I can just call the house or go over there if I need to."

"Good. I'll call you later then. Feel better, Kim. I love you."

"Love you too, Mom." Kim hung up the phone.

She tried to stand and found herself more steady on her feet. She put on her slippers and went to the kitchen. She felt slightly dizzy, but okay. She made herself some tea and a slice of toast. She ate the toast slowly and sipped the tea. It appeared to want to stay down. After she was satisfied that she wasn't going to vomit, she headed for the couch and turned on the TV. Shortly after, she fell asleep on the couch in front of the Giants game.

Carl got home from the afternoon game at seven. He let himself in and found Kim still in her pajamas in bed, reading her novel.

"Hey, Kim," he said, approaching her. "You okay?"

Kim managed a grin. "I'm a bit better now, but to be honest, I was feeling pretty rough earlier," she told him. "I called my mom, and she made me promise to call and make a doctor's appointment tomorrow, just to make sure I don't still have anything going on from when I was sick. But I think I'll be okay to go to class tomorrow. How was the game?"

Carl sat down on the edge of the bed. "It was fun. The Giants won, 4–3." He took her hand. "Kim, I'm worried about you. Do I need to be worried again?"

Kim could see that Carl was already worried by his furrowed brow and intense stare. It was a new experience for him, and it scared him. She gave him what she hoped was a reassuring smile. "I think I'm okay," she told him honestly. "I really do feel better than I did right after you left. But I do think it's a good idea to get checked out anyway. Just to make sure I don't need more antibiotics or something."

Carl rubbed her hand. "Okay," he said. "Do you want me to go with you to the doctor?"

Kim shook her head. "No, I don't think you need to. I'll be okay to go by myself."

"At least let me make you some soup," he offered.

Kim looked at Carl's face, and he looked like a sad puppy. She could not say no to that face. "I would love some soup," she told him gratefully.

CARL MAKES SOUP

Kim called Seska Family Care the next morning and was told they had a cancellation that she could fill that afternoon. She went to class and was able to get through her lectures without falling asleep or leaving to vomit. She saw that as a good sign. But she still did not feel well.

"I'm here for a 2:15 appointment with Dr. Thomas," Kim told the woman behind the sliding glass window when she pulled back the panel at the doctor's office. "I'm Kim Drake."

The receptionist checked her schedule book. "Yes, I see you here on the schedule. The nurse will be out to get you in a minute. Any change to your insurance?"

"No, not since I was here last," Kim said.

"Please take a seat," she was told.

Kim sat down in the row of chairs and picked up a magazine. She was leafing through the pages and stopped on an article that she realized was written in Spanish. She threw the magazine down and decided not to try again. She was tired, and her stomach hurt. She just wanted the doctor to tell her she was fine so she could go do Brain Studies lab, go home and eat, and go to bed.

"Ms. Drake," said a nurse as she opened the door to the back hallway and exam rooms. Kim followed her back to room 3 and sat on the exam table. The nurse took her blood pressure, pulse, and temperature. Then she asked what brought her in. She made notes in Kim's chart, then told her the doctor would be right in.

Kim waited for ten minutes, kicking her legs back and forth under the exam table like she was sitting on the rim of a swimming pool. Finally, the door opened and Dr. Thomas came in.

"Hello, Kim," she said, glancing up from her chart. "It looks like you've been getting more symptoms that you think might be related to the strep infection or the virus you had last month. Tell me what's been happening?"

"For one, I've been feeling queasy," Kim told her. "Kind of like when I was taking antibiotics. I don't have much appetite, and I'm really tired. Sometimes, I feel like I'm gonna fall asleep in class. But then I've been having trouble falling asleep at night. I haven't been vomiting as much as I was before, but sometimes I get really nauseated. Do you think maybe I need to take more antibiotics? Maybe I need another few days."

Dr. Thomas nodded. "It's one possibility," she said. "Some bacteria are more resistant, or perhaps we didn't give you the right type." She reached out to feel Kim's neck. "Do you have a sore throat at all?"

"No," Kim said, "that's gone. I think the antibiotics knocked that out."

"Open and say aah," Dr. Thomas said.

"Aah," Kim said obediently as she felt the tongue depressor in her mouth and felt she might gag.

"Throat looks good," Dr. Thomas agreed. "Let me listen to your heart and lungs real quick."

The doctor completed her exam, and then sat on the rolling chair and rolled over to Kim.

"Kim, it is possible you have a relapse of your infection," she told her, "but I'm in no hurry to get you back on antibiotics until we get more information. Especially if you are having nausea. I'm going to order some labs, just to be sure. Did we get a pregnancy test last time you were here? Oh, yes, I see it here. It was negative. I'm going to do a repeat of that to rule it out based on your symptoms. If I see anything concerning, I'd be happy to prescribe more antibiotics, but if not, let's just wait it out a bit. It could be a virus, and as you know, we don't treat those with antibiotics. Those take rest, hydration, and time. You can start right now with rest and hydration. Try to drink six to eight glasses of water per day. So why don't you stop at the lab before you go, and we'll call you with the results when they come in, probably tomorrow afternoon. Sound like a plan?"

Kim nodded. "Okay, thanks. I just won't worry about anything until I hear back."

Dr. Thomas smiled at her. "Alright then. Have a good afternoon, and call if you have any questions going forward."

Kim jumped off the exam table, slipped on her shoes, got the after-visit summary from the nurse, and headed for her neurology lab.

When Kim came home from her lab at dinner time, she wasn't feeling very hungry. "Do you mind if we just have another can of soup for dinner?" she asked Carl, placing her purse on the table and sitting down in the chair.

"You're still not feeling well?" Carl asked, grabbing the saucepan and a can of soup from the cupboard. "What did the doctor say?"

He opened the lid with a can opener, poured the contents of the soup in the pan, and added a can of water from the tap. He put it on the burner and turned on the heat.

"She said that it could be the same thing I had last month. It might just be another virus," she told him. "The strep is gone, though. She took some more lab tests just to be sure. She told me to rest and drink lots of fluids."

The phone on the wall next to the table rang. Carl stirred the pot while Kim got up to get the phone.

"Hello?" she said into the receiver, twirling around to untangle the long cord.

"Hi, can I speak to Kim Drake?" asked a female voice.

"This is Kim Drake."

"Hi, Kim, this is Dr. Thomas from Seska Family Care. I met with you earlier today? I'm calling with your lab test results."

"That was fast. Was everything okay?" Kim asked nervously. She had never had a doctor call her with lab results. It was usually a nurse or a receptionist. Carl looked up from the stove and they made eye contact.

"Everything else looks good, Kim," the doctor told her, "but there's one result we need to discuss. Your pregnancy test came back positive."

Kim felt all the blood rush out of her face. "Excuse me?" she said. "I guess I had forgotten you even ordered that. Did you say it was positive?"

"Yes, Kim, it's positive. You're pregnant." She paused for a moment. "I can tell this is an unexpected result. I'm thinking we should set you up for a follow-up appointment so you can get more information and we can make a plan going forward."

Kim was silent for several seconds. "Can you hold on a second?" she asked the doctor.

"Of course."

Kim took the phone from her ear and covered the mouthpiece with her hand. She looked at Carl. He looked right back.

"I'm pregnant."

The spoon slipped from Carl's grasp and hit the floor.

"What?" he asked, although he had clearly heard what she said.

Kim put the phone back to her ear. "Doctor, I don't understand," she said. "I'm on the pill. I take the pill every day. How could I be pregnant? I've been so careful!"

"Kim, the pill is pretty effective," Dr. Thomas said, "but it's not one hundred percent. There are lots of variables involved. You say you haven't missed a dose?"

"No! Never!" Kim insisted. "Not since I started when I was fifteen!"

"We had you on antibiotics several weeks ago, and some people think those can interfere with the pill," Dr. Thomas told her, "but there's just not enough conclusive research to prove that yet. When you were sick, you still took your pills?"

"Yes," Kim said. "I made sure to take them every day, even when I was so sick, I couldn't keep any food down. I didn't want to miss any and get off track."

"Kim," Dr. Thomas asked gently, "think about it. Did you vomit after taking your pills? Is it possible you weren't keeping those down either?"

"Oh," Kim said, and she sat down hard on the kitchen chair. "Oh my God, I'm such a moron. I never even thought of that." Carl knelt down beside her on the kitchen floor and watched her face.

"Well, no matter how it happened, Kim," the doctor said, "the fact is, you're pregnant now, and you need medical follow-up. Let's go ahead and make an appointment for you to come in and see me later this week, and we can talk, and if you want, we can make you a referral to an obstetrician. We have wonderful OBs at our clinic. I'll have our scheduler call you tomorrow morning and we'll get you in quickly. In the meantime, just relax, okay? Take it easy, and know that you are a healthy and strong young woman. We'll make sure you have the best possible outcome. We'll talk soon, okay?"

"Okay, thank you." Kim ended the call and hung up the phone. She turned to Carl and stared at his face.

"Oh my God, Carl," she said, squatting down on the floor and covering her face with her hands. "Oh my God, oh my God!"

Carl put his hands on both of Kim's shoulders to steady her. "Oh my God, Kim," he said.

Kim's breath came faster until she felt she was starting to hyperventilate.

"Carl, I can't breathe," she said, falling on her knees on the floor and flailing her hands in desperation. "There's no air, I can't breathe! Where did the air go?"

Carl got her to her feet and slowly walked her to the bed.

"Sit," he said. She did.

He ran to the kitchen and got a paper lunch bag, then ran back to Kim. He handed her the bag.

"Here," he said. "Breathe into this if you need to." He sat down beside her and put his arm around her shoulders. She looked at the bag, and then at Carl, and then leaned against Carl's chest. She took a few deep breaths, and slowly, over a few minutes, her breathing started to go back to normal without the bag.

"I'm okay," she told him, and then she closed her eyes and took another breath. "I'm okay," she said again.

Carl realized that he had been holding his own breath. He exhaled and followed Kim's lead with slow breaths.

"You're okay," he told her. "You're okay," he said again. He pulled her closer and kissed her hair above her ear. They sat like that for some time, breathing.

Kim's head jolted up. "Did you turn off the stove?" she asked in a panic.

Carl nodded. "I did," he assured her.

Kim leaned back against his side. "Okay," she said. They sat in silence.

Carl finally broke the silence. "I'm gonna go finish heating up the soup," he said, "and then we're both gonna eat the soup, okay? We need to eat the soup."

Kim looked at Carl's face and nodded. "Okay," she agreed. She was glad that he had come up with something for them to do. If he hadn't, they would have had to just sit on the bed for the rest of the night.

Carl finished heating the soup and poured their portions into their bowls. They sat down at the table and ate spoonful after spoonful until there were just dregs left in their bowls. Kim sat at the table while Carl cleared their bowls and spoons, and then washed them in the sink along with the saucepan. Then he turned to Kim, who had been staring at the back of his head.

"What should we do now?" he asked her.

It was a loaded question. She chose her answer carefully. "I want to watch TV. Let's go watch TV."

"Okay." Carl reached out for her hand and she gave it to him. He pulled her up and into his arms and hugged her tight. They stood like that for a couple of minutes in silence. Then Carl let go. "TV now," he said, and he led her to the couch. He turned on the set, changed the channel to a program they both liked, and went to the bed to get the quilt.

He set the quilt down on top of Kim, then cozied up close to her under the spread. She laid her head on his shoulder. Tiger jumped immediately on the couch and stretched across both of their laps, purring. They took turns patting his back, wordlessly watching show after show, and only getting up to use the bathroom.

Eventually it was time for bed, and still no words were spoken about the call from the doctor. Carl assumed Kim was in shock. He was in shock. They both got up from the couch and went into the bathroom to get ready for bed. Kim took her pill pack out of the medicine cabinet like she did every night, stared at it in her hand, then dropped it into the trash can.

Finally, they crawled into bed. Carl curled around Kim like a spoon. They both lay awake and silent with their eyes focused straight ahead in the dark until eventually they were both mercifully taken by sleep.

I HAVE TO TELL YOU SOMETHING

The next morning, Carl was up and showered and ready to meet Laine at his truck before Kim even woke up. She didn't have class until one and would be going to Head Forward at nine. She stirred as he was heading toward the door to go.

"Bye, Carl," she called out groggily.

He went over to the bed and kissed her on the forehead. "Bye Kim," he said softly. "I'll see you tonight. We'll talk about it then, okay?"

Kim nodded as her eyes closed again. "Okay," she agreed. "We'll talk about it tonight."

Laine was already in the truck when Carl got there, and he started the engine. "We're heading over to Carsonville," he told Carl. "Heating and cooling system failure at the hair salon. They had someone else from Severton doing their ongoing maintenance. Not anymore." He put the truck in drive and headed to the next town over by the back streets.

Laine made small talk as he drove and told a funny story about something that Claire had done the night before. Carl did his best to act like everything was normal, laughing when he was expected to.

They arrived at the job site, and Laine handed equipment to Carl to haul up the stairs. They entered the building and were directed to the problem area. They found the breaker box and turned off the power to the system. They climbed the stairs and entered the crawl space in the attic. Laine barked instructions to Carl. Carl did what he was told and handed Laine tools before he asked for them. Laine asked Carl what next steps he would take, and Carl predicted correctly each time.

Laine came out of the crawl space to inspect a wire under the light. Carl stood still and watched silently. Laine made a face at him. "Something's different about you today," Laine said. "You just don't seem like yourself. I usually have to shut you up at some point so I can concentrate on the work, but you've barely said a word all day. What's going on with you? You and Kim have a fight or something?"

"No," Carl answered tentatively. "No, we're getting along great." He wasn't sure he could say it out loud. He hadn't said it out loud yet. Saying it out loud might make it real. "It's just that Kim is . . . pregnant."

Laine turned to face him, but his expression didn't change. "Kim's pregnant?"

It was like Laine asked him if it was going to rain that day. "Yeah," Carl answered.

"Hmm," Laine said, turning his attention back to the exposed wire. "So what are you going to do about it?"

"I guess we're gonna have a baby," Carl said. "If it's a boy, I wanna name him Pedro."

Laine's only movement was a twitch at the right side of his mouth. "Pedro?" he said. "Pedro *Bishop*?"

Carl shrugged. "Well, my name is Carlos Bishop, and my mom is Puerto Rican," he explained. "I do have other relatives besides the Bishops and the Farmers, you know."

"I know your name is Carlos, Carl," Laine said. "I have a copy of your Social Security card in your employee file. I might also have your birth announcement in a box in my attic somewhere."

He reached back and handed Carl a pair of work gloves. "Put these on and help me hold these back," he instructed, moving aside to make room for Carl and pointing at the mass of wiring in the crawlspace.

"But what I meant is, what are you gonna do? Have you talked about it? Will you get married? Move back to Massachusetts? Is Kim even okay with having a baby? Last time I heard, women still had a choice about these things."

Carl kept his eyes focused on the job before him, although his thoughts were scattered in all directions. "No, we really didn't get much past the panic attacks last night when the doctor called and said the test came out positive," he admitted. "We both didn't even know it was a possibility. I had to help Kim stop hyperventilating. Then it was like nothing had happened the rest of the night, except both of us were walking around like zombies."

"Yeah," Laine grunted from inside the crawl space. "I hear the best way to deal with an unexpected pregnancy is just to ignore it, like it never happened."

"All you Farmers are the same," Carl lamented. "Always making jokes, but never laughing at them."

"That's called deadpanning," Laine explained, taking a step toward Carl. "Hand me that spool right there and watch what I'm doing."

Carl watched as Laine replaced the frayed wire and took mental notes. He thought about someday mentoring his own son and teaching him all his electrical skills. Since he currently had only basic electrical skills, and exactly zero parenting experience, it was a tough picture to draw in his head.

"Pick up that trash and carry it out with you," Laine instructed a few minutes later. "We're going down to turn the power back on and try not to burn the building down in the process."

Carl followed Laine down the stairs and into the basement. He threw the garbage in the large can and watched as Laine flipped the breaker switch. He could hear a whirring noise coming from the environmental system above them.

"So, I take it you and Kim are gonna talk about it tonight?" Laine asked.

"Yeah, we agreed to talk later," Carl said. "I don't know what that's gonna look like. I mean, I'll support her, no matter what she wants to do. If she wants to have a baby, we'll have a baby. I mean, I'll do whatever I have to do. But you know, we've never even talked about marriage and kids. I mean, we're right out of high school! It's not something I've really considered. I mean, I'm not saying it's not something I would ever consider, but I'm not sure I would want to get married just because she's pregnant. I mean, I think we have a pretty good thing going. Maybe we should just wait to see what happens."

"Carl," Laine said, giving him a serious look. "What do you think is happening here? You have this girl, this wonderful girl, who was willing to pick up and follow you across the country so you could have a better shot at a good future. She was willing to leave her family, her friends, her home, to come all the way here with you, to support you."

"Yeah, I still don't get why she did that."

Laine gave him a look of concern. "Maybe it would be a good idea to ask her that question," he suggested. "Maybe the two of you should talk about what you both want. About where this is headed. Carl, this is serious stuff. This isn't a game. You're talking about a baby. If you both want the same things, great. If you don't, you should decide that now. Don't put it off until the decision is made for you."

He patted Carl on the shoulder. "But first," he said, "I think there's something else the two of you need to talk about."

Carl nodded. "Yeah," he agreed. "We'll talk. I just hope I say the right thing."

Laine smiled kindly at his cousin. "Just remember, Kim may be tough on the outside, but that little girl is probably scared to death right now. Just ask her how she is. Let her talk. You'll have your turn to talk, but let her go first. Listen to what she says. And respond to her based on that. If she feels heard, she'll be much more willing to listen to you. And by no means should you tell her what she needs to do. That's not your call."

Carl nodded. It wasn't easy for him to listen without talking. It would be new for him. But so was having a pregnant girlfriend. All bets were off now.

While Carl was in the field talking to Laine, Kim was sitting at her little desk at Head Forward, staring at the wall and thinking. She figured that thinking was better than the blank mind she'd had the previous night.

She couldn't believe she was pregnant. It was as though the doctor called the wrong patient and made a mistake. But she knew that it had to be true. All the pieces fit into place, and she was still feeling like crap.

She had been so careful, for so long. She couldn't understand how she had messed this up so bad. She finally had something good going for her in her life; she liked her classes, and she loved her internship. Things were going smoothly for Carl at his apprenticeship. They were getting along so well. Throwing a baby in this mix seemed almost impossible.

But she loved Carl, and this was his baby. She had the potential to grow Carl's baby inside her, and someday hold it in her arms. She wasn't going to lie to herself; she'd thought about it from time to time back in high school when she saw Carl with kids and thought he would make a great dad. *This could actually be Pedro Bishop,* she thought.

She knew she had a choice. She lived in a country where women could make decisions about when was the right time to have a baby. But one of the reasons she took the pill so seriously was so that she'd never have to get to the point where she'd have to make that choice. But now, ironically, there was no choice; she had to choose.

This wasn't a decision she would make lightly. She needed to talk it through. She knew that she would not have privacy at the agency, but she had to talk to someone before she saw Carl after school, so she could have an idea what she wanted to do, so she could present it to him in a little package, wrapped with a tight bow.

Kim decided to head home after her internship hours and before class. If she was late for class, she'd be late for class. She was always on time, so she would be forgiven.

At 12:15, she stepped into the empty unit, made sure the door was closed and locked, and picked up the phone.

"Mom," she said when her mother picked up. "I have a very big, big problem, and I really need your help."

"Kim, are you okay?" Mrs. Drake asked.

"Mom, I went to the doctor like you told me yesterday, and I'm okay, well, sort of. Mom, somehow I managed to get pregnant."

"Kim!" her mother exclaimed. "Oh my God! I was not expecting that. Oh, my. Are you okay? Is everything okay?"

"I'm fine, Mom. I'm still a bit queasy, but not as bad right now. Mom, I've got to decide what to do. I don't know if I'm ready for this. I'm only nineteen!"

"Oh, Kimmy," her mom said. "I know. I know exactly what that's like. It's so scary. I remember it like it was yesterday. Have you told Carl?"

"Yes, Carl knows. But we haven't discussed anything yet. I kind of froze up after I spoke to the doctor on the phone, and we just, well, kind of ignored the whole thing last night. But we said we'd talk tonight. I don't know what to say. I mean, neither one of us signed up for this. We haven't talked about what would happen. . . . I didn't think we'd need to!"

"Oh babe," Mrs. Drake sighed. "It's such a good thing to have the ability to make a choice like this, but that doesn't make it easy to choose. Do you have any idea what you want to do?"

"Mom, I don't know. I was awake most of the night, and my mind was either empty or cluttered. I mean, this is Carl, not some random guy. What would it be like to have a baby with Carl? But on the other hand, what would things be like if we didn't?"

"Kim, do you want my opinion, or do you just want me to help you work through your thoughts?"

Kim thought about it. "From anyone else, I'd say no on opinions, Mom. But I do want to know what you think."

"Well, I think you could go forward either way," Mrs. Drake said. "I think you and Carl have a strong relationship and could weather either choice. But I want to let you know, Kim, that if you do decide to go ahead with the pregnancy, I'll do whatever I can to help you. I'm not sure what you'd need, but you would just need to ask. I think you and Carl would be able to do it. And for what it's worth, I think you would make good parents. And on the other side, if you don't go ahead with it, I'll be here for you, to support you. Again, whatever you'd need."

"You really think we'd be good parents?" Kim asked.

"I do, Kim, either now or in the future. Whenever you decide to have kids, you'll be great. Remember, I've seen you with your brothers and sisters. You have wonderful instincts."

Kim paused. "Mom, I don't know. I think I need to spend a bit of time thinking about what I'd feel like if I made either choice. I mean, this isn't like choosing a prom dress. It's a big deal."

"It is a big deal, Kim, and one that could turn the course of your life. But I know you'll make the right decision for you. You're a smart woman. You'll work this out."

When they ended the call, Kim sat on the couch and thought. She thought about what it would look like to have a baby crawling around the floor of the apartment unit and sleeping in a crib by the bed. She imagined herself boiling bottles on the stove. She thought of Carl, holding a tiny baby in his arms, and rocking it back and forth. She smiled. Then she looked down and realized she had her hand over her belly, and tears were running down her face. She went into the bathroom and splashed cold water on her face, combed her hair, and got ready to leave for class.

FINGER-LICKIN' GOOD

Carl had Laine stop on their way home for a bucket of chicken, cole slaw, mashed potatoes, and rolls. He arrived home before Kim and set the food on the small table in the kitchen. He took out two mismatched dinner plates, serving spoons, and forks. He poured water into two large drinking glasses. Then he sat and waited. His stomach growled as the chicken aroma wafted around the kitchen, but he wasn't going to start eating without Kim.

Five minutes later, he heard the screen door handle click, and Kim walked in through the kitchen door. In her hands was a bucket of chicken and a bag full of sides from Kentucky Fried Chicken. She looked at the table, looked at Carl, and looked back at the table. Then she laughed.

Carl smiled and released his breath. They both loved fried chicken. It was one of the things they totally had in common.

Kim placed the second set of food on the table and sat heavily in the chair. "Talk and then eat, or eat then talk?" she asked.

Carl looked at the food. "Eat then talk," he announced.

"Right answer," Kim agreed, and they dug in. They ate silently until there was a pile of discarded bones and drips of gravy on each plate. Then they sat quietly, almost daring each other to speak. Carl wanted to fill the silent void, but he bit his tongue.

Kim finally spoke. "I'm pregnant."

"I heard that somewhere," Carl responded.

"So you're kinda pregnant too," she told him. "But not really, so I don't want to hear any complaints from you about morning sickness or sympathy weight gain."

"I won't say a thing," he promised.

We're having this baby, he thought. *She decided. We'll have to tell people we're pregnant. There's gonna be a baby. I'm gonna love this baby as much as I love you, Kim.*

He waited.

"So we don't have to get married or anything," Kim announced. "I mean, we should only get married someday if it's something we decided to do. I mean, I'm not even sure how I feel about marriage yet."

Except that I don't ever want to marry anyone but you Carl, she thought.

Carl nodded. "Okay," he said. "But it's always there if we decide to do it. But we don't have to." He hadn't said anything stupid so far. It seemed that hardly saying anything was the trick.

"I didn't get pregnant on purpose," Kim said defensively. "I just want you to know that."

Carl put his hand over hers and squeezed. "Kim, I would never think you would do anything like that. I hope you know that. "

She nodded. "I know. But I just needed to say it. I'm pretty thrown by it. I mean, I was on the pill. I didn't realize what had happened when I was sick. If I had known . . ." She shook her head. "I just feel so thrown. I mean, I was always in such control of my body, you know?"

Carl continued to hold her hand. He realized Laine was right. Kim was scared. He knew what to say now.

"Kim," he said gently, "I'm scared, too. I know it's not the same thing, but this changes everything. But the good news is, you're not in this alone. We're in it together. All the way. This is my baby, too. And I can't wait to meet him. Or her. We're gonna both be here for this baby. I'm not going anywhere."

Tears crawled down Kim's cheek. Carl wiped them away with a clean napkin.

"Carl," she said. "My biological father left my mother when she told him she was pregnant. I've never even met him. My dad's first wife left him after they had their second baby, because she just didn't want to be a mother anymore. My dad, well, he didn't mean to leave me, but he had no choice. And your parents . . ."

"I know, Kim," he replied. "Some really shitty stuff happened to us. Still happens. But we're not them. We're us, and we will be here for each other, for the baby. I can tell you want this baby, and so do I. This baby will be loved. By so many people."

Say the words, Carl, say them, Kim thought.

"Kim, between the two of us, there will be so much love," Carl said sincerely. "We have a lot of love to share with a baby."

And no one will ever love you and this baby more than I do, he thought.

It wasn't the words she longed to hear, but it was close. Now he was looking to her to say something.

"Yeah, you're right, Carl," she said. "I agree. We have plenty of love to share with a baby."

Because I love you so much, the baby won't be able to help but feel it, she thought. *Why are we still tap dancing around the words? What is wrong with us? Why can't he say it? Why can't I say it?*

"If it's a boy, we'll need to name him Pedro," Kim said.

Carl laughed. "You remembered!"

"Of course I remembered," she replied. "I remember everything you tell me." *Everything.*

Carl smiled. "Pedro Bishop. But we don't have to decide right now. We have a long time to decide a name. Maybe he won't look like a Pedro. Or maybe he will. Or maybe she'll be a girl."

"I've already spoken to my mom," Kim announced.

"I told Laine," Carl confessed. "He guessed something was up. He asked what was wrong. He thought maybe we'd had a fight."

"That's okay," Kim said. "This is a no-gossip zone. He'll keep it to himself. Even if he tells Beth, she'll wait for us to say something. But let's not tell anyone else yet. Not just yet. Not until after my doctor's appointment."

"Okay," Carl agreed. "We tell no one."

"It was in the car," Kim said.

"What was in the car?" Carl asked.

"The baby," Kim said. "We made the baby in the car. In Modesto. Under the quilt. On my fake birthday. I'm sure of it. I just know." She touched her stomach. "But we'll just keep that completely between us. It will be our little secret."

START SPREADING THE NEWS

Kim received a clean bill of health, and a due date of December twelfth. She called Darlene as soon as she got home from the OB's office.

"Hey, Kim," Darlene said, excited to hear from her. "How's school?"

"Great!" Kim told her. "How about you?"

"It's good," Darlene said. "I'm loving my Intro to Sociology class. I never thought learning about how people act could be so interesting! I'm gonna register for some more next semester. If that goes well, maybe that will be what I choose for a major. So what's new with you?"

"Well," Kim said, "I'm just trying to plan my own schedule for next trimester."

"Don't you mean se-mester?" Darlene asked.

"No, Darlene, I mean tri-mester." She giggled.

"Kim, what are you saying?" Darlene asked. "Are you saying what I think you're saying?"

"Carl and I are pregnant!" Kim said, and she squealed.

"OH MY GOD KIM!!!" Darlene exclaimed. "If you're joking with me, I'll kill you! It's a little too late for April Fools!"

"I'm not joking, Darlene. We're having a baby! We found out two weeks ago, and I just went to the obstetrician today. I'm due on December twelfth. The pill failed me. Always remember, if you get sick and you throw up after you take your pill, use another form of birth control for the rest of the month!"

"Kim!" Darlene said. "Have you told your mom? What did she say?"

"I told my mom," Kim told her. "She was pretty freaked out at first, but now that she's adjusted to the idea, she's excited! She was nineteen when she had me, and now I'm having a baby at nineteen. I don't know, I guess it's kind of cool."

"What about Carl?" Darlene asked. "How did he take the news?"

"Well," Kim said, "he was there when we found out, and he took it better than I did. I had an actual panic attack on the spot! He's psyched now, but you know, it's scary! We weren't expecting this at all!"

"And you're so far away!" Darlene said. "Are you gonna move back to be close to your mom? Are you two gonna get married? Kim, have you two even said the 'L' word to each other yet?"

Kim was silent.

Darlene gasped. "Oh my God, Kim, you haven't, have you? Oh my God! You're having a baby! I don't even know what to say anymore. Kim, do you love him? Just say yes or no."

Kim paused. "Yes, I do," she admitted. "So much."

Now Darlene was rendered silent in thought. "Kim, does he love you?"

"I'm pretty sure he does," Kim said. "I wish he would say it. I do. I wish I could too. It's like it's gone too far now."

"It's not too late, Kim," Darlene said softly. "You can't go forever without saying it. You're gonna have this baby, and it's gonna look to the two of you to learn about life. Are you just never gonna tell each other how you feel?"

"I want to," Kim said honestly. "I want to shout it from the rooftops. And I will. I know it will happen. I just have to figure out the right time. There's got to be a right time."

"Kim," Darlene told her, "there will be a right time. Just do it before you have this baby, okay? The baby deserves to be born to parents who love each other, and say it out loud. Just tell him the truth. Tell him he's your prince."

When they hung up, Kim thought about what Darlene had told her. She owed it to her baby, she owed it to Carl, and she owed it to herself to express her love to Carl. But right now she had something else to think about.

She was thinking about what Darlene said about moving back home to be closer to her mother. Because the trust in the universe still wasn't there. There was still the chance that if she told Carl the truth, if she told him she loved him, told him everything, he would somehow disappear. And she knew she wouldn't be able to survive with a baby if she was left alone.

WHAT ABOUT YOUR FRIENDS?

Kim's morning sickness eventually faded away. Once she had known what it was, it hadn't gotten too much in her way, or stopped her from going to class or her internship. She didn't tell anyone at either place about the baby, and Carl, Laine, and Beth kept their silence. It was a fact that once anyone in Seska knew, everyone in Seska would know, and Carl and Kim were not quite ready to be known as "those teens that got knocked up out of wedlock." They knew the day would come eventually, but they didn't want it to just yet.

But that didn't stop them from telling their family and friends back home. Chris was beside himself.

"You've got to be kidding me," he told Carl on the phone. "We all made it through high school without anyone getting pregnant, but you two just couldn't keep your horny paws off each other, could you?"

Carl laughed. "No, Chris," he admitted, "it's a problem for us. But as far as problems go, I've had worse."

"Please break the chain, Carl," Chris begged. "If it's a boy, give him his own middle name, okay? I think Jerome needs to be retired."

"You've got my word," Carl promised.

Sally was not quite as shocked. "Kim, your babies will be the cutest!" were the first words out of her mouth. Then she spoke to James, who was with her. "Carl and Kim are pregnant!" she announced.

Kim could hear James responding in the background. "Well, that was just a matter of time," he said. "Tell them I said congratulations. No, wait, tell Kim to put Carl on the line so I can tell him myself."

"When I'm done talking to Kim," Sally answered.

"Hello?" Kim said into the phone. "You two can talk any time! I'm still here!"

They waited until the last possible moment to call Gram Missy. They got on both phone extensions when she answered.

"We need to tell you something, Gram," Carl said.

"You're engaged!" she guessed.

"No," Carl said.

"Oh!" Gram said. "So it's the other thing then. Well then! Congratulations to you two!"

Kim laughed into the phone. "Really?" she said. "That's your reaction? No scolding? No sighing into the phone with exasperation?"

Gram chuckled. "To what end, Kim?" she asked. "Would that make you any more or less pregnant?"

"True," Carl agreed. "But you don't sound very surprised."

"Carl," Gram said, "when you get to be my age, and you have as many children and grandchildren as I do, nothing surprises you anymore. Plus, I know you two will be wonderful parents! This is good news, and we celebrate good news!"

"Thank you, Gram," Kim said with relief. "We just don't know how people will respond. Everyone seems excited, but concerned. I mean, yeah, we have some stuff to plan and work out, but we're gonna manage it just fine."

"I know you will, Kim," Gram agreed. "You are both smart and resourceful. And you've got a lot of folks on your side. I'm really not that worried about you. You'll be okay."

Kim waited until Carl left for work the next day before calling her mother.

"Mom, I just want to let you know that we told Gram Missy about the baby yesterday," she told her. "So I'm sure the word will be out now. I didn't want you to be caught off guard if someone walks up to congratulate you."

"I appreciate that, babe," her mom replied. "But what about Carl's parents? Do they know?"

Kim sighed. "Not from us," she said, "and they won't hear it from Gram, either, so I don't know who would tell them."

"I feel sorry for them," Mrs. Drake said. "Not only did they miss out on so much with Carl, but now they're going to miss out on their grandchild."

"I know, Mom," Kim agreed. "But at this point, I really think we're better off without them." She paused. "Mom, I wanted to talk to you about something else, but it's something I haven't talked to Carl about yet."

"What is it?"

Kim took a deep breath and then blew it out. "I've been wondering what it would be like for us to move back home to Eastboro, you know, before the baby's born. To be closer to you."

There was silence on the line. "Kim, is that what you want?" Mrs. Drake asked.

"I don't know yet, Mom," Kim said. "People keep asking me if we'll move back home now. I'm not sure what I want, but it might be easier to be near you, and grandma, and Gram Missy. And to be able to see my friends more."

"What about Carl's apprenticeship?"

"Well," Kim told her, "he committed to staying for a year. His birthday in September will be a year. So I don't know, I guess it would have to be something we'd talk about."

"Kim, if you came back," her mother said, "you'd always be welcome at our house. You know that. But with three of you? It might not be the most ideal situation."

"Oh, I know," Kim said. "I think we'd want to find our own place. I guess we'd have to work all of that out. I mean, it's kind of just an idea I'm throwing around, y'know? I mean, Carl might not even want to go. And I don't know if I'd come back on my own. . . ."

"Are you and Carl having problems?" her mom asked with concern. "Would you move back here without him?"

"Oh, no," Kim said quickly. "I would never want to come back without Carl. I just . . . I would just want to know the option is there, you know, if anything ever happened."

"Kim, nothing's gonna happen," her mother assured her. "Carl is going to be there with you through this. I talked to him. He assured me. I can always talk to him again."

"No, Mom, that's not necessary," Kim said. "I'm just thinking out loud to you. Everything's gonna be fine. But I am going to talk to Carl. I want us to talk about our options. I might just want to be close to my mom when I have my baby. That's not so unusual, is it?"

"No, of course not, Kim. I'll support whatever decision you make. It's just a big move for you, and it seems that things have been going well for you there. I'd hate for you to give it all up just on a whim."

"I'll think it through," Kim promised. "If we decide to move back, it will be because we thought about it and weighed all of our options and it's what we want. But I just wanted you to know what I was thinking."

"Also think about the logistics," Mrs. Drake said. "How would you get back here? Would you want to drive back when you're six or seven months pregnant, or would you want to hire movers, and fly back? And if so, you'd need to make arrangements about your cars, and the cat. I'm not trying to talk you out of it, Kim, just so you know. I would love to have you here with your baby. My grandchild! It would be wonderful. But I just don't want it to be too hard on you."

"I know, Mom," Kim said. "I appreciate that. I have a lot to think about. Like if I want to leave my internship and my school. And if Carl will be happy if we leave. I'll think about it. And I'll let you know."

WHAT COMES NEXT?

As June slipped into July, the mercury started to rise, and Kim's shorts began to pinch at her waist. "It's about that time," she told Carl. "I'm gonna have to go buy maternity clothes. People are gonna start to guess."

"Kim, there's no stopping the momentum now," Carl said, coming up behind her and putting his arms around her. He lifted her shirt and rubbed her belly. "Hello, little Bishop baby," he said. "We can see you now."

Kim laughed. "And we can feel you, too," Kim said, putting her hands on top of Carl's. "At least I can. You feel like a little butterfly flitting around!"

"So do you want me to take you to the mall to go shopping?" Carl offered.

"That's very sweet, Carl," she said, turning around to face him so they could embrace. "But maybe I should ask Beth to come with me. I think she would like that. And I don't think it would be as fun for you."

"Probably not," he agreed. "I'd probably try to get you to wear plaid with stripes."

Kim shrugged. "I might just wear it, if you chose it for me," she said. "Go ahead, call my bluff."

Carl smiled and reached down to kiss her. "You are so sexy when you're tough. Should we go take a little afternoon nap together, except we'll be naked and not sleeping?"

Kim laughed. "I like that you don't assume any of my horniness has gone away just because I'm with child. I'm gonna go ask Beth if she wants to go to the mall later this afternoon. When I come back, feel free to be in bed, all ready for our nap!"

Kim and Beth went to the mall later in Beth's Taurus and brought Claire along for the ride. As expected, she fell asleep in the car and stayed asleep through Beth transferring her to her stroller. They walked the length of the mall and stopped at a store called Stork. They stepped inside, and at that moment, Kim's pregnancy became public.

She chose several tank tops, shorts, skirts, and dresses to try on and joked with Beth that she should just get a shirt that said Baby with an arrow pointing at her belly instead of making people guess. She opted not to in the end.

Kim chose several items to purchase, and then she and Beth walked back out to the mall with each of them carrying one of two huge yellow bags from Stork. "It will keep them guessing which one of us it is," Beth teased.

They decided to go get haircuts and then pedicures before going home. They brought their fresh hair to the pedicure chairs and sat down to be pampered.

"I used to get pedicures with my mom when I was pregnant with Claire." She glanced over at Claire, still snoozing in the stroller.

"Beth," Kim said cautiously, "you moved to Seska to be near your mom. I've been thinking about what that would be like."

Beth turned to look at her. "You're thinking of leaving?" she said. "I didn't know that the two of you were considering that as an option."

"Well," Kim said, "I haven't really talked to Carl about it, but it's just been on my mind. Please don't say anything to Laine. It's really not out there yet. I just want to talk about it. How did she help you when the kids were babies?"

"Sometimes I think she thought she was more helpful than she really was," Beth admitted. "I would have to redo things the way I liked them when she left. But it was just about her being there, you know? I mean, who knows more about what you're going through than the woman who went through the same thing, and with you!"

Kim nodded. "And my mom went through the exact same thing as me. Nineteen and unmarried."

"But she didn't have a Carl like you do," Beth pointed out. "And Carl just adores you!"

Kim looked at Beth. "Adores me?"

"Of course!" Beth said. "Carl would do anything you ask him to. He loves you!"

"Has he told you that?" Kim asked.

"No, not technically," Beth admitted. "But he doesn't have to. Have you seen him look at you?"

"Yeah, every day. But why does everyone keep asking me that? I mean, there's more to love than the way someone looks at you, or the light in their eyes."

"Yes, I agree, Kim," Beth said, "but there has to be a foundation, something to build on. You have to start somewhere. And sometimes, it's just the way the person looks at you."

"I wish I felt like that's enough," Kim said. "I wish I could trust that love is something that you can touch, or can see, or hold in your hand."

"How about hold in your belly?" Beth asked. "How about how your man takes care of you when you're sick, and worries about you, and calls your mother for you, and offers to go buy you Pepto Bismol?"

"Yeah," Kim said, "Carl is amazing and sweet. And I would not want to be apart from him, ever. He's awesome. But he's never once said he loves me."

Beth looked at Kim with concern. "He hasn't?" she asked.

"No."

"Have you asked him?"

"No."

"Have *you* told *him*?"

"Uh, no."

"But do you?"

Sigh. "Of course I do."

"Oh Kim."

Sigh. "I know."

When Kim got home, Carl looked up from the couch and smiled at her large yellow bags. "Success?"

"Yes," Kim said, placing the bags on the table. "I'll model for you later."

"You got your hair cut?" he asked.

"Oh, yeah, I did," Kim said, touching her hair. "I forgot!"

"It looks so great," Carl said as he got up off the couch and came to greet her. "I really like it." He gave her a kiss and then touched her hair.

Kim smiled. "Thanks!" she said. "What have you been up to?"

"Playing video games with Benjamin earlier," he said. "And then Gram called. She said the strangest thing."

"What?" Kim asked.

"She said if we decided to move back to Eastboro that we would be welcome to stay with her as long as we wanted. I mean, it was kind of weird. She said that maybe you would want to come back to have the baby and to be near your mom."

Kim sat down at the table and looked at him seriously. "Well," she said and then stopped.

"Wait," Carl said, sitting at the table across from her. "Have you been actually considering moving back?"

"Not so much considering," Kim said, "but more just thinking. Maybe out loud to my mom. But I haven't spoken to Gram, and I don't think my mom would do that. Maybe Gram's just putting herself in my shoes and trying to guess what I might want."

"Is that what you want, Kim?" Carl asked. "To move back to Eastboro? To be near your mom?"

Kim sighed. "I don't know, Carl. Maybe. Maybe not. But it's on my mind. It's complicated."

"Yeah," Carl agreed, "it is. There's a lot of things involved. But Kim, if this is what you want, we'll do it. We'll find a way, and we'll do it. I mean, my year is up in September. And I need to think about you. And the baby. What's the best for us. I'll do whatever you decide you want to do."

Kim nodded. "That's good to know. I'll think more about it, what I want. I'll know when I decide. It will feel right. I won't keep you in the dark, I promise. I think if we decide to go, we will need to go by October, at the latest. I don't think I would want to travel at seven months or after. It's something to consider."

"Yeah," Carl said. "There are a lot of things to consider."

YOU CAN BE SO COLD

Late July was hot, and Kim was uncomfortable. She knew everyone was hot, so she tried not to complain, but it was hard to keep it inside. Beth kept the kiddie pool set up in the yard and kept it filled up during the day so Kim could cool her swollen feet.

Laine obtained an old, non-functioning air-conditioner from a customer who was willing to pay him to haul it away. He brought it back to the shop, and he and Carl spent most of a Saturday morning taking it apart and trying to figure out how to make it work. They replaced the electrical cord, repaired and replaced wires, and changed out parts. They replaced filters, then started again. Carl took it apart again and stared at the individual pieces for several minutes. He moved things around. He drank a glass of water. He went for a walk outside. He went back to the shop where Laine was repairing a microwave. He looked at the air-conditioner again, and then sat down on the floor in front of it. And then he put it back together. Laine watched in silence from his worktable. Carl plugged the air-conditioner into the outlet. He flipped the On switch. It started to purr.

Laine bolted to his feet. "What the hell, Carl?" he said. "How did you do that?"

Carl shook his head. "I don't know," he told his cousin. "I've been looking at it all day. We took it apart twice. We tried to put it back together. All the pictures were in my head. They just kept moving around. Then I just knew what to do. Kim needs an air-conditioner. I had to make it work."

"Carl, you are a wonder," Laine said, shaking his head back and forth. "A natural wonder! I can't believe how lucky I am that you chose to come and work with me. It's like I get to watch this amazing work of art being painted right in front of me, every day."

Carl looked at him silently for a moment. "Laine," he said tentatively, "Kim might want to move back to Eastboro, you know, to have the baby at home, near her mom."

"What?" Laine asked, looking up quickly from the unit at Carl's face. "You might be leaving? When?"

Carl shook his head. "It's not for sure yet, but it would be sometime after my birthday, probably in October." He paused. "I don't really want to go, Laine, but what choice would I have? If Kim wants to go, I'm gonna go where she is. Where the baby will be. I want to be where Kim is. We would stay with Gram until we figured out what to do next."

"Oh," Laine said quietly, looking away from Carl and back at the air-conditioner. He hesitated before speaking again. "I see. So you two have put some thought into this."

He pondered the idea briefly, scratched his head, and then looked back at Carl. "Of course you would go where Kim goes, where she wants to be. You need to take care of your family. There's no question. If Kim wants to go, you go, Carl. I mean, I would hate to lose you. You have so much more to learn, and to teach me. But you have your priorities straight, man, and that's good."

Carl nodded slowly. "Kim said she would let me know what she wants to do, so we can start to make plans if we need to. I'll let you know as soon as we decide."

"Yeah," Laine said, walking back to the microwave he was working on, averting his eyes. "I'd appreciate that, Carl. Keep me up to date. We'd have some paperwork we'd need to do, and I would want to help you figure out your next move in Eastboro. I could help you find a new mentor if you wanted. Or whatever you decide to do, I could help."

They worked quietly for several minutes. Then Carl spoke. "I would really miss you, Laine. If we left."

Laine nodded and gave Carl a strained smile. "Yeah, Carl, I'd miss you, too. Hey, why don't we head back home now and install that a/c in your apartment unit, okay? Let's make it comfortable for that pregnant girlfriend you have over there. She deserves to be comfortable."

Carl turned off the unit and unplugged it. "Yeah," he agreed. "That's the goal. I really want to do whatever I can to make Kim comfortable."

FORWARD AHEAD

Kim was hot and sweaty, so she decided it was time to wear one of her new maternity dresses to her internship. She picked out a black babydoll dress with a tiny pink floral pattern. It wasn't her usual style, but it was cute, and comfortable, and she looked good in black. She headed to the office to start her day. No one there knew she was pregnant. They would most likely figure it out now.

The first person she came upon was Cassandra, the social worker. She was making copies of resource lists in the clerical area. She looked up at Kim when she walked in. She glanced at her dress, then at her face.

"Hey, Kim," she said, with a warm smile. "I'm just about done here. Wanna come to my office, and chat for a bit?"

"Yes, please," Kim responded gratefully.

Cassandra carried the piles of paper back to the office she shared with Robin and Rose, who weren't due in until later. Cassandra closed the door and sat at her desk. Kim sat down at Robin's desk and turned to face the social worker.

"Sooo," Cassandra started, "tell me what's new, Kim?" She gave her a look that said she absolutely knew what was new.

Kim laughed. "I'm due on December twelfth," she revealed. "I know that's what you really wanted to ask. This was unexpected, but not unwelcome. Carl and I are both getting psyched about it."

"Congratulations, Kim!" Cassandra said, and she reached out to hug her. "I'm so happy for you! I think you'll be a great mom."

"Thanks," Kim said, relieved that someone else knew. "I waited as long as I could to put on the maternity clothes, but it's just so damn hot out! I couldn't put anything tight around my waist anymore!"

"It's super cute, Kim," Cassandra said. "But it wasn't the dress that gave it away. It was the look on your face when you saw me looking at the dress. But I'm trained to observe things that other people might not see, so everyone else might not figure it out right away. But they might. So you'll have to decide if you want to announce it, or just wait for people to ask."

"Ugh," Kim groaned. She slouched in her chair. "I'm not ready for this yet. Do you really think they'll ask?"

"They might," Cassandra admitted. "They shouldn't, but they might. But you don't have to tell them anything you don't want to share."

"That's gonna be awkward," Kim said. "I'm nineteen, unmarried, and living with my boyfriend, three thousand miles away from my family. And this is a tiny little town."

Cassandra nodded in agreement. "It comes with the territory. We have good schools and friendly neighbors, but gossip abounds. If you want to talk it out with me, you're welcome to, but you don't have to."

Kim paused. "I kind of do," she admitted. "It's not so much the marriage stuff. I mean, my mom was nineteen and unmarried when she had me. I know the drill. And it's 1987. Things have changed a lot since 1968. At least I hope so. It's more people asking me if I want to move back home."

"I'm guessing this is something you've been thinking about," Cassandra said. "And you're not sure of your answer yet."

Kim shook her head. "My friend put the idea in my head when I told her I was pregnant back in April, and I haven't been able to stop thinking about it."

"What does Carl want to do?" Cassandra asked.

"That's just the thing," Kim said, and she sighed. "He said he'd do whatever I want to do, but I don't know what he wants. He's very close with some of his family, but not his parents, who live back there. And he's doing so well with his apprenticeship."

"So he has reasons to go and reasons to stay," Cassandra summarized. "What about you, Kim?"

"What do I want?" Kim asked. "I don't know. I want to be near my mom and my family, but I also like being here. The bottom line is, I want to be with Carl." She paused. "But I have to think about what would happen if there were no Carl."

"No Carl?" Cassandra asked, looking confused. "Why would there be no Carl?"

Kim shrugged. "I don't know. Lots of reasons. He leaves me. He gets sick and dies. He has an accident."

"Oh," Cassandra said, nodding. "I see. So hypothetically, for some reason, sometime in the future, you're worried that Carl won't be there for you. But not because of anything that's going on now."

"No," Kim said quickly. "Nothing is going on now, but how do I know that everything is always gonna be like this?"

"You can't know that, Kim," Cassandra said softly. "No one can say that. It's not possible. We don't have a crystal ball, and we can't control what happens. But we can make wise decisions about what happens now. Is it possible for you to think about what you want now? Not next week, not next month or next year, but now?"

"I don't know," Kim admitted. "I don't know if I can separate now from the future. They seem so entwined."

"Kim," Cassandra prodded, "what do you want *right now?*"

Kim looked up at Cassandra's eyes. "Right now? I want my mom."

Kim's talk with Cassandra left her feeling even more confused than she felt before, although she knew that was not the intention. But one thing she did decide was that she was going to tell people her news before they started to guess. She figured it would be a good idea to start with Dr. Singh.

Dr. Singh was sitting at her desk in her office. Kim knocked on her open door, and Dr. Singh looked up and smiled. "Come in, Kim," she said. Kim quickly came in and sat in the chair in front of the desk before Dr. Singh could take a good look at her. "What's up?" the medical director asked her.

Kim had no idea what to say. She cleared her throat. "So, I have some news," she said. "So it seems I might be almost five months pregnant."

Dr. Singh's hand flew up to her face. "Oh, Kim!" she exclaimed. "Is that why you were so sick a few months ago?"

"No," Kim said. She laughed. "This might be too much information, but it's more like I'm pregnant because I was sick. But before you ask, this is a good thing. I'm happy about it. And so is Carl."

"Oh, Kim, then I'm so happy for you!" Dr. Singh stood. "Can I hug you?" she asked.

Kim nodded. "Yes!" she said. Dr. Singh came around her desk. Kim stood up and let herself be hugged. She was getting used to people wanting to hug her.

Kim filled Dr. Singh in on the details and her due date. "So how long will you stay at work?" she asked Kim. "I know some people work right up to going into labor, and others decide a certain date to stop."

Kim didn't know how to answer this question. "I have no idea," she said. "I haven't even thought about school. I mean, I'm due December twelfth, and school doesn't end until a week later. I don't know how I'd finish the semester. I don't even know yet if I'm gonna stay in Seska. I might want to go back to Eastboro. I just, we just, haven't decided yet. I don't even know if I should register for the fall. I guess I have a lot of things to decide."

Dr. Singh nodded. "Babies don't work nicely into schedules," she said. "They aren't very convenient at the start. But it gets better. Eventually. But it's August, Kim, so you probably need to talk to your school to find out your options soon. Maybe they'll work with you on a plan. And it's probably a good idea for you to talk to Fred to let him know, too."

"He's my next stop,"

Pretty soon, the news was out, and staff approached Kim and offered congratulations. No one asked her about her plans, and she was relieved. By her next day at Head Forward, talk had already died down, and eventually things seemed to return to normal.

Kim was taking two summer seminar classes: Intermediate Spanish, and Brain Disorders of Childhood. Tami was in her Spanish class. Since seminars only met once a week for longer periods of time, Kim had not announced to Tami yet that she was expecting. But Tami had already heard when Kim told her.

"Jackie at Stork recognized you when you went in there because she had seen you at the grocery store with Carl," she said. "She mentioned it to her cousin Grace, who was in David's class at Seska High, that she saw you in the store buying maternity clothes. At first, she thought you were there with Beth because she was pregnant, but then you were trying on the clothes, so of course she figured it out. Grace told her boyfriend John, who then mentioned it to David, who of course immediately called me from the bakery to tell me."

"Wait," Kim said, confused. "So when did you find out?"

Tami smiled. "The same day you got the clothes," she said. "Probably before you even left the mall. But I didn't tell you I knew because I wanted to give you the chance to tell me yourself. I figured you would eventually."

"Ah," Kim replied, feeling weird that the chain of gossip had gotten to Tami before she did. "I need to go talk to the registration office to see what to do about next semester. I'm not sure I'll make it until Christmas break starts, and Carl and I are also trying to figure out if we want to move back to Massachusetts."

Tami frowned. "You might leave?" she asked sadly. "That sucks. I like having you around and hanging out. And I want to see your baby, too."

Tami was the first person to actually say how she felt about Kim possibly leaving, rather than asking her what she wanted. It was refreshing.

"I know," she said. "We've been here a year now, and I really like it here. It will be weird if we go back home, even though it would be great to be around my family."

"I understand that," Tami said. "But you'll be kind of like me back there. All of your friends have left for college. They only come home for random weekends, holidays, and vacations. Some of mine didn't even come home for the summer. It's never the same after high school."

"I know," Kim said. "I have to keep that in mind when I decide. There's just so much to think about! Massachusetts winters are so cold and snowy. I'm not sure I want to go back to that. But I'm also not going to rule out going back just yet. You don't know what it's like to be so far from your mom and the rest of your family, especially when you're having a baby."

"No, I don't," Tami agreed. "And even if I ever did leave Seska, I probably wouldn't go any farther than Sacramento. So yeah, you have to do what you need to do, but I'd miss you. And I'm sure Laine and Beth would miss you and Carl a lot."

"Yeah, we'd miss them, too," Kim said. She felt a sudden lurch in her stomach, and wondered if maybe the baby was kicking her in one of her vital organs.

The registration clerk listened to Kim's story, and they came up with possible solutions. Kim could register for and start the fall semester, but she would have to disenroll by the end of September if she decided she wouldn't be staying. Otherwise, she risked losing financial aid. And if she did decide to stay, she would need to meet with each of her instructors to make a plan to finish her work prior to her due date so wouldn't get Incomplete in all of her classes. She could work out her internship details with Fred at Head Forward.

Kim was relieved to have a plan. Now she could spend her mental energy on getting by day to day and deciding the course of her and Carl's entire future. She started back toward home and planned to take some Tums when she got there.

I JUST WANT TO BE WITH YOU

Kim told Carl about her plan for school in either scenario. Carl could tell that she felt better now that she had choices.

Carl didn't want to leave Seska. For the first time in his life, he felt totally at home. He loved the town and the people in it, and he loved his work. And he loved having Kim all to himself in their little house.

Being so close to Laine and Beth and their kids was the closest thing that Carl had ever had to being in a functional family. He enjoyed the family meals, the banter, and the fact that they could all have fun together. He loved that Laine and Beth could disagree on something, and neither one would storm out of the house and not come back that night, or maybe even that week. He loved his clan back home, especially Gram Missy and Chris, but he knew they would always be there for him, and they were busy living their own lives.

But he knew that he had only one choice. He would do whatever Kim wanted to do. He would do what Kim thought was best for the baby. He would never leave her, and he would never let her go alone. Even if it meant he needed to find his way in the world again, he would follow Kim to the ends of the earth. And back. But he wanted to make sure she was making the right choice, and for the right reasons.

He called Chris, who was still home with his family for summer break. "Why do you think she wants to go home?" he asked.

"Her mom," Chris answered quickly. "She's having a baby and she wants to be with her mom. Girls are just like that."

"Why can't her mom just come here?" Carl asked, knowing the answer already.

"Carl, you're doing that thing again where you act like you're not a super genius," Chris scolded. "Don't do that, okay? Dude, you got an awful mom. Kim got a good one. She gets something out of being near her mom when things get hard. And she probably wants to be near her dad, too. I don't know if he would even be able to grasp her having a baby. He'll probably need to see the baby, and he can't really go to California."

"That's true," Carl conceded. "I wish there was some other way we could do this, though."

"You don't want to come back, do you?" Chris asked.

Carl sighed. "Would you, if you were me?"

"Probably not," Chris agreed. "But I'm kind of surprised Kim doesn't want to stay. She's done so well out there. She has like a whole community of people. She probably could get a job pretty easily after she finishes school, and really like it."

"She is happy," Carl told his cousin. "That's what makes it so hard to understand. It's like she's torturing herself trying to figure out what to do."

"Maybe she wants you to make the choice for her," Chris suggested. "Maybe she's scared that you won't be happy with what she decides. You two are so squirrely when it comes to telling each other how you feel."

Carl thought for a moment. "You could be right," he said. "Not about the squirrely thing, but about wanting me to take the lead. I was reading in one of Kim's pregnancy books from the library that pregnant women can get like a foggy brain. Maybe she just needs some help. I can do that."

"Yeah, but don't mention the foggy brain to her, though," Chris said. "She knows a lot more about brains now than you do. She might not appreciate it. And for what it's worth, bro, I hope you guys do come home. I miss you both."

Next, he called Gram Missy. "So if we did come back," he asked, "what would that look like?"

Gram gasped. "You've decided to come back?" she asked.

"No, Gram," Carl said, "not yet. We're still deciding. I just need to know what it would be like if we came back. We would have to stay with you, at least at first."

"Of course, Carl," Gram responded. "I would put you in your dad and Uncle Ted's old room, and we could either put the baby in with you, or we can make one of the other rooms into a nursery and you could stay as long as you need to."

"I'd have to find a job," Carl said, "or a new mentor to get my hours, and both Kim and I would want to stay in school. So we won't have much money coming in, just financial aid and whatever I would make at work."

"That's okay, Carl," Gram assured him. "Cissy and I can help. We'd be happy to. And you could take your time until you get settled. There would be no rush."

Carl wasn't sure that was a good idea. The last time he took his time, nothing happened. He responded well when held up against the wall. But Gram didn't need to know that.

"Gram, I don't have to tell you," he said, "but babies are noisy, and messy, and loud. And they can get expensive, with diapers and clothes, and all the laundry. You really would want all that in your house? I mean, you finally have peace and quiet."

"Carl, let me tell you something," Gram confided. "I'm a twin, and I come from a family of nine children. I didn't even have peace and quiet in the womb! I don't like peace and quiet. I don't trust it. I prefer a joyful noise!"

When he got off the phone, Carl realized he had just gotten two votes for moving back, and no one was trying to convince him to stay in Seska. He wondered if maybe that was his answer. Maybe he was supposed to go home. He had to talk to Kim.

Kim was babysitting for the Farmer kids until dinnertime, and she came home hungry. "I figured I would grab some dinner with them and call you over, but they already have plans with Beth's mom tonight. I guess her aunt is in town." Kim sat down at the table. "Would you mind throwing some frozen fried chicken on a tray and sticking it in the oven? And maybe some fries?"

Carl went to Kim for a kiss, then right to the freezer for the chicken. As he dumped the pieces on the cooking tray, he laughed. "Our baby is gonna be made mostly of chicken and fries," he quipped. "He, or she, had better like frozen chicken or they'll be out of luck!"

"Or Kentucky Fried Chicken," Kim added, propping her feet up on the other kitchen chair.

Carl put the chicken in the oven, lifted Kim's feet, and sat on the chair. He laid her feet down on his lap, removed her sandals, and rubbed her feet, one by one. Kim moaned from the relief.

"Kim," he said, while pulling lightly on her big toe, "we need to talk about what we're gonna do."

Kim sighed and closed her eyes. "I know," she said. "We're running short on time. It's just so hard to decide what to do. I want both things, but we've got to pick one, and it's got to be the right one."

"Yeah," Carl agreed. "It's tough. On the one hand, we both like the programs we're doing here, and being with Laine and Beth. On the other hand, we have tons of family back home who will help us when we need it, and probably even if we don't, and they'll love the baby so much. I mean, so would Laine and Beth, but they're only two people. Plus we have our friends, who would be much closer, even if they were at school. They would be like aunts and uncles."

Kim laughed. "Like this baby won't already have a thousand aunts and uncles. Okay, so you said a lot of good things about moving back. What about how noisy it is there? You like the quiet here. I can't really say anything about the gossip, because it's just as bad here as it is there. And the weather? Remember the words 'snow cancelation'? And it gets so cold." She paused. "But that's where my mom is. And my family."

"And my Gram. And all my cousins. And Chris."

Kim felt the lurch in her gut again. She rubbed her belly. "Hand me the Tums?" she asked Carl.

"So what do we do?" Kim asked. "Where do we have the baby? Where do we raise our baby?"

Carl still got goosebumps when Kim said "our baby." It was still hard to wrap his brain around the fact that they were having a baby together. A baby that they made. This would still be true no matter where they lived, where they went to school, or where they worked. That made the decision easy.

"What does your gut tell you right now?" he asked Kim.

"Aside from telling me to eat Tums," she said, "it's telling me to go to my mom." She felt the lurch again.

"Then we go home," Carl told her.

"Okay," Kim responded. "We go home. It's settled." She popped another Tums in her mouth.

SHOWERS OF FLOWERS

Kim registered for Fall classes, even though they planned to leave by mid-November. She figured something might go wrong, or she might go into premature labor and have to stay longer, so she didn't want to take the risk of sitting out the whole semester.

She and Carl went to see the OB, Dr. Stein. Dr. Stein strongly advised Kim against driving cross-country in advanced pregnancy. "Who knows where you'll break down, but trust me, it will happen, and you'll be in the middle of a corn field in Nebraska."

And she told her not to fly after her eighth month.

"Just don't," she said. "People sometimes do, but people do stupid things all the time. Just don't do it."

Otherwise, she said Kim and the baby were doing just fine.

So Carl and Kim planned to hire movers for their cars and anything else they needed to bring home. It was going to be a speedy venture, so they held off on buying baby supplies. "We'll get them when we need them," Kim said. Carl could tell she was just itching to hold baby supplies in her hands and start nesting.

So when Tami called him at the store to ask if anyone else was planning a baby shower because she wanted to throw one, Carl quickly agreed. "But just clothes or small toys for gifts," he told her. "Remember, anything we need to bring with us back to Eastboro has to fit in the cars."

It was still slightly early for a baby shower, but they planned it for September fifth, three months and one week before Kim's due date. They decided not to have it be a surprise so Kim could be part of the planning. She and Tami went to the party store and picked up invitations and thank-you notes. They made a guest list, and decided that they would invite men, women, and children to the event, since it would most likely be sort of a goodbye party, too. Tami secured the Rotary Club Hall for the afternoon. Beth agreed to be in charge of decorations, and the bakery would cater the food.

Kim brought an invitation to Head Forward and tacked it to the staff bulletin board. She didn't want to leave anyone out. Tami invited some girls from their classes, and her friends Katie and Sarah from USF. Carl invited some of the customers that he had gotten especially close to over the year, including the Campbells and some friends he'd made in town.

Kim thought that now that they had decided what to do, and told everyone, she would be able to settle down and feel relief, but the lurch in her stomach sometimes woke her up at night. She would get up, eat a Tums, and go back to bed, but it kept coming back. It was annoying, but it wasn't bad enough for her to have to call the doctor. But it made her uneasy, like she had forgotten to study for an important test that she was just about to sit down and take.

Kim and Carl started childbirth classes at the medical center and learned all about what to expect in labor and delivery. They were by far the youngest couple in the class. But they were overachievers and learned the skills faster than anyone else. They would need to learn it all before they left Seska. Kim particularly liked the breathing. It was so simple. You just had to breathe. And she found if she breathed at night when she got the lurch in her gut, it helped, and she could go back to sleep without taking Tums.

The day of the shower finally arrived, and Kim spent a long time in the shower, shampooing and conditioning her hair and somehow shaving her legs without losing her balance. When she got out, she dried off and rubbed lotion on her skin. She put on her black dress with the pink flowers, only now it didn't hang so loose. She brushed and dried her hair and put on her makeup. Carl looked up from reading on the bed and smiled at her.

"You look beautiful," he told her as he got off the bed to embrace her. "You are so beautiful."

"I'm getting large," she said, rubbing her belly. "I take up more space now."

"It's a beautiful space," Carl whispered in her ear.

Kim laughed. "You need to get ready," she told him.

Carl looked down at his T-shirt and ripped jeans. "I thought I was ready," he joked. He dodged as Kim reached out to poke him in the stomach. "Okay, okay," he said. "I'll be ready in five minutes."

Kim wandered out to the kitchen. She sat at the table to wait. Carl had been sitting there earlier, doing some research on moving. She picked up a brochure he had left there from a local moving company that might be able to help them ship their cars. Kim looked at the picture of the truck and then clutched her gut. The lurching again. She breathed in through her nose and out through her mouth. The discomfort eased away. Carl came out in his khakis and his navy-blue polo shirt, Kim's favorite outfit on him. He saw her there breathing with her hand on her belly and grew concerned.

"No, I'm fine," Kim said. "Just a little heartburn. I'm used to it."

"Okay," Carl said. "Are you ready to go?"

Kim exhaled one more time. "Ready as I'll ever be," she said.

Carl drove them to the Rotary Hall, and they parked in the lot. When they went inside, they found the room filled with elegant decorations. Beth had used white, silver, and gold streamers and tableware and had placed bouquets of flowers from Callie's as centerpieces on the tables. Kim was glad that the decorations were adult themed and not goofy baby themed. Beth and Tami bustled around the room, putting last-minute details in place, while David rough-housed with Benjamin and Claire on the dance floor in the corner.

"It's like a private prom," Kim said, looking around. "Just for us."

"No dancing, though," Carl said. "And no spiked punch."

Kim laughed. "You didn't bring your flask?"

Tami and Beth came over and hugged them both, and soon, the guests started to file in. Small packages piled up on the gift table, and their friends and coworkers came up to say hello. Pretty soon, the room was crowded, and guests were helping themselves to small sandwiches and snacks.

After some time, Tami called the group to attention. "Thank you all for coming," she said over the murmur of the crowd. "We're all here to celebrate Kim and Carl, and their future baby. Kim, I just wanted to say, I'm so glad you sat down next to me in English Lit class a year ago, almost to the day, and became my friend. I never thought I would meet anyone new in Seska, being such a small town, but you arriving at school and in my life was a true gift. I'm so sad to see you go, but I'm so happy for you that your future is going to be so bright. I hope you come back here someday and bring baby Bishop so we can meet him. Or her. Best of luck to your little family." She raised her cup of punch. "To baby Bishop."

"To baby Bishop," everyone cried out and then sipped their punch.

Carl could see Kim starting to tear up. He was prepared with some tissues in his pocket, and now he handed one to her. She smiled at him and dabbed around her eyes.

Laine came up to the front to speak. "I met Carl when he was first born," he said. "I was a sixteen-year-old junior at Murphy High in Eastboro, Massachusetts, and my parents made me go to this baby party for my newest cousin at my Aunt Missy's house. I had a thousand cousins, and believe me, I was over meeting new cousins."

Everyone laughed.

"But I didn't know then what I know now," he continued. "That one day, almost eighteen years later, Carl would move out to Seska, California, to be my apprentice, and at the same time, become my all-time favorite cousin. Carl and Kim came into our lives like bulldozers last year, and our family has not been the same since. Carl, Kim, I'm so proud of you guys and all you've accomplished in the one year you've been in our lives. You are both amazing people, and you're going to be amazing parents."

Laine's voice became shaky, and he stopped to clear his throat.

"Don't be strangers, you guys. You're always welcome in Seska. And our home will always be your home."

"Hear, hear!" Beth yelled out, and everyone cheered and clapped.

Kim was quietly crying now, and Carl put his arm around her. He was working hard to contain his own emotions when Benjamin came up and grabbed his arm.

"Why are you leaving?" he asked Carl. "I thought you liked it here. I like having a cousin here. And a boy cousin. I like playing video games with you. I don't even have my own game system."

Carl squatted down to make himself the same height as Benjamin. "Benjamin Jerome Farmer," he said, "I do like it here. I like playing with you, and I'll miss you. But we'll be here two more months, and we'll play together a lot before we go. And when we do go, I'm gonna leave you my game system."

Kim turned her head sharply. "You are?"

Carl shrugged. "Sure," he said. "We don't have enough room for it in the cars anyway. I'll just pick up a new one when we get there."

Kim closed her eyes and the tears squeezed through her lids. Carl's game system was the pride and joy of his high school years. And he was willing to leave it behind for his special cousin.

Suddenly, she felt a nasty lurch. "I've got to sit down for a sec."

Carl walked to the table with her, and they both sat down. Benjamin stood in front of them.

Kim took two long breaths. "I'm okay," she told Carl and Benjamin. "Just a little kicking, that's all."

They stayed at the table quietly while Kim continued to breathe. Then Tami silenced the crowd again.

"Time for presents!" she called out. "Kim, just stay where you are. We'll bring them to you."

Tami, Laine, and Beth started to carry piles of gifts to Kim's table. Then Beth brought over a notebook and pen and sat beside Kim. Claire came over and jumped on her lap.

"We're gonna make a list for thank-you notes," Beth told Kim. Laine and Tami started snapping pictures.

Kim and Carl took turns reading cards and ripping off wrapping paper. They showed their guests the gifts and passed them around the room after Beth wrote down the vital information. There were mostly little jumper suits and outfits in yellow, green, purple, red, and white. No one dared to give pink or blue clothes before they knew the gender of the baby. Kim thought that was silly. Kim would have liked some navy-blue outfits, but she figured she could always pick some up herself. There were a few toys and small items, but everything would fit in a few large bags to go back in the cars.

After gifts came cake from the bakery. It was chocolate with white frosting. Kim and Benjamin had two pieces each. Everyone milled around the room, ate, drank coffee, and talked, and Kim was pleased that there were no shower games. She held court at the table with Carl, and guests came up to sit and talk, or shake their hands before leaving. Kim knew she would see everyone again before they left, but it still felt like a small goodbye as guests walked out the door. The closer friends stayed longer, but eventually, it was time to clean up. Tami insisted that they load the gifts in the car and Carl bring Kim home, because the guests of honor should not have to worry about the garbage. They brought Benjamin back with them, and he helped them carry in gifts and leftover cake. Then he and Carl played video games while Kim looked over their gifts.

"These are so tiny!" she said, holding up a short-sleeved white onesie. "How can a whole person fit inside this?" She squealed.

Carl laughed. Benjamin shrugged. "Babies are really small," he told them. "Even you guys were that small when you were babies."

"Not me," Carl protested. "I was born five-foot-ten. I was very advanced."

Benjamin looked at him skeptically.

Kim laughed. She hoped her baby would be born with Farmer humor. And she hoped the baby would one day get to meet his or her cousin Benjamin.

KIM MAKES A DISCOVERY

On the Monday evening before Carl's birthday, Carl was watching the New York Giants play the Chicago Bears with Laine in the Farmers' den. Kim was playing *Sorry* with Benjamin at the dining room table. Beth was on the floor with Claire playing with action figures while dinner was cooking in the oven. When halftime started, Laine turned to Carl.

"Hey, Carl," he said as he stood. "It's still pretty early. I have it on my list to finally fix that light fixture in the downstairs guest room. But I think I'm gonna let you take the lead on this one. Let's go take care of it now. I can talk you through the steps if you need it."

"Okay," Carl said, standing up to join him. "I think I remember what to do. I watched you do that one last week at the Campbells' house. I'll give it a try."

"We'll be back before the second half starts," Laine announced to the room. "Don't change the channel." The two of them walked toward the back hall.

"It's pretty cool that Laine keeps letting him try new stuff on his own," Kim told Beth. "Especially in his own house! Carl gets excited about learning new things. I hope he stays so excited after we go."

Beth looked up. "Laine says Carl picks up on stuff faster than anyone he's ever met," she said. "He's really impressed with all the work he does. He hates to be losing him so soon. He still has so much he wants to teach him. But Carl will find another mentor back home. He'll still learn. I'm sure he'll excel, no matter where he is."

Kim felt the lurch in her gut. Laine was Carl's mentor, and his friend. It would be a hard transition for both of them when they left.

"I need to go to the bathroom," Kim told Benjamin as she stood up.

"Again?" Benjamin moaned. "You've already gone twice since we started the game! I haven't gone since I got up this morning!"

"Benjamin!" Beth exclaimed with horror on her face, but Kim laughed.

"It's okay, Beth," she said. "He's right. Benjamin, I'll be back in a minute. Don't cheat while I'm gone."

Kim walked back to the restroom, which was next to the guest room. When she was done, she peeked in and could see Carl working on the overhead light.

"That's right," Laine said, looking over his shoulder and holding the work lamp. "So what do you do next?"

"I connect the wire back to the fixture, and secure it here," Carl said, making room for Laine to watch his work. "Then, I put the top back on, and we switch the breaker back on." Carl got down off of the step ladder. He stepped out of the room, smiled at Kim, and went over to the breaker box next to the back door to flip the switch. He went back into the guest room. "Now we see if I did it right, or if we burn the house down."

Laine reached for the light switch on the wall and flicked it to the On position. The light went on. "Hey, hey, look at that!" Laine said with a chuckle. "It worked. You did it, Carl. I only showed that to you once, but you picked it up like a pro! This work really does come naturally to you. Good job, kid!"

Kim looked at Carl. He was beaming with satisfaction, and he looked at Laine with pride in his eyes. He was happy to please Laine. He was proud of his work and the praise it brought him from his cousin and mentor. Carl was doing a great job learning the skills, and he really liked what he was accomplishing.

Suddenly, the reality of the situation came to Kim as if someone had handed it to her in her cup of pregnancy-safe herbal tea. The lurch in her gut wasn't from the baby. It was something else inside her, trying to tell her the truth. Carl was happy. He loved his work. He loved his cousin. Laine was the brother that Carl always needed, always deserved. Carl was happy in Seska. Carl was going to leave Seska because Kim had asked him to go. He didn't really want to go.

And, as Kim knew, people don't pick up and move across the country for just any reason. They did it because they couldn't stand the thought of being away from the person they loved, even for a minute. A warm sensation flowed through her body. Carl loved her. She knew it now, for sure. He didn't want to leave. And Kim didn't want to leave either. Now she didn't need to.

Tomorrow. Tomorrow was the right time. She would tell him she wanted to stay. She would tell him everything. Every last truth that she knew. Some of it would be hard. But it was time. Even if it was his birthday.

BIRTHDAY MIND BLOWN

Carl had to work, and Kim had school on the morning of Carl's nineteenth birthday. Kim had greeted him when he woke up with slow pregnancy cowgirl sex, and now they had gotten up to make breakfast and prepare for their day. More birthday celebrations would come later, but for now, Kim had more important things on her mind. Last year, she had promised Carl she was going to blow his mind on his next birthday, and she was about to fulfill that vow.

Kim stood by the open cabinet and took two deep, cleansing breaths like she had learned in childbirth class. Then she turned toward the table.

"Carl," she said when she sat down with her bowl and a box of Cheerios. "I don't want to move back to Massachusetts anymore."

Carl froze in the middle of a bite of banana. He chewed and swallowed.

"What?" he said. "I thought you wanted to go. I kinda thought it was your idea to go back. To have the baby near our families. To have a family support system and all."

"No," Kim asserted. "Not anymore. I've sat with the idea for a while now, and I've changed my mind. I know I don't want to go. I want to stay here, in our tiny little maroon house with the purple flowers out front. Every time I think of going back, I start to panic and my stomach hurts. I don't want to go back there."

Carl laid the rest of the banana on the table. "We need to talk about this," he said. "I need to know more. You need to tell me what changed your mind. If we're gonna stay here, I need to know what you're thinking, Kim. There's more than just you and me at stake here now."

"I know," Kim admitted. "But I've really thought this through. In Seska, we have our own life, Carl. Our new friends, and Laine and Beth and the kids have already become our family. And Laine has really taken you under his wing, and I can see how much you love working with him. In Seska, we don't have to depend on the Bishops, or the Farmers, or even the Drakes or Lesters for anything. And then there's Chris. You know I've gotten to be better friends with him in the last couple of years, and he's really changed a lot. But still, I always have this fear of losing you again to Chris, and I wouldn't be able to stand that. You stand out in the sun here in Seska, Carl. You, Carl Bishop, all on your own. You shine. You aren't Chris's cousin here, or Missy's grandson, or part of the legendary Bishop-Farmer clan. Here, we're Carl *and* Kim. Not Carl *or* Kim, or Carl and *sometimes* Kim. Not just friends. We are a couple. A team. We mean something special. And now we're having a baby. Our baby. I don't want to go back to Massachusetts and have all that disappear into the crowd."

Carl looked at her with confusion. "What do you mean about losing me to Chris again?" he asked. "When did you ever lose me to Chris?"

Kim got up from the table, her breakfast abandoned. She walked the five feet to the couch, sat, and let herself sink down into the cushion. She put her feet up on the coffee table. She resigned herself to telling Carl the truth. Finally. She was going to tell him everything. She grabbed a throw pillow and held it against her belly like a shield. She was in storyteller mode.

"I was seven," she started. "You were still six. We had just started second grade. We had Miss Freely. Up until then, you and I had been in the same class every year, but Chris wasn't. Second grade was the first time you two were together. Pete and James were in our class, too. It was the year that Chris formed his little bad boy posse. The year that everything changed.

"Before that, Carl, you were my buddy. Literally. In kindergarten, Mrs. Francis appointed us as hallway buddies, remember? We would hold hands walking to the art room, the library, and the bus line. Your hand was always warm and sweaty. I looked forward to those walks every day. We played together every day on the playground. I remember you pushing me on the swings. We did our art projects together. For two years, it was Kim and Carl against the world. Even when you weren't around, I was thinking of you. I adored you. You can ask Darlene. We would play pretend when we were six, and I always insisted that we play princesses. I was always the princess, and I would make Darlene pretend she was you and you were my prince. Prince Carl and Princess Kim. She still reminds me to this day that you were my prince."

"I never knew that," Carl said softly.

"Of course not. Because I never let you know. And Darlene was sworn to secrecy. But then in second grade, everything changed. Chris was in our class, and he pulled you away from me. He made you his second-in-command. He demanded your time on the playground. He had all of you sitting at the same art table by the end of the first week of school. He convinced you guys that girls had cooties. You might not realize it, but you started to act differently toward me then. You worshiped Chris. You always had. Your older cousin, but only by six months. Your families were so close. I couldn't compete. I finally gave up trying. I started following Darlene and Michelle around on the playground during recess and demanding they play with me, so I wouldn't be alone. Pretty soon, we had a posse of our own.

"I think that's when I started to get sort of mean. Remember on the playground, we used to play that stupid game, Boys Chase the Girls on some days, and Girls Chase the Boys on others? When I would catch up to one of you guys, I would push you with both hands. I remember pushing Pete once so hard that he fell over and scraped his knee. He cried. I laughed. I felt so bad, but I felt the power, too, for the first time. People reacted when I hit them, especially boys. Not usually a positive reaction, but a reaction of some sort."

"I don't remember all of that," Carl said, "but I do remember the time in the sandbox when you pushed me over."

Kim sighed. "Yeah, not my best look," she said. "Pretty soon I was the leader of my girl posse, and I had the girls doing whatever I wanted them to. Those poor, sweet little girls. They had no idea what they were getting themselves into back then. Like the time we laughed at you when you fell down skating. Darlene had nothing to do with that. That was all me, and she just followed my lead. But the whole time, every single day, I never forgot that you had been my buddy for two years. My prince. I wanted that back. I wanted my friend. But the more I wanted it, and didn't get it, the more I resented Chris, and the meaner I got to you."

She sighed. She was getting closer to the hard part.

"It got better when Mom and Dad got married and we were all happy. It settled into more of a toughness after Dad's accident, but it was a toughness I needed to survive. I settled down a bit more in high school, but by then, I didn't know how to come back to you. The tough-girl routine was too ingrained in my personality, I guess."

She paused and looked up. Carl was watching her, rapt on her every word. She sighed again.

"Carl, I have a big confession to make. I lied to you. I didn't make that prom pact with you sophomore year because I was afraid no one would ask me to the prom. I made it because I wanted to go to prom with you so badly, I was willing to make up a scheme. I didn't want to go to prom with someone else and see you there with some other girl. It would have destroyed me. So I made up the idea about the pact. I felt so clever, so sneaky. To be honest, I actually did get asked to the prom that year."

"By who?" Carl asked.

"Sam Johnson," Kim said. "I told him no because I already had a date. My pact date. I never intended for us not to go together. You know everything that happened after that, but you don't know this. Prom was the night I fell in love with the grown-up Carl Bishop. That's why I cried when I knew I had hurt you."

Kim stared at her feet, and then looked Carl in the eyes.

"I love you, Carl. I can't remember a time when I didn't love you."

Carl stood up from his chair at the table and sat down hard on the couch next to her. He sat silently. He looked at his hands. Then, he reached out and took one of Kim's hands. Kim noticed it was warm and sweaty. They sat there on the couch for several minutes not speaking a word.

"I love you, too, Kim," Carl finally forced out through his constricted throat. The sound of the words out loud startled him. "We've always been friends, but since we, uh, got together, when things got weird with us at prom, I have loved you. I just never thought that you could love me back. I didn't think I was enough for you. I always felt like second best, especially when I found out about what happened between you and Chris. It's something I learned from watching my parents. There might have been love there once, but by the time I was old enough to notice, it was long gone. It was replaced by anger and resentment, and it was too painful to watch. It was at its worst at home around junior prom. So I just kept waiting for the other shoe to drop with you and me. And then you wanted to come out here to California with me. I didn't understand why you would do that. Why would you want to move across the country with someone like me? Why would you choose me? But I think I understand now.

"I know how it feels to think about us being apart, and I never want that to happen. Kim, of course I remember being your buddy. I remember holding sweaty hands. I also remember second grade. I remember the pressure from Chris. My dad encouraged me to follow Chris's lead. He wanted us to be best friends, just like he was with his cousins growing up. You know our family has really weird boundaries. My dad thought Chris was tough, and he wanted me to learn to be tough too. And Gram wanted me to look out for Chris, to make sure he didn't get *too* tough. That was a lot to put on a little kid. So since I always thought I was second best anyway, I became second fiddle to my cousin. I would much rather things had stayed the way they were before, with us as buddies, with the boys and the girls playing together, and none of that cootie stuff. But it's like you said once. Chris was all about charisma. When Chris spoke, you responded. I got lost in all that charisma. It was easy to do. I never had to make a decision, or take responsibility for anything. People knew I was just following Chris's lead, that poor little dumb Carl wasn't to blame for anything. I was kind of a joke. And I was okay with that, until junior prom, when suddenly Kim Drake wanted something to do with me. Something big and important. It was huge, but it never felt real, you know? I was always afraid that any minute, it would all disappear, and you'd turn to mist and float away.

"I remember the first time I realized I loved you, or at least acknowledged to myself that the thought was there. It was after my first day of work on the lawn crew. You were rubbing my shoulders, and then you did some things that absolutely blew my mind. The words 'I love you' popped up inside my head, like a neon sign. They almost came out of my mouth, and it terrified me. I stuffed them right back down inside me and vowed to keep it to myself. But even if I said nothing, it was there, every moment. I wish I could go back and tell you I loved you every single time I felt it. You would have been so completely buried with I love yous. You always would be."

Kim didn't bother to wipe the tears from her cheek.

"Carl," she choked out. "I've loved you all my life, but it became real at prom. It became like something solid that I swallowed and got stuck in my throat. But I was so scared that if I told you, something horrible would happen. You would get taken away, by someone else, or some sort of cruel, horrible accident. I tried to lie to myself, but I knew all my own tricks. I couldn't fool myself. Carl, I love you. I love you so much, it makes my stomach hurt, and I promise, it's not just the baby kicking! Oh my God, Carl, look at us! So afraid for so long of losing each other, that we could have easily pushed each other away forever. Think of what things would have been like, if one of us just said it, way back then!"

Carl wrapped his arms around Kim and held her tight.

"That's all over now," he assured her. "I can't promise you that nothing will ever happen to me. I can't predict the future. But we're together, and we know

now that we love each other, and we don't have to go back. Not if you don't want to. I just want to be with you, and the baby, wherever you are, and I am happy here. And Laine and Beth can be our family support. They love us."

Kim let out a long breath and felt instantly lighter. "I love you Carl. And I want to stay."

"I think we should get married," Carl announced, completely surprising himself, but knowing it was what he truly wanted. "And I don't mean because of the baby. Well, sort of because of the baby, but also because we're a family. And we're best friends. And I never want to stop being your best friend. And because I love you."

Kim's mouth dropped open. "Carl, are you proposing to me? And on your birthday?"

Carl's eyes widened. "I guess I am! But I should do it right."

He slid down to the floor onto his knees and reached out for Kim's hands.

"Kim Drake, will you marry me?"

"Moron, you're supposed to be on one knee, not two!" Kim laughed.

"Oh, sorry!" Carl lifted one knee. "Kim Drake. I love you and I will love you for the rest of my life. Will you marry me and make me your moron for life?"

Kim laughed through her tears. "Yes, I will!"

She reached forward and put her arms around his shoulders and held him tight.

"And now, like so many engaged couples, we need to decide if we want to get married before or after our baby is born!" They both laughed.

"We need a ring," Carl declared.

"I don't think a ring would fit on my finger just now." Kim held up her swollen hand. "I think that can wait."

Carl looked around the room. He saw a bread bag with a twist tie on the kitchen counter. He got up to retrieve the tie, then fell back to his knee in front of Kim. She held out her left hand and Carl twisted the tie lightly around her ring finger. Kim laughed through happy tears.

"Who should we tell first?" Carl asked after their first long kiss as an engaged couple.

"Ha! We should call James and Sally!" Kim joked. "None of our friends in high school expected either one of us to be the first to get married. Especially to each other. Although no one really seemed all that surprised when we told them we were having a baby out of wedlock!"

"My family's not gonna be happy that we're not moving back," Carl said.

"Screw them," Kim said. "Let them all come live here if they want us around so bad!"

"What about your mom?" Carl asked gently. "I know you wanted to be with her."

Kim nodded and wiped a tear from her chin. "I'll talk to my mom. We'll figure it out. We can visit. Or she can visit. We always work things out somehow."

Carl smiled. "Y'know, let's go tell Laine and Beth right now. It will be nice to give some good news to someone who will genuinely be happy for us."

They joined hands, slipped on their flip-flops, and walked over to Laine and Beth's door, still wearing their pajamas. Kim knocked. Beth answered.

"Happy birthday, Carl!" she said with a smile. Then she noticed Kim's tearstained face. "Is everything okay?"

"Everything's great!" Kim exclaimed, and she lifted her hand to show Beth her perfect engagement ring. "Guess what?"

MINDS ARE FOR CHANGING

They decided to get married before the baby was born. Kim wanted her husband there for the delivery. Which meant they needed to make some phone calls back east to let everyone know what was going to happen.

"Mom," Kim said to her mother on the phone the night of their engagement. "We're getting married! Carl proposed, and I said yes!"

"Oh, my, Kim," Mrs. Drake responded. "This is a surprise! But a wonderful surprise! Are you happy?"

Kim could hear her siblings' voices piping up on the other end of the phone. "What happened?" "What's going on with Kim?" "Did she have the baby?"

She heard her mother shushing them, and then, muffled, "No, she didn't have the baby, she's getting married! Now hush! I'll tell you all about it when I'm off the phone. So sorry, Kim, I'm back. I was asking if you're happy."

Kim smiled at Carl to let him know her mother had responded favorably.

"Yes, Mom, I'm happier than I've ever been," she told her. "But Mom, I have to tell you something. We've decided to stay and make a life for ourselves here in Seska. We're not moving back." She braced herself for her mother's reply.

"Kimmy, if that's what you want, I support you one hundred percent," Mrs. Drake said. "I mean, I miss you, I always will, but this is your life, your choice. Remember? We had this talk before you left. We all choose our own path for ourselves."

"Thanks for getting it, Mom," Kim replied with relief. "I would love to be around all of you, especially with the baby, but this is just the right place for us right now. We're happy here. We fit in."

"I know, babe, I can hear it in your voice. I think you're making the right choice." She paused. "But I would really like to come out there when the baby is born. I want to be there for you, to help you."

"I would love to have you here, Mom," Kim said, "but how? What would you do about Dad?"

"I think I can work it out," Mrs. Drake said. "I just have to make a schedule. This is important, Kim. You know me. I can make it work."

Kim nodded even though her mother couldn't hear it.

"Mom, there's one more thing. Carl and I have decided not to wait to get married. We want to go to the courthouse and just do it there, just us and Laine and Beth. We can always have a ceremony and reception sometime in the future, but I really want to get married as soon as possible. You can understand, right?"

There was a pause. Kim sucked in her breath.

"Oh, sorry, Kimmy, I dropped the phone," her mother said. Kim exhaled. "Of course I understand. That's okay, babe. We can plan to have a real wedding for you later, when the pressure is off. You just need to worry about getting that baby born healthy, and taking care of yourself. All the details will work themselves out."

Kim smiled and gave Carl the thumbs up. "Mom, I really want to come home and have a ceremony there, maybe when we're feeling the baby is old enough so we can travel. I want to have Dad there. I want him to walk me down the aisle."

Kim could hear a catch in her mother's voice as she replied. "That would be wonderful, Kim," she said. "That would be perfect for you. We will make that happen, I promise."

"Mom, we need to call Carl's grandma now to tell her the news. I hope she takes it as well as you did. Maybe we can get the two of you together. I'm sure she'll want in on the wedding planning."

"That's fine, Kim," Mrs. Drake said. "I'll call you next week and let you know about my plans to come there for the baby."

"I'll let Laine and Kim know you're planning to come," Kim told her. "They have a guest room. Please tell the crew I said hello and I love them, and give Dad a big hug for me."

"I will, babe. I love you to the moon."

"And I love you back."

She hung up the phone and reached for Carl. He wrapped her in her arms. "She's coming here, to help me," she said, in disbelief. "This is really happening, Carl. We're really having a baby. And we're getting married!"

Carl smiled. "See?" he said. "Everything's working out. Now I have to call Gram Missy. Wish me luck. And pray for me!"

The call to Gram Missy started out stressful but turned out successful; she loved the idea of planning a wedding in Massachusetts, even if Carl and Kim were already legally married. And she would contribute to the cost. And she would let them, and Mrs. Drake, participate equally in the planning. The most important thing was their happiness.

"I would have loved for you to move back here, Carl, so Cissy and I could support you more, but you have to do what's right for you," she told him. "I know everyone thinks that I think I know what's right for everyone, but I know when to step back and mind my own business. You're a very smart man, and you've grown up so much in the last couple of years. You've had to overcome a lot, and for that, I am so sorry. I should have been paying better attention to what was going on at your house, and I wish I could make it up to you."

"It's okay, Gram," he told her. "One thing I have always known was that you loved me, and knowing that really helped get me through. If I didn't feel that I could have handled things, I would have come to you. And it's all good now. I'm happy, and I have my own family to take care of."

He smiled at Kim, sitting next to him on the couch. She took his hand and squeezed it.

"Gram, we'll call you every week to let you know what's going on, and we'll call you right away when the baby's coming. You can be the Bishop-Farmer town crier, okay?"

"I'd like that, Carl. Tell your bride I said congratulations, and give her my love."

"Bye, Gram. Love you."

The last call of the night was to Darlene. It was after 11:00 p.m. in Ithaca, New York, and a school night. But Kim knew that Darlene would not mind being woken up for some happy news.

"Hello?" Darlene sounded alert and not at all sleepy.

"Hey, D, did I wake you?" Kim asked.

Darlene laughed. "Kim, it's eleven on Thursday at Ithaca. I haven't even gotten started yet! What's up?"

"I told him," she said. "I told Carl that he's my prince! I finally did it!"

"Kim! You did it!" Darlene exclaimed. "What did he say?"

"He said he loves me," she answered softly. "And then he asked me to marry him!" She squealed.

Darlene squealed back. "Kim!" she said to her with warmth. "Prince Carl is finally making you his princess!"

They talked more about the details, the courthouse wedding, and the ceremony that would take place in Massachusetts, hopefully in the spring or summer. Kim promised to let her know more when she had details but assured Darlene that she was definitely still her choice for maid of honor. Darlene squealed again. Kim asked her not to say anything to Michelle or Sally. Kim planned to call them the next day to share the news. She had a lot more squeals she needed to get out.

COURTHOUSE ROCK

They rode to the Seska courthouse in Beth's car. Kim sat in front, and Carl and Beth sat in back with Claire. Benjamin was at school until three. Kim could not believe she was getting married on a Monday. She was skipping school for the day, but the Seska courthouse only made wedding appointments on Mondays. Her instructors had understood. They were already working with her to prepare for when the baby came. Her school was being very supportive, as was Head Forward. This was Seska, California, and one of the reasons Kim had wanted to stay.

They parked in the nearly empty parking lot and trooped to the front door of the city building. They were dressed in their most formal clothes, and Claire had insisted on wearing her patent leather shoes and a purple ribbon in her hair. Kim wore the one dress she had left that fit, a long-sleeved solid sky-blue A-line with a scoop neck, and pulled her hair back out of her face in a loose braid. Carl and Laine wore ties, both of them belonging to Laine. Beth was dressed primly in a Sunday-go-to-church-style dress that had never seen the inside of a church, and she had managed a bit of mascara.

When the clerk saw them enter, she knew immediately why they were there. "Hello, Laine," she said, recognizing him as the city-contracted electrician. "I'll go get Morton. He's the JP today. Please, all of you have a seat."

They sat down anxiously, and Claire jumped off her mother's lap and started to run in circles around the spacious lobby. The tapping of her fancy shoes made echoes throughout the cavernous hall. When Claire realized she was causing the eerie noise, she started jumping up and down and laughing with glee at the sound she created.

Carl and Kim clasped hands, and Kim started tapping her foot on the floor. "Why am I so nervous?" she asked him. "I feel like we're here to take some sort of standardized test!"

Carl laughed. "Yeah, it does kinda feel that way," he agreed. "But remember, I'm really good at standardized tests. We'll get a really good score."

Kim smiled, allowing herself to relax. The baby moved tightly on the left side of her belly, and she placed Carl's hand over the area so he could feel it, too.

"He's awake for the wedding," he said. "Or she. I'm glad the baby will be there with us."

There were heavy footsteps in the hall, and a gray-haired man in a somber gray suit appeared before them. "Drake-Bishop?" he called out.

They were the only ones there.

"Oh, hello, Laine," he said when he saw him sitting there. "I didn't realize this was a Farmer family wedding. You can all follow me back to my office."

Carl and Kim trailed behind Laine, Beth, Claire, and the Justice of the Peace as they walked the length of the long hallway.

"Carl," Kim said quietly as they walked. "I've kind of been thinking of the baby's name. I was thinking it might be nice to name the baby after my father."

"Gerald?" Carl asked. "That's a bit too close to Jerome."

"No," Kim objected. "I don't think it would be very nice to name a baby Gerald in 1987. But I'm changing my last name to Bishop, so I was thinking, what about Drake?"

"Drake Bishop?" Carl tried out loud.

Kim cleared her throat. "Drake *Pedro* Bishop," she corrected.

Carl smiled. "I love it," he said. "I really do, Kim. It's a real tribute to your father. And my grandfather. And there's no Jerome in there anywhere. That's a good thing."

"Drake is also the word for a sexually mature male duck," Kim admitted, "but luckily hardly anyone knows that, so I never got teased in school. But it's good to know anyway."

"Well, at least it would be Drake Bishop, and not Drake Farmer. That would be unfortunate!" They both laughed.

They had reached the office of the Justice of the Peace, and they all stepped inside. Morton closed the door. When they came out ten minutes later, they were officially and legally Mr. and Mrs. Carl and Kim Bishop, both with thin gold wedding bands on their left hands. Beth snapped pictures in the hallway, and Morton joined in for a group shot. The clerk took the picture. Then they said goodbye to the courthouse staff, got back into the car, and went home.

LAINE DROPS A BOMB

Beth made them a lunch of sandwiches and soup. Then Laine left for the store, giving Carl his wedding day off. Carl and Kim went back to their home, and gently and lovingly consummated their marriage. Then Kim fell asleep, and Carl got dressed and went for the mail on the Farmers' front porch. He found Beth on the porch, looking at several packages, four very large and about a dozen smaller, that had been delivered while they were at the courthouse.

"These are all for you and Kim," Beth told him. "They all have a return address of a baby boutique in Shrewsbury, Massachusetts. A nice one. It looks like baby furniture and supplies."

Carl examined the boxes, not knowing where to start. He found one that appeared to contain a shipping list and invoice. He ripped it open. There was a notation on the bottom that indicated the purchase had been made by Melissa and Cecelia Bishop. The Grams. He should have known. The items listed were a crib, a dresser, a changing table, a baby bath, and various linens, toiletries, feeding supplies, and baby toys. Carl was kind of blown away.

He was able to move some of the smaller boxes back to the apartment, but decided to wait until Laine got back to help him lug the big ones. He noticed that Kim was still sleeping and opted to wait for her to awaken to break open the boxes. He took a congratulatory call from Chris, and then took off his shoes and pants, pulled back the sheets, and crawled into bed with his wife. Her body tilted slightly toward him but was stopped by the bump around her belly. She leaned against his side. Her warmth was comforting. He slowly started to doze off, feeling content and secure.

Soon after, he felt Kim stir, get slowly out of the bed, and struggle to put on her clothes. He could not imagine what she went through to even reach her swollen feet to put on her socks. He would have to give her a foot massage later.

"Carl?" she said softly.

"I'm awake," he told her.

"What are all these boxes?" she asked.

"Gifts," he told her, "from the Grams. And there's more on the porch. They pretty much sent us everything we'll need for the baby."

"What?" Kim said in disbelief. "Everything? We were just gonna get things as we needed them. When we could afford them."

She reached down slowly and lifted one of the smallest, lightest boxes. She went into the kitchen and found a box cutter. She tore the tape, opened the flaps, and pulled out the contents. There were crib sheets and hooded towels.

"Crib sheets?" she asked. "We don't even have a crib!"

"Uh, we kinda do," Carl told her. "Front porch."

Kim let herself fall into a sitting position on the couch. Her eyebrows lifted close to her hairline.

"Wow," she said. "The Grams. I guess they're my Grams now, too. Everything has changed!"

"For the better, I hope," Carl said, smiling. "Dude, you're a Bishop-Farmer now. Remember, it comes with perks."

Tears came to Kim's eyes. Then she started to shake with sobs.

"Oh, my God, Kim, are you okay?" He rushed over to her and kneeled on the floor beside her. He grabbed her hand.

"Yes, I'm fine," she said, fanning her face with her free hand. "I'm just a bit overwhelmed. I can't believe everything that's happened. We're married! Carl Bishop is my husband! I'm Kim Bishop now! We live in California, and we're mere weeks away from being parents. And Missy Bishop is my new Gram!"

She started to sob again. Carl put his arms around her and held her.

"I'm just so . . . so happy!" she sobbed. Carl held her for several minutes until her chest stopped heaving.

He smiled at her. "I'm happy, too," he told her. "And I'm also really happy that only one of us has pregnancy hormones. Pretty intense, huh?"

Kim sniffed. "Yeah," she agreed. "Pretty intense. But you know what would help? Opening these boxes."

She handed him the box cutter, and one by one he opened the boxes and handed the contents to Kim.

The phone rang, and Carl dashed to answer it. It was Mrs. Drake. He handed the phone to Kim.

"Mom!" Kim said, "we're married! And I'm a Bishop-Farmer!" She started to sob again.

Carl decided to give them some privacy, so he walked outside and headed back to the porch. He examined the boxes from all sides and slid some of the smaller ones toward the sidewalk.

Just then, Laine pulled into the driveway in his truck. He saw Carl on the porch and came to help.

"Beth called earlier and told me about your delivery," he explained. "Thought I'd give you a hand hauling this stuff back. Looks like the Bishop girls outdid themselves." He grabbed one side of the crib box, and Carl grabbed the other.

"Kim's a hormonal mess right now," Carl told his cousin. "I left her in there with the smaller gifts and her mom on the phone. Let's just get all these to the door, and we can bring them in after."

"Good plan," Laine agreed. "We're gonna have to assemble all this stuff, too. And rearrange the furniture in the unit to make room."

"Yeah, I don't think the Grams know what a small space we're working with here," Carl admitted.

They put the crib box down gently by the door. "Carl," Laine said, using his hand to brace his lower back. "You know you and Kim are welcome to stay in the unit as long as you want. But maybe you should start thinking about your next move. You're gonna need a bigger place at some point."

Carl sat on the concrete stoop. "You're right," he agreed, "but I don't see how we can do it. I'd love to be able to buy a small house, and pay a mortgage instead of rent to a landlord every month, but houses are expensive. We can't afford one yet. I think we're gonna have to stick it out here a bit longer and come up with a budget so we can save some money."

"C'mon, let's go get another box," Laine said. They started back toward the porch. "Carl, what if I told you that the unit back there is paid off?" Laine said, grabbing the end of the changing table box.

Carl hefted his end up off the ground. "I'd say congratulations?" he responded.

"Are you being a moron on purpose, or is it just natural for you?" Laine said with a smirk as they crossed the driveway.

Carl looked at him in confusion. "What?"

"Sorry, you just make it too easy sometimes," Laine said. They leaned the table box up against the crib box. "What I'm saying is, you've been paying me rent since you moved in here last September. But I don't need the money. I've been putting it in a special escrow account the whole time, and it's been earning interest. Carl, that money is meant for you and Kim, and now your baby, for when you decide it's time to find your own place. It's not a ton of money, but it might make a nice down-payment on a house."

"Laine, I don't understand," Carl said. "I mean, why would you do this for us? You barely even knew me when we moved in here. Why would you even consider—"

"Carl," Laine interrupted. "Did you ever notice that you never question when something bad happens to you, but you always question when something good does? Like when Kim decided to come out here with you, you were baffled. But when your parents made choices every day to leave you on your own, and not be there for you, you never batted an eyelash. You just expect the bad things to happen, but you doubt the good stuff. When it comes to parents, Carl, you were dealt a really bad hand. Your dad turned out to be a real fuckwad, excuse my French, and your mom, well, she started out okay, but she's just broken. What happened to you was not fair. Things might have turned out a whole lot different for you had you been raised in a different environment. And your family has noticed. People want to help you, Carl. They want to make up for not being there for you when it really mattered. Farmers are generous people by nature. They like to help. That's why Jerome Farmer was so revered as mayor. He was a mayor for the people. That's why he got a statue. And like thirty baby boys with the middle name Jerome.

"So anyway, the Farmers want to help. They want you to be able to live up to your full potential. That's why my dad thought of you for the apprenticeship. He knew you had a gift, for knowledge, and learning, and you were languishing in that house with no direction. So I made you this offer. I took a leap of faith with you. And you've lived up to all of my expectations. You've gone beyond my wildest expectations. Your Gram Missy, she wants so much for you. I think you remind her of Uncle Cecil. You look like a Bishop, and you're smart like a Bishop, and you have the heart and humor of a Farmer.

"Carl, it's your birthright to have a chance to shine. And we all want you to be able to shine. Good things should happen for you, all the time. That's why Aunt Missy and Aunt Cissy have been matching your rent every month. You have a nest egg of over fifteen thousand dollars in the bank, there for you when you're ready to use it. And I'll help you with anything you need in the house. I built this unit almost by myself, and as you may know by now, I'm pretty handy with electrical work."

Carl was struck speechless. He heard a noise behind him, and when he looked back, he saw Kim standing behind the screen door, holding a stuffed giraffe. She had heard the whole thing. She also had no words. They both stood silent and humbled.

"So," Laine said, clapping his palms together. "So there's that. Think about it. You don't have to make any decisions right now, but I just wanted you to know that you have choices. Happy wedding day, you two. Go get dressed. Beth and I are taking you and the kids out to Roma for dinner."

He walked back toward the porch.

"We'll get the rest of the packages later," he called over his shoulder. He stopped. "Oh, and I almost forgot." He turned around and came back.

He reached into his back pocket and extracted a small package and handed it to Carl.

"This came by special delivery at the store today. I needed to sign for it. It's addressed to you. From Aunt Missy." With that, he walked away.

Carl peeled the brown paper off the box and opened the lid. Inside, he found the engagement ring that his grandfather Cecil had given his Gram Missy, all those years ago, leading up to the infamous Bishop-Farmer wedding. There was no note. He held it up to show Kim.

Carl stared at Kim through the screen door. She stared back at him. Then she opened the door and stepped outside. Carl took the ring out of the box and slipped it on Kim's finger. It was a bit tight, but it would fit perfectly in a little over a month. Kim stood silently, staring at her new ring and moving it around so the sunlight reflected off the diamond. Then she looked up.

"Look," she said to Carl, holding up the stuffed giraffe in her other hand. "It was in one of the boxes from the Grams. It's the same exact one as mine. The baby and I will have matching giraffes."

DUCK, DUCK, DRAKE

December twelfth was approaching quickly. Mrs. Drake made plane reservations for December tenth, which could be changed if the baby came early. She would stay for two weeks. Her sisters-in-law would take turns staying at the house while she was gone, and they made arrangements for care aids from the state to come over during the days while they worked. The kids were scheduled for multiple play dates and overnights. The calendar page was scribbled with notations of plans. Copies were made for family and the schools. Baby Watch was on.

They planned a small Thanksgiving celebration with Laine and Beth and kept it quiet and low key. Kim complained of heartburn all night and chewed on Tums tablets before bed. But she admitted every bite of pie was worth it.

Kim worked with her professors to get ahead on her schoolwork. She did all of her assignments and specially assigned projects and essays. The semester would end just days before Christmas, and she wanted to get credit for the work she had put in. Her goal was to get everything done by December seventh, in case the baby came early. She was able to meet her goal and finally started her unofficial maternity leave. She would be taking the spring semester off and returning to school in the fall. She had resigned herself to the fact that community college would be more than a two-year venture for her.

Carl brought his car to work every day instead of riding in with Laine and drove home at lunch to check on his wife. They made emergency plans in case she went into labor and couldn't reach him. He took her to doctor's appointments and rubbed her feet as she watched TV at night.

Carl and Laine assembled all the baby furniture and placed it around the unit. Kim and Beth washed all the towels, sheets, and tiny baby clothes and put them in their places. A mobile was hung over the crib and another over the bassinet. The cat sought extra attention and affection, as he sensed things were about to change drastically. He liked to take naps in the crib. Everyone was as ready as they could be to welcome Baby Bishop.

Mrs. Drake flew into the airport on December tenth. Laine drove to San Francisco to pick her up. Kim wanted to go, but everyone told her no; she would see her mother when she got to Seska.

When Laine pulled into the driveway, Beth came out to meet them. "Hi, Mrs. Drake, I'm Beth Farmer," she said. "Don't bother getting out of the car. My mother is here with the kids. We're going to the hospital." She opened the back door to the car and got in. "Welcome to California," she told Mrs. Drake. "You're about to be a grandma."

Kim had started having contractions early that morning, but they hadn't been distressing. "I think they're just those Braxton-Hicks things they're always talking about," she had reassured Carl. "Nothing to worry about."

By noon, the contractions started to have a pattern. "It's nothing," Kim had told Carl. "My mom will be here soon. We can call the doctor's office if it makes you feel better."

The doctor had told them it was something. The contractions were getting closer together, and the intensity was increasing. These were not practice contractions. Kim had started labor. She was having to focus on her breath, but she wasn't getting relief.

"It's time for us to go," Carl had told Beth, and they helped Kim out to the Escort with her bag.

"But my mom—" Kim protested as she doubled over with pain.

"We'll bring her right over when she gets here, I promise," Beth said.

Now Laine, Beth, and Mrs. Drake were making the ten-minute drive to the Seska Community Medical Center, and every second felt like hours.

In her hospital room, Kim was feeling nauseated. She was grasping Carl's hand, and he was trying to help guide her breath, but she was panting.

"Count with me, Kim," he told her. "One, two, three." The contraction passed and Kim relaxed.

"It hurts," she moaned to Carl. "Why didn't anyone tell me this would hurt?" she protested.

"I don't know," Carl lied. "What a bunch of assholes."

Kim laughed. Everyone had told her this would hurt. There was just no way she could have anticipated this level of hurt.

"Kim," Carl went on, "you are the bravest, and the strongest person I have ever met. It's because of you that we're together in the first place. It's because of you that we made the leap together, and told each other how we felt about each other. You left everything behind to make a new start for us. You can do anything, Kim, I know you can. You can do this."

Kim loosened her grip on Carl's hand and rubbed his palm. "I can do this, Carl," she told him with determination, "because you're with me. We can do this."

The Farmers and Mrs. Drake had arrived at the maternity ward and checked in at the desk. The doctor was with Kim, doing a quick exam, and Mrs. Drake would be allowed to go in when she was done as long as it would be okay with Kim.

"Why don't you two call me Victoria," Mrs. Drake insisted. "I'm guessing we're probably about the same age. It's weird for you to call me Mrs. Drake."

"Victoria," Laine repeated. "I didn't even know you had a first name. It's always been Mom or Mrs. Drake. What's your maiden name?"

"Lester," Mrs. Drake stated.

"Victoria Lester," Laine said. "Did you go to Murphy or McKinney?"

"Murphy."

"Did you know any Farmers there?"

"There was a Janine Farmer in the class above me."

Laine smiled. "Jan's my oldest sister," he said. "She's Jan Peterson now. Wow, it's amazing how connected we all are, Victoria. And you're gonna be a wicked young grandma. What are you, thirty-eight?"

Mrs. Drake smiled. "That's right," she told him. "I had my first baby at nineteen, and she's having her first baby at nineteen. If this baby has a baby at nineteen, I'll be a fifty-seven-year-old great-grandmother!"

The nurse at the desk called out for Kim's family. They were escorted to her room.

Kim had just met with the doctor, who did an exam. "You're eight centimeters dilated, and ninety percent effaced," she told Kim.

"Is that good?" Kim asked. She was bracing herself for the contraction she knew would be coming. She breathed into her stomach muscles to try to relax.

The doctor smiled. "It's very good. You're progressing nicely. When you get to ten centimeters, you get to start pushing. I think you will be meeting your baby very soon."

Kim and Carl made eye contact and smiled. She was still grasping his hand like a lifeline and didn't dare to let go.

Dr. Stein wrote some notes in the chart. "I hear you have visitors," she said, "so I'll clear out and let you visit for a bit. I'll be back in about an hour to check in on you again."

The doctor opened the door to leave, and Kim's guests came into the room.

"Mom!" Kim called out, and her mother rushed to her bedside and embraced her. Kim immediately started to cry. "Mom, I didn't think you would make it on time. I need you. Mom, it hurts so much."

"I know, I know," Mrs. Drake said, stroking her daughter's hair. "But pretty soon, it will all be over, and you'll be holding your little baby, and it will all seem like a distant dream. I promise. It's true."

"Mom. I can't believe you're here."

Kim's muscles started to tighten, and she felt the start of another contraction. Carl held her hand, and Mrs. Drake held her other hand, and together, they both talked her through it.

They gave her ice chips, and Carl rubbed her hands and feet. They talked about the family at home, and the wedding they would be having in the spring. Contractions came, and contractions ended, and after an hour, Dr. Stein came back.

"Kim," she announced. "You are now fully effaced and dilated. We can start having you push this baby out."

They cleared the room besides the medical staff and the parents. Laine, Beth, and Mrs. Drake returned to the waiting area to await the news. Laine and Beth talked quietly while Mrs. Drake tried and failed to read her book. She got up and paced the room. She chatted with other families waiting for news of their own babies arriving. Laine went to the cafeteria and got them all coffee and muffins.

At 10:00 p.m., Beth called her mother, who agreed to spend the night. Mrs. Drake, who was still on Eastern Time, dozed off in her chair. Carl came out at 11:00 with an update that Kim was doing well. She was exhausted, but still pushing like a champion. When he went back, Laine and Mrs. Drake started to compare names of friends and relatives back home and found out they had several mutual friends of friends.

At 12:16, Carl came back out. "He's here," he said, his voice ripe with emotion. "Kim did it. He's beautiful. Everything is perfect, and Kim is fine."

"It's a boy?" Mrs Drake asked.

"It's a boy," Carl confirmed. "I knew it would be. Drake Pedro Bishop. He's 19 inches long and 7 pounds, 4 ounces. Born on 12/11 at exactly 12:11!"

"You named him Drake?" Mrs. Drake asked softly, reaching out to touch Carl's arm.

"Yes," he said proudly. "Kim wanted to honor her father in some way. We both agreed it was the perfect name."

Mrs. Drake wiped tears from her eyes.

"Congratulations! When can we see them?" Laine asked.

"I don't know," Carl admitted. "They were just cleaning him up and Kim told me to come out to tell you all. I'll go back in, then I'll come to get you when I can."

Fifteen minutes later, they were all introduced to Drake Pedro, a small, swaddled bundle in his mother's arms. Kim looked serene as she stared at her son. "He tried to nurse right away!" she marveled. "He knew just what to do. He's a genius, like his father."

Carl beamed, and Kim encouraged him to take the baby. He held the sleeping child in his arms and instinctively started to rock. "He looks like a Bishop," he said.

Laine peeked at his face. "I see some Farmer in there, too," he insisted.

Now Mrs. Drake piped in. "He's got the Lester eyes. Lesters have beautiful eyes."

"It will take some time to see if he has any Valdez in him," Carl said softly. "I hope he does."

The baby was passed around the room, and everyone got a chance to meet him and say hello. Soon, Kim yawned, and they decided to call it a night. Laine, Beth, and Mrs. Drake all kissed and hugged Kim goodbye and promised to return tomorrow after they were all rested.

A nurse came in and offered to bring the baby to the nursery so Kim could get some sleep. She would bring him back when it was time to try nursing again, so she had about an hour. Carl climbed into a large convertible recliner near the window, and before he could even say good night to Kim, she was asleep. He was very close behind her.

HOME BEFORE THE HOLIDAYS

The Bishop family came home two days later and were greeted by an indignant Tiger. Kim sat down on the couch to try to nurse Drake, while Carl sat next to her, patting and soothing the cat. No one of any species was to be neglected in his home. Mrs. Drake bustled in with Kim's bags and supplies and went straight to the kitchen to start organizing meals.

Drake nursed like a pro, and Kim was always ravenously hungry and thirsty. She craved fruit and ice water, so Carl and Mrs. Drake made frequent trips to the grocery store to fulfill her needs. She was not allowed to lift a finger to help clean, organize, or plan. Her mother put the ottoman under her feet and told her to stay. She obeyed. They were up every two hours with the baby, and by the end of the first week, they were all exhausted. At his checkup, Drake was declared to be a healthy little boy, and he was growing right on target. Kim breathed a sigh of relief.

They got on a routine for feeding, waking, changing, and starting again. They bundled Drake into a stroller and went out for a walk on a cool California December afternoon. Although she didn't know where it was all coming from, Mrs. Drake was doing laundry almost every day. Babies were work-intensive, even for an experienced mother of five.

On day eight, Mrs. Bishop got a call from her sister-in-law Karen. Kim could hear her on the phone using hushed tones but couldn't make out the words from the bedroom. When she hung up, she came back and sat on the bed next to Kim and Drake.

"Kim," she said. "That was Aunt Karen. She told me that Dad had another seizure last night and they had to call an ambulance to bring him to the emergency room."

"What?" Kim exclaimed, sitting up straighter and shifting Drake in her arms. "Is he okay?"

Mrs. Drake nodded. "He's okay. They adjusted his seizure meds and made him a follow-up appointment with the neurologist. They sent him back home. But Kim," she continued. "He's been having seizures more often over the past few months. They may be nearing the end of what they can do for him with medication changes."

"What does that mean?" Kim asked desperately. "They're giving up on him?"

"No, no, no," Mrs. Drake assured her. "No one's giving up on Dad. But what they might need to do is give him some other medication or treatment to keep him safe and comfortable, and he's going to need twenty-four-hour supervision. And not the kind of supervision he can get from Stella and Chip after school. He needs professionals."

"A nursing home?" Kim guessed, tears welling up in her eyes.

Mrs. Drake nodded. "A nursing home or something similar. Where they can take care of him, and know what to do when he has seizures. And he won't have to go to the ER all the time, either. That's so hard on him. And on the rest of us, especially the kids. But it's not for sure yet, okay? We're still going to see the doctor next week, and we'll learn more. And we'll see if he has any more seizures before then."

"Do you need to go home early?" Kim asked.

Mrs. Drake put her hand over Kim's. "No, babe, I'm not changing my plans. It doesn't really matter if I'm here or there. Karen will keep me informed if anything changes. I just need to make sure I'm home in time for Christmas, for the kids."

"Mom?" Kim started, afraid to ask what she was thinking. "If Dad goes to a nursing home, will he still be able to walk me down the aisle at my wedding?"

Mrs. Drake smiled reassuringly. "Kim, I will do everything in my power to make that happen. The worst-case scenario would be that we wheel him down with you, or use that as a backup. But this is the one thing you asked me to do for your wedding, and I'm planning to make it happen."

PLANNING OUR FUTURE

Mrs. Drake left on December twenty-fourth to be home and play Santa for her younger children on Christmas Eve. Kim felt lost and alone the moment Carl's car pulled out of the driveway to deliver her to the airport in San Francisco. Beth came over and they chatted while folding laundry, and after a while, Kim stopped and sat to feed the baby.

Starting that day, they switched off spending time together at the Bishop unit or the Farmer house while their husbands were at work. Claire adored baby Drake and worked his existence into her pretend play. After school, Benjamin tolerated his little cousin, but also watched him protectively from his perch in front of the TV and sometimes showed him his LEGO creations.

Kim wrote letters to her friends and sent them photos from their courthouse wedding and of baby Drake. She let them know that a real wedding was coming up in the spring, and just like they all vowed, the whole group would be invited, even Traci. Darlene called her once per week to check in. Sally wrote to her from Providence College. She and James and Michelle would be at the wedding no matter what. And Chris, of course, would be the best man.

Carl spoke to Chris at the end of February when he called to say happy birthday to Kim. "We just went out for Kim's birthday," Carl told his cousin. "It's like you have to pack luggage to go out with a baby, even for like an hour!"

Chris laughed. "Gram showed me the pictures Kim sent last week," he said. "Drake's a moose! He's pretty cute though. You did good, Carl."

Even after being gone for two years, that sort of remark still made Carl feel proud. "Thanks, man," he said. "Yeah, we're pretty happy. Kim's a great mom. I expected she would be, but she's really taken to it, you know? She's pretty awesome." He paused. "So have you heard anything about Scott lately?" he asked. He hadn't spoken to his brother since he moved to California.

"Actually, yeah," Chris said. "I did hear from Gram that Scott started doing shift work over at Aries! Can you believe that? And you'll never guess who his boss is. J.D. Newell!"

Carl gasped. "James's dad? That's unreal! I heard he's a hard-ass at work, but if he takes you under his wing, you're sure to get promoted. Maybe J.D. can whip some sense into Scott. It could be a good thing for him. Maybe," he went on, "if you ever see him, like at one of the Grams' houses or something, you could tell him how I'm doing, and maybe find out where he's staying, so we can invite him to the wedding?"

"Of course," Chris promised. Then he said more softly, "What about Jack and Rosa?"

"No, that's okay," Carl said quickly. "They've made no effort to be in touch with me the last two years. I told Gram not to include them at all. I don't know if they even know about Drake. I don't really have any need for them anymore."

He could sense the relief in Chris's voice. "Second-best decision you've ever made," Chris said. "The first, of course, being . . ."

"Kim," they said together, and they both laughed.

"What?" Kim called from the kitchen.

"Come say hi to Chris," he yelled back at her.

Kim came into the room and grabbed the receiver. "Hey Chris, how's life in the dorm?" she asked.

Carl saw the baby wiggling in the bassinet and saw his eyes trying to focus on the mobile hanging above his face. His legs kicked in the air, and he raised and lowered his arms, making a cooing sound. Carl scooped him up and held him closer to the floating animals so he could get a better view. Drake smelled like a baby, and Carl inhaled the scent like perfume.

Kim hung up the phone and came to join her family in the living area. "Chris sounds good," she said. "I told him he could bring a date to the wedding, and he said he'd think about it, but I think he'd rather come alone. That way, he can spend time with the gang and not have to be distracted."

"Sounds like a good plan," Carl agreed.

"I spoke to Gram Missy earlier," Kim said. "She said she found a really nice indoor/outdoor non-denominational venue we could use, both for the ceremony and the reception, and they do have an opening on Memorial Day weekend.

That's three months from now. They're gonna pay for our plane tickets. Should we just go for it?"

Carl shifted the baby so he was cradled in the nook of his arm. With his other arm, he pulled Kim close to him, and he stood there with his family, the only family he really needed, enveloped in his arms.

"Yes," he said confidently. "I think we should definitely go for it."

THANK YOU, DAD, FOR EVERYTHING

Kim entered the room, and Carl came in behind her. Mr. Drake was sitting in a chair by the window, watching other residents of Eastboro Nursing Center moving around the yard.

"Hi, Dad," Kim said softly as she approached him.

He looked up and smiled. "Kimmy! Oh my! It's so good to see you! You look wonderful! When did you get here?"

Kim reached over to give him a hug, then stepped aside and let Carl stand beside her, holding Drake. "Dad, Carl and I are here to get married. We're actually married already, but tomorrow, you're going to walk me down the aisle so we can get married again in front of our friends and family. Dad, Carl and I have a baby. His name is Drake."

Carl stepped closer to his father-in-law and bent so he could see his grandson.

"We named him for you," Kim told him proudly. "Drake Pedro Bishop."

Mr. Drake looked at the baby. "Oh, what a beautiful child. I'm glad you named him Drake instead of Gerald. Gerald is such an old man's name."

"And we bought a house," Kim told him. "It's about two miles away from our apartment in Seska, so we'll still be close to everything. We're gonna start moving next month. Drake will have his own room, and we'll have a lot more space."

"That's so exciting, Kimmy," Mr. Drake said. "Did your mom help you with the real estate stuff? She's really good at that. I know from experience."

"She did, Dad," Kim said with a smile. "Dad," she said hopefully, "do you remember my eighth birthday party?" She didn't know how much time they had left before he would fade back away. The time they had was a gift.

"Of course, Kimmy," he answered. "It was an ice skating party. We had such a good time."

Kim felt encouraged to continue. "Do you remember my friend Carl, and how you helped him when he fell on the ice?"

Mr. Drake thought for a moment. "Carl. He was your special friend. Your hallway buddy. He was one of the Bishop-Farmers."

"That's right, Dad. And Carl and I stopped being close for a while. But you helped him. You told him to be patient and I'd come back to him." She gestured to Carl.

"Mr. Drake, you were right," Carl told him, stepping closer. "It took some time, and I had to let a lot roll off my back like a duck, but I never forgot what you said. And now, we're married, and we have our little boy. So thank you. Thanks so much for the best advice I ever got. Someday, I might give the same advice to Drake."

"I remember, Carl. I remember that sad face. She came back to you. I'm so happy to hear that." He laughed. "Kimmy! I can't believe you married a Bishop-Farmer! You always loved that story!" He smiled warmly.

"I know, Dad, I really did!" Kim said. "Sometimes, it's all like a dream."

Mr. Drake glanced out the window as if distracted by some movement outside. Then he turned back. "Kimmy!" he said when he looked at her. "When did you get here? And who's this with the little baby?"

Carl grabbed onto Kim's arm, as if fearing she would fall. She didn't. She stood tall.

"I love you, Dad," she said firmly.

"I love you, too, Kim. I always have. You're my firstborn."

Tears sprang from Kim's eyes but she remained composed. "We'll see you tomorrow, Daddy," she said.

"Bye, Kimmy," he said, turning back to the window.

Kim turned and fled from the room, Carl close behind. He handed Drake to his mother-in-law in the hallway so he could attend to his wife.

"That was rough," he said and he put his arms around her.

"Yeah," Kim agreed. "It was. But Carl, it's all in there. He might not know it right now, but all those memories, they're in there. Now Drake's in there, too. Even if he never realizes it. We're part of him. And you got to tell him what you wanted to say. And he remembered. You're in there too. And that's everything."

Carl nodded slowly. "Yeah," he agreed emphatically. "That *is* everything."

Acknowledgments

This is harder to do than the first book. I want to thank all the same people. Everyone who has been supportive of me as I've gone on my journey to develop and create the world of Eastboro, Massachusetts and Siska, California. So thank you to all of my friends and family who have encouraged me and given me love even when I had my head buried in my laptop any time I wasn't working or sleeping.

Thank you Jonathan Meltzer, for all of the hard work you have done to help me get the word out there about my series. Thank you for reading every single one of my books as soon as I finish each section.

Thank you to my mother, for unconditionally supporting me from three thousand miles away.

Thank you to Melissa Barnes, who is not Michelle, but inspired the little red-headed firecracker with her hair and her love of new age music in art class.

Thank you to Jai Design for my logo, cover design, and all the marketing tools a girl could need. Thank you to Nicole Frail, editor extraordinaire. Thank you to the best and most dependable beta reader to ever exist, author Clint Chico (look him up on Amazon. His books are inspiring!). Thank you to Meg Stratton for helping me with promotions. You are also an awesome author!

And of course, thank you to my husband Al, who is trying to get through my first book, and my daughter Tory, who will soon be a Duck. I love you both endlessly, and I sure can tell you that!

Debby Meltzer Quick is a full-time social worker in Portland, Oregon. She has been writing for fun since age twelve. Growing up in Massachusetts, she became a huge fan of Boston sports, especially the Red Sox and Patriots, and she aspired to be a sports reporter. She is an avid reader of fiction. She lives with her husband, daughter, two cats, and one rabbit. She plans to release at least five more books in the McKinney High Class of 1986 series.

Don't miss the next installment in the

McKinney High Class of 1986 series:

Absolutely and Totally Smitten

Coming in February 2024

Please enjoy the following excerpt

Prologue

I DO, DO YOU?

They had all wondered who among their friends would be the first to get married. Everyone had a pretty good idea of who it would be. They were all, of course, wrong. It was a beautiful outdoor venue, with flowers in large vases and lining the aisle. There was a view of a small pond with swans and geese flying above, and ducks floating on the water. The sun was shining bright between a few white fluffy clouds, and a light breeze blew through the seventy-five-degree afternoon. Dozens of guests sat ready and waiting as violin music filled the air.

Two identical twin grandmothers, wearing fancy dresses and ornate corsages, one carrying an almost six-month-old baby in a tiny tuxedo, made their way down the aisle and sat in the front row. Thirteen-year-old Stella Drake and her ten-year-old sister Sophia walked down next in matching dresses, carrying small bouquets of spring flowers. James Newell and Sally Bachman walked down the aisle holding hands. They both spent a moment imagining this was their wedding. Then they dropped their hands. James went to the right to start the line of groomsmen, and Sally to the left to be the first of the bridesmaids. They were followed by Pete Cooper and Michelle Gorman, then Chris Mahoney and Darlene Feinman, the best man and maid of honor. The music stopped. Everyone stood. A string quartet started playing "Pachelbel's Canon," and everyone watched the back of the aisle in anticipation. Slowly, they were rewarded with the vision of a beautiful brown-haired woman in white. Grasping her arm on one side was a sandy-haired man looking dapper in a black and white tuxedo, and on the other, another woman in a corsage, talking softly to the man as they walked. He smiled brightly as he escorted his daughter, his wife continuing to coax him along with her soft words. The bride was radiant.

Mr. and Mrs. Drake stopped at the foot of the aisle, and both gave Kim a kiss on the cheek. Then they took their seats next to the Grams and baby Drake. Kim's face was already wet with tears. Carl Bishop took a step closer to her, took her hand with a smile, and together they stepped up to the officiant to speak their vows of everlasting love, for the second time.

Chris Mahoney could not remember another moment in his life when he felt so proud and so happy for someone he loved. For two people he loved. This was their moment to shine, their moment to show the whole world how their love conquered everything. But this was not the story of Kim and Carl. Or of James and Sally. This was the story of why, at that moment, Chris turned his attention to the girls he knew in high school and smiled warmly at one of them. And she smiled back. And he felt something new inside of him stir.

PART ONE

Our True Brothers

Chapter 1: Bad Boys Are Made, Not Born

"He has Farmer eyes," Kate Bishop Mahoney said sleepily as she gazed at her newborn son's face.

Her husband Ken nodded. "He does," he agreed. "And if he has even a tenth of the intelligence, compassion, and charisma of Jerome Farmer, he'll do really well in the world."

Chris Mahoney was born into an Eastboro legacy. His maternal great-grandfather, Jerome Farmer, was the mayor of Eastboro, Massachusetts, many, many years before Chris or his mother were even born. He was considered a brilliant man before his time, beloved by the people. He even had his own statue downtown in front of city hall. Chris had inherited three things from his great-grandfather: his eyes, Jerome as his middle name, and his overpowering charisma.

Chris was not the only one in Eastboro with the legacy. The Bishops and the Farmers were prolific breeders, and there were three generations of cousins in every nook and cranny of Eastboro and surrounding towns. There were cousins at school, cousins in the government, cousins working at the auto mechanic shop, cousins in the police force. And even cousins in jail. Anywhere you went in Eastboro and met a Bishop or a Farmer, you could be assured they were part of Chris's famous family.

In the middle of all the pomp and circumstance was Chris's grandmother, Cecelia, and her identical twin sister, Melissa. The Farmer girls. They were affectionately known as Gram Cissy and Gram Missy by their grandchildren. They were made famous countrywide for their storybook double-wedding to handsome and charming brothers, the Bishop boys, Cecil and Clyde, thus securing the Bishop-Farmer legacy for further generations.

Chris seemed to know from the time of his birth in March of 1968 that he was destined for some sort of greatness. He was a charming baby, and people gravitated toward him. As he grew, Chris got to know his cousins, aunts, and uncles, their habits, and their quirks. As a small child, he knew who kept candy in their pocket or on their coffee table. He learned which cousin got a discount at the toy store, or who could set him up with free samples of new sneakers or demo music tapes from the radio station. In junior high, he knew beyond any doubt who could hook him and his friends up with joints or six-packs of beer, or free tickets to R-rated movies. The cousins didn't need much convincing to do these things for Chris. They liked him. He took them seriously. He listened to their stories, and he told them his tales, both true and far-fetched. He was interesting and friendly. It was all about the Farmer charisma.

Chris developed a group of school friends in second grade, and they were his troop, his posse of bad boys. He was their unofficial leader, and he made his second cousin Carl Bishop, Gram Missy's grandson, his right-hand man. Carl was a lost little boy with no sense of confidence and neglectful parents. Chris liked having a lieutenant, but he also knew instinctively that Carl needed protection from the world. He needed Chris to help him navigate through social situations and to keep him safe. Chris was not sure back then why he needed to keep his cousin safe. It would not be clear to Chris for years why he made Carl come to his house several times per week, made sure he was invited for dinner when he was there, and included him in everything he did. He made sure the posse was tight. They were a team: Chris, Carl, James Newell, and Pete Cooper. And Chris ensured that nobody, *nobody*, messed with Carl.

They made it through elementary school and most of junior high before the walls started to crumble in on their bad boy careers. Chris, James, and Pete were caught sneaking out of school to go smoke a joint by Carson Lake in ninth grade. It wasn't their first time sneaking out, but it was their first time getting caught. Chris was holding the joint. He was suspended from school for three weeks, his friends for three days each. Their parents began to tighten the reins. The boys endured tense meetings with their parents and the principal. There was talk of Chris being expelled if anything even similar to this ever happened again. James and Pete were grounded after school for a month and kept away from Chris's influence. Chris had to beg his parents, with promises of being good, to help him get his friends back. Eventually things settled down, and his friends were allowed back into his life, but they had already changed. They had lost some of their recklessness, their good-natured bad-boy innocence. They became more careful, more mindful of the rules. And that was the incident that led James to decide to live the sober life that would later help to define his character.

But all along the way, there was still always Carl. Carl had not gone with them to the lake that day, had not gotten in trouble, and had not dealt with any of the consequences. Even if he had been with them, his neglectful parents were not too interested in his bad-boy ways. They probably wouldn't have cared. He probably would have still been free to do as he pleased. He was always still up for trouble. He was still Chris's loyal sidekick. They still engaged in harmless mischief, but just not enough to get in trouble at school.

In tenth grade, Pete went to Murphy High, while Chris, Carl, and James all went to McKinney High, thus breaking up the quartet. The latter three started high school as a close-knit trio. Carl and James turned to Chris for guidance on what to do, how to act, and how to fit in. It was a role Chris was born to play and had provided to them for years. But soon after their first year of their high school career began, Rhonda Jenkins made her first move.

Chapter 2: Help Me, Rhonda Jenkins

Chris knew of Rhonda at Randall Junior High. All of the boys were aware of Rhonda from a distance. She was the first of the girls to experiment with tight sweaters, sexy bras, and lavish makeup. She had a very fortunate growth spurt between seventh and eighth grade and came back on the first day of school tall and curvy, dressed in brand-new designer jeans and a halter top. Chris was sure all the boys in his class had similar sexy dreams about Rhonda that night. They never talked much about girls, and especially their sexy dreams, but their eyes started to drift down the hallway when Rhonda passed by. She was like something you'd see on a movie screen but was way too far away to touch.

On the first day of sophomore year, their first day at McKinney High, Rhonda closed her locker door, turned to look at Chris standing nearby, and smiled.

"Hey, Chris," she said, and then started to walk away.

Chris dropped his thick math book on his foot. He waited until she disappeared around the corner to wince, curse, and pick up the book. Chris was too cool to show his pain in front of Rhonda. Carl, who witnessed the whole event, laughed heartily.

"Dude, I wish you could see the look on your face," Carl told him. Chris wrote off Rhonda's smile as a fluke and went on with his life.

There were other small signs throughout the fall and early winter months that Rhonda might be interested, and Chris stowed them away in the back of his mind, one by one.

"Hey, Chris," she said before the bell rang in history class. Chris looked up. "I can't find my pen. I have more in my locker, but I don't have time to go back there before class starts. Do you have one I could borrow?"

Chris quickly dug through his own bag. He found a stubby old pencil with no eraser at the bottom. He kept that for himself and handed his good pen to Rhonda.

After class, Chris was walking toward the cafeteria, when he heard Rhonda calling behind him. He stopped and turned around.

"Chris," she said, scurrying up to him. "You forgot to get your pen from me. Here." She handed it to him with much ceremony and a smile.

"Thanks, Rhonda," Chris said. "You could have given it back to me tomorrow, you know."

Rhonda shrugged. "But you might need it before then." She gave him a little wave and turned to walk away. Chris watched as she moved down the hall.

Rhonda's friends started saying hi to him when they passed him in the hallway, which they had never done before. Rhonda complimented him on his baseball shirt in the cafeteria, even though it was almost exactly the same as his other four baseball shirts. His friends were starting to notice the attention, too.

"She's totally into you," James told him as they hung out in the crisp mid-November air at the Store 24 after school. "She's always looking at you and turning away when you look at her. She doesn't have a boyfriend. You should ask her out."

"You should," Carl agreed. "She's hot, and she's popular. And I bet she's experienced. Maybe she could hook us up with her friends."

"I don't know, maybe," Chris said with a shrug. He wasn't going to tell his friends, but he was worried that if he asked Rhonda out, she would say no. No one had ever said no to Chris before. Most girls were impressed with his confidence and surety. He may have only gone out with most of them one time, but he never got an initial no. But Rhonda was in a whole different league. One of the differences was that he didn't care if those other girls said no, so there was never anything to lose. But if Rhonda said no, he would feel it. And people would know. It was a calculated risk. He kept it in the back of his mind.

It wasn't until after Christmas break that they finally connected. They had to choose partners for a project in history class, and Rhonda turned to Chris. "Hey, Chris, wanna be my partner?" she asked. Then she gave him the smile.

He knew he had a golden opportunity at that moment. He could say no. He could publicly turn down Rhonda Jenkins. He could show her who was in control. Then later, he would ask her out and not care if she said no, and she would be unable to say no. But the smile turned his brain to mush. He nodded. "Sure," he answered as nonchalantly as he could manage.

"Great," she said, and then turned back to the front of the room. Chris realized at that moment that Rhonda knew all the same tricks as he did. Just throw it out there like it doesn't really matter if they say no. And they never say no. It was the first sign that he didn't have all the control in his relationship with Rhonda. It wouldn't be the last.

Their schoolwork relationship morphed quickly into a romantic relationship while they worked on their history essay in her bedroom the first day, when she shoved aside their books, pushed him backward on the bed, and kissed him.

"My parents won't be home until five," she whispered to him. Then she started to pull his shirt up over his head.

Their relationship was largely physical at first, because it could be and they wanted it to be. But as the weeks went by, Chris realized that he really liked Rhonda a lot. She was funny, and interesting, and she liked heavy metal and rock music. She was also smart and had nice friends, who really seemed to like him. And she seemed to like him, too. The sex became more intimate as they talked more, and asked questions, and cared about the answers. They started to spend more and more time together after school and on weekends, until Rhonda clued him in on a problem.

"Chris," she told him, "you're neglecting your friends. Your posse. Especially Carl. Carl seems lost. I've seen him just standing there in the hall sometimes just looking around. And something's going on with James. I don't know what, but he just seems so angry all the time. Haven't you noticed that something's off?"

Chris had to admit to himself that he hadn't. He'd been completely swallowed up by his relationship with Rhonda and only really thought about his friends when they were right there in front of him. Even then he was likely thinking about Rhonda. He felt a pit develop in his stomach. He thought about Carl being alone and lost and suddenly wanted to go back to find him. He wanted to know what was up with the normally agreeable and amicable James that was making him so angry. But he also wanted to be with Rhonda. She understood.

"Chris, I'm not gonna just disappear if we're not together all the time," she assured him. "I mean, you know I still spend time with my friends. You just need to make some time for yours. I'm okay with that. I actually respect that."

Chris liked the idea of Rhonda respecting him. It felt good. He wanted her to respect him, even if it meant doing things that made him feel uncomfortable. Even if it meant he could no longer actively pursue the bad-boy lifestyle.

"I'll talk to them," he told Rhona.

Later that day, Chris found Carl in the hallway, standing alone. Rhonda was right. He looked lost. Chris approached his cousin.

"Hey Carl," he said as he leaned up against the wall next to him. "I was thinking we should head over to Store 24 after school. We can grab James and just go hang out for a while like we used to."

Carl nodded. "I'd be up for that," he agreed. Carl's expression was flat. Chris hoped he hadn't waited too long to re-engage him. He'd have to work on getting him to joke around with him later. Carl was usually happiest when he thought he was being funny. And sometimes, he actually made Chris laugh.

He saw James last period in Spanish class. "Wanna go hang out at Store 24 after school today?" he asked him. "Carl's coming. Maybe we can ask Pete to meet up with us next time."

James nodded. "Yeah, man, that would be good."

"Is something going on with you?" Chris asked him, noticing James did seem all tensed up. "You seem kind of off lately. What's up?"

Much to his surprise, James appeared to relax a bit after Chris asked him what was wrong. "Yeah," he said. "There's some stuff going on at home with Howie and my parents that's really bumming me out. I haven't really had a chance to talk to anyone about it yet, but I think hanging out today would help a lot. Y'know, just getting away from it all for a while."

After talking to his friends, Chris was feeling even better about his relationship with Rhonda. She was insightful, and kind, and tuned in to what was going on with him and his friends. Which is what made what happened the first day of senior year all that more confusing.